Book
of
Dreams

Book
of
Dreams

Jack Kerouac

Introduction by
Robert Creeley

CITY LIGHTS BOOKS
San Francisco

Cover photograph: "Jack Kerouac"
© 1958 by Robert Frank, courtesy Pace/MacGill Gallery,
New York

Cover design: Yolanda Montijo
Typography: Harvest Graphics

Library of Congress Cataloging-in-Publication Data

Kerouac, Jack, 1922-1969.
    Book of dreams / by Jack Kerouac.
        p.   cm.
    ISBN 0-87286-360-8
        1. Kerouac, Jack, 1922-1969—Diaries.   2. Authors,
American—20th century—Diaries.   3. Beat generation—
Diaries.   4. Dreams.   I. Title.

PS3521.E735 Z484 2001
818'.5403—dc21   00-065635
                                                    CIP

CITY LIGHTS BOOKS are edited by Lawrence Ferlinghetti
and Nancy J. Peters and published at the City Lights Bookstore,
261 Columbus Avenue, San Francisco, CA 94133.
Visit our Web site: www.citylights.com

Dream, When You're Feeling Blue
Dream, That's the Thing to Do . . .

Robert Creeley

I always felt embarrassed that I could never remember my dreams—or more than just two, it seemed. One had me at a classic sixties long table with lots of others, all eating out of a great bunch of pots filled with various stews along with bowls of rice. Finally, we seemed to have eaten everything and there had been a lot—yet there were still people yelling for more. I remember turning to the woman next to me and asking, how come these people are still hungry after all the food we've eaten? Ah, she said, we were hungry and so we could be fed! But they, they are possessed with the idea of hunger and so they can never get enough. I carried that dream for years as a talisman against confusion and obsessive desire.

The other dream was equally terrific. At least I thought so. It occurred on the way out of Albuquerque, driving to Prescott, Arizona, in the middle eighties. I dreamt I was in a pueblo somewhere along the river, but the year, or even the century, wasn't clear. All the men were about to go hunting, and I could see them getting their stuff together, the horses ready, weapons, food. Momently they had ridden out, the women went off to their work, and I found myself sitting on the ground with the children, who were playing usual games, tag, making little houses, sitting in a scattered pattern around me. I was not with them as someone might be who was taking care of them. I wasn't there to teach them or to tell them anything. I wasn't really with them at all except that I was there too, placed as they were, simply on the ground. Waking, I thought the dream told me to accept myself as a child, to stay with that hierarchic place, to keep my vision, such as might be, clear and initial.

Years later, in much pain with confusion of self and with an increasing inability to keep faith with my family's needs, I went to see a useful adviser in such matters, a Freudian psychiatrist who was about my age and a colleague at the university where we both worked. I loved his name, Marvin Hertz—*does Marvin hurt?* Actually, he did quite the contrary and helped me a lot.

But he did damage my first dream, which I told him quite proudly, thinking it showed him how perceptive and wise I was, even while sleeping. After he had listened, he said, "You must never get what you want." *But I am the one who does get fed,* I pointed out, *it's me who can't understand why those others are still hungry!* "Who do you think 'they' are," he said, "where do you think 'they' are but in your head? They are all *you*, one way or another." I don't think I ever told him the second.

Are all these dreams, then, "Jack"—one way or another? Is this extraordinary book just the same reiterated person— and are persons, to begin with, only a walking explanation of themselves? Is it still the case that Marvin, whoever and wherever he may now be, still *hurts*, still hears his name as pain?

A slogan for our generation was Yeats's "In dreams begin responsibilities. . . ," to which I'd now add the poet Robert Duncan's useful corollary, "Responsibility is the ability to respond." For Jack especially, dreams were a remarkably significant source and resolution for all his life as a writer, and for all and any of it otherwise. As late as July 11, 1967, he writes an admirer, Calvin Hall (*Selected Letters 1957–1969* [New York: Viking Penguin, 1999]):

Dear Hall,

Thanks for letter. No longer write down my dreams on waking, too lazy for now, but used to, between 1952 and 1960, all in Book of Dreams. But do make definite practice of mulling them over in detail on waking nowadays, and am keeping track of strange recurrences and even have a dream novel in mind. So many locations, mixups. Fact, I like to sleep so I can tune in see what's happening in that big show. People say we sleep a third of our lives away, why I'd rather dream than sit around bleakly with bores in "real" life. My dreams (like yours) are fantastically real movies of what's actually going on anyway. Other dream-record keepers include all the poets I know. "Free association" of dreams are really road signs showing you to another location. It's *placey*. People in dreams just wander said landscapes and room places and city ideas. etc.

Jack Kerouac

Dreams must be recorded as they come, spontaneously.

Jack's early listings of manuscripts for possible publication invariably note the present book. For example, a letter to his life-long agent, Sterling Lord, dated January 23, 1955, and written previous to the acceptance of *On the Road*, refers to it as "~~Gray~~ Book of Dreams" ("Unread, in my possession") (*Selected Letters 1940–1956* [New York: Viking Penguin, 1995]). Perhaps most telling is his letter to Malcolm Cowley, the editor at Viking Press who was finally to arrange for *On the Road*'s publication. Cowley had been a significant poet in the twenties, most identified with the expatriates, and he planned to do an introduction for the novel. So Jack writes him (Feb. 4, 1957):

Dear Malcolm,
   Two things we failed to insert in your notes for the introduction.

(1) That as a "recording angel" however I have to do it in a necessarily birds-eye personal-view form of a legend, which is the DULUOZ LEGEND, to which all the books belong except first novel naturalistic fictional Town & City. "Duluoz" is Kerouac, as you know, but might note.

(2) We forgot to add BOOK OF DREAMS to the complete list of works, which is a 300-page tome of some excellence, spontaneously written dreams some of them written in the peculiar dream-language of half-awake in the morning.

If you have the time, let me know what you think literary-spiritually and then professionally of DESOLATION ANGELS, and if you decide for that or DOCTOR SAX as our next venture.

Hoping you're having a pleasant rest,—

as ever,

Jack

Such emphasis as I make here may well seem more than is necessary. What, after all, does this curious, digressive, endlessly circling, insistently returning cluster of brief narratives have to do with the "real" books of Jack Kerouac, the novels we think of as his master work? One expects a writer to have his or her own preoccupations, a memoir perhaps, an account of some exceptional relation, even a collection of essays. But this dense, obsessively detailing collection of "dreams" can hardly find an apt place with *On the Road* or *Dr. Sax*?

If the boundary of narrative, the story one hopes to tell, must of necessity end at the usual limits of consciousness, or, put more clearly, be ended by our own understanding, the fact of what we think we recognize and know, then it becomes a story that will be, paradoxically, forever an awkwardly willful "dream," a fiction that only a limiting intention has made. Despite we think to stay within such a daylight world, we nonetheless summon characters and occasions, which must always implicate far more than we know literally, or can in any sense finally imagine. As a fellow writer, Fielding Dawson, makes usefully clear, it's when the story takes a turn on its own, when someone in it does something we, writing, cannot anticipate, when the place and time and company become circumstances we enter unknowingly, just as the reader must, it's then that our story begins.

Not only was Jack Kerouac's intent to open and map this human place, but he had also to discover a language for it, an address that would not displace its information in the fact of entering. So he writes of Freud, the authority then beyond all others for such an undertaking:

> Dream analysis is only cause-and-condition explanation (such, as, cliff from symbol during waking day, like murderer with knife because window left unlocked)---dream analysis is only a measurement of the maya-like and has no value---- dream dispersion has the only value---Freudianism is a big stupid mistaken with causes & conditions instead of the mysterious, essential, permanent reality of Mind Essence. . . .

His irritation and hostility to Freud's mode of analysis can be quickly understood if one recognizes that Kerouac, as a writer, was not working to understand or "explain" the substance of dreams. Rather, he wanted that dream content, of presence and feeling, of place and its multiple resonances, to join with the narratives he had composed as "novels," "visions" or "poems." He wanted the world to be all that he recognized as its defining experience, all places of mind, and so of dreams. "I am only a recording instrument," his friend

William Burroughs writes of his own work. Just so Jack Kerouac wants to bear witness, to be in all the places of his life "the great rememberer," as Allen Ginsberg calls him, the intense and completing expression of a human life rather than its displacing discretion, its reflective attempt to objectify, "to impose"—again in Burroughs' phrase—"plot."

So what then does one encounter here? For one thing, some 200 dreams have been added to the initial selected edition (1961), bringing the original imagination of the work back to its primary dimensions and content. At one point fairly early in the book, Jack has this characteristic instance, ending with a note as to the dates of the first year of his writing them down:

> boulevards or Montreal or my truckdriving honey-colored love New Haven pier crash days with pows of seas, dry muds, spiders, slants, pits, trestles, caves, necktie racks, Swiss, rock, smosh, pot, pone, poll, pall, pill, pell, purl, pash, posh, Tim, Tyler, Tom, Reading the Daily News, Finding the Shrouded Stranger, the desert, the arrow, the rat in the CLIMD (paste that in ya hat)---the actual wooden house with red sun on grade school in the first morning of the world, when even on the canal there had been no activities yet, dew sat unruffled everywhere, no footsteps of any action had crossed the spit face of time, I was infant rising to chime the paradise. I'm on the road to heaven (this marks the first year of dreams, begun in Easonburg Aug. 14,1952, and it is now Aug. 14,1953 in New York.)

There is the melding and playing of sound patterns, of the familiar particulars, the "red sun on grade school," the always present "Shrouded Stranger"—and then the sense of a quiet, a pervasive resting of things, a freshness and innocence—"no activities yet."

So the places of the novels and poems, their means of escape and securing refuge, are here too, but now the land-scape is not sequential or linear. Rather, it moves as weather, confronting, repetitious, and never entirely anticipated. What appears, often again and again, has never a simple explanation despite particular persons who are suddenly there, much like the rabbit in Carroll's *Through the Looking Glass*. There is a cast of apparent characters—his mother, sister, father, his friends as Burroughs and Ginsberg, women who are a part of the com-pany in some ambient manner, recurring. There are also partic-ular locations that have a curious "time machine" effect—as the many places of Lowell he returns to, intimate and flooded with echoes. So the "wrinkly tar corner" of Moody Street becomes a communal meeting ground not only for the childhood cronies, the initiating friends of Jack's life-to-be. It's also that place where dreams begin, and so they return there, over and over:

> Nobody's explaining the trip of the world to us but there's the spectral Riverside hiway offward going as if God had been a malicious creator of dyers and sufferers and hopeless throatchoken ant ish bedazzled *ees* in this impossible bril-liance heart & horror of the hole on high---Gad I wish I could find my way out of these dreams as in--death's begin-ning to occupy my thoughts again---Straj!

The "Jack" I found in this book was not a consistent or necessarily integrated presence—but this was not just the result of his being so variously met, one moment a child, next a son, then a musing spirit, say, or else a usual working man, walking a familiar street home. He was of necessity the multi-ple, the many in one, the all that being one is. Of course, not one "Jack," there was *he* as he must have been, lying in bed, sleeping, then coming awake to write down what his dream had been. He loved the muffling, displacing edge between consciousness, as it's called, and the dream-filled sleep one leaves to come back to it. One time, when all of us had collected at Locke McCorkle's house in Marin for Gary Snyder's farewell party—he was off the next day to Japan—Jack and I slept out at the top of the hill in sleeping bags, the cabin being full of parents and kids. I remember him waking me momently the sun was up with a great shout, *"Are you pure?"* "That's like asking water to be wet," I somehow answered. He laughed.

Dreams are like *asking water to be wet*, which it is, always and forever. Dreams are where Wynken, Blynken and Nod still set off to, each night, in their wonderfully thoughtless shoe. Each night they return to fish those unimaginable depths and distances, common to all who trust their lives, believe they are not only their own understanding, not just sole fact of the conscious, literalizing world. So Jack listened and believed:

> All night long their nets they threw
>   To the stars in the twinkling foam—
> Then down from the skies came the wooden shoe,
>   Bringing the fishermen home;
> 'Twas all so pretty a sail it seemed
>   As if it could not be,
> And some folks thought 'twas a dream they'd dreamed
>   Of sailing that beautiful sea—
>   But I shall name you the fishermen three:
>   *Wynken,*
>   *Blynken,*
>   *And Nod.*

Now go to sleep.

Editor's Note

"Dreams must be recorded as they come, spontaneously," wrote Jack Kerouac about his *Book of Dreams*. The editor's job is never spontaneous, and dreams of the perfect book are never realized.

For the 1961 City Lights edition of *Book of Dreams*, Jack Kerouac typed a manuscript based on the dream notebooks he had been keeping for several years. His publisher, Lawrence Ferlinghetti, made a selection of a little more than half of the entries or episodes to reduce the manuscript to a size that the small press could manage. Then Kerouac handcorrected those selections to fix a few typographical errors and to more or less systematically change the names of identifiable persons.

Now here is the complete book. I have attempted to edit a book that reflects Kerouac's intentions. I assumed that Kerouac would have wanted the complete manuscript published — and his careful typing and the correspondence seem to attest to that wish. I also assumed that the name changes that Kerouac made for the 1961 edition should be extended to the previously unpublished and unedited sections. Easier said than done, of course, with the task made more difficult by Kerouac's own inconsistencies in renaming.

On the subject of names, the wise reader will easily decipher the fictions in which the famous are lightly clad. Neal Cassady is "Cody Pomeray"; Carolyn Cassady is "Evelyn Pomeray"; William Burroughs is "Bull Hubbard"; and Allen Ginsberg is "Irwin Garden." These are public persons whose biographies are nowadays common currency or, better, shared myths. Ardent Kerouackians will have no trouble using their secret decoder rings to reveal the real names of many of the other characters who populate Kerouac's dream accounts.

We have tried to follow closely a photocopy of Kerouac's typescript (furnished by Kerouac's longtime agent, Sterling Lord). Wherever possible, peculiarities of the author's spelling, punctuation, and spacing have been retained. An urge to correct obvious typographical errors was resisted for two reasons: (1) Kerouac had ample opportunity to make his own corrections in the sections chosen for publication in the first edition—and refrained from doing so, in most cases. (2) In dream accounts, what could be more expressive than "errors"—slips of the tongue or typewriter?

The manuscripts of Kerouac's own "Foreword," "Preface," and "Table of Characters" have not been found. They are published here as they were in the 1961 edition, except for the correction of two typographical errors in the preface.

In this unabridged edition, the shape of *Book of Dreams* is clearer. There's the dreamy introduction to the voyage in the opening pages: "I can't see the end of it on all horizons, this is the book of dreams." The book then takes the reader on an odyssey of Kerouac's nocturnal wandering in search of love, adventure, and eventual safe harbor in that moment when the narrator comes to: "New England haunted houses of old white cracked white paint, with stark trees of November.....It is such a sensational and sensitive and charmingly Garden-like intelligent dream I woke up amazed....."

James Brook

Foreword

The reader should know that this is just a collection of dreams that I scribbled after I woke up from my sleep—They were all written spontaneously, nonstop, just like dreams happen, sometimes written before I was even wide awake—The characters that I've written about in my novels reappear in these dreams in weird new dream situations (check the Table of Characters on the next page) and they continue the same story which is the one story that I always write about. The heroes of "On the Road," "The Subterraneans," etc. reappear here doing further strange things for no other particular reason than that the mind goes on, the brain ripples, the moon sinks, and everybody hides their heads under pillows with sleepingcaps.

Good.

And good because the fact that everybody in the world dreams every night ties all mankind together shall we say in one unspoken Union and also proves that the world is really transcendental which the Communists do not believe because they think their dreams are "unrealities" instead of visions of what they saw in their sleep.

So I dedicate this book of dreams to the roses of the unborn.

Preface

Book of Dreams was the easiest book to write—When I woke up from my sleep I just lay there looking at the pictures that were fading slowly like in a movie fadeout into the recesses of my subconscious mind—As soon (one minute or so) as I had assembled them together with any earlier dreams of the evening I could catch, like fish in a deep pool, I got my weary bones out of bed & through eyes swollen with sleep swiftly scribbled in pencil in my little dream notebook till I had exhausted every rememberable item—I wrote nonstop so that the subconscious could speak for itself in its own form, that is, uninterruptedly flowing & rippling—Being half awake I hardly knew what I was doing let alone writing.

But an hour later, over coffee, what shame I'd feel sometimes to see such naked revelations so insouciantly stated—But that is because the subconscious mind (the *manas* working thru from the *alaya-vijnana*) does not make any mental discriminations of good or bad, thisa or thata, it just deals with the realities, What Is. It is only with our conscious mind (the *mano-vijnana*) that we judge and make arbitrary conceptions, that is, that we arbitrate and lay down laws about should & shouldn't be written or done. So I wrote these dreams with eerie sleeping cap head & now I'm glad I did.

Everybody interested in their dreams should use the method of fishing their dreams out *in time* before they disappear forever.

—Jack Kerouac

Table of Characters

OH! THE HORRIBLE VOYAGES I've had to take across the country and back with gloomy railroads and stations you never dreamed of---one of em a horrible pest of bats and crap holes and incomprehensible parks and rains, I can't see the end of it on all horizons, this is the book of dreams.

Jesus life is dreary, how can a man live let alone work---sleeps and dreams himself to the other side---and that's where your Wolf is ten times worse than preetypop knows---and how, look, I stopped---*how can a man lie and say shit when he has gold in his mouth.* Cincinnati, Philarkadelphia, Frohio, stations in the Flue---rain town, graw flub, Beelzabur and Hemptown I've been to all of them and read Finnegain's Works what will it do me good if I dont stop and righten the round wrong in my poor bedighted b---what word is it?---skull. . .

Talk, talk, talk---

I went and saw Cody and Evelyn, it all began in Mexico, on Bull's ratty old couch I purely dreamed that I was riding a white horse down a side street in that North town like in Maine but really off Highway Maine with the rainy night porches in the up and down America, you've all seen it you ignorant pricks that cant understand what you're reading, *there,* with sidestreets, trees, night, mist, lamps, cowboys, barns, hoops, girls, leaves, something so familiar and never been seen it tears your heart out---I'm dashing down this street, cloppity clip, just left Cody and Evelyn at a San Francisco spectral restaurant or cafeteria table at Market and Third where we talked eagerly plans for a trip *East* it was (as if!) (as if there could be East or West in that waving old compass of the sack, base set on the pillow, foolish people and crazy people dream, the world wont be saved at this rate, these are the scravenings of a---lost---sheep)---the Evelyn of these dreams is an amenable---Cody is---(cold and jealous)---something---dont know---dont care---Just that after I talk to them---Good God it's taken me all this time to say, I'm riding down the hill---it becomes the Bunker Hill Street of Lowell ---I'm headed for the black river on a white horse---it broke my heart when I woke up, to realize that I was going to make that trip *East* (pathetic!)---by myself---alone in eternity---to which now I go, on white horse, not knowing what's going to happen, predestined or not, if predestined why bother, if not why try, not if try why, but try if why not, or not why---At the present time I have nothing to say and refuse to go on without further knowledge.

AND MEXICO CITY, A SPECTRAL ONE WITH WISHED FOR PIERS sitting at the base of gloomy gray Liverpool-like Ferrocarril---I and a horde of young generation in suits with prom flower girls attend a melee, a gathering, at a building, a tower---so crowded, I, among bachelors, have to wait outside---rousing applause, speeches, music inside---Strange how in my dreams it doesnt seem that everything's already happened in a more interesting way, but awe, sweet awe remains---for my rage is eating my heart away. What am I doing in this sinister North Carolina as a clerk getting up at 6:00---a clerk among sinister oldfaced clerks in an old gloomy railroad office---no dream could be as frightening and more like hell.---I finally manage to get in the party---no, the idiot dog woke me up at just the point where I might have made a story of the deal---and lately anyway I wake at dawn with the horrors. In New York they're stealing my ideas, getting published, being feted, fucking other men's wives, getting laurel wreaths from old poets ---and I wake on this bed of horror to a nightmare only life could have devised. To hell with it.

IN A STRANGE LIVINGROOM presumably in Mexico City but very much and suspiciously like a livingroom in a dream of my Ma and Pa in Lowell or Dream Movetown--- June (Evans) is telling me the name of a great unknown Greek writer, Plipias, Snipias, how his father ran away with the family money so Plipias, queer, went to live on an Island with the boy he loved; and wrote: "I never go on strike against man, because I love him"---June recommended this writer highly, and said: "You can spend an hour a day hassling over small things but in the larger sense you can see what he means, never go on strike against man---" Meanwhile I'm about to go in the bathroom but Bull's already in there---has made no comment---

DIGGING IN THIS WOMAN'S CELLAR to plant, or transplant, my marijuana---under clutters of papers (just a minute before was going thru my own things, in a huge new room, Peaches'd just left Hal)---clutters of rubber bands, etc., and digging into dirt to make plant bed but realized how deep her hole was beneath her junk, thought to myself, "The old lady's---the older you get the deeper your cellar gets, more like a grave-----the more your cellar looks like a grave---" There was a definite hole to the left---a definite saying---

I was foraging for my stories and paper for Peaches---earlier I was in a room, working for a man as secretary, he was a masquerader, a fraud---and an evil pulp magazine crook genius leader of some evil---My mother visited me as if I was in jail---I turned over in my bed, my cot, interested in these things---

HORRIBLE HASSELS IN CHICAGO---with young seamen and Deni Bleu, in a car, Boston-like going up and down bright traffics---stopped by cops, the youngest kid throws 2 quarts beer out window and smashes them---"Goddam him!" we all curse---I make note of my pockets, nothing but a rubber---But cops find a roach, but I'm going to say it's just thyme, or Cu-Babs, and that's what it really is---thyme not valuable but culpable---a plainclothes taxidriver cop has me stick my tongue out to check on Cu-Babs, I do so, he makes as if to slap me but doesnt---On the radio we'd heard big seaman union broadcasts with that silly wiper from the *Pres. Adams* giggling over the air---also making angry union speeches---Deni gloomy as ever---*used* as ever---

Then in the olddream Frisco of hills again but still related to the Bunker Hill of the white horse and altho it hasnt happened since I *actually* went back to Frisco---

4

Cody is driving jaloppy, a swank apartment house hill (he pulls throttle from floor without seeming effort to reach)---he's telling me something but unpleasantly, everything is now unpleasant, everybody wants money or earning power from me, the sweetness is gone---Cody has a harried, unpleasant, sullen expression--- The jaloppy reminds me of the jaloppy I had parked in a quiet Ozone Park street last week, a buddy sleeping at the wheel, and a guy began shooting at us with a shotgun from 2nd story window of a leafy Calabrese home and I ducked in gutter gritting my teeth for feel of shot burning me but he missed---then I run down street, he begins shooting at me deliberately (first shot was aimed at woman June Ogilvie woman on sidewalk)---now he wants *me*---I run---I'm tearful and terrified that he's after me---Jaloppy is mine---he jumps in, "he's going to steal my truck now!" I moan--- "Goddam this world!" And my buddy didnt move from behind that wheel---was this because he was killed by the first shot? He was Don Jackson of Mex City---I wished I hadnt left carkeys in car---I'd been driving and driving, thru that spectral railroad station Rainycity---The madman shot again ---I was in that Ozone Park that sometimes at night on a vast boulevard I'm riding a bus to my mother's davenport porch house---all rattling, all haunted by the dead---lost lost lost in the infinite eternity of our doom---

LAST NIGHT MY FATHER WAS BACK in Lowell---O Lord, O haunted life---and he wasnt interested in anything much---He keeps coming back in this dream, to Lowell, has no shop, no job even---a few ghostly friends are rumored to be helping him, looking for connections, he has many espe-

cially among the quiet misanthropic old men---but he's feeble and he aint supposed to live long anyway so it doesnt
matter---He has departed from the living so much his once-
excitement, tears, argufying, it's all gone, just paleness, he
doesnt care any more---has a lost and distant air---We saw
him in a cafeteria, across street from Paige's but not
Waldorf's---he hardly talks to me---it's mostly my mother
talking to me about him---"Ah well, ah bien, he vivra pas
longtemps ce foi *icit!*"---"he wont live long *this* time!"---she
hasnt changed---tho she too mourns to see his change
---but God Oh God this haunted life I keep hoping against
hope against hope he's going to live anyway even tho I not
only know he's sick but that it's a dream and he did die in real
life---ANYWAY---I worry myself. . . (When writing *Town
and the City* I wanted to say "Peter worried himself white"---
for the haunted sadness that I feel in these dreams (PA-G-X-
4327) is *white*---) Maybe Pop is very quietly sitting in a chair
while we talk---he happened to come home from downtown to sit awhile but not because it's home so much as he
has no other place to go at the moment---in fact he hangs
out in the poolhall all day---reads the paper a little---he himself doesnt want to live much longer---that's the point---He's
so different than he was in real life---in haunted life I think
I see now his true soul---which is like mine---life means
nothing to him---or, I'm my father myself and this is me
(especially the Frisco dreams)---but it *is* Pa, the big fat man,
but frail and pale, but so mysterious and un-Kerouac---but is
that me? Haunted life, haunted life---and all this takes place
within inches of the ironclouds dream of 1946 that saved my
soul (the bridge across the Y, 10 blocks up from 'cafeteria'---)
Oh Dammit God---

A LONG QUIET ALMOST WAKING TALK WITH EVELYN---almost real---about how hopeless her "love" is and what's going to happen and not happen----I dont understand love at all---but I sit there eagerly talking and supping up the hours of the angels---by the clock---

THE STRANGEST PLACE IN THE WORLD is that little fairyland old Colonial house on a narrow street in back of my father's old printing shop near the Royal (therefore Market street) but also in England and gray---cobblestones ---many dreams there, vague marriages, girls, maybe something to do with the other life I sensed in the Frisco Market Street Vision---(*Market* street? Of *Greeks?*)---On a very strange other street semi Aiken or Lilly in Centralville but also a big mysterious maindrag in a tremendously important city like New York (Bronx St?) or Montreal---but really Aiken St.---but really Juarez at the Prado---(New Haven! That's What!)---a young kid, a boy, well dressed like the round-the-world-$80-hitch-hiker is riding a horse over the trolley tracks but is holding the reins so loose I, from the curb of Scoop's store, say "Hey, that rein's too long---he's gonna lose control of his horse---" But gravely the kid trots up the street, thru traffic, but then starts galloping either to show off or lost control and as he gallops the reins slip more and more thru his hands till he's leaning way back and rearing to fall backwards with hands up holding futile long flap-reins as the horse gallops across a dangerous intersection where the light has just changed and armies of cars and trucks who'd been playing the light, bearing down on it 60 m.p.h., now ball right thru and barely miss horse and rider but I can see he's going to get killed pretty soon down the street---and I'm yelling "Grab those reins shorter! pull!"---he's no baby, I'm saying to myself, he has enough strength to pull that horse up if he wants to---aint he got sense? *THIS IS NOT ME*

Also there was Garden and schools on the side rawls, but I paid no attention and dont remember, except, a dawn, waking, I saw the vision of 3 words in my mind. . "urp rain again". . .the return of the urp rain again---

("A bullet fell in ya!" says Little Paul)

THEY WOULDNT LET ME WORK on the ship even tho it had just sailed from the North River pier where Joe and I've many times walked---a gray, dismal pier---rickety, hive-ish, with "Julien's reformatory" as I call a certain strange Arabic tenement and the place where Ma and I stood on the warship deck in that famous dream of face-towel crabs float-ing in the water that Hubbard analyzed in 1945---I'm in my quarters, we're already at sea, I feel lonely, awful, lost in mazes of fresh-paint rooms and lockers and bunks and worried about the gray cold sea and the officials come in to check my papers and he, the head one, young, grins---I call him Mate, meaning First Mate, forgetting the Sir---"You cant sail with-out a so-and-so paper," he says with incredulous smile, "You'll have to sail this trip but you cant work"---I'd helped with lines at tight dock---in fact I'd run on board the very last minute as the ship was moving down the crowded canal, I could see its funnel passing roofs---how I got on is unclear, I was returning from a spectral ball in the huge-room places like the Mexico Harbour City Tower with mixups of everybody---O haunted poorboy John Kerouac but you are headed for a long sad dream---

The smoke is on the Tar River, the sparrow does its delicate flutter---

IN DENVER NOW---I dream I go in a store place and there's Joe Gavota and Joe Melis and I go up dramatically to poke Melis on his LHS thicksweater and he's not surprised at all but as if I'd been known to be around and in fact Gavota (who delivered me the '38 Lawrence game football) doesnt even look up---and they are casual but as tho aware, and I feel guilty and silly about something---at a big wild party, after loves in a sideroom slatwindowed bed (I think in a house on a dirt road, the same perfect future wife love I dream'd long ago, clarity is perfect)---we, love and I, girl with beautiful young tawny body drives me mad, we sit on floor, our love supposed to be a secret, she snuggles up, I say "Not here dont you think?" (it's all taking place in Australia!) and like Edna she tinkles laughter and throws herself back and over with her pretty little ass no panties naked crack and all to the party of watching jealous women dancing with men who dont care---one way or the other---or a jealous suitor at the kitchen in back---the dirt road of the Shrouded Arab and of the high school late gold afternoon when my mother bought me a baseball bat and Gavota and Melis (of the Lowell High School football team) were there---

Deni Bleu appears, we've been sliding down a hill but not on snow, D's in good mood---breaks window ---whole section of wall---slats fall out like yesterday's ruined shack house under Denver Viaduct---Deni on a stepladder

---laughing---and my girl-love there---more like Edna than anyone---but her ass is just like June Evans's! (and yesterday on phone I said "Evelyn Pomeray's more like June Evans than anyone") (to Mannerly)---mysteries aplenty right here. (I shall survive them and love them or they love me or it's hate, war & death---)

IN SAN JOSE NOW, Sept.7, I'm riding the yellow local Lowell bus home to Pawtucketville and as the driver comes into that last fast stretch to the corner (wrinkly tar) I say *now roll*---but it's on Riverside instead of Moody, the homestretch is changed because I've heard of the new superhiway---As he (there's a kid or two riding with me, heads out the window, we've just come off adventures on a ship which was shaken by depth charges and Boisvert was on board)-----blam, there's a dead run-over dog near the stop, as I get off I notice it is still alive tho contorted and run over---"Oh God he's still alive and suffering---Officer!" I yell to one of the two busdrivers "that dog is still alive----shoot him, kill him"---and out of nowhere he ups with a revolver .38 and aims it down the stairwell and begins the shooting of the dog, about 4 times, the ineffectual dreambullets only fairly surprise the dog, he twitches, gets up, and comes for me and the kids---We run backwards across Moody to avoid it---"Keep to the right!" yells the busdriver---I don't know what he means---The dog may bite me but his deathness I dont want to touch me---I can choke it, stop it, but not his deathness---he is a dirty gray Fellaheen dog, with some brown in the neck, and an old tragic collar of some blearfaced owner in blank and blind sternity,--- his teeth, his eyes---Then I see G.J. and he's complaining that

Scotty or somebody is still the same old Scotty, it's NOW, 1952, morning, the old dream of sad G.J. in the morning getting ready to go to work in the Navy and griping---I tell him about the dog, the ship---as I'm telling now---

THEN I'M WORKING ON THE RAILROAD, as I've been doing now I realize for *years* in dreams of the Barrostook Crock & Crane R. R. that runs side wise east and west from Lowell to Lynn pot and other such places along a dry almost Mexican SP desert ground with tragic brakeman shacks, the road to some All Boston---now I'm almost California SP and Cody and my father mingled into the One Father image of Accusation is mad at me because I missed my local, my freight, I fucked up with the Mother Image down the line, I did something childish (the little boy writing in the room) and held up iron railroads of men---I finally get to the track but the freight is rolling so fast by that time I'm afraid to try jumping on--- grimy Pop-Cody is already at work, he may fuck up in his own tragic night but by Jesus Christ when it's time to go to work it's fucking time to go to work--- There are also angry faces of seamen on ships, I screwed up at the potato pump---W C Fields in switchman's overalls by the tracks, the doll-like brakemen are jumping on the fast train,---I'm left gooping in my own sor-row---groping in my own dull Tit---

A LONG ALL-NIGHT AFFAIR WITH A WOMAN supposed to be Marlene Dietrich---"because of her mouth you can tell"—but other people seem skeptical she's Marlene, though I believe it or insist on believing it---I go to some parkinglot and tell the owner of the used cars that Marlene's my girl---it's located on Bridge St. Lowell across the street from the big gray warehouse--- There, I am shown a Life magazine with a big 3-page spread of pictures of me in a raincoat (tan, tailored) cutting along like a "lonely writer in sadness" in various angle shots----darkhaired, gloomy, line faced---I'm displeased because I'd have preferred closeups and also because I didnt know these pictures had been taken ---by Marlene, presumably---her *mouth* which was the key to her identity was tragically muggled and almost with buck teeth, like Bill Wagstrom's mouth in Mexico City or the mouth of the used car man in Rocky Mount (he was a big tall man with Panama hat) (and's in dream) and Shorty's Clarence's wife in Easonburg, and Nina Foch's mouth some- how tho she's not muggled but like real life Marlene.

AN ENCAMPMENT OF ALMOST PROVINCETOWN SUBTERRANEANS (Monterrey hipsters) around a fire, Peaches, etc., I'm with them but getting up to hit the road (the night traffic) for Canada, back to Canada and early pale Twenties furniture (sad beads of afternoon) scenes of my childhood where my mother is---it's a long trip, a sad trip, I start but come back to say something, they dont care, there's a cat in the road, I've had a dab of Immortality in this dream ---This is opening chapter of real "On the Road"---

A LONG VOYAGE to Mexico City, I leave my California railroad work before it's even started (like I did the Carolina r. r. work) and en route get involved in houses and small dirt

streets like you dont see any more because they made the
automobile to ride 5 miles down the broad dead road with
for what they used to slink across the street for---I make
goofy tape records with Eisenhower, he condescends, but is
actually friendly and has fun and doesnt mind leaving his
goof words to posterity unlike real life politician---arrive in
Mexico City, with Al Green, go to Hubbard's house and plug
up my new longplaying phonograph and play the tape for Al
---he is Eisenhower himself---he appreciates and digs and
laughs---but the door bursts open and in staggers Hubbard
roaring drunk, he---I say to him, to "apologize" for breaking
into his house uninvited, "I got this new phonograph and lots
of money"---as if, *aren't you grateful I am here?*---but he staggers around, makes only cutting comments, spits on the floor,
goes to his room, every time Al (who's heard so much about
his greatness from me) tries to talk to him Bull is absolutely
stone silent as tho deliberately---affronting Al terribly
because he has sensed that I prepared Al for him and he
ignores everything and is silent with that half smile---I'm
mad, never want anything to do with him either any more,
fresh paranoias follow me to every travel terminal, I also feel
guilty and foolish and importunate for leaving that railroad
work so soon, now I'm fucked, all bridges behind me burned
to dreary eternity---Earlier my father had returned, to West
St. but was also now a drunkard and didnt answer or give a
shit---Intractable as a bad child---and I with my mother is
the lost spectralities of a 4th of July Grool stand in criticism
of him, fireworks on First St., nameless events waving in the
road towards Joe's on Bunker Hill and down to Centralville
center---the rose lattices on the porch, the drear light of
the house like the light in the Cody-copwoman-oval track-

13

children dream of moths---the Mystic Celt is far from bloomed, he's tied a Slavic knot around the Fellaheen band of the world, the Aramean Spring time is shoving underground the Iron Americas of Fellah---

COMING IN A KIND OF WAGON TRAIN of movement, with lots of people and Al Green, into a rippling new land of Fellaheen mystery and Gypsy women---an exact spot on the plain, the scene instantly changed to Fellaheen, just like at Nogales Ariz. to Sonora---and just like the sudden truckload of section hands at Santa Margarita (on my student run) ---we turned and saw the colorful people on the corner, the whores in bright gaudy (but Fellaheen dirty) dresses, the muddy streets, the stores, great trees enormous as Time, cottonwoods, uprooted at the old man's corner---I'd clearly been there clearly before this uprootin----the vast roots were displayed to the sun, the old man was at his bench talking to the old women, there were several other smaller trees uprooted up and down the Main Drag which was the demarcation point between where we'd been and where the rippling mysterious land began---Then I was telling a smiling Julien and Irwin about Bull and me in Mex City whorehouses and adventures, as we strolled in that Mexico City "circle" the other night I rode on that "switch" block---In pretending to show my ignorance of Spanish in the story I keep saying Spanish words to show off--- At first I came thru that "rippling Fellaheen entry town into the Fellaheen Plain" with Al,---then the Bull adventures, then re-visited and found Trees uprooted---so tragically---and with great silence of Time and Reality, dreamed in a caboose the night after I got trapped on the roof

14

of the boxcar at 60 miles per hour in the foggy dark of the Watsonville and Moss Landing sea marshes.

I'M SNEAKING AROUND IN THE FRAGRANT DARK of some night, I cant find location, very like ideal Denver night of scrivenings (and High Point North Carolina salesman's story of dorms, lacquer furniture Jewish guy) and only vaguely related to Delmar and probably with Cody, but a rickety house, trees, dark, and suddenly June Ogilvie appears in door radiant and beautiful and awful and *sees me* (to my horror) ---I was sneaking back to get something, some papers, belongings, ("belly belly dilly" I explained to myself in half sleep, or "dilly dilly belly," *one*)---now in the 20th St. pad which suddenly clicks into the New York Dream Place as near the FBI tea dream village and Sheridan Square---and Times Square V-Movies---I'm sneaking, smelling at door in dark sweet night (like the night of Rosario)---Garden's around---I think I foresaw this pad in dreams---she's not there, but imminent---recently I went in there and even slept (like with that little Lesbian)---the whole night mysterious, creaky, breathing, I'm really sneaking and hiding in that steeltrap brain---the big horror of seeing her and her seeing me, shiney like an angel, as if I was the black Antichrist after all and a sinner against the Virgin Mary---Blow your top and roam like Joan of Arc, *Babe,* and I'll come back to you---unworthy too---

IN MEXICO, BUT EN ROUTE IN THE PALE DUSTS of dirty dobe towns by the railroad---Hoppy is there, we've stopped in this town everybody, I steal things from a boxcar

---it's a long run, it has its dream place in an up and down vertical movement of the Mexican rib-neck and sadder, North American, if Indian very weird Indian---like the Nogales section hands, but in a gray dust Guadalajara---my mother, cats,---cant make out what happened---

WITH A BLOND KID like the Kansas City Oldsmobile 88 soldier and Willie Hubbard grown up I am riding thru the railyards in a spectral circle in Mexico or someplace up and down South---"riding on a switch," right on the black square knob, which is "dangerous" because when it goes over switch points it may spark like a toy train and burn and throw me off---fast, too---and the passenger coaches in the yard are like houses, people inside, strange homes like the boat of the Boston Canal---where also I remember in the Greenland Bay the blond kid, and Dorchester drummer blond kid---we ride to a row of houses on Orizaba (at park) or Lowell Margaret Cole Highlands and big empty lit up houses with house-size windows, no sight of my mother---we're going to move into one of them---gradually we're coming along Riverside St. right to Wrinkly Tar Corner and but the bank of the Merriscrack is gone, they've cut it away to provide a Wista (including Textile Field) so it's huge and bluff-like like the Ohio was at Louisville with Blondy last month,---lights, spectral, the dump is now glorified as during the airplane war with glitters of far down light, huge, like the Missouri River ---it's eaten away Pawtucketville, a glimpse into milleniums and aeons!---Blondy wants to cut thru the funny really rickety alley back of grocery store (which Sax didnt remember!) and but a bunch of people in a new 1952 car, hoodlums, yell

16

harshly at us and Blondy's like to cry "I cant do anything I want, they wont let me" and I sympathize and we do cut thru over barrels and soft humps---come out on Moody at Destouches' store and Lo! Moody street is modern and pink-neon in regularity just like Sunnyvale Calif. and I'm amazed, a change, awful, like Marie Bernadette---level pink lights of new bars and stores, no more brown glooms---Lowell widening in the gyre---(Sept.26 first day on railroad board). . .

DREAMED OF BEING IN SOME KIND OF HARD-SHIP PILGRIMAGE with a man and woman in some Mongolian harshland and when we got to the (again) Fellaheen town (of the Fellaheen-rippling dream) which had a gray cement factory color and dismalness I said "However in your town here I could pose as a prisoner of yours---in fact, in reality I am your prisoner, according to the facts---"

"Yes, that's a fact," they said much, and innocently, pleased, especially the woman---they might have been Mongolian---I walked on the sidewalk ground carrying my rifle stock down as befitting a prisoner and they rode the point of our vehicular or animal travel-gimmick that had carted us across the wastes---I secretly mistrusted their joy, we had started on some Jesus pilgrimage, now they were letting their thoughts be affected by matters of war---but I trusted them finally---

THEN A WHOLE CREW OF US WERE MOVING FURNITURE in a house but with the same procedure as a crew switching boxcars and riding the brakes, so the tagman

17

boss says to me "Ride that one" and it's a shiny mahogany sofa-table that I push over the smooth hardwood floor into a room on the right (like into Track 2), and it's a bedroom, there are relationships among us like those of children, we're in a sense prisoners, or children, and innocent but have done wrong in the past---The area is wild with possibilities of scenes just recent, the Mexico Circle (Orizaba Park houses around a sweet pond pool at night, window lights) and the blond kid of the 88 (Willie-like) and the new Fellaheen land------

I HAD THE TOLSTOYAN DREAM, a great movie, with the Bolkonsky-Boldieu hero officer, in the stress of events, stomping out of an officer's milling ball and giving himself away thereby and they shout like Russians with toasts and arrest him on the spot and he indignant and meaningful--- Meanwhile I've been told to note the particular excellence of the performance of the "Peasant"---the old Fellaheen Hero ---He is in Cossack soldier uniform, a soldier comes into his strange room to arrest him, the Peasant is just standing there,---with a sense that not only I but my father is watch-ing this film, and it's in the 42nd Apollo and it's like the great lost Lost Father chapter of now-naturally out of print *Town and the City* and I remember my pre-tea joys, strengths and knowings God bless the purity of the Martins, the Kerouacs of my soul, still unfulfilled---we are all to watch how the Peasant handles situations, he takes the gun from the soldier's hand, in a funny way, with an enigmatic opaque remark, and points it floorward, makes a face, the soldier is non plussed by this brother peasant,---the audience laughs with anticipatory tears in its eyes, it's the great Tolstoyan Movie.

The peasant has a big head and wears a huge hat & vast sadness in his face just as the officer has vast rage in his---

ON A RAILROAD OR RAIL TRAVEL MACHINE or just flying straight thru the rail of space I see California in the night along the way, a chaingang of very recognizable hoboes and winos like on 3rd street and with ordinary but flushed-with-drinking American faces like Conductor Fields, they're in chains, sadistic fat guards have them completely sick & trembling, I see them being pushed and maltreated just for fun, but only vaguely in the gloom and I distinctly hear a loud cry *"You win! You win!"* as apparently a guard was tor-turing a poor devil just to hear some such outcry---I feel sick---just 2 blocks along, where cars are parked on a slant like in the Middlewest wheat towns but in pink neon California Road I see two separate fist fights between tiny children, with adults watching, fighting between the cars---young kids & children---it is the Machine in all its glory---I wake up horrified---nightmares are paranoia---

THE TRAIN PULLS INTO THE ROUNDHOUSE, I'm riding the engine, which is like a Mallet with windows, etc. & Cody, Evelyn & kids are riding the rear cab of the engine ---I notice other trains pulling in, & sailors, lots of sailors got rides (are getting rides) from trainmen & are stepping off with their bags, talking to the trainmen---it's early morning, all night in the engine bed & in the dark rooms of the mysterious Montreal house we (the whole family) been

wrangling moth-like dramas, like Cody is like Joe etc. & I'm
tired, pull up engine, & just then poor little Gaby that lately
I get so mad at & who apparently loves me now is climbing
sorrowfully slowly & tragically into the cab with me to say
Good Morning---& what do I do but turn my bleak face to
the day with that harried-anxious-flows-to-east face. . .

EVERSOTRAGIC FURTHER DREAM OF THE
"INCENSED NOBLE" of the Great Tolstoyan Movie---
here I see him in his family life in a house located in the
strange truckdriving New Havens or whatevers of old dreams
and he's got a family, particularly a beautiful blond child, very
Scandanavian, "like the son of the Kansas scientist with blond
hair, the land reclaimer"---(one in hitchhike of Aug 1952)---
everybody wants to kiss him except me, they're kissing him
on his erotic rosy lips, the Noble (somewhat Bull-like) takes
peculiar pleasure in waiting for his turn & in kissing kid---
he's "queer as the day is long," like Hubbard---in fact right
then I see a vision of Bull as developing into a final old goodnatured lecher with no thoughts---just "waiting for his blub-
bery kiss" from Rainbow Lips---& Bull was in dream much
earlier, but somehow in the same house, which has a lot of
overstuffed furniture brown, gloomy & to me beautiful---
fact, I talk about furniture with somebody, we're sitting, there
are other events in other rooms---the whole house spectral
& almost a boat again---but definitely located "in Maine"---
or at junctures near a tremendous embrillianted Kansas, with
sideshows of Fellaheen Gypsies off the main highway, down
Mexico like dirt street like near the Rastro at Dave's, the cars
flash east & west beneath great whiteradiant skies, Mexico is

"south" off that (as in Geography)---the house is on the right, on a knoll, suddenly as we pull up to the house (Aunt Whozoo's inside) me, my father, the Noble, & a driver, a mob of men surround the car to beat us up---open the door, say to me "Get out"---I think of rushing out in a wild fury slugging faces, then I think of my poor pop in the backseat with me, they're going to beat up that poor old sick man?---(when I woke up I pleaded "You cant beat up my father!" "He's got cancer!")---but they dont care, something the Noble has done has grimly set their purposes, they dont care about personalities & fathers, just as I wake up I realize I shall get kicked and beaten & probably killed but somehow the Noble--no, he too will be killed and beaten I guess too---the fool's done something---my father says nothing---Ah what's happening in the world!---that now the men come to beat us up!---what will the horrified women in the window say? Where's the pretty child? the angel? Dreamt in Cameo Hotel.

IMMENSE SAGAS ALL NIGHT LONG, fantastic detailed nightmares of me losing my pants twice in a row & being sought by the police also as a sex pervert because I have so much to do with young high school boys and girls while losing my pants---I talk to them eagerly with some flimsy scarf over my thigh---ugh---a strange exultant queer saint of some kind---The first time I'm getting on a local passenger train, it's going down the line of white radiant land, commuting school kids are jammed in it---I've already been up to something all night---involved with youngsters in the same way as the flophouse of Chicago dreamed in the Greensboro Salvation Army---I get on the train a sort of official brake-

21

man but somehow I lost my pants, I try to cover up but the cloth or scarf keeps slipping to show my thigh, my cock with no hardon, I hope no one sees---it's "just like" the dream in the crummy 5 nights before, Waldo Walters' wife is in a caboose with me, dotty, we talk excitedly and intimately and suddenly just as she's going to show me the important point Waldo comes in and simultaneously her skirt falls open to reveal a tiny cock which is "a woman's" nonetheless I insist--- a woman with a cock, that's all---and Waldo sees what we've been up to in a "wrong light," we had "no sexual intentions" ---same way, my little cock shows---and I'm blushing to cover up, my milky thighs without hair---somehow I get into the yard of a great lost school like the Horace Mann of my dreams but situated in a radiant New Britain California Land and there still pantless I'm plotting to get them back and some kids see me from the classroom windows (like the windows of the Queens General Hospital which were in an orange wall that bore the imprint dust stain of a former huge portrait there hung, picture of my diploma or brother or mother I forget, or me)---teachers are dissatisfied, call police (all the talk the details, forever elude us!)---I sneak around looking for my pants---Then in a gigantic house with hundred foot ceiling I have all my poems, manuscripts, all of them sexual, crazy, revealing, skewered around among records and books and a whole bunch of high school kids with me laughing at my antics and description of when I lost my pants but now they know I'm crazy and are cruel in jest, the cops are coming, I sneak back down there to recover my culpable revealing manuscripts, "shh" I say to Emil Ladeau, "the lady upstairs'll hear you!"---we look up, in a 4th floor window is poor harmless Mrs. Garden!!!!!---(Emil Ladeau I insulted once for his nose,

22

in that John MacDougald workshop dream)---Mrs.Garden
wont say nothing, I'll have time--"It was horrible, I had no
pants here the last time, cops are after me naturally, *twice* an
offender" I'm saying---and a thousand rattly crazy things also
---I have the same terror as in an old Henry Street dream
where I murdered somebody or was a witness, and hid a
revealing manuscript in a trash basket, it was pink, like lob-
sters, towels and walls of hospitals---Only yesterday I was
feeling guilty for writing *Doctor Sax, On the Road,* a sheepish
guilty idiot turning out rejectable unpublishable wildprose
madhouse enormities---Ah, come to papa do,---the high
school girls were cruel, the boys too---it wasnt my fault I lost
my pants, they eluded me on the Aiken St. bridge somehow
---it is such a terrifying bridge, you walk on narrow cables,
it's immense as the world---At the end, I'm watching from a
tenement top window like Julien's Dostoevskyan loft, like the
George Jessel New York tenements on the upper east end---
all the children are playing on the opposite roof, nets are
stretched across the court to catch the ones that fall, when
they do the other kids watch smiling---the fallen one cries in
the net---*I told you it was cruel*---the mothers are not too
concerned---"why cant they play on the sidewalks," I say---
"*there's no room,* civilization is too vast now"---Guilt is a
dream, pity is the only reality. . .

BIG CHICAGO SALVATION ARMY with wild young
gang with me, and girl---horrors of my wallet, Salvation
Army underwear---incredulously all over me I see six inch
long and thick sponges of fungus growing off me---so awful
I dont believe it even in dream---the silence of it---spectral

happenings, cellar, stairs, rooms, bathroom, girl, boys, wallet (I had it in my pillow case so Red mightnt steal it)--

A TREMENDOUS FAMILY SAGA, it takes place in a huge high apartment by the sea, the same sea of Tidal Waves and Sea Battles---there are intelligent child girls, earlier in the opening of the Saga, in a big room, after something to do with the Girl of the Huge Room, Halvar Hayes holds a kitten by the neck choking it and me and someone else (Joe Gavota was around) try to break his grip---"You're choking that cat to death!" I cry---and try clawing Hal's face, pushing his nose in, pulling his hair, everything, kicking him in the balls so he'll leave that kitty go and he wont---both of us are pummelling and pulling and torturing at him and he wont let that little dying kitty go---my heart is breaking all over---and Hal has such pitiful guts---I dont understand what, how it ends, there are dispers- ings and gray scene shiftings in the Shakespearean stage of my dreambrain---and the next day the kitty is still alive and play- ing! I am astounded, hosannahd, resurrected---and poor Hal was tortured for nothing?---that Judas choking Jesus! or that Jesus being tortured by Judas for a chimerical cat! Then the Saga swings to the high apartment, there are bargain base- ments below, a veritable Radio City, or Paramount Theater, a Jewish winter resort, crowds,---great company visits us, we have rich furnishings (like Kereskys)---smart little Margaret O'Brien girls---I protect them---we have inheritances--- crises come and go---suddenly in the midst of a big cocktail party the depth charges start exploding on the beach ten sto- ries below (this is the front of the Newspaper Building in New Britain I dangled off of)---"the depth charges" we all yell---

"Or is it just a joke, just fireworks!" Bedlam---Great clouds of black smoke spurt with each blast 10 stories high---Me and the two girl prodigies or one grownup girl and prodigy and the male other-hero are rushing down the hall to flee, but I warn them "Have we got our precious belongings?" No---we didnt---we all teeter in thought---then start rushing back to get our precious things (into our rooms like the rooms where I'd lost my pants, as if I had had a Tolstoyan childhood in castles with great sun pouring in thru Versailles Palace windows with noble trees outside)---(near Andover St. of Ernie Malo) ---but now we're hungup trying to decide what to save and meanwhile the tourist movie crowds are rushing to the elevators and we join them empty handed and as we "pummel" down floor by floor with floor indicators on buttons I worry about a depth charge suddenly breaking the cables and killing us all---In the general family lostness, here, it's like night Gerard died and the yelling relatives in the upstairs bedrooms and the fireworks crashing outside (ours, sneaked and set off by my cousins)---yes, Nin, young Nin of olden childhoods is one of the girl prodigies, she and I must have thought what to salvage in the general wreckage to bring to the Baileys with us ---I must have thought it was the end of the world when Gerard died---Yes, the milling tourists are clearly stomping thru our apartments in a wake, one of my heroes of the Saga has apparently died (Hal? cat?), and we the little ones are working out tiny salvations in the huge detonations of world adult disasters, ah me sad life of little souls come back---

IN THE BIG HOUSE ON LAKEVIEW AVENUE in the Centralville Olden Night there is a Mannerly but the

Conductor Young-Mannerly type Salesman chatting with
me and waiting for his interview with the Board of the
Southern Pacific Railroad which will include Cody and
decide whether the salesman ought to be hired and retained
---but he's so eager and sadly so that I'm all of the opinion of
course he should, who else could sell the samples better and
in fact "He's already sold a number of them and is so enthu-
siastic for his work--Good God why not?"---Also the salesman reminds me of Good Old Jimmy Bissonnette-Emil
Kerouac French Canadians of Lowell and I'm all for him, I
stand around in the kitchen in my slippers just like in 1928
when Blanche's husband was there in sad spats---
"Recommend him for hiring," I tell Cody---right there at
the foot of the hill where I'd gallopped so recently (Bunker
Hill) on that Eastward White Horse---Cody just "Yeahs" and
"Awups" as usual though in a dream he retains a little more
humanity, like a not quite empty wine bottle---The Board
arrives to convene: a big official blank and sayless like Wayne
Brace, and subsidiary asskissing brakemen with no brains.
Meanwhile "Salesman Mannerly" has already been across the
street in the Old Teachers' Home and even discussed me with
some of my old grammar school teachers, one of whom
however disclaimed a real remembrance of me because it was
so long ago---"Well,"---I say--- The board convenes. . .
Cody isn't going to vote one way or the other because he's
not concerned. Brace will vote *against,* as a representative of
Management of course; the brakemen following his suit. I'm
not on the board but nevertheless I'm going to make a stir-
ring memorable speech anyway recommending Mannerly for
obvious, practical reasons for the railroad (as I'll show) and
because I like him as a poor lost human being of the night

and might as well help him---but it all ends in a waking day-dream and I've only slept 3 hours in 2 fucking days on this fucking railroad---they can ram America up their ass and all rails and iron machines with it---I'm going back to Brittany and warn my fishermen: "Dont sail for the mouth of the St.Lawrence, that's where you got fooled before---*ils vous on joué un tour.*"

I GUESS IT WAS MY BIRTHDAY PARTY and for some reason like my marriage I was honored by a great gathering of the members of my generation, the scene was in a big one story house which has elements of the Kellostone house on Hildreth when I was 5, and the Gershom Iddyboy house and also elements of Sarah Avenue because of layout with kitchen pointing towards street thru parlor and also the little cottage across the court has Alice Kerrigan qualities but not in the end--- My mother's around, may have arranged the party but wont be in it to interfere (Ah Gaby Jean!)---elements of N.Y. of course keep creeping in--- Wine, beer, all kinds of drinks are ready--- Jim Calabrese is coming, and Cody and Evelyn, and groups of Subterraneans but well dressed and cool I dont even know but heard about the party and come, almost hos-tile to my fame. . . Watson must be there, and Madeleine is there--- Julien---but the people, the friends are powerful, intimate composites instead of actualities, for the poor brain yearns--- Everybody arrives---it is quiet, polite hubbubs as befits the beginning of a party--- But does everybody recall my saying "Something that was supposed to happen just didnt happen?"---(I'm a writer, a sad figure)---and without a warning the party begins to crumble---no laughter---bad

27

sign---the Subterraneans just sit embarrassed not talking to anybody---Garden is trying to talk-----Cody is stony silent---there are arrivals and dispersals, not much gayety or drinking ---Groups pull out "momentarily" to hit the bar across the street---It starts to snow---The sadness deepens---soon everyone realizes the party is a sad failure-- Sympathetic expressions appear on some faces-- Small groups get in huddles discussing the party anxiously-- Some girls come to me with condolence faces---Of course *I'm* not worried because I have already arranged for a small private party in Lionel's pad in a tenement not far in the snow and have already cut in and out of there several times and back to the "official" main party---at Lionel's there's been records, tea, a few girls, Danny Richman, Josephine---but always these heartbreaking composites and not actualities---Cody has been in and out of this side party, like when we flew in and out of Deni Bleu's with Lionel and Danny---in fact Deni is there, has just returned from a ship, has bought (undoubtedly) a lot of the wine and beer and is deeply disappointed, as always---Finally almost no one is left at the party---Such silence and incommunicativeness has existed between the partyists that it's become a heated, shocked topic of the evening among the handfuls of intimate, rapidly-getting-drunk friends left in my parlor---I'm a little worried because all the efforts of my good mother to give me a nice birthday party have gone in vain--- Cody rolls up some tea in the kitchen, leaves Buckle and me 6 sticks each sitting on the table and departs (without much comment, that is, he's not involved in my trouble or with any of the people, and I'm not actually in trouble anyway, just anxious to hear Cody's opinion which will not come because even as a composite he has lost his contact

with judgments of this kind)--- I'm standing out in the little
court, most of them have left, took the drinks with them---
in the little open court, snowing on me in the night, I gaze
fondly at the little shuttered cottage (like neighbors back of
Cody at 1047)---I tell Buckle, who's smoking his tea, "This is
the little house of my past---How odd that one of the fruits
of my being grown up and successful is to have this little
house of eternity in my backyard, ah spectral night! Oh holy
snow! These mysteries---my father---what shall we all do?"
I consider smoking that tea to dig my little house better---
the neighbors who live in it are not in at present, an "old
couple"---but no, I've laid off tea, it alienates my soul from
me "as it has done Cody's from himself"---the little house
has old gingerbread eaves, brown, a fairytale house of lost
infancies in some kingdom of the past--- Sad, I go back to
the last drinks, the last guests at my party--- I have my overcoat on and sit in a chair, glooming--- The piano, someone's
at the late, last piano, among empty glasses---Everybody
is crushed to realize that people could have made such a disastrous mess of a poor party, not being able to talk or communicate to the point where it embarrassed them to
realize. . . the whole generation afflicted. . . Up to me comes
the brunette I loved, and still somewhat love-- She's "Jim
Calabrese's sister" or maybe even Jim Calabrese but "definitely not Marguerite," more Maggie Cassidy, sexy, sad, inti-
mate---She is also so strongly Madeleine Watson that I
shudder to think of these Names;- She says to me, brooding,
"Come on, let's go spend the morning somewhere---the
party's over, dont be sad-- Comfort me."

        "Comfort you?" I say with a dawning joy.
"How?"

"Just comfort me---anyway you can think of." Immediately I picture myself eventually devouring her in kisses and love--- I'm all heartbroken to love her---and grateful---and hang on---and incidentally hastily reprimand myself: "Her family would have liked you to marry her a few years ago---she was in love with you then---You'd have not only her but lots of money now"---"But you let it all go for some chimera about yourself, concerning sadness, and so your party *is* sad, fool"--- Meanwhile June Ogilvie has been in and out of my party, with the Subterraneans, like a stranger, an onlooker---she talked of other things with them---But my intimate group in which Madeleine is included talks only of sadness and is a fine group---I go out with Madeleine, to the waterfront; there one of her seaman friends is on the corner of a pier, goodlooking, muscles, strange long arms---he grabs her and pushes her against the wall and goes into a deep kiss---her hand reaches out to me, at first I think with horror of this "comfort" of hers but it's for the quart of port wine in my arms---she takes a slug, back to wall, thug to cunt,---I'm amazed---it seems I know this guy, too, and yet of course I'm jealous---A minute later I try to push her against the wall too, for a kiss like that, especially so she'll be soft and out-hipped to me just like she did for him, but she resists, slips out, I end up groping at her cheek for a lost kiss---("Damn your dreams!" says Evelyn---) I'm afraid even to ask what she wants for "comfort" and I have somehow betrayed her request, too,---This is the Maggie Cassidy part---her rich parents was the Marguerite Calabrese part---

Back at the party, it's now another day, the house has changed into a working office, all the people are there working at desks, it must be Monday morning, gray skies press in at the windows, it's like the Hospital ward at Kingsbridge for location (overlooking New York) (in "Albany")---My desk is at north end, like my bed was--- Wallington's desk south of that, where the Negro Johnson was and also the dying Mr. Kaiser---(was)---Elements of the party are still around, but all at work now--- There are brochures, folders,---issues,---now Madeleine is busy, not as dark, working, not as sexy,---mysterious happenings,--- Even the Subterraneans come in and out of the West hall with papers--- But Wallington is quietly and steadily talking, or dictating, at his desk and isnt confused at all---I've been confounding at mine--- I hear him say "We've got to work in love or not at all---" These confident words I see also printed on his brochure which I have in my hand--- "WE'VE ALL GOT TO WORK IN LOVE, NOTHING ELSE"---in love, AT love---LOVE---he is preaching this strange thing in a solemn businesslike office and's not even embarrassed, I recognize him now suddenly as a great man, a saint, he is steadfast and almost mad in his insistence on this---and particularly because of my party, which gave impetus to his conviction, and everybody knows it---Great Wallington Preaching Love in our midst, from his desk in Our Office---but at the back of our minds we all know the authorities wont listen, Wally is already some sort of crank in his "Love" work---but I am moved, and wake up in the night full of awe and realizations---

THAT GORGEOUS BLONDE DANCING BARE-BREASTED on a golden stage before the sullen Charlotte N.C. audience, that Zaza-like Gabor beauty---at one point

31

she began pulling up her panties, you could see the brown hairs of her Venus hump starting to show between her sensuous thighs so sexy-tossed---Old ladies began leaving the theater in civic excitement, finally even young men rose and held local caucuses among their seats and I even heard some of them calling for a committee, a rope, a lynching---uproars gathered---the blonde danced on, her huge bulbous soft white breasts with pale pink nipple bouncing in the golden footlight glow--- I began to cry out "Stop this furor, this is a beautiful woman---enjoy and watch her---never mind your lynchings and laws---Is that *all* you're interested in? There's life and love staring you in the face, sip it while you can--- besides you dont want to harm a nice woman like that---"No one hears me; angry Southerners are shouting with Southern accents and it seems I never knew they were so mysteriously vicious and organized in that---there are rushes out of the theater---I run to the stage door, I run after the blonde who's now put on her blue slacks and is hustling to her bus with her traveling bag---across a field in back of the barracks theater--- shaking her head and saying to me "Well I guess it didnt go over in Charlotte---Elmira's my next engagement---I've been on the road with this act for a month---grossed pretty well in Kewark---" and so on with showbusiness gravity and "innocence"---of issues in the real, political world---and she's short, God so tall and statuesque on the stage and so buxom, and here a short businesslike little showbusiness blonde cuttin along in slacks---fast, fast walker, I can hardly keep up---

THEN I REVISIT SELMA CALIFORNIA scene of my 1947 cottonpicking and living in a tent with Bea and child---

but buildings all over the cottonfield now, strange brown grocery store-cabooses on the tracks rolling, wide as a real house, lights inside, goods on shelves---for the "use" of section hands---I go across these litters, enter a store, a beautiful sexy brunette says turning to her father "See, all the men go for me"---this after I appraised her with appreciation and said something---

"Alright Irene," her thin Okie-like father says, resigned---I sit inside the stationary bench at the table waiting to be served---I realize she's "Irene Wrightsman" and this is "Wrightsman the oil millionaire," her father---I realize I can come into money with her---

"Do you know so-and-so?" she says to me---"Cousin of so-and-so?"

"Sure---the one---"

"That cousin'll inherit a million in oil--" (which I know beforehand.)

I start to wake up and forget all about her sex to speculate with myself and with them about these millions---(Railroad call, knock on door)---

And that very day I see for the very first time a brown ranch style prefabricated house being rolled out on wheels at San Mateo---right out on the road---and mention the dream to brakeman Neal McGee, who laughs and says, "Well must have been a *nightmare!*"

I WANTED TO STEAL A PINK WOOLEN SWEATER from the outside counter of a Jewish clothing store across the street from the park---right on the spot where I was when I watched the boy with the runaway horse and loose reins---

New Haven, but also the Chicago of Parks and just as I woke up the realization that it was only the real Frisco and the park was just a Boston addition to it---but I grabbed the sweater, just like a can of Spam in the store, tried to fold it under my coat, or in my arms, walk casually across the Montreal traffic to the Park, but as I woke up it seemed he saw me and also that I only dream-daydreamed stealing it---pink, wool, I dont even need a sweater, Edna had a pink one, I had a red cashmere one for awhile (where?)---(when?)---(Barbara Dale in Greenwich Village)---it is the middleclass security of pink wool sweaters I wanted.

MY POOR SAD MOTHER ANGIE is trying to get off a crummy, I see her up the track, she's carrying burdens, she's "followed me on the railroad," it's hard for her with her old legs to jump off the high caboose step, but she does---How short, squat, sad she looks---how long suffering, that now in these last tired years she "follows me on the railroad"--- Finally, after a series of "moves," in the night, she's standing by a switch, we're finished for the night---she looks so tired, old and grayhaired and finally weary now, heavier, much slower, no longer bubbling---my heart breaks when she says "Ride ton *point*, Jean---and dont walk on your poor legs--- ride---and come back home." I'm going to "ride my point" to the other end, that'll be the end of my day's work, we'll rest now---worked so hard---my heart is broken, God, by this sad lonely mother you made me come from and by the poor way she used the railroad word "point" with a French Canadian accent and sadly as if talking to her baby---having to use this harsh Okie word under the stress of earth's harsh

inhospitable circumstances---Ah Lord, save her---save me---
she is my Angel and my Truth---Why does it tear my heart
out that she pronounced it "pwaint"---that French Canadian
way of using English to express its humility-meanings---no
non-French Canadian knows this---

THEN (SEVERAL WEEKS LATER) (at Cody's again) I
dream I'm in Mexico City with Cody but there's a wild
Kearney Square just like and in fact Lowell, except for strange
dark faces like the faces of Armenians or Syrians but really
Mexicans arguing angrily on the square, and the darkness
beyond the lights of the Square has that dense soft ink-like
quality of the Great Mexico City Night---it's Kearney Sq.,
there's the corner of Merrimack and Bridge, the Post Office
and Auditorium to the left, but the neons are soft deep colors
like blood red, night blue, ink pink, jade green,---especially
that night blue, that dye blue pervades the mellifluous air in
the Lowell Redbricks beyond the Square, and I'm so amazed
that Lowell and Mexico City are the same---but then, at
Bull's house, located back on Bridge Street, in his gray flat, he
seems listless, "only wants his money back," doesnt want to
come out, is not much interested in this fact that I am there
(just as in his last letter)---and Cody is already gone, I have
said "But we didnt even go to Organo Street!"---he only
stayed a day, or a matter of hours, but it really doesnt make
any difference to me either, "speech was our concern, is our
concern no more," all that's left is that incredibly dense, soft,
dark, rich Spanish night or Indian night or New World City
night---the blue of tombs is in the neons, the secret of the
Old Fish is on Old Fish street, the dark spoor of real pro-

found red throbs from the lights of the Merced shacks, all Lowell Mexico City has become a slightly alien, ugly but soft and kindly night for me to roam my head in alone---I wind up at the Organo Street whores, there's two of them, the usual cot with rat-eaten drape of burlap, there's a hassel over something, money, Cody or somebody just went, says, "Ah but they're *really* filthy" but which I know they're not really, being Indian Beauties with greasy hair is all---("Then it couldnt have been me!" laffs Cody.)

Just before waking I'm at table, kitchen, with Ma and Nin but at Cody's table here in San Jose, and I pour olive oil out of a huge can onto my toast, "Easy!" they say but I spill it all over an inch deep, but to make up for it I say "Alright save that olive oil for tonight, we'll butter our toast with it and use it on potatoes, dont worry, save it, I never waste anything," ---which I dont.

THE MOST INCREDIBLE BEAT DREAM in the world, it's near St.Rita's church, on that street from Moody, but as my mother and sister Nin and I are traveling up Mammoth Road on some kind of train a woman rushes up shouting "I want to see Dinah Shore!" ---She, Dinah, lives right up the street, right at the location of that grammar school---in a house---she has a "canary yellow" jeepster or convertible, which I point out to the lady saying, "That'll be her house there, Olivia DeHaviland has a canary yellow car"---(confusing the names)---My mother and sister accompany the woman: but I stay behind in a kind of suddenly transplaced Sarah Avenue house, it's Sunday, I'm the 30 year old beat brother and loafer of the family---"Dinah Shore" is standing in front of her house, and, seeing that I had directed the woman autograph hound to her she says, bleakly looking at me in an "official" or "Hollywood courteous" way---"Wont you come in with us?" (for a bleary visit)---

"Oh no---I'm busy--" but, they can see that I'm yielding and in my head I've started calculating advantages I can get from knowing "Olivia de Haviland"---So I give in, but in such a beat obvious way, and we go on in---

"I'm a novelist," I announce forthwith, "you shrould read my book," I say to the hostess---"Your husband is a writer too---a very great writer, Marcus Goodrich." Then the persistentfiction I have that Dinah Shore is really Olivia De Haviland has to break down here and I say "Oh well, of course, yes, you're Dinah Shore, I keep thinking you're Olivia de Haviland"---but this is so gauche---and I havent shaved and stand there in her parlor, she is bleakly attentive, I'm like a thinner younger Major Hoople who really had a small taste of early success but then lost it and came home to live off his mother and sister but goes on "writing" and acting like an "author"---on the little street---But now, my sister sees that I am botching everything so she steps in and in an even more beat awful gauche way begins to try to impress Dinah with a kind of halting Canuck-English speech (attempts at 'social smartness') (and really painful to hear) goes into some speech about how this and that, and so on, to show how really chic she's been at one time, we've been, our really more elegant real backgrounds than what shows (and in spite of this pitiful brother, and she's spoken up really to cover me up and also cut me, as she has her own ideas about how to impress people like Dinah Shore) to which Dinah listens even more bleakly---and my mother standing by like the original lady who wanted an autograph---it ends on this bleak beat note. . . with me all anxious and chewing my nails---the comic opera of our real days---

I'm also a neighborhood self-styled roué ready to make all the housewives but they dont really want any part of me, except a few of the older ones who want to have something on my mother---

A WHOLE 13 HOURS NIGHT OF DREAMS---I visit "Eddy Albert's" house on a kind of Andover Street, incredibly rich house, also previously dream'd, "Ernie Malo's" house which is of course the Andover, and "namelessly" connected to that dream-house where I'd lost my pants---New Britain, the football stadium, the river, the levee, the Hartford-New Orleans glittering-dark boulevard, the roominghouse I lived in---Eddy Albert's father who in real life showed me a $100-bill is in this dream, in rich Mackstoll livingroom, I come in from Andover street, pause to admire rich modernistic front like Spanish style but simpler, "these people have millions," a great Tolstoyan house of halls and events and patriarchs by the fireplace, I say hello to everybody in that nameless New York which is in Keresky's San Remo or whatever Towers---Gad the Jewish millionaires I've known to whom a thick rug means more than all the Salvations of 2 Billion suffering mortals on the groaning world---the evil intelligence of Bill Keresky! In the Eddy Albert bathroom I pause, looking out, as his sister 'Jacky' (after Jacky Keresky) comes home in an old car and steps out with a pet turkey---very pretty, pale faced, dark eyed, little sensual rings under her eyes---I'm watching, like a masturbator in the bathroom, mindful she'd never dream within this dream I'm watching her---the rich Jacky, I could have her and have millions but she'd never gave me a look and never would (I remember her bedroom near the bathroom when she was 17, 1939, now she must just be a randy old pet bitch of time with a demand for minks turning over whole industries)---but here she's still a young girl---and it's gray outside, somehow raining, like the tragic Andover Mansion--- Also, at the Phebe Avenue house there's been a kitty soaked in cement, thought to be dead he was left on a branch to decay in his pitiful cast, but suddenly I saw him try to move and still alive, I cried out, I ran to my mother to ask her to help him, she got a knife or stick to scrape him with, wet him with hot water, he cried from the pain of this, he was supposed to have been dead for 3 days---I tried to imagine who were the beasts on Gershom or Phebe or Sarah who had pulled such a stupid gag---(like, of course, the cat in Life Magazine)---on the green porch where I'd played jockey (stirrups on rail) my mother worked hard to save the little cat---her face drawn in the strain but she wont give up---the cat stirs with life, it's amazing how his little spirit managed to live anyhow---

There were other dreams, sagas of them,---I cant remember but these 2 for tonight---they come close-packed in one cunning steady stream from the same fount--- I woke up rejoicing in the music of the little birds and had a vision of the Indian squatting in the soft brown land of the brown mountain in the blue sky not Spain but Mexico--- prophetic dream of 8 o'clock a Spring morning on Sarah Avenue Lowell---Why write, rejoice unendingly like humble St. Francis---return to New York on foot followed by the children, come to kneeling Irwin and Stavrogin-eyed Julien in an East Side Street---keep within yourself the fund of love and rejoicing, be in your soul the child the same child again, forget literature and English after these next 15 years of Art, and retire to fasting and prayer in the desert and descend to the sweet villages of Man

LOUSY DREAM that I'm back with June and am standing around in gray dull suites that cost a lot of money but are necessary as she's temporarily with "My Child" having to live someplace, the chimera of money-spending is now official on account of My Child, the understanding is now official on account I'm to be slave and goat to this all my life, no question any more of the bard and his apple branch,---also understood there's to be no love lost between us but My Child is supreme so I'm standing there, it's an interim arrangement, it's located somewhere near that sad Sheridan Square of my dreams, she's got pins in her mouth for diapers, I dont actually look at the baby even once, dont know what it looks like, dont care but am somewhat apprehensive to look into all that radiance of flesh---I guess I am haunted by the Radiance of her appeal in the pit---but already in back of my mind I realize it's impossible, this hypocrisy and adult hate superimposed on innocent foundations of children who should get a better building but mainly I'm sore and want to leave and am planning to get a duffle bag within the hour, throw everything in, and be gone by morning because she's already beginning to suspect my intentions and will call the cops again within 24 hours--- America: in Silone's Italy Bastiano throws chairs at this weeping wife, in America the woman has the Police State Telephone in one hand and My Child swathed in incredible bills in the other---Bastiano may murk and scream, but

Milquetoast Jones the Sucker is a poor cunteater being devoured by the thing he eats, in the glare of white neons, with his balls cut off by the Amazons and Lesbians of the Support Court, Life Magazine, Good Housekeeping, the Bureau of the Interior and Dwight D. Eisenhour's serious countenance and manly fists---ah Kafka you never had it so good.

Also I've been playing around, or pursued by---a---sexy cunt---Alice Arsenault, or whatever her name, an evil doll with a hatred of June, she's trying to make me to foment girl trouble between them, they're Lesbians---I know this but I am amazed by the sexiness of this doll but smoke tea and try to really ignore her but spend most of my time trying to ward her off, we're in a room right around the corner and by God she looks no different than June in her snaky pre-marriage days with me---it's all gray, hopeless, I'm gonna put my head on the rail if this ever comes about---

LAST NIGHT IT WAS MY FATHER, in San Jose yards I'm coming back from a chain gang freight run, he's there in black railroad gloom vestments, looks like that sour old hoghead with the cigar (Greaves)---carried a lamp---everything dark, the black railroad earth, shining rails, soot, dim brown lights, and red and green, in this hopeless plain I say "Hey Pa where'd you go? What'd you do at home? Where's Ma?" and sundry questions, trying to talk to him, and he turns away without a word, refuses to talk to me---I'm sad---But when I wake up I pound the pillow and say "This father and son business has gone far enough!" ---(What do I mean?)---My father is so obviously Cody in this dream and reminds me that they both wear (sometimes) the same expression on their faces, the mouth inpuffed with indignation that's held in, the face bleak, the jaw grim, the eyes stone---mainly a stiff-necked refusal to talk. . .my father pulled that on me many's the time---Who am I?

"MY MOTHER IS PREGNANT" and she'll have to go to Chicago for an abortion so I'm going to be alone in the city awhile and I'm cuttin out of this poolhall on a Friday night, I'm wearing a white shirt with starched collar, and a tweed sports jacket and clacking along like I used to do in prep school and college, at first I take a quick view of the doings of the boys in the borwn poolhall, the card tables, then I hit the glittering city night and I'm free to do things on my own for a week or so, and I'm young and happy---

AN INDESCRIBABLE SERIES OF EVENTS IN A HOUSE, I'm about to put on a green sports jacket and a green knit tie very bright and throbbing green and almost as tho painted and glazed green over the twills---I'm going to put it on with the coat---but I have no clothes on, I'm sick, like measles or whopping cough---the snaky necktie is central in the picture.

BLURRED PLACES AND EVENTS have been throwing me off my dream track---like the hullaballoos and sad mysteries going on in the gigantic basketball court like Fenway Park but with steep balconies frightful to fall down like a great Metropolitan Opera House---reminding me of old

42

1943 dreams of a place like that in Liverpool with my father and the boys from the ship and many crowded narrows of shipping and rusty bridges outside---wild---great shouts of crowds, events, games, track meets, sometimes I'm all alone in the great dark corridor in back of the gallery doors and I'm wandering around looking for a great room like in Joe Fortier's house and his mother's room and his spectral cellar vast like Lowell High School below, the whole thing sometimes a boat floating on water---(did I tell about the hardwood floor in that 'new city' apartment and my father sick and I have to go to work?---These dreams---and another one just as vague but connected, for the balcony of the stadium is also the movie balconies of Brooklyn and baseball bullrings of life in general---tho from what hant to come and *how* is this to come?---the lemon bay stretches out---timeless eternity of Debussy maidens beyond---and on---

SO I'M GOING THROUGH EL PASO, a clear dream and vision, it's all wild and merceds and shacks jumbled like Thieves' Market and just like it with green shacks, fruit littered dirty mud walks, Arabic filth behind, squatting brown ragged figures, blocks and blocks of it under the clean blue sky of Indian City morning, smoke rising from a thousand noxious pots, strange hidden robes, wild, orange peels, bananas, the end---I'm driving through with somebody and cry out "Look at this wild Es Paso!---the cat told me it was the wildest place in America if you live downtown!---this is sure downtown!"---and blocks to the fore began the skyscrapers of a spectral city but it wasnt Mexico City it was on a plain in Texas and not only that the Texas of raw snow and moons and mountains for suddenly I saw Apache Navajo Indians with their shaggy ponies at a dismal rack, in front of almost buffalo tents in the general rueful wreckage of the market shacks and they wore floppy rider hats stained and rolled by snows of the Texas plains, and brilliant big blankets which also were thrown over their mournful little paints---the Texas, the St.Joe and the Independence of the Old Real America, dismal, cold, vapors rising from their brown mouths, feeble thin smoke from fires not warm enough, the cold blue keen February morning sky---El Paso of the frontier border, of the Navajos and Indians, of the market shacks and dung heaps and ponies, of the sad Indians and dumps of poverty---downtown wild huge Merced El Paso---I was stoned! I wanted to get off the car and live there, work on the railroad, dig it, like I'd planned---Get *high!*---

LONG BEFORE I WORKED ON THE RAILROAD, in earlier dreams of traveling down the ribneck Mexican continent, it was always rails---railroads---sad mountains---the railroad, the yellow ground---long sad trips---Now I'm in Mexico City, I go to live in the sumptuous apartments of Bull and June, June is still alive after all---They have rich brown furnishings, but somehow they got hungup to live with a paternal older couple and awful bores, an Okie 40-year-old painter or carpenter, goodnatured but suspicious, mock gay, and a funny type middleaged thin whacky woman with (like Vera Buferd) a husky voice, Tallulah like, sexy---I go into the bedroom with an understanding with June that we're gonna do some fucking, we get in bed together, June rambles and talks, but suddenly the woman jumps in bed too and that brings the

Okie and it appears he's not pleased about that or something's wrong and dammit I'll have to leave the comfort of this house---so I never get to bang poor sad June---and Bull is somewhere in the house, silent, isnt interested in those El Paso Navajo ponies of mine---(like when I lay in bed beside June one time in the dark at 118th street on benny and Bull came in and sat talking to us, I guess)---The wacky woman doesnt really want to screw but to create an issue that will get me out of the house, as I long suspected of E. So I'm out in the Indian cold again, and return to El Paso, and walk in the dirty snows with angels in my soul, whoopee! That Es Paso!!

ALL THE GAY LITTLE BALLET DANCERS OF ECSTASY are around---it's the Theater, I'm there, that old spooky opera house and high school auditorium and class-meet hall of all my days, with hints from all the stages of Time's earth and actors too, and behind is all the corridors, props, dancing girls, phantoms, sceneshifters, stagehands, Lon Chaneys, Ernie Malos and Madeleine Poopy Dolls of poor time---I dont know what happened, seats, darkness, lights, crash, events, hooray, blah, wah, went backstage, falling sand-bags, the Marx Brothers---if it could have been the twig that was on that white wall, Crist Sakes the buses dont wanta growl fer leaves or let kiddies yell while the record turns and the machine drowns everything out sucking as it goes sugar, spice, matches, ragamuffy dusts---shit! It was the Theater, it was the Vast Dream, too much to understand and cant wait till the day! Phnark!

Dreams in Mexico

A GREAT BIG MANSE, I live in it, the railroad's nearby---
a wandering stranger is trying to make me or buy me---but
I'm glad---Great trees in the yard---a well---swings---the
first clear dream in Mexico, but I didnt remember it----Joe
was there---and it takes place in the lost America---

WE'RE IN FRANCE, Cody and Evelyn and I, driving cross
country, I'm in the back of the station wagon on blankets and
sheets, the sun shines thru the glass, I say "It's hot waiting
here, let's get on to Paris!" but Cody is at the gas pump, busy,
and intends to stay in this rolling part of the country for some
time; the Country has Dali road signs strung about, Mutt and
Jeff cartoons in the shade, a crazy place, with a central ribbon
road rolling over the hill to Paris. But I cant believe we're
really going to Paris and I'm terribly impatient. What a dark
dream to have in a cold room. In a cold cell.

Dreams in Richmond Hill

A BARE BLEAK HILL "outside Mexico City" and I'm hiding in holes, looking towards the ocean for which it is also a
strange beach, people come looking for me in the rippling
winds---Finally I get a nice bagful of tea and feel it with my
hands, smiling---A friend is near---Events---

THE BUGLES WERE BLOWING in a white sand court
and I was there with the same soldier who crossed the

General MacArthur artilleries of the hospital dream and there's tents,---To the right, in dark stall, we got caught doing something; the hospital had red brick---I might have been wearing a polkadot shirt but more gray canvas and something from the field of elephants that tore up the dust of carnival field, the stands, the night, the people waiting---for the fireworks---I was given a white sheet, or shroud---In the yard the tents, the bugles---we were leaving for some kind of England---they had soups brewing in great stewpots in pig fat copper Kitchens of the Prime Roast of Rib and great omnivorous odor of boiling water so flavored---with beef. But nothing for us, a couple wasters. It had faintly to do with the hill house the other night when I was a child, under pines---not as clear as those original pines beneath a very early morning school of the hill at Hildreth behind where bakery stood---the young teacher, who also, (pretty as she was) had a place with a lake---early primitive woodchips--- and later, boats. . .but I'm just a little kid and I just woke up to the fact of the morning of life---and stand in the yard, dew wet, pink from eraser sun just come up over the school hill, a tot, bleak---I really did watch an Armistice Day parade in the cold red morning from my 3rd story wood porch, crying because I wanted to go back to the woods of all that summer

IN BULL H'S BIG AIRPLANE we're all gonna go fly---he has big wings, a DC-whatever, he takes off from our grand estate near the Pine Brook Woods and off we go---arriving at the Carnival City in the Strange Mexico, setting her down he does without a flaw on the big rubber tires over the black ground, rolls her right in---We have drinks in the plane---A

47

woman at first wanted to put her coat over my seat but I picked it up, sat, put it on my lap, she apologized, we finally laid it over a back rest of the seat, and throbbed and shivered on across the air---Where are we? doing what?---Just a little intimate group of us going up in the plane---The runways are waiting for us---There had been events in New York apartments, we flew off---the place we're landing at is that Mexico of Navajo Smokepots, merceds and sad ponies of El Paso; banners are rippling:- we've come to our business there---it's also the Gen. MacArthur hospital grounds---and Canada---always dreamy weird---place of last night's tents---

WILD AS SEEN FROM THE TOP OF A GRASSY HILL outside town, it's Mexico City, where are elephant water holes, funny shepherds, me with a huge well not huge medium sized bag of tea in which I'm running my hand as though gold but it's just weed, and the day's bright, flowing clouds, the Plateau North of the Great America of the World is fine and white like a beard of a patriarch in the Popopapacetl Sky---my silk and lace-able you---Events---

IN A NEW YORK LOFT LIKE JULIEN'S or Finistra's but it belongs to Watson who's been making money writing thrilling love sex stories etc., there's one, huge proofs on a table with illustrations, starting, "It was just another day I was starting as usual with nothing on beneath my flimsy dress"--- with illustrations, I'm there, by the fire escape, alone, but it's also Evelyn who wrote it and is Watson and she's out with Cody right now. The "proofs" are a gigantic bound book long about three feet, wide one foot---like my father's Spotlites and ballooned to great size---Alan Minko's around someplace, it's also some missed Paris---

ROLAND BOUTHELIER is driving us, Ma, me and a bunch of kids in the back seat, from some festivities---We were at a springtime town with a castle and wooden tenements---I daydreamed of living there, in huge rooms of castle, of my sister being amazed by the size of my room and Ma's room---Also I wanted to live in the tenements and I looked up and some of them were abandoned, broken windows, looked burned---(We traveled thru Maine, incredibly sad the land--) I walked around, the grounds of the castle, the town,-- In the castle itself was Bertha Fortier Joe's sister all alone there with him and Philip---family gone yelling---and a little Mexican child they owned who climbed up way high on the facade and fell down landing in the courtyard with a tragic plop bouncing on hands and knees on his belly flop knees and I thought "Oh he'll be crippled for life like that!" ---like a paralytic swimming but Joe didn't seem to notice nor the Mexican child hurt---he'd just hung down and dove off his perch---Then I asked Bertha for a sandwich, considered sex with her, thought of her big figure on the couch etc.---wandered around the big halls back of the kitchen--- The "main" family was gone away on some celebration--- Then I took a cab and had to rush to find a lawyer in the little side street shopping district off the hill of Moody---I was on the hill, hailing cabs, got one, big car, in which the driver had his wife or woman with him up front but in the backseat her huge coat and bundles took up all the room and

I had to push hard everything over, cursing, so I could sit but they didnt notice---When we got to the show I paid the fare, leaped out, and realized I didnt really know there was a lawyer at this shopping-movie-district, had only heard--- There were swinging doors, a saloon, people, noise---the name of some dentist or lawyer on a plate---melting snow-banks in the street stores---

Joe---Roland---O lost---He, Roland, was driving us back to Lowell in the '29 Model T Ford, pretty soon we'd see the dreambrick factories over the pines again--- and it would be Sunday---and the Pawtucketville of the radar mystery air raids, of terror---the Royal Theater is dark even right now--- My Ma sat in front with Roland as he drove the Lakeview Road which is like the spectral Mexico Road--- My father not there---As tho once Joe, Philip, Ma and I went driving alone with Roland---

Pauvre Roland, he's also Cody---It was warm, sunny, earth-springing melting in that Castletown, we'd gone South, the snow was trickling, humidifying, mak-ing muds fragrant in the fine air---Events---I was sent for the lawyer merely, wasnt the hassler in dark halls---All this is gone forever. What is the name of our death?

All that we lost will come back to us in heaven.

I'M HURRYING OFF into the sandbank in back of the old ladies' house, naked, dont want nobody see me---I see a bunch of little kids coming, I sit in the sand, buried half to the waist, till they pass, they look at me curiously---Then I resume my hegira in the woods---Back at the old ladies' redbrick place there's been a big party, banquet, Audace and the other dames set the table for huge roaring gettogethers, Mel Torme was there even and played the piano and I leaned my head eyes closed on the upper keyboard to hear him play, Mel didnt mind, played wild and good on the rest of the keyboard---

A BIG PARTY in Mexico City mixed in with the Mel Torme party but not the same, a fabulous gathering, John Labine, Worthington, Watson etc.---a lot of coats---Hubbard somewhere---drunk I stagger out of this party, Worthington and Watson send me a telegram which gets to me some way ---It was worded by Watson, a friendly telegram, ordinary, but the sound, the tone of it is so--semi-sissified--or what-ever--that I get mad and do not respond to it---So that when later I accidentally run into W & W in a little bar off Times Square (I'm with Garden or somebody) and we all have a happy reunion and all's forgiven still I take the crumpled telegram out of my pocket and read it with frowns and shakes of my head---I'd almost thought it sarcastic, insincere, hypo-critical---but now we're reuniting gladly over brews, it's just a little bar, brown oldfashioned, like the wonderful bars I dream behind Scollay Square Washington Street Boston and especially deep among the lost mills of Lowell, little dark *bouges*, wonderful, and in fact the Labine party was in a London-type apartment, duplex, upstairs, over one of these old bars,---and the lights of the city are shining all around like in a vivid cartoon--- Some guy at one point wanted to start a fight, at the party or in the bar now---But we're all gay and glad and reunited and Watson is shrewdly scrutinizing and devouring everyone of my visible outward expressions as

51

still I frown and wonder over the wording of the telegram---
I think Hubbard had seen it earlier and said "Hyah hyah
hyah!" the way he laughs, slapping his knee, that much
absurdity, and Irwin had gravely discussed it (semantically)
with me on the sidewalk.

BIG HOUSE ON THE EDGE OF THE COUNTRY, "Jim
Calabrese's" house but at the same time my house because
Ma lives there finally---but with rippling Africa trees and lots
of land in back leading to Colorados and New Britains and
New England dreamlakes---(of the mind) But one time, I'm
there when Jim lived there, his father John Calabrese is with
us in the well furnished livingroom, we have cocktails, there's
some kind of joke, we're all laughing--- It goes namelessly
into a Sunday afternoon jazz session in a nightclub I guess in
Mexico City with Slim Gaillard and Bull Hubbard is there,
we have no drinks but are waiting, turns out ice cream and
cookies will be passed around on trays, no drinks---
The musicians are gathering---Bull is talking to me---
Demosthenes the Greek kid from Lowell is there, and others,
standing around talking--- Slim Gaillard sits at tables and jaws
with people---Bull is polite and excited---looking around,
like John MacDougald---But later I'm in Africa, in an estate
in the middle of great rolling grasslands, my "parents" are
there whoever they are, the front yard is a lot like Joe's yard
on Salem Street and come to think of it Joe was also at the
"Jim Calabrese house" tragic and quiet and just out of the
hospital but now in the Africa house he seems to be transformed into a Negro buddy and together we, after many
preparations, play, talk, and smiling approvals of my smiling

hunter trader Mau Kuwi father set off with a water buffalo in our wagon to hit the long grass---some enormous adventure that'll take us around the world eventually through Russia, Europe---it's all like the back of the Bartlett Junior High, I see maps of the world---It's like my old cartoons, dreaming of myself---That's our destination, the spectral Europe---We have spears, we've had athletic contests with them and in a funny way now I realize Joe-Negro-Spearman-Buddy was also at my other "Jim" house where my mother lives, and stayed with us awhile---In the brown bleak kitchen, with doors open to summernight, trees dark-waving, poor pale sick haunted Joe! He's been sick lately---always trying to get on with the game---like little Michel of FORBIDDEN GAMES---meanwhile the generations jazz on in Sunday afternoon nightclubs eagerly gabbing like Pat Fitzpatrick---Is this all I can remember of all these events, talk, seething feelings, mysteries?

FINALLY I'M AN OLD WHORE waiting in my bed, sexless, knowing the only time I'll wake up is when young boys are brought to me---instead of the usual round of old ladies---apparently I'm a male---I wake up surprised---there is no scene, just my bed, me in it, 11 o'clock Sunday morning---dismal like the 'beat brother' on the little gray street with the house, but my sister's not around, and from a horrible tired-out brother I've turned in my shame into a Silly Dylan Thomas old whore. . .old whore alcoholic and told everybody so. . .a silly Jack Kerouac whore with that same old tired old gasafaycagoo.

STE.JEANNE D'ARC CHURCH the long low basement cellar church on the hill at Crawford and Mt Vernon in Lowell,---gloomy masses, vespers, gray, the kids, me, people--- There've been holdups in there, gangs of thugs walk in from various doors with guns and conduct holdups as the priest continues with his *ad altre deums* and hardly anybody notices except a quiet gossippy panick---I'm there during one, with my little chums, the young men in gray coats in the doors--- after (no money taken, nothing that I can see happening) we all rush out to the dark street to chase and find them---they're gone---there's snow, kids, sliding in the gray air---I walk along home down dark Moody, dark Gershom, discussing it, to my dark house on Sarah---everything has that darkness of things buried in the ground decomposing---it's ME---I see my tree sprouting from my hand now, I see Novenber through the bone, I'm waiting for further Springs and blossoms for my black, I'm the Frankenstein of my own 6 foot grave goodbye little golden children of the glee mad world.

A HORROR CAVE becoming a horror boat of some kind, there are alleyways, monster, knives, iron bars, grates, worst of all iron spikes that close in and trap you and multistab your Jumping-around of these horrors on a gray day---I dont know what for, finally the river the boat's anchored on rises gray and fast and on the bank is the sand beach like the Boulevard and instead of taking off for Africa now that I've conquered the monsters and Bela Lugosis below, my boat (with attendant tied-on rowboat) capsizes and sinks utterly and I'm left swimming for my life to the shore in the strong seaward run of waters but make it surprisingly easy like

swimming in a bathtub and reach the sandbar with one playful last little kick---

Meanwhile I've also been on Amsterdam
Avenue at Columbia U. where bookstalls are established right
on the Livingston Hall sidewalk, I steal a couple of brand new
tho small art books, walk around, look for Edna in her grandmother's window---bookstealing now added to my spectral
missing of classes---nobody notices---

Later I see vision of a present I gave Nin, a
big rose colored wood bureau, and a smaller present on top
of it, a chest, box, furniture of some kind, it's in an apartment,
brown, dreary, talk, events---it's all too much to remember---

WE WERE IN TRAINING---we had to pass under the little plank with our bicycles, everybody made it but me, I
couldnt even bend down let alone pass myself or the bicycle
under, tho I did succeed to some extent,---"Well this guy's
got too many muscles," laughed a sub coach---"Yeh, I'm
muscle bound," I said, "I cant even bend---" It's because I'm
wearing my big thick wintercoat---and "muscle bound" is
the fat around my waist---Frank Leahy seems to be the head
coach, the place in Julien's loft, dark---a woman in an old
house is looking at us from the window---A bakery nearby---
We're learning to be Secret Service Sneakers---God the
mangled impossibility of those 'bicycles'!---

TRYING TO PLUG IN MY WEIRD LITTLE ELEC-
TRIC SHAVER in a bathroom wall plug---it's just a little tin
gadget with pieces of insulation,and sorrowful---People

come and watch me---There have been long, lost hegiras of trouble in troubled rooms, dark airs---I hope I dont get a shock when I put the "shaver" against the plugholes, I wait with anticipation.-(So that day Al Green presents the Ray electric shock lamp at me quivering purple and the little electricities *teek, teek,* and I feel it from across the room, in "anticipation" indeed---)

A DANCE, at the Commodore or some ballroom, a group of girls are haggling over boys, go out and aim at them when the music starts---one is a thick roundfaced boy in a tweed jacket all gloomily interested in himself and the dreary ages of his ego just begun---in rosy void night of balls---

AT THE GREAT BIG HIGH SCHOOL CHURCH SER-VICES in a gray dark Ste. Jeanne d'Arc basement type church which Eisenhower is attending and even making a speech and I at one point met a beautiful honeycolored girl and in some kind of ante room wrestle and moan with her, she has nothing on underneath, I force myself on her and finally surprise her by really getting her and completing the job---it has dreamlike unreality but charming and juicy---When the church service is over I file out with everyone else and there she is by the door in the aisle, I brush my lips on the sleeve of her coat, she says "You'd better!" (and we've already made an appointment for later)---Out on the church porch instead of going down the steps in the Pittsburg rainy town gloom I go over the balcony of Ernie Malo like and oldlady-MelTorme-like party houses in back, alleys, board fences, I climb down to avoid slow crush of crowds and come somehow to the tremendous sea, iron purples brood on its fantastic scape, clean, clear, I rush down the sand, the waves of dawn are enormous, our boat is to the right waiting, I'm signed on---we're going to that cold desolated spectral Greenland---the purple clouds, the gigantic waves---I jump in and dash around scared---the cannons are booming over the surf---Morning and new seas---

IMMENSE DREAMS OF AL GREEN and Frank Shephard ---Keiths' Theater---Red Rodney---the little pretty girl that sings for Godfrey is in some kind of foreign Paris with me (in a rickety roominghouse), her girlfriend's in love with Red Rodney, he undresses and they jump onto the couch together to bang---it's in some (there were jam sessions, Wig played bass) spectral Lowell---There's a high sandbank that I get caught on the top of, afraid to move, steep sides, sheer cliff drops but soft sand---G.J. with me on top---I lose my belongings (briefcase)---Later, in a Paris suburb, on twin cots in a little house Al and Frank are chatting, I've just arrived--- I want to buy a ticket to somewhere, to do so (take a walk talking with Frank then) go to the bar where Johnny the Bartender works, he's "off duty" today, standing at rear, I go up to him, "Are you off duty?" --- "No I come on at 12--- whattayou want to buy a ticket for?" (Johnny is Roland)--- He wears a hat and coat-- Earlier I was at Keiths' Theater in Lowell, an afternoon matinee, all the Strange matinees I've seen in gray dreams there---The Red Rodney dream and sandbanks is not far from the Bunker Hill of the Cody-Evelyn white horse that started all these dreams---Also, the little girl I have is reminiscent of the "Italian young gang" of fountains and Beautifulness dream'd long ago---dreams are prophesies--- The Maggie-Marguerite-Madeleine dream has all come true: I wrote "Maggie (Cassidy)", loved "Marguerite," and Madeleine will see soon---

The old Buferd park dream has obviously fulfill'd---(Wig drove by it---Wig is in Italian fountain girl dream)---

The huge dream and inevitability of the faces of Sebastian, Marguerite, La Negra---La Negra who will get me a kilo---

THE HIGH CLIFF OF GREENERIES, trees, buildings, rails, overlooking the down low plain of the world with its pale river and factories---I'm living on cliff, working railroad, they call me for a local down the cliff on the plain, I dont like it---The atmosphere is sad, advanced---

MA AND I ARE IN "NEW JERSEY" on a bright Saturday morning, we go into an abandoned roofless lot, find in tubs a great smoked ham, a box or pail full of living moving white sponges, a crate of pasta, all kinds of food---nobody around--- Ma takes the huge ham and goes around the corner to an outdoor sink in the lot and boils out---"You dont have to do that," I say--- "Oh yes!---it'll be (cleaner) better---" Meanwhile I work on the other stuff---in the bathtub---pas-trami like---Suddenly there's Van Johnson sitting there watching me--- "Is this your stuff?" I say---He seems no commentish---In two cottages at the end of the street his own huge mother is roaring mad---It's all the Saturday morning market merced New Jersey of the Navajo Indian El Paso too----My mother and I are tremendously happy, we've found $50 worth of non perishable food, we'll take it home to Long Island---and say "What is this place, a store they started and abandoned?"

EARLIER MY FATHER WAS BACK among the living--- very pale---but sure of his own health---and had just got a new job in New York---but I know he's going to die---especially from his face---He's been down to the Union--- Meanwhile I'd been high on a great building overlooking infinitesimal harbors, unafraid---The history of the Kerouacs in huge spectral dream New York.

★ ★ ★ ★ ★

SAD EPIC OF THE RAILROAD, I'm a brakeman, young, inexperienced, working across vast illuminated lands with my bird on a leash---Bird Handlers of the railroad take it from my hand after each trip---I do my work, finish a run which was up in some side country (of which more later)---arrive at end of run at sea coast, get off train and suddenly I lose the bird and it flaps up into sky with leash---"Hey!" I yell---it's happened before, you get demerits---"Where will it go?" I ask the Handlers whose sad work with cages and seed in dark Railroad Bird Roosts I'd never realized before-- Maybe I'll find it again someday roosted in a gable still with the leash around its little neck---or in a sand nest of the shore---but until then---It goes into a George Sanders sentimental comedy, he owns an antique store, is a bachelor, a beautiful girl comes to buy something, a romance starts, he takes her to

59

lunch, makes her a gift of one of his expensive doodads wrapped in a box (a present 'before lunch' and which to me seemed irrelevant)---his partner fetches it---and all the time you know someday George will re-find the bird---but he seems reluctant to continue in such a sentimental movie and tho my heart thrills, my spine shivers in the hope George Sanders will find his bird. . .he snuffs off the idea and is already displeased with this script and his part in it and you know the movie will not be a success---somewhere in his antiques, in his store, attic, loft, in the sadness of the dream, the leashed bird will reappear, the brakeman epic youth of George Sanders be roused up again---tears---The illuminated land to which the railroad ran. . .a man was driving all of us in a car, to a picnic, he swung off the road and over a double track for a shortcut but with a dead end curve so that you could never tell if a train was coming or not and tho I'm just a little boy nevertheless I worked long enough on the railroad to feel obliged and also licensed to yell 'O dont ever do that! it's the most dangerous thing you could do---find some other way to cross the tracks!' and everyone listens respectfully even my father, Pop, who might have been annoyed that I yelled at an old friend of his but they know and respect my railroad knowledge and nod and agree but suddenly I see that around the curve the doubletrack ends at a double deadhead block so it wasnt dangerous at all and I say "Oh well then it's alright, I thought--" and down at the station meanwhile trains are loading, arriving and departing--- We're having a big picnic, I'm under a grandstand in the rubble finding lovely fresh apples, fruit of all kinds for Ma and especially I want plums for her but only find one but a good one and bring it all back to her at the sand picnic very proudly and she thanks me---It is all during this time the bird is becoming mine and I work it---till my work leads me to the shore, and the loss---I see it fluttering weakly in the sky with the heavy leash---gray skies---

THE OTHER---ONLY LAST NIGHT---I was at the Mexican little border with drunk John MacDougald, still working for the railroad I kept re-crossing border with my pass easy as pie, Mac kept mauling at me drunkenly---I saw old Dave Orizaba my connection and we went into Mexico together talking---the border town was like Watsonville, with bank, restaurants, downtown streets---and rickety Mex out-skirts---in the border toilet MacDougald kept yelling and pulling at me, drunk, goofing, laughing harsh Falstaffian, etc.,---my bird, my bird--- O that cold minded George Sanders will never go to heaven!

DARKEST NIGHT ON THE COLUMBIA CAMPUS corner Broadway and 116th on the Barnard sidewalk, no streetlamps working---a dim mist of rains---shadows pass-ing---by my peanuts I stand waiting---warm April night---mystery of the West End Bar, the corpse in the Hudson, Edna in a Russian darkness over the campus---I'm almost afraid of marauders in this gloom, look around---Timeless the world waits---I wake up---wondering---

IN CODY'S HOUSE in San Jose sleeping on 'third floor' hard bed in middle of mysterious night---A long view of

East Santa Clara street with neon, thirst quenching softdrink and ice cream grocery store freezers, supermarkets, tokay liquor stores, California cocktail glass neon bars, TV---We were all in car, talking, around the corner---

OUT DRIVING IN JERSEY FENS, looking for farm land, the Great Lost Sea of Jersey is a marsh---bleak---Later I'm working in a filling station with 2 guys, oil trucks come, driver helps himself to gas from ground well pump---I have my wife, tall brunette, and three children meet me at 12 o 'clock but at 12 I'm rushing to Lowell and back in quick 20 minute walk though this is California,---on business---I'm 25 minutes late---fellows sitting in office in coveralls are nice, dont bother me because I dont know business yet---"Time for my lunch," I say getting my lunch out of drawer--- "Try some *Westchester* beer, Jack, that's *good beer!*--" (at across street tavern). "Okay I will!"---Wife strolling with kids I rush to meet, explain my lateness, no smiles, no kisses, I am about to take my first look at my children---I wear coveralls, street is sad---

JOE AND I ARE RIDING HIS MOTORCYCLE, I'm sitting ass back, heels of my new crepesoles dragging in the Southern town street---I want to ask Joe to slow down so I can turn around but he doesnt hear or care, it's Rocky Mount or Kinston, we cross the railroad tracks and go out and go speeding over the countryside but suddenly it leaves us and a great gap of nothingness and sand hundredfoot canyon yawns beneath us and all we can do is fall but Joe has that wild crazy hope the wheels'll stay upright which they more or less do, we ride the saw horse, at the bottom is a dry creek, another climb up sand steep bank like those we tumbled on Lawrence Boulevard *nightmarish* vast waiting---a little house shack occupies the opposite slope, we go in, a beautiful girl named Ann Buee or such is living there with her Ma---has a tape recorder, books, is lonesome---I go in there cockdangling naked---I start talking to her, Joe disappears, I have to go away to get money or work but I'll come back and marry her---she is honey colored, innocent, sixteen sweet---cluttered bedroom--- sad sandbank sunlight fills her eternity windows---

Earlier it was the Lowell High School football practice field in spectral outside-Lowell---Tewksbury Road---Coach Keady---Kids of team---me coming up--- from sand hegiras to Boston---it's too late I'm too old but I still wanta play on the kid team and those imaginary jumping up and down Billerica hills leap into Lowell suburbs like motorcycle hill and Italian fountains of Frisco---the honey-hearted girl lurks for me---Milk!

GREAT SAGAS that begin in my Phebe Avenue yard with I'm in the Army and soldiers are resting on their backs in heavy rain from full exhaustion---they haven't got all their gear yet but nevertheless have been sent out to hike and exercise some still in just pajamas---same applies to me so I hide in huge hospital house, tell myself I'm waiting for my gear---Many beds like dorm at far end---I go to mine---No raincoat, nothing, just my pajamas with a big hole in the ass,---Pat Fitz comes to visit me and reminisce about the Army---I desperately figure ways of sneaking out---return to railroad in California under cover somehow---relates this dream to old

Navy bootcamp madhouse dreams of regimented life I hated so much---

SUDDENLY I'M IN "NEW ORLEANS" down on the piers, hundreds of ships, thousands of people walking cobbles, I go to Acapulco lines and ask for a job, he asks if I'm union, I say "Used to," doesnt hire me, he asks if I'm union, I say "Yes," show him papers, he hires me---I sail as handsome ship's officer with blond hair, map shows our route down Mexico East Coast---At Frisco suddenly all the wooden houses and hills---I want my Ma to see them, too vast I'm being rushed half awake through halfbaked dream tho at New Orleans a great sight: walking in one tight melted together but stiff group Scandanavian ships' crew officers in front men and maids in back the short ones in back walking against tall North Sea tweeds of tall others, swinging Nazi arms march from consulate to shore, shore to consulate, grim, glad, I catch fleeting glimpse of blondhaired cabinboys with golden hairdos gathered in buns at back---wild health of the sea and Scandanavia---

A BIG FOOTBALL GAME being held in basketball floor loft in Lower East Side---Julien in game, Zoumis---2 teams---my cat Rondu with me, after game I afraid I lost him but look in bedroom closet and he's there's sleeping in dark corner, all the furor washed over him, the game was like a drunken party---Earlier I'd been rushing up to the elevated Long Island Railroad-like tracks to work---late, I figured on catching my train as it pulled out, but yard is so complicated and big with commuter trains and third rails I realize hopelessness and lost train, job like old hooky nightmares---Later I'm writing a novel and call Julien "Sam Vedder" and he likes that name, I also thought of "Roger Beauchamp"---It's all happening in the same bone weary bleak---

CODY AND I ARE COPS working on top of a steep frightening pyramid like hill where some people cause trouble and we send for 2 more cops---as they come up they can see me sitting writing in the cab window, Cody is down the hill, I think to myself "They can see my uniform, they know I'm a cop, now they'll find out about me, this is my first duty"---the hill is clear, high awful, I'm afraid to look down at all those worlds but here goes. . .

SIX THOUSAND DIFFERENT DREAMS, I cant piece them all together but I was in some city with a neck out to sea, had a room in a hotel, warm nights, my father was around---my life is too confused for any more simple solid dreams---I was supposed to sleep---All in that Provincetown California sea shore---

NIGHT OF MIRACULOUS DREAMS March 16 Sunday night---There had been a national catastrophe, it was announced over the radio at gray rainy dawn, it was riot of so great proportions it was some kind of revolution---over "police brutality" ---bandages were strewn in the street--- people had revolted against the police---survivors were

65

stretched out in annexes---announcers were grimly announcing everything in quiet voices on the dawn radio---I knew something would happen when I went to bed the night before---this would change the course of history, America and the world---no school no work---Like days when I was a boy, rain, I'd stay home with Ma and see before me sweet hours of playing with my marble horse races and papers and as in Gloomy Bookmovie in *Sax* she'd occasionally look in on my games, bring cake, milk, fresh pies, show socks she was darning and *assure* me it would rain much too hard for this afternoon too and so like the national riot catastrophe now she cant go to work (if so I'll walk her to the bus, there may be bricks flying----but it's a good idea not to---but she insists, "I dont wanta lose my job, it's the only security I have")---

Then there was Lowell, the Gershom street house, Iddyboy looking young and thin now that he's in his 30's came rushing in in a white shirt, with Rudy Loval---I had been all around the world and away from Lowell, I was back, with Ma, in the 34 Gershom street house "Hee thee Boy!" cried Iddyboy joyfully so glad to see me---sweet sun and flowers outdoors of a Sunday morning everybody Pawtucketville going to church---Rudy Loval as ever eager, warm---this is the happiest dream of my life ---

There are visions of the Lowell Sun Sports page, stories about yesterday's Red Sox game all the lost players with their names intermixed, Jim Piersall goofs of other times proving that the future is every bit as rich as the past; also there are old stories of me writing sports articles for the Sun curiously intermixing the triumphs of 16 (athletic) with the workaday tragic job of 19 on the Sun---somewhere there I took the wrong road---I left Lowell in March of 1942, to go to Washington---returned (after construction job in Pentagon, and Jeanie, and throwing gin bottles over the moon) in May or so---and ship't out to Greenland---on which ship rough seamen who saw my child's soul in a grownup body broke my spirit by spitting and cursing at me---and in October 1942 the ship sat in New York harbor and I tried to tell Archie Sleepyhead Hainesy that I was on the Columbia Varsity and he didnt believe it, so 2 days later I was back at Columbia practising for the Army game---but was satisfied enuf---and left that too, again, disgusting everyone, for to go to heaven deviously I had to cut and dodge institutions, plans, schools, formalities and be silly---and in Xmas 1942 I came home with a radio under my arm to rest, but the war took me away in 3 months and drove me crazy ---mad---in a madhouse, they stroked their chins seeing me write---the book was *The Sea is My Brother* and it was a dreary attempt at Naturalism with a sea background---When I came home again, June of 1943, with Navy clothes on my back (for my original clothes'd been sent home before they shaved my heads and all our heads and that is why the police riot was so great, such emancipation)---now Ma and Pa--- my love for my father is greater hidden---now it was New York, they had a little apartment over a drugstore in Ozone Park, the druggist's name was Sam, there was the old Piano--- my mother'd brought it from Lowell at great expense, my father cursed but loved her---like George Burns and Gracie Allen---now no more Lowells, no more rainy days of no school, but cities, sodomists chasing me, girls and women who tried to run my life. The--*Town and The City* is not yet written. It must be written again. Irwin Garden was right. So M--but also there were voyages, to California, lying on the ground, to Mexico, walking among the whores to the desert, the peotl and the t, to San Francisco of the endless green night---all for nothing---I was back in Lowell, Sunday morning, the birds singing, and Iddyboy in a white shirt thin and handsome and the father of four children whose picture was in the paper and Iddyboy look't different there but it was him and all children are gorgeous because they are the beginnings of our evil, make golden foundations for mountains of crap our later years multiply and ferment our early childhood years are not years at all but a sweet outpouring of eyes---Thus Iddyboy also beautiful look't out gladly at the world for the Love of God and his wife was not in the picture she was in the background somewhere, I was ashamed in the midst of all my roaring happy friends of heaven of succumbing to the sexual invitation in public of the girl or woman who wants to prove that men are not priests---And they are not beasts, they have bodies wild and hungry upon the golden rod of their being the flesh wrapt around---homely---Women have folds of milk around the depth of their womb---and let me think of the best the most beautiful---It is not fair for anyone to accuse me of not loving women---least of all myself who knoweth---that what I reach in the woman's heart is thru her flesh and she misconstrues the idiot child to be the monstrous beast---Around the world on ships---and swirls of that behind me---, my attempts to understand the world on every level it has---and so Iddyboy and Rudy knew without my saying all these things---and greeted me back home with cries of joy--- "Gus and Lousy and Scotty and everybody knows you are back---They'll be here soon---" My interesting little backyard is still there, I can see it through the back window---from the depths of hell I know that I can make

68

wilful confessions of evil but in heaven are wilful hopes of God's good love and this latter is what I choose, Genêt---poor Jean---my brother---In the newspaper in my joy suddenly I see my picture in a baseball uniform wearing a pitcher's purple jacket, squatting in a 3rd base box, cleated foot, hard brown athletic profile,---apparently I'd been a star in further dreams than this one of actual conscious life and activity---It is only when dreams lose their importance that the dirty business of evil begins---by dreams I mean what you saw in your sleep---not what you wished in your day revery---Carloads of Lowell guys as usual were driving to Fenway Park in Boston for the ballgame that afternoon---Irishmen---I read stories about the Red Sox---When Cody saw me in San Jose in the kitchen with his son on my lap he shuddered, I saw his hand quiver, his eyes were wild, I never saw him so glad---This is almost Iddyboy and Rudy---We start gabbing and talking at the kitchen table the round big one, Ma's around, putting up new shelves, talking to her own kind of neighbors again---we should never have left Lowell---but now we're back and everything saved again---

BUT THE DREAM HURRIES AND SHIFTS---I'm in Baker Field Columbia in my football uniform practising alone, I sprint 80 yards dodging in the heavy suit, my legs drag like lead,---that was another mistake leaving football because at the expense of just a little physical weariness I could have convinced everyone that my heart was in the right place instead of this writing which is so dangerous to my sanity---so that I may have to stop soon and just work on the railroad in the dark---No coaches, nobody watching---I go into the showers and change---some of my old team mates are there, no ones from the freshman class wonder who I am---they dont realize how old I am---and that so absurd, the coach doesnt even know I'm back and would take the uniform off my back---I am temporarily secretly back on the team---Ben Wirt is there, contemptuous---on a Main Street in Pennsylvania he once squatted and took a big crap, crying---he was drunk---talk about your Sinclair Lewises---he wore contact lenses---he used to cry and curse trying to catch me on the wing around KT70 run---I had to squirm out of his reach to get by and make my way down the field to the goalposts of reality---The Coach would laugh---we were all tired---The big game came, crowds roared, behind the grandstands secretly I ran up and down in my stolen uniform hoping I'd wake up---I walked down the steps of the 215th St. El with Cliff Battles, at the bottom step I dropped my milk bottle, this is how I almost made the Columbia team and they said I was another Cliff Montgomery proud name-----now they'll say I'm another Wm. Blake---

AGAIN THE SHIFTING DREAM, and I'm on my back on a cot on a summer night reading the sports page, I get up to go buy another paper, the city is like New Orleans, it is also Gershom Avenue---Then I'm lying on my back on the sidewalk with a baseball hat like a railroad brakeman resting between freights and a brunette girl is jostling and joking with an older couple, she slams a mail box, they laugh, she looks over their shoulders and down at me and I remember hoping she'd fall in love with me at first sight---Also a little kid walks by and I poke him with my toe and he has toys and plays, as tho I was on the parlor floor on the funnies and he was my son---I've forgotten everything---I'm sick, I'm sweating OPE THE CRACK OF HEAVEN when I first woke up it was all there, I waited too long, wrote too much, hid too much, the open crack of heaven closed again---but I hadnt eaten for 2 days I was feeble I made coffee using precious minutes and also drowning my delicate blood in caffeine and now---The warm night cot---is something that happened I dont remember---and so I'll stop for today---

I'M ON DARK MOODY STREET with Billy Artaud, I lend him 50¢ and a book, as agreed, he walks off home without a word, I yell "Okay Bill?", he doesnt answer, I say "Hey!" ---no answer---and panicky I suddenly realize he's mad and means to keep book and 50¢ both and never return them--- he is striding away, his face is red, his ears burn as I hurl curses at him and run after him, he disappears in his house---on the street I'm yelling at the crowd all my grievances---

SOME KIND OF LYNN. . . I live alone, around the corner from newsstand Mainstreet, I'm waiting for something--- There are girls around---cats---I have a transom on my door---I make lunch, and go to work---Up on top of the Fellaheen hills overlooking the sea finally I live in a swank expensive cottage with Peaches, now I go to school with her with my prepared lunch but something is deceitful---like we at night we make love but she holds a piece of steak to her cunt and I have to come into it on the edge in the slit she made so when I feel my cock throbs in spring pushing thru

71

the membrane of the silly meat I can well tell the sham but she in her childish daydream insists---by day we sit together in the same double bench in school and it seems the whole class is expectant of our lovemood, when it's good the class buzzes excitement and accomplishment reigns---when no and I slump in my seat. . . tenseness, waiting. . . A famous guitar worth $1350 or more had been given to me in my Lynn bachelor transom days (very like the transom of the Mel Torme old lady party)---(redbrick etc.) With this instrument by day on the sea hill I gaze at the sea, waiting---I go down towards the village, a beautiful middleaged Fellaheen Flamenco woman sees my guitar, disengages herself from the women washing at the Pawtucketville hillbottom creek--- comes over---she too lives in a hilltop cottage with her old man---I say "How much is worth?" --- "You wouldnt get more than $350 for it"---She starts playing it---it is a great guitar---her playing is so gorgeous my eyes fill with tears---a little boy so high also listening also stares up with tears---her hands work swiftly so swiftly and magically at one point she lets go and alone the guitar continues a shower of heavenly strums complicated rich according to the arrangement she prepared with her magical knowledge and technique---I am in the Fellaheen Land of the Great Guitar---there are pale hills---dusk---the even star and her saucer cup moon make bright couple in the keen pale edge of oncoming blue---I am happy---I go up to the hill cottage with the woman--- she feeds me huge meals and so when I go to school I cant eat my lunches and the man in the seat in front of Peaches and me, a distinguished middleaged New York manabout town, gives me a lunch bag saying "You left your lunch in the seat yesterday"and I realize with horror I been eatin so many big meals---etc.---and the whole class is wise, all except Peaches---it's only when I wake up I begin to think "I gotta make Peaches realize this steak is silly to give me herself not a piece of meat"--- So huge and timeless, the events strung out from some intenser center and forming vague distant points only to be found again when centers and universes shall shift in other dreams---

BRIEFLY,--I HAD TWO CATS in Amsterdam Spectral, little yellow bouncer, bigger gray, kids with me---I go down the street looking for the tragedy which is somehow related to that pregnancy of Ma's when I clacked out the poolhall---the moon---I hear noises, I look back, Good God a great commotion, a huge thin Giant Hound is bounding across the street with my cat in his mouth---I start to run to stop it---I know it's too late---my poor personable kitty is gonna be dead, my little Bouncer I know *it's* already inside that Baskerville Beast's throat---O from where came this horrible canine of ghost??!!---I scream as a huge bus balls by---I hear my child weeping inside---I pantomime in the street at jeering men looking out the back window that I know my little kid's in there, I make the signs, they laugh, but a stern woman inside prevails and has the bus driver stop---it stops---it has baggages like airport buses---the plate says QUEBEC---I open the back sidewell door, jump in, ark, loud and foolish, "Is my daughter in this bus?" and as I ask I realize I made a big mistake and was only paranoiac and though they're all (except stern woman) laughing a dead silence falls over bus as no answer comes and it's in the negative---and my little daughter of course delusionedly is somewhere else not here I am crazy and realize it and all they too---So I step out and back---that's when I look up the street and see my tragic little cat in the great dog's mouth---my children helplessly screaming chasing it with its long spindly ghost legs chiaroscuroed against dream-dark horizon of Amsterdam mothswarmed---

THEN I'M IN A LUNCHCART---record store narrow, with gang of friends, 2 uniformed doormen come in, I give a Chaplin military salute goofing backhand to brow---but suddenly 2 real cops rush in---we have T---I sneak out door unnoticed and rush down street in back of George Wicksner and caution him and we hide in doors and I really beat that rap---he disappears---I go (halfworried about fate of friends in store) into a beat bar, a blonde whore is sitting on floor facing wall, I stoop and hug her and put cheek to cheek and she says "Just that, just that, nothing else"---she's been wail-ing blearing crying at whore wall of dark sad saloon kicked beaten--- "Just hold me like that please" ---we are heroic Russian lovers in a hovel---but suddenly she starts stretching and spreading legs on floor, says "Hmm," snuggles, says *"I have prick trouble, man,"* and I say "How much?" "Five" --- "That's too much---how bout 3" "I cant" ---I wont give five---I hold her---she lusciously stretches---

MADELEINE AND I are in old James Watson apartment, I'm sitting on couch in corner, suddenly I look and she's taken all her clothes off, has perfect little hourglass shape and black Italian cunt and I jump her to the floor and start right in eyes closed elbows to each side of her ribs pounding in an elastic strange box that stretches as tho my cock was stuck inside pajama pants urging out, which it was---(as I awoke)---and all Madeleine did was *talk* sprightly and little girlish as I worked wordless---In Montreal I dreamed something and woke up sneering at the ceiling---about "the deception of the female"---making horrid gesture with hand at hole void of red room in Ste. Catherine bordello---Also other nightmares of drink now forgot---and no Montreal of runaway horse parks---how strange reality of the bleak endless world which has no destination or meaning or center and the sweet small lake of the mind

RIDING IN A CAB with friends and Bob Boisvert, talking about Chaplin---when we get to Harcourt office Bob is saying that sometimes Chaplin comes in solemnly in dark glasses, or sometimes tips his hat gayly his homburg smiling and Bob walks off thru the office to do something pulling a little wagon and I follow turning to friends doing that tipping gesture to explain how-Chaplin and jump on wagon and ride it thru office goofing (like a young Chaplin) as office workers stare and Bob doesnt notice or care---At a rack are various big Pages covered with current publisher's cover designs and photos, I look at Scribner's for GO but realize it's been already published---Did this woman upstairs kill my cat? No, the kid's back and has it hidden like he used to do---poor kid---

I'M AT THE BEACH with guys---Julien---suddenly I see Al Eno and Albert Lauzon, God how Lousy's changed, fat, puffy, he lisps, has regressed to a silly precocious child, he sits on my chest and tells me what's happened since---only the other night I'd seen him in front of Destouches' store---Swimming in the beating waves we'd had a big ball, it floated far out, I went out to get it---Later I want to show 2 of the guys how well I play mambo drums, we're in a house, they wait as I rush out to get a proper drum, a kettle---I practice 10 minutes by myself in the street to be ready---I play well, my fingers race and rat ta tat---then I go in but en route find an old broken real drum and try *it* but it's not as good---by the time I get in the house they've lost interest and left the parlor where we talked about it---semi Phebe St house, semi by the sea---

I'M GONNA GET A JOB IN THE STEEL MILL, dark horny iron pieces are taken out of an oven and somehow slatted up on a long bar and a poor grimy ghost has to lift that bar to a horny bier hot, everything hot, with hot clothes he pushes against hunks of iron and somehow pulls slat bar back and disposes them---I anxiously wait my turn to start this work, fear's in me---I see now they have a gray gloomy iron treadmill will bring the steel to my feet, my slat-bar---not only impossibly heavy but red hot---experimentally in this hell I lean over the bier counter to test distance, it too is hot---

I have a sexy Italian girlfriend on the little street tho---we neck---people are off on a trip---so I go buy her a halfpint---of whisky---cause I drink wine---She has hips---Earlier a group of phoney literatteurs with Dick Beck-Ed Williams cultish cool manners have me visit them, hint at trips, advantages---finally allow as they'll let me join their organization and announce it gravely and impressively---I'm afraid to ask what it'll cost me---and afraid to tell them I

dont want to join anyway---"I never join organizations"---
The 3 Negroes that tried to run me down in a car are somewhere out in rain, driving---"Only last week we came down
from Montreal," hints literatteur darkly, "from the Northern
Boulevard we drove in"--- Ah that poor bleak hell mill of
horny iron doom

I'VE BOUGHT A TICKET ON THE S. S. EXCALIBUR
sailing from a hilly Mexico to Havana so I can see Bull who
is there---I go to the ship, see my dull brown lonely stateroom like the ones in doomed Dorchester---one of the officials is queer and is trying to rub my hand beneath the desk.
so I look down there and say "Hey there's a rat down there!"
feigning innocence---The ticket is high price, I learn the
ship's also going to North of New York in all kinds of dream
gray ports---it's sailing at 12:45---Meanwhile I go home to
make a lunch, get ready---a stone's throw from the big slip
and ship---I'm completely alone, I sit and daydream how I'd
tell the story of the queer steward to Bull and others---I
decide not make a lunch since there's three meals a day
aboard ship----Suddenly I realize I'm late and have no decent
clothes---sweating, my legs dying, hobo pack on back, I'm
hustling to my house, uphill, downhill, to get remainder of
my gear---big whistles blow---I see the ass end of a ship passing a pier---I rush to the bridge, it's going very fast, *it's my
ship*. I mistook 12:45 for 12:15----Oh the world is sailing
away and not a sound----I watch from the bridge but it isnt
the Excalibur, I realize I was correct, it's still 12:45 sailing
time, I have a half hour but I cant see the Excalibur in her
berth any more---I dont look long but rush home struggling

to get my final tomatoes and pack them----I take a shortcut and get hungup on unnecessary steep hills----a funny sunny hilly Mexico like Frisco----there is a golden silence in afternoon naborhoods----I dont know what's happening----

SOMEBODY'S GOT A HOLY CHALICE of some kind in his hand and just then (calis!) (caw-*lis!*) in a mirror we see someone----impersonating the Devil---from the rearview ----and the chalice, having a Cross, makes the Devil hiss & shiver back----

EXCUSING MYSELF FROM DINNER I rush up to make a scheduled phone call----The colored girl is watching me from her bedroom door---as soon as I finish the call I rush into her room and we wrassle & love & soon she's on my lap black & naked & I'm working up----then I turn her over to her back & we work----ecstatically, madly, gladly----I wonder what the people downstairs will think of my long "phonecall"----

I'M IN FRANCE, tryin to be amazed----in a bed in a room, Seymour has the other bed, we're traveling with his mother ----I'm looking at wallpaper, thinking about France, the waiters downstairs, etc.----earlier it had been long motor trips over mountains and along canyon rivers somewhere---

ON VAN WYCK BOULEVARD before it was built---CALL ME MADAM or some such show has been a big hit, everybody's talking about it, I see it (marquee)---walking home, I see a telephone pole climber with spikes go running up a pole and start snipping at wires, amazing how fast he climbed, little kids watch awing---A thousand things happening up and down the crowded Boulevard---I'm blasting, curse cause I lose an ash---I find a sidewalk in front of a house with a thousand pretty little decorated stones in little boxlike places---I steal six or seven, carry them in my hand, drop one under a car bumper, recover it,---My mother whom I just call'd is come to meet me instead of waiting at home so I blank butt and suddenly across the street we see a popping fire racing and snapping out of the ground along the gutter---a car follows and drives over it for fun---fire goes right through a pole and traffic light and on in a straight line thru pavements of a big intersection--- "It's the telephone power!"---A happy dream full of life---

★ ★ ★ ★ ★

Dreams in San Luis Obispo

GUY GREEN AND I and Marguerite standing on corner of "72nd and Broadway"---to show her how a guy does, he falls over in a tremendous fall landing on his side on the pavement just missing hitting his head, comically---on the raingrit cement---people stare---but I am suddenly remembering something I missed or had to do or have to catch and just as Guy hits the sidewalk and Marguerite's laughing I take off sprinting up Broadway like a madman and without a word leave them there---I say to myself "People will think I tried to outdo Guy's fall." Later I start down a dangerous incline but feel it's safe because it's dry, a dry sidewalk---but it turns into a rack a hundred feet high, I try to hang on to my nervous cat---I feel he'll do better by himself with his claws---a crowd is watching---I throw him to a beam---he claws wildly missing and hissing and hits another one and tumbles off and falls to the sand way below---(like a rollercoaster at the beach)--- I cry---I'm afraid---I can't come down---Later I'm sick---in a house---back from the hospital---events---people swirling around---why don't they leave me alone---etc.---a mixture of wax images, real blood and sad floors---

DRIVING THRU SPECTRAL LITTLE CANADA with Easonburg Annie and Ma and Nin in back seat, and me too, Annie is asleep or drunk, "Put on the brakes!" I yell---"you stupid sot"---she doesn't know where it is---I dont either--- I reach for the wheel, guide the car swerving and crazy over sidewalks, inside lampposts, around corners, other cars, hospitals, canal, night---I aint worried, I do well from the backseat----Later Good God I'm walking with Nin and Ma in the Textile Mill alleys back of Prince and Aiken and Ford and Cheever---dark, cobbles,---that old dream there---Suddenly we see a grimy dark little man, "It's Dave!" I tell myself joyfully---Dave Orizaba the Mexico City connection---Nin and Ma are *terrified*---"Come on! dont talk to that man! Oh!" ---but I rush up, only see it's not Dave just an old greasy hat ghost bum of Lowell alleys---but he has a package---tea?--- he follows us, and the fleeing women---madly I reach back and feel his package, it's solid like meat no marijuana---

BROOKLYN---strange sad scenes haunted with guilt, that began long ago at the age of 4 when I FIRST went to Brooklyn with Ma---Now it's the grownup LATER just as in a dream and I'm trying to tell Ma if she takes the El and gets off at Juralomon she wont have to spend so much time gettin to work---She worked in a shoe shop when I was 5 and we lived on Hildreth in the Kellostone and when we took the first coldnose trip to black New York---something there is wrong on that end of the line of life---also the Marquand girls are around---the work is towards the Park, the Island, the Ozone, sunny haunted Els---of old dreams---Ma Evans Lynn-haunted redbrick house, still---Ma and I are on the street waiting for buses, it comes around the corner but doesnt stop but a halfblock further, we run after it---I remember Denver---all, all haunted and mixed up---Wesley Martin is much much clearer---There was a girl, hauntedness, guilt, nakedness, shyness---her sister---a lost dream. Earlier at dusk in Columbia South Field I'm heaving in long throws to two kids but like in a dream I wont and cant get em off and wind up and run and never let the ball or rock go---till later--- when there's no more force---but I high hard em in good at times---Where's Edna? Jule? Franz? and Pan American Bull? What am I doing in San Luis Obispo? *rain*-----no raincoat money---that's what I'm doin in San Luis Obispo

RAILROADING THRU THE SAN JOSE MAZE of tracks with some kind of Lil Abner Indian buddy like the baggage-room Indian in Frisco---and he has a buddy himself who is all gold, we go downstairs to a crowded meeting basement hall full of poor workingpeople, there's a party of some kind,

81

a ritual, something they dont have to do but do it anyway---
Indian's buddy is wearing tights and performing on a platform, I think "If any non Indians walked in here now they'd
think it was a queer party" --- Indian and I are doing the
Railroad Company a favor---"Guys like you and your buddy
are one in a million," I tell him, and mean it, as we leave to
go back to our Engine---At one point I'm on my knees
mopping some spectral corridor with that red tile floor like
on old passenger cargo ships---We have rods, clean out the
engine, go down steep nightmare grades---At one point I'm
on the Centralville Hill trying to crawl hands and knees
down a steep hill and rack---argh!---helping ladies---My
Buddy is like Iddyboy, Lil Abner,---like yesterday's fireman
on the Guadaloupe Local---The San Jose yard looks east like
that lost Bunker Hill of the White Horse Riding East Out of
Frisco From Cody and Evelyn in the Market Street
Cafeteria---commence, finis.

MY MA HAS ACHES AND PAINS, I tell her to take a little whiskey to ease it,----a minute later I see the old man
sneaking out of the house and going to the drugstore----for
aspirins, those same old aspirins----I'm mad, I tell Ma again,
she pretends to brighten up "Oh, whiskey?---then what do I
do?"----"Take it with aspirins and go to bed"---The scene
is somewhere in the East, sad----

       Earlier it was Pete Menelakos greeting me
on a Lowell corner, begging me to come back to Lowell, it's
the same impossibly warm Lowell that doesnt exist (I
remember cold mornings of oatmeal and hostile school)----
G.J. is with me, & good old Scotty----I tell Scotty about

himself----G.J. is friendly, & anxious----It is now 8:30 A M Sunday morn in San Luis Obispo, pristine & bird-sweet----O Lord what shall I write? how bend these sinews of my art & on what anvil? what harp? what frosty window Beethoven hope secure? what SEA draw? and the mind inbend?----Pete Menelakos who was there in the Moody Street saloon the last time I saw Maggie Cassidy and when Moody Street was still thus named----in fact when Lowell Sat nite Summer was one great riotous scene on Kearney Square of bus waiters for the Lake, shoppers, dancers hurrying----up there in just one corner of vast America----now TV-itis I think has ruined the culture cold----

IRWIN GARDEN---somehow always a vague aura of murder around him---a Manhattan pad----a long talk----his finger up----I had gone to bed with the first clear vision & definite message of the necessity of my death----I'm walking on a beach among crowds, it doesnt matter that the scowling stocky muscular man of 30 should die----one of two billions on the dead bilious world----with its burden of time, tedium----Woke up realizing sex is life----sex & art----that or die----

GOING THRU A WORLD OF SAD DEBRIS as a train ----myself a train, the front of one----down some track----thru plasters, dusts, whole blocks & plazas of disaster & wreck & junk & cellars----Finally I start hiding in this junk----in broken cellar rooms----I go with my mother to the shoe factory to collect her Xmas pay check, there are signs on the wall, one of them says "Angie's Son is Back From California" ----I feel tremendously insulted that those people assume I just want her money----I picture her gabbing happily about my imminent arrivals----Slaves in a shoe shop, slaves on a rail, James Watson made a tragedy of the day Town and the City was accepted and "Frankel" rejected and now he has 20,000 dollars to my one----Gad, what were those broken Roman cellars----?----along what Lowell canal route---- They ran right straight by the Y----along the Boston & Maine tracks and out to the Princeton Boulevard yards where Joe and I explored old locomotives in the 30's old pots of old 1915's rusting in the weeds----The old sad plaster of haunted houses of Lowell, the cellars of the Rat beneath gaping no-more-floors----the horror of the death of a house and a family once in it----a pristine leader made it----lost it---- has none of my sympathy

SOME ATTRACTIVE WOMEN with Bull and me in "Mexico City," we're going to have lunch in a place----and cocktails----or dinner----I'm well dressed, I go in, it's a kind of tower (!) bar & I start from downstairs self consciously swinging up the first flight with one hand on pole slowly swinging & rotating to the stares with bashful eye flutters and posing surveys of the group in basement----on up to second floor where are interesting young men drinking----I'm about to recognize some of them----faces, names, the incredible perfection of interest people offer in bars in early evening before dinner!----Later it will all hangle and grow frowsy----

Now pure morning birds sing the San Luis Obispo blues of dawn----I'll go off and be an impure drunk

84

and leave this tanned, bored perfection of health peace comfort----comfort 's for dead----peace for mountains----"Why didnt I make great friends with Kells?"

LIKE NOTRE DAME in Montreal is the Cathedral, the church that the train of some sort is pulling into and I'm with Bull----a giant dog runs alongside in the aisle, by pews, it's the "Hound of the Baskervilles" ----Suddenly he takes off impatiently into the air, becoming a giant black bird, and flies over the altar and descends at the vestry doors where hurrying theological students pay no attention to him & he lands upright on his feet like a man----& humped with wings walks to a vestry door looking like Satan, black, sad, but also like a humble vestry janitor---

        Later I'm with Bull and some youths, I say to one of them "I look like a hoodlum too when I'm dressed sharp" He doesnt believe it, looks at me, an older jerk talking crap----I feel silly---

        Ah so our bird is tripping into a vestry door----behind altars----

        I woke up, looked in the mirror with disgust at my fattening oldish face----the giant bird limped----the kid who looked at me with suspicion was Don, was blond----(Don Johnson I met in Mex City)----

        That limpish Angel Gabriel sooty bird----

ROLLING ALONG THE SIDEWALK in (it's the place of the mambo drum practice on sidewalk) New York suburban downhill sidestreet on a little toy wood wagon affair I come to two children, boy and older girl, and with very few pushes make circles around them and then give them the wagon ----after which the little girl wants to go into the house with me, I say "You're too young" but is she ever pretty!----and really not too young (urgh) in India----I give her lil brother the wagon----I go in the house, upstairs, talcumy eternity mother bedroom, waiting for Evelyn---- "O---she's not here----it's Friday----she's gone to see Cody at the hospital" ---- I wait----soon the little girl comes knocking----I debate with myself in the masturbatory master bedroom----Earlier I'd seen that little girl with Raphael Urso at the beach, foot of low cliff----the Lakeview Avenue beach on the dump----gray----they'd told me to wait for them there, they'd be back----it's the same eternity dump of my first view of the world from Lupine Windows----the Merrimac Sea----tic tic tic----

THOSE AWFUL AMAZON WOMEN of Rome have got me as one of their slaves dancing in their torture chorus, a ritual, in the Circus----people watch laffing, clapping----the sexual dance----they'll stick you with a spear if you dont dance----the big brunette runs up, grabs me, pulls me, makes me do lewd suggestive stuff with her, all a formal written dance but I'm a reluctant slave, unhappy paramour----the crowd roars glad----it's also a kind of basketball floor, the St.Louis Parochial floor----

I BRUSH AGAINST EVELYN'S tit reaching over for Cody in the bed (at 1047)----her upstairs bedroom "talcumy" was second story, my mother's bedroom facing sea at West Haven and at Sarah Avenue facing sun----Reaching for Pa----

ME AND THE BRAKEMEN are playing catch in a lot, ----for fun I make sensational catches falling softly on my face, diving around, over my head, backhands and backhand backthrows, all with a flying ease----what a ballplayer I could have been!---if the professional A&P's hadnt been so grim and anxious!----the tall brakeman, Mulles, Bostrell, Schaefer, amazed, makes me hard throws----still I stab them, impossible----finally I miss one----it saddens----in vast quiet the force of the sun is burning out, dusk birds sing----up through the vast tree we see rays of gold, and smoke----I throw the ball up through the hole as immense music plays slowly----The old conductor's putting in his last report, the day is done, the train is done----This is the way the world will end, in rays, red, people watching, silent, tired----The world of the mind is the real world----the rays of the mind the real rays-----

RIPE JUICY ORANGES are fallen from the trees in Cody's driveway, lie cracked on the ground----I bring their attention to it for the first time, on the curb across East Santa Clara St. I bring Evelyn an orange, smiling----

Dreams in the Cameo, 'Frisco

UP IN THE GRAY MOUNTAINS around Joe's yard Ed Buckle appears on a broadcast with the President of the Senior Class and answers questions with the same nasal lost voice *I* have on tape and recordings----and the announcer introduces as follows: "Helen Buckle was born in Paris & came to America in 1930----troop-troop----& started her career & business" and he goes into some spiel about the Buckles' Success Story and I'm there in the grayness saying to myself "They always being to assert themselves late those who have waited in their humble cocoon so long and they always come on like the last vulgarity----after them will come not barbarians but necessarily cultures again." (In this vein----and more wild, subsconscious,----) I woke up realizing I have no more enthusiasms

★ ★ ★

Dreams at Sea

I'M IN MY BEDROOM onSarah Avenue, home from some kind of work, night----Ma's in the kitchen downstairs playing radio----It's a sports event to which all the rebellious high school girls went just to clap in great rhythmic unison ----louder, louder, madder, more terrifying----haunting my nap in the dark bedroom of Gerard's green desk---(sleeping out on deck in Pacific on cot)----Ma comes upstairs to turn my light on----to talk----alone in the spectral house----The poor mad girls cant get men who are always sleeping at home in their mothers' house, I remember thinking----

        Later it's a weird San Luis Obispo, guys, girls, rooms, events, a sudden murder or discovery of murder ---- I'm walking down the street with a guy ---- later I'm destroying evidence, throwing things away----sorting objects ---- unrememberable horror but it always happens.

MA AND NIN AND I are back living in Sarah Avenue house, I come down Sarah, go into Alice 's house where they all are ---- Alice has largened and improved her house --- great thick rugs, furniture, a Christmas tree as ever----

I'M CARRYING LITTLE LUKE or Little Tim in my arms, little children of the spectral gray Liverpool hotel after some offense of some kind are clawing around my body trying to reach up and tear him to pieces and so while I hold him high there he is sucking on my nose----The women are around but there's a big fight, a riot, a big plane had just took off from Cow Field---night----I hold the baby, turning, struggling, he blithely goes on sucking my nose----

IN THE REAL NIGHTSOFT FRISCO of Al Damlette Chinatown later I'm with Irwin Garden----we're walking to his room, talking----he is darker and older----there are involve-ments----girls----it's the same tragic Frisco of Charley Low nightstreets and now with an authentic Gardenian sadness replacing the early joyous white spectrality---

THAT CRAZY HORACE MANN Jewish kid----a great wit----in my dream past it seems I knew him----he was very wild and interesting----I was at a girl's, a Jewish girl's rich New York apartment----he came to woo her sister ----she didnt want him----but he spieled----amazing the things he said----I got a few letters from him----I knew his funny father----but so many things were happening in those days I hardly had time to answer him and after awhile abandoned his correspondence and friendship in the press of events----in real life I never knew him----except a composite of Musselman in the nuthouse and little fat wits of Horace Mann----but this one was clear, powerful, real---the mind invents like God----He was a sex fiend---he spieled sex to the sister, in such a way she couldnt accuse him---and too fast and too complex for her to understand---I'm there thinking "What an amazing guy---Someday he'll be a producer----I should be amazed by the Eternity of his huge funny complex soul---" Marty Churchill, young Blatberg----Ah inescapable---

Caribbean Sea

I'M HAVING AN AFFAIR WITH A COLORED GIRL like that heroin girl in Frisco---I work in a kind of bakery, where she is some kind of supervising office girl-----the hours are long----part Crax factory, part Lowell Hi School machine shop in the basement, part Rocky Mount Mills ---part, too, some dream garage like Blagden's on Back Central street where I parked cars----gray, dreary, like Lowell vocational schools on raw drizzly days---She lives in the East 70's not far (in N Y) from where Al fell down to impress Marguerite and I ran---We--it's about 4 A M----arrange to have a fuck----but linger over something, like heroin, and by the time we come to the door of the joy room she has to go open up the bakery, 5 A M----and it's not she doesnt love me, business and circumstance compel her to leave---(she loves me, she loves me not)---

IRWIN GARDEN HAD GONE TO FRISCO I heard, I'm
in Mexico City or somewhere, I go look up Bull Hubbard at
his new apartment house pad----His name is misspelled
Jurroughs on the metal plates---June is still alive in the old
New Orleans-dry canal-Florida-glittering boulevard associ-
ating of it---but actually not for when I ring, no one in, and
go around corner to a lunchroom and call from a wall phone
while waiting to be served, it's 2 snickering hipsters answer
the phone and Bull doesnt seem to be in----They are "Don
Johnson" and "Phillip Lavalina" or Wagstrom of Mex City
----they goof on phone---I get mad and sound like old
friend of Bull's anxiously enquiring---I say "Did you hear
about Irwin G. going to Frisco?" and they say "Oh he's back
already---"

SUDDENLY, in same town, with little friend Jimmy Low-
like, I cross street to see the crazy girl---She happens to be
my ex wife June and looks like Paulina Cole also---At door
she snickers, rushes little Jimmy into her room, I hear him
giggling insanely as apparently she's undressing and tickling
him as she does every day---I get exasperated not only
because she's my ex wife but she should have more taste---
When she comes out I take her arms seriously and say *"Why
are you crazy?"*

A change takes place---she melts, agrees,
seems sane---sad--- "Nothing else to do---I'm lonely---"
She says something profoundly philosophic about it, something beautiful I cant remember---She is beautiful---I wake
up on the steel boat realizing I still love June.

DRIVING IN TWO CADILLACS one a '52 one a '47 Limousine, with a gang of friends---the driver is Jim Calabrese-Mexican kid---we're going Lombard St Frisco and part Lowell, go down a very steep hill, stop all to get out and buy cigarettes---Lousy, Al Green, lots of girls---Jim is smiling---We went over some canal---Later I'm back in the West Street cottage with Ma wondering if the organ is still in the shed---Not the family that followed us "in 1931" but "the one after that must have sold the organ"---"the Chalifoux"! ---seeing gardens of Montreal and Rubens beyond backyard, *so glad*---Relishing the roomy rooms, the yard, porch--- whiteness of cottage, the old Aiken Street First Street dreams of Centerville---walking in soft dark dusks---by Presbytère ---evening on the rosy porch---Good God where's Pa?---Say Pa, say Ma---forgot how to say *Pa* now---will forget Ma, will forget Mer, will be grave merde.

AT A BIG HAPPY afternoon party at my aunt's house in Lynn---we're making lemonade lunches---for my uncles & aunts I personally a little 11-year-old boy prepare to put grapefruit juice in their peaches by squeezing an incredibly dreamunbelievable juice-y grapefruit without end to its fruition & flow---it overflows a coffee mug---Ma comes in with other aunts, they've been having a little gay side party of their own, with rum, in the yard-- I'm glad they could manage that---Nin is there---it's the same Lynn-Ma Evans Brooklyn redbrick vase house of that Mel Torme piano old-lady party dream---

MAN AND I are running some kind of big rooming house in Frisco or Lowell or N.Y.---Al Damlette has a topfloor room, Ma says "While you're up there take the key out of that lock, it doesnt ever work, he doesnt have to keep his room locked" ---but what she doesnt know is that he has a gallon can of pure heroin, gotton from Bull, thru me---We have jolts up there--- It's also the Textile Lunch tenement---gray, dark, gloomy like the Fortiers but makes me very happy and is full of mysterious rooms to read in , full of old books, a dream of mine (which Watson has in Saybrook, also old King chairs even, to read in, and bronze busts)---only this Collier-ish manse is in the thick of cities and dope addicts and interestingness of the wild void heart and the can is an ex gallon ice cream container!

I'M WALKING ACROSS SOME PARK, there are children playing, by fountains---one lil girl stops me in a copse, says "Mister will you tie my buttons on top?"---she is about 7 but with little breasts or a breast, it seems---I am dark and lasciv-ious as I look at her, her honey color, the little body---I start to tie her top bottoms as she talks---I am going to try her innocence---I feel guilt as deep as the sea---I wonder if there are any mothers around-- I prepare to kiss, or take her to kiss her little thighs, gently but right on the cunt---gonna be careful not to tip her over---she vaguely senses my intentions with a blithe blabbering smile---I dont move---I am old.

        Who am I?
        STAVROGIN

★ ★

I'M LIVING WITH MA AGAIN-- there are gangsters downstairs, I'm watching one all the time-- one day I trail him---at the Gangsters' Club library to cover up I grab the first book I see on an over-the-door shelf and turn to the librarian to check it---He's the 2nd cook and baker of the S S William Carruth---eventually---at first a gangster--- Suddenly I see a shelf I really like and a volume I really want, Allen Tate's "The Invasion of the Latin Temperament," a huge new yellow book---

"Hey can I check this one out too?"

"Sure"---

Beyond I see the gangster going in to see the boss---I go into the 2nd Cook's bedroom---he has to dress before I get the books-- Meanwhile Ma's still waiting downstairs for us to go to church---Beyond the bedroom I see that behind the library all the gangsters are sitting in a big sittingroom with books, and newspapers, including my victim who has always been suspicious of my watchfulness but now I'm not even thinking of him & looking right thru him & I'm aware of this---It's the kellostone house on Hildreth, of thegreat Maggie-Marguerite-Madeleine dream--

IT'S THE PHEBE AVENUE HOUSE , Ma & Pa & I and one of Pa's friends are doing something in that fresh paint green kitchen but there's a war on just like the time I saw the exhausted soldiers in the yard and suddenly the first of the bombing jet planes comes over and drops a bomb a few blocks away that shakes the house-- I yell "Let's put the table in the cellar!" and grab the cloth under my arm and pull the table en masse---Father and his friend are rushing in the sideroom wanting to finish something before they have to hide in the cellar---I yell "Come on---in the cellar!"---My Ma is annoyed--

"You're disarranging my whole table and I just put it up! *Eh twé!*" but it's got to be done---but she's not worried about bombs so much as household chores---

JUNE OGILVIE IS IN A TAXI on Park Avenue with 5 small cats, guys, Porto Ricans, one of them myself---She's pick't them up one by one with wily ways, they're all smilingly anticipating something but at corner of 44th she gets off and hits another cab---They discuss her anxiously---

SOME KID OF GARBAGE OR DISHES to be washed on the side---cups, glasses in a sink, brown water---events on a ship---

IN A BIG BASKETBALL HALL I'm with a young friend, we're taking tests at some table---crowds of kids around--- Everybody rushes out to sea but we salvage our tests & take them to another table---notebooks & paper---

WE'RE ALL SITTING on a second story wooden porch in a keen cold snow---moon night in the butte desert West of "Montana"---myself, Ma, and a bunch of others either like Nin and Luke or some such composite of the future or melt-less past---the stars shine on the cold rock of a mesa, it's the West---it's still---we're in our coats but sitting and talking about Flying Saucers, the spectrality of the universe---also I feel so warm and happy I reach out and kiss my mother on the cheek---We're apparently moving away from this house all of us---tomorrow---and waiting for our car ride---Earlier there'd been hegiras and megiras with at first Wild Bull Lee coming on board and then transformed into a Julienesque character so profound and mixed up with autos swirling in our yard and two tall girls one of whom I couldnt make and all the yak gabbling blah talk of gray diffuse eternity complicated beyond recall---so that at the end he disappears nostalgically and we all mourn and miss him and remember his sweet blond thinness---And the clear keen western night, starry-- flying saucer men wear helmets and carry ray guns and are bulky and dark peering out of bushes. . .

I'M IN DRACUT TIGERS FIELD in a drizzle of rain or sleet, I go to the part in short right field where a spring's welling and bubbling in the snow and wait there for a sign from the shroud of Arab eternity who is going to give me the secret of the frost, on a tablet of ice---I'm amazed to see my old left field tree over which Al Roberts'd hit homeruns and myself once hit one, 450 feet---All Lowell is shrouded on the horizon by the sad sleek murk---I've just come back from big adventures sailing thru tropical canals of the South---

THEN DOWN FIRST STREET in Lowell go June, Bull, Irwin, others---right by Boisvert St and the old Dupuis house and I'm saying "There they are in pulsing life going by the symbols of their past and dont realize it but are enriched by it"--- Even tho I know the great gray mystery block house on the corner is gone and in its place I see a modern apartment rosebrick building with all conveniences and in fact Bull lives there---,-we all go in---He's on first floor, the lucky usual bastard---Modern door, *Hubbard* in white on black plate---indirect lights continually on in bathroom, thick creamy bowl and tub, throw-rugs, fixes on shelf---I'm carrying the communal boloney or stuff and walk right in depositing it in proper icebox or hidingplace, as Bull says "Drink?" and I say "Thanx I dont drink no more" and then he wants me to go downstairs and call the blond motorboat hero, shows me his name and number, has number all mixed up as ATtabury 77 273 when it's actually ATkinson 7-7273 and as I go downstairs I repeat it over and over again "Atkinson seven seventytwo seventy three"---I have to circle around in identical hall to the phone which is under Bull's floor and very modern---I make the call, dialing-- I'm thinking "Bull has just arrived and here he's with a terrific $100-a-month pad and thinkinnothing of it and as of yore has house full of friends and kicks and has me make calls for him, stands there issuing stiff dollarbills from his long pockets in the excitement of the afternoon of life---and this is the spot where I was an infant haunted by gray heaps and dark corridors but now overbuilt and modern in the Eternity of Lowell"---

AT YANKEE STADIUM I'm an attendant standing around in a white jacket, behind foul screen---a whole bunch of loafers are watching game, and yelling---something drizzles---

a little Athletic rookie says "Does it always rain in California?"---I guess it's California---I fall asleep or something for I wake up on my feet and the game is in late innings and the boys are yelling more but what a lacksadaisical seedy crew we all are, even the ballplayers who play pepper between innings are lazy, modern, no-good----I dont even know what the score is, less care---

EARLIER IT'S THE RIVER SHORE, the great ship tied to it, I've got a tall girl, a short girl and a colored girl and I try to make em all---I take the colored girl and tell her " Let's go down by the river and I'll show ya" ---Somehow the house of dreams where Gerard died is nearby---the Gangplank to the ship is level over mud shores and wood piers, I dont use it as all crew files back ghostlily but jump to the ground and up on pier, ratwise---I recognize members of my crew in the zombie parade---Ladies and gentlemen and then I'm in a moonlit yard of long ago winter schools maybe in the Highlands-- pigtails---lips---

THE WHALING MAN AND I are crossing the little Caribbean island which is not far from the mainland and greatcity of some land, we can see the lights and red neons across the darkness as though it was part of the island, and in fact that's what I think but the whalingman says no---we 've been sailing and seeing great whales dormant in the water in the day sea---Now it's night and he wears a hat and we hurry to our ship in the dark and those spectral bigcity lights over there-- we talk---In fact all this is but a story I'd been read-

ing in a book, in a 4 Volume Work and this was 3 Volumes of
it, I'm in a terrible Skid Row suffocating hotel room in back
of Bill Mink's record store and I'm drinking hot water and
whiskey the last slug of which makes me so sick I spit out and
empty the glass in the sink---I'm supposed to go see Danny
Richman, I feel miserable--- I wonder if I should take the
canvas camp pack to France or just leave it in the room---

MA HAS GONE TO FRISCO ahead of me and is staying
in some beat hotel like the Cameo again---I'm terrified to
rush up and save her, fearing she'll hate the city for it---I'm
in Lowell and am obliged to return to high school on Kirk
Street which I do in the pristine sunny October or May
morning but I'm late and walk up and down the corridors
smiling realizing *for the first time* that I dont have to go to high
school at all because I'm a great writer, in fact 3 years of H S
has been enough and I will always say "I didnt even finish
high school"----No, whaling in the Carribean and going to
Frisco is more important and I've got to hurry and get to Ma
before she gets disappointed out there---I can see her however enjoying the white hills, blue sky---

LATER I'M WITH BULL telling him I shipped out and
sailed thru the Panama Canal---I tell him he ought to ship
out-- but I cant picture the work he'd do on board and certainly not serving officers' mess---or dishwasher---There's a
dump outside illuminated by great sun and Saturday Morning
whipped by great winds, along a night's river, where in the
vastness of structures I've been climbing around in truancies

so elastic that the river changes to a sea, with surf,---the dump
changes to a gigantic construction job with me running under
stationary and also moving lashed-together pipes---and my
hookey-from-school becoming a great coastwise swim with
my own human arms and legs from North in Frisco to here
South in Bigshore Spectral, a guy watching me---O South
City of my Dreams---and Shore of Oceans---my throat aches
to find my way back to the place where I am mourned and I
cant even remember any more where that is---

SHOTPUTTING THE 16-POUND BALL in some gym
where also there's a ditch, a Chinese kid is trying to sleep on
the floor, I tell a big Chinaman "Hey get him out of there I'm
throwing the shotput" ---Like Parry O Brien I'm facing to
rear and swinging clear around---Another kid tries it,
exclaims "Hey! it improves my distance!" ---There's also a
huge pile of my writings including self written newspapers
commemorating myself and my novels, with pasted pieces of
headline---such a sorry mess of scatalogical absorption it
makes me sick---A whole bunch of guys have been visiting
me in the second story of this wooden I-think-seaside house,
Nin's been there---now they're waiting for me downstairs, at
the car, to travel, and I'm cleaning up final matters such as my
muffcap instead of baseball cap, khaki jacket with fur collar---
"Aw go on out there with just a shirt and breathe in the cold
air!" advises Irwin Garden excitedly---it's Maine---I'm writing myself to death---I have so many crates of crap and paper
and writings I find an original typewritten copy of a novel
the carbon of which I'd been working on, thinking it the
original---poor funny sonofabitch.

100

I'M INVESTIGATING A WHOREHOUSE in Mexico City or Paris, I walk right into a courtyard and go down between windows, screened, seeing inside the round buttoxes of Negresses reclining with magazines sometimes eight whores in one little room---My buddy snickers at the entrance--- Then I'm sitting on the whore house porch with Maggie Cassidy watching two whores who are standing against the rail watchin and waitin to be propositioned, one of them a brunette with imperfect features, the other her fat ugly pal that you have to buy also, like girls in the sailor park---the brunette applies rouge and suddenly looks much prettier, her eyes and eyebrows stand out exotically like Indian beauties of Organo Street---I look at Maggie, she is unbelievably cute with her rosiness and dark hair and eyes like black agates--- "Maggie" I say, the whores pretending not to listen, "this is one of those times when your eyes are *black*" ---Maggie is interested in digging whore life and goes on chewing her gum in rapt absorption---

JUNE OGILVIE AND I GOING TO WORK, earlier, for a woman in the sweat shop, we sat at the same table and started, my job was easier than her folding job so I offered it to her ---she is frightened and sad and bitter to work and because we have to work, I'm amused--- I'd been (I know it's a dream) considering going to Albany to work the railroad but decided I wouldnt have time for anything---our furnished room is dreary, our lives dim, unfriendly---the place where we're working was scene of a big carousal the night before, it's where the Liverpool bombs dropped also---

WALKING THROUGH SLUM SUBURBS of Mexico
City I'm stopped by a smiling threesome of cats who've dis-
engaged themselves from the general fairly crowded evening
street of brown lights, coke stands, tortillas---Unmistakably
going to steal my bag---I struggled a little, gave up---Begin
communicating with them my distress and in fact do so well
they end up just stealing parts of my stuff, I dont want them
to take my shoe tree, (Ed. note: Shoe shapekeeper) one does
take a piece of metal---We walk off leaving the bag with
someone---arm in arm like a gang to the downtown lights of
Letran, across a field---I feel it's because of my betrayal of
Ennrique Villanueva of Vera Cruz who'd given me a rabbit
foot which must mean something to an Indian---the Indians
are mild but dangerous---I cajole, feel hemmed in, losing my
"belongings" in the real world and have to become crucially
involved in it---

WE GO DOWN INTO THE UNDERGROUND SAND
CAVES of India, me, two women, a boy---there are Burmese
snakes, idols---we get lost and cant find the opening to get
out---It's all near Lowell-like sandbanks---purple eve out-
side---

LATER I'M BACK LIVING AT WEST 20th street and I'm
sitting at my writing table after some friends have left, writing in red ink in a large flourishing hand the final lines of
Doctor Sax and suddenly I realize Irwin is still there, still
awake reading on his cot in the corner---

ON A SHIP IN THE CARIB we go zooming 60 miles per hour down Main Street of a town, Georgie the Polock says it's Santa Rico, Porto Rico, but I cant believe it because the houses are American, the signs in English---I claim it's Galveston but suddenly we see the KEROUAC HOOK AND LADDER COMPANY---Outside town on the black sea a great boat rowed by fifty Negros is alongside, they're hardy young singers who want to come on board---I want to get off---Georgie says "I seen em before, they're all young and well built" --I think "They ought to be with that rowing"---"Galley slaves of song"---That town was really Kansas City Kansas---

AFTER A BOB CROSBY CONCERT Ma and I get the job of cleaning up in the hall which is also our apartment---During the concert which includes drum solos by three drummers and songs by Helen O Connell I play with my cat in the bedroom and my other cat is terrified out of his wits shivering by the noise and comes catapulting from the vicinity of the bass drum---After it's over Ma is using a push broom up and down the floor, there's another broom for me, and a cardboard box---She has the $20 in her hand---A leftover watchman of the concert is in the Main Hall---It's like the first page of JENNY GERHARDT---

THE UPSTAIRS BEDROOM WITH THE BARE BULB BURNING, on Gershom at Sarah, the scene of BROTHERS KARAMAZOV, a pale pimply thin ascetic sickly John MacDougald is with his be-stockinghatted father arguing, they have a half gallon jug of Tokay---Cackling craftily the father asks him over to the bed to adjust his sheets and suddenly slowly unfurls a folding sword of some kind and slowly playfully slices gently on John's brow till even it penetrates and cuts the brow skin a little--- "You crazy old fool Karamazov!" I think---In a rage John picks up the halfgallon and throws it across the room, hooking him right in the face and the old man crashes down bloody and dead off his bed ---Downstairs in the lobby of the Gershom Hotel there's excitement first about some fire or disturbance, then about the murder---I walk off to my house across the street---

AT THE 42ND STREET HIGH BUILDING on a Sunday I'm debating way up on the roof whether I should go see Irene the colored girl or call her---the building is twenty stories high, gray, shroudy concrete with ramps running continuously up and great sections along sides with names or words written denoting name of--like puzzle---Earlier I'd been in the sweet Santa Clara valley with Cody and some others, bums, roaming, trying to decide whether to take showers before the big trip, demonstrating our three TV canvases to the women of the Richmond Hill morning. . .

BOISVERT INVITES ME to visit him over the holiday weekend in upstate New York, up the river, I agree---time comes for my bus I still cant remember if it's St.Peter's or St.Whatever's he's at and whether I'll take a bus or train and anyway it's too late and I'm walking across a great snowy Chicago park in San Jose all lost and confused in my plans---

finally I find out it's near Saratoga and that's too far---
Meanwhile I've also missed work or missed collecting my
check and I spend the weekend goofing in somebody's apartment alone, Danny's probably---eating ice cream, at one
point with Helen Buckle---I'm feebleminded lost boy of 32
with wild hair---I go down by the Royal Theater in Lowell
to the pawnshop where everybody's cashing their weekend
holiday checks, I have none---the checks are pink---I see
Jake Spender in the hall, say hello, after he's passed I call him
back to tell him I've got a lot of weak tea I been smoking---
" I've got some too," he says disinterested, not smiling---
" Oh, okay,!!" I say sheepishly---There's lostness in the cold
grandeur of the world failing to meet for my lost hopes, my
sweethearted futility---but not only that, it's the gray light
falling on purple winter granite without care, the gloom of
combinations such as the tiny fury of the bus stations of holidays from far across a snowy park in the void---the way souls
dont meet but clonk stones brow to brow cold eyed---poor
Peter Martin has come back---

I SPEND A WHOLE AFTERNOON IN THAT
BURMESE CAVE or cellar, that rat horror with its impen-
etrable hideaways and traps, with Marguerite, trying to make
her---can't---in the evening it's the beginning of the big holiday weekend, I tell Ma and Pa I'll meet them in Boston at
12 A M---But I go to Keresky's house in the Village and
knock on his apartment door, he's not up because naturally
it's almost two A M but here he comes from the street all
bleary and so tired he wont talk to me scarcely though it was
he sent for me to renew friendship after all these years---

another Horace Mann guy lives next door, and joins us in the gray hall---Outside is the big holiday weekend, with lights, people, sadness, near 6th Avenue---Minetta Lane-- I go to my house to sleep and dress-- I go to Al Green's house for dinner, there's pink cream ice in glass cups---I keep spilling them---Al wants to know if I have anything to do---"No" I say, then I suddenly remember the appointment with Ma and Pa in Boston but can it really be them?---in exasperation I say "I'm supposed to meet somebody in Boston---I havent got time---it's too late anyway"---Al's mother is making din- ner and suddenly an old bum is at the kitchen door trying to close it on the kittens and mothercat---I rush infuriated at him---he's apparently a neighhoor and even friend of the Greens but I dont care, I push him back and try to hit him but with strong hands he holds my arms, complaining--- every time I free a hand I hit him, which disappoints him and he retreats saying "Aah!" and snarling but really intelligently looking at me every time I hit him, as though he was myfather with his blue eyes understanding that I'm hitting him on account of a hangup on family cats and we both know I'm a big futile child and he could hold my hands but I swing him those slow punches, a gelatinous fight---he finally retreats in his door---I go back, spill all the two ice creams from a chair and start crying but immediately leap with a spoon to rescue it from the linoleum and put in cups-- Al is helping me intelligently saving the ice cream, making little jokes---I'm amazed what his mother must be thinking of me by now----One ice cream did not spill, the other only par- tially and rescuable except for the little part touched the floor---they set the big round table for supper, there seems to be n'o room, I say "What? We'll get two little tables? a little

chairs for us, Al?"---"Oh no, we all sit together," he smiles---
His fat sister asks me some question which I'm reluctant to
answer and I wish I could sit alone with Al instead of having
to be social around one big table.

> the cave was a
> lost scene in the
> hidden world,
> a motorboat scene
> in the gash of
> the lake---

an abandoned house, the bottom of a boat---

> Apocalyptic? Apocanothing--- a pock on

you---

WE'VE BEEN STRAGGLING ALONG THE STREET
talking, been in lobbies goofing, me, Irwin, Al Green, Bull,
the Ordinary on the S.S. William Carruth-- Danny---at one
point in a lobby Irwin stood up in the corner seat to look
around---Coming down a sunny broad street I involuntarily
overturned and pushed and dragged to the middle of the
street a big long tool table, the workers dont notice at first
and when they do their table is on its side in the middle of
the road and Bull says "Now theyre coming"---my gang has
long dispersed up ahead in fear---I pick up an armful of
rocks and run, arriving hiding in Brockelman's store on
Kearney Square where as I'm trying to come out through a
narrow opening and vault over an iron spike grill and have
already lost and dribbled my rocks one by one especially on
the sloping concrete causeway before the grille, the Ordinary
stands there ready to pelt me with rocks as I try to teeter out

---He's joined the enemy camp---I'm enraged---The opening isnt big enough for me to throw back at him strong---He comes in around the back, followed now by my gang who are trying to stop him---the Ordinary is a thin kid with a lisp---As he comes in I duck a rock he throws, and wait, he turns to look at Al and them coming in and I reach out to get him in a movement so fast a loud WHAP wakes me up as I've laid my hand over the windowpane by the bed and almost went through it, as though I'd clamped my hand over the dreamman's mouth to shut up his activity, and so fast I wake up with satisfaction

HUCK AND IRWIN are staying with us in the Richmond Hill house, they're in my room singing Jewish hymns, Irwin in a high quavery synagogue choir voice, Huck a huge bass---Irwin's just found him a job as waiter in a synagogue home---Huck concludes his song with a big socko showbusiness finale bass, heard everywhere, while I'm washing my teeth in the bathroom---Applause---Pa's in the livingroom---There's been lots of people at the house all weekend, including, earlier, Vinny, GJ, Scotty and Lousy as of yore and it's NOW and I'm telling them about the railroad and in a great epic poem and they listen to the New Zagg---Later I do go to work at the Boston and Maine Yards, Lo!---Shaggy Northern Indians in dirty striped robes are gathering the lettuce waste in the pile field, their sad dark women are walking off all clinging to one another in the coming winter wind, O Sad!---and it's right down the yard over the heaps are the boxcars, there's the brakeman stepping off, looking for his sign, I have to go up and ask where my local's made up at---Also men Indians in

the middle gathering the junk and waste---I say to myself
"Ah, not only California Indian section hands, but the
weirder ones of Home and North and this iron ruddy loss---"
---The big weekends at home at 94-21 have included
Rachel, people, big tree shades, just like in New England in
Lynn, that's why Pa was there---O I wish humanity would
come visit me like that, I wish my dreams were true, I wished
I could work on a railroad like that---it's nothing but the
same Boston-to-New Hampshire-to-Lowell one I've
dreamed of since so high---

THERE'S A GUY IN OUR HOUSE MAKING A BOP
RECORD, very strange tenor horn that at times sounds to
me like bop voice and I look up and see he's playing a few
notes poorly a-la-baw-baw like Cody on his alto in Frisco
and then voice-riffing the rest---"Hell I can do better than
that" I say to him and his recording engineers when he's
done---he looks like "Al Cohn"---to show what I mean I
riff---they listen---Nin wearing dark hornrimmed glasses is
there, says " Let my brother make a record like that"and leans
her crazy face right next to the fan as it rolls towards his face
and back, to see him closer and persuade better, following the
movement of the fan, sayin "Ah? Ah? Huh ? Let him??" He
agrees!---Earlier I'd tried to show Georgie the Polock
Meiducki how to run his new tape recorder in the YMCA
in Lowell where we'd stashed it but I'm not able to having to
hold.it teetering and crooked on one knee while I fiddle
with knobs I cant quite read or see---earlier it was some great
prison house on a hill overlooking towns, I escaped---

A GREAT HEGIRA OF MANKIND IN AMERICA has crossed the wilderness, is almost in Washington but the recently martyred revengeful Indians are close by and coming---It all began somewhere in a theater, I was there, in a seat, there were girls, eating in booths,--- Now the great parade goes over the Potomac River bridge into Washington as just then the Indians upriver dive in the water and swim it--- "They're going to surround us on the other side!" ---Some of the bridgecrossers start popping the Indian swimmers with rifles, some women shoot---the swimmers are suddenly not Indians but ordinary people trying to reach the same shore---I can even recognize a girl who'd been in a booth with me in the war land---I see someone aiming at her to shoot but changing his mind---Others do shoot, the swimmers lean their head into the water, floating drowned--- Suddenly also at the safe end of the bridge great crowds of people are hurrying in the shallow water along the bank, apparently further enemies, one well dressed man throws his silver dagger up at the bridge as he walks under---it goes over and down in the water on the other side right near himself---the masses all melt, the war is confused, we're all rushing pellmell into a new peaceful life, the river made the difference of the war---or the difference of war----So now my mother and I have a little grocery store on a drowsy street in neighborhoods, one afternoon I go for a walk under the shady goldgreen trees---Five blocks up in the New Orleanslike drowse I suddenly faintly hear her "Deni Bleu!- --Jacky just went for a walk---he'll be right back!"---By this time I have a seven foot salami on my shoulder, it's shaped crooked like a twisted branch, I struggle back to the store gleeful with this great weight---I pass the same girl of whom

I'd been so bashful in the long-ago booth of the war places, I'd been left alone with her temporarily and I remember, I wouldnt talk or look up---I come into the store, Deni is thin, he jumps up as I make a hey face---"Who'd you think it was?" he cries shaking my hand---"Want some salami?"--- and as my mother laughs Deni starts on the salami but suddenly he starts shaking olive oil and vinegar on it with the frantic action of a kid jacking off and spills pints of it all over the floor---"My God not so much" my mother says----"Oh I love olive oil!" he laughs, and smears his mouth with it, glad---I gaze rueful at all my oil on the floor---Anyway war's over, (this was dreamed and written July 26 1953 Korea Truce day)---

UP IN HUCK'S ROOM on Times Square Irwin and I are taking some books and things and leaving some on his bed- --we're going up to his other higher room in the Times Square Dormitory Attic like the one on San Juan Letran street in Mexico City where all the street boys sleep and take benny and have big rapports, big talks in the excited hepcat nite---"Where's Huck?"---"Well, he's in jail."---"How long has he had this room---years now!"---"Yeah but he's never in it---they dont even let him scratch his name on the door any more---" The door is the bathroom door, a plate, many times many names scratched among them Huck biggest and over and over again as the supra-occupant of this spectral death hotel in the brown New York----Irwin and I have just apparently returned from the Coast---

JULIEN DIED---we have him at the wake, we the subterraneans, it's Julien's house on lower Fifth Avenue but our
wake, it even gets in the paper and it's mentioned how Dick
Beck's antiquated stationwagon always parked in front sprung
a leak and flooded something and he got a summons---Julien
is not on his back in a coffin but sitting up on a chair in the
corner---everybody talks and drinks nevertheless, even
gayly--- It's also Gerard and my house on Beaulieu Street and
sadly brown---I remember going in there the "second night"
of the "wake" after having seen the television program
announcing Jack Kerouac reading Children's Tales and after
long interminable horrors and sorrows at Pennsylvania
Station's marble corridors waiting during hot holiday weekend nights for trains, around johns, getting in trouble with the
cops, inexplicable, sad---I see Beck's car out front, go in---
The side door is open but also the vast front one with its
blinding apocalyptic spotlight and I go in that one eyes wincing and bashfully crooking my shoulders and sticking my
hands awkwardly in my belt as though anyone might think
I'm taking the *second* night of Julien's wake lightly---thus I
shamble in, he's still in his corner but this time in the freedom
of choice I dont look---the kids are sprawled around, I sit on
the couch with Roger Barnet who shows me a clay bottle of
Gin and Gypsum---GIN & GYPSUM---"Should we drink
it?"---"Sure, *I* would." The girl (Shelley Lisle's wife) already
has her glass and ice cubes ready---the wake had much gayer
been the night before, now the publicity and the seriousness
of Julien's imminent burial begins to weigh on us---Irwin's
somewhere around---How still is the grave displeased youth
of death in his festered corner chair, how solemn, still
unyielding, still disapproving, priggishly prim, *mort*---

112

A WOMAN HAD A BABY, in a wooden house in the suburbs we all rush upstairs for the christening or to show it to
somebody---but it's not just-born, it's about one year old I
can see as I look at it, a boy, pretty---We're all in the hall land-
ing--- This is the place like the Aunts of Winchendon and
Maine and touches of the Joe tenement when the porch was
crumbling and I was sick and Jeannette was there, touches of
that place of hills with country cars and stores and maybe
nearby that Lakeview Chet Tipka Lake---rural, joyous,
healthy, New Englandish, familial---Autumnal---fecund---
also on a sad red Sunday I'd gone there through country town
or village squares, and talked with the children of my aunts. . .

BACK AT LOWELL HIGH SCHOOL in sunny morning or
maybe Bartlett Junior High but it seems I'm back from lifelong
worldwide sea adventures and in fact I'm on a ship bound *again*
as if not remarment and cart chap toed enough for once and
here she is bespelding the mordelore---as if not enough *again*
---the valley of the dead, the dead houses, the North Pole
silence and as ever those bleaky gloo gloo Eskimos hanging
out the red ice on thong wars, the mist from meskimoxo's
ladysmouf---So I'm in the class and have newfound intelli-
gence, talking to the kids---There's Pete Menelakos asking,
"Where you been?" ---Girls---the same lost morningness---
the same guilt and helplessness in the well lit void of this
world---Cant worry about every gull in the sea---

SUBTERRANEANS AT A JAM SESSION in the Open
Door, which becomes a great theater and I'm in the cellar

trying to figure the way to sneak in free, I see a giant stairway without steps that turns out to be an escalator for the theater employees and I say "All we gotta do is climb that, jump up" ---- "But no" says the kid with me, Dick Beck or Lisle or Gerard Rose, "you've got to show your goddam pass and badge at every door, at the top of that escalator----" It's the big eternity Brooklyn movie still---We see a few of the employees, their heads motionless rising from the vast punch-clock cellar of Lon Chaney and St.Louis Bazaar 'Sale' Hall gloom-prop backgrounds of screen and stage, to the plush lobbied heights----one an ordinary Negro workingman--- There are jam sessions, wrangles---girls---cops---Later I'm at the beach investigating a historic landmarked famous old cottage and in fact so old they've only bothered to put two or three notes at certain places like in the pantry, by some old moldy cups, a note---I vandalize and bust up the cups and think of tearing up the notes---It's just an old house and moldy and small---I'm afraid to go in swimming because of the same reason that foodwater was charged the other day, as if radioactivity or disease---not drowning I fear but some nameless salt sediment or disease in the mud of the water itself---It's like spectral Lakeview beach on the side when I got that Pale Sun Sunburn of WPA baseball days and the ancient beach of Gray Glook Lake where I refused $5.00 to go in swimming (age of three)----Danny Richman with me at the cottage which is also like the wrecks and ruins Ma and I found Pastramis in, in New Jersey---the "Van Johnson" time----Later I'm eating in a restaurant (after a namelessly long night at the Fortiers and my mother saying "They never make us a place to sleep" but the truth had been Mrs. Fortier'd arranged my bed in a middle room of this "Sarah

114

Avenue Fortier house", a big double bed but Donnie was in it---Bill Tenor's Donnie---and immediately was on me and what with Ma in the front room and the Fortiers in the back and Nin and all the lights on and the closeness of all the walls and the aversion and horror I felt and Donnie loud and crazy to blow and jump all over and strangely like Joe I rushed out to find another bed to sleep in which was when scene changed to gigantic upstairs rooms empty and gloomy like rooms of Salem Street Manse)---in the restaurant (after submitting my Cortons porkscraps to the Contest Cook who slopped them into a big pot and prepared them as I waited anxiously by the sea outside his kitchen)---I go in, aint hungry, sit at table with owner (Johnny the Bartender) chatting (and like when Johnny was "in France" in that other Restaurant-by-the-Sea Dream) and in comes that awful blond hooknosed brakeman of the SP from Frisco whom Cody hates and thinks officious, he sits down and orders coffee and as soon as my friend the Owner goes off to get it leans to me trying to borrow money on the sly (which I aint got) (and owner Johnny notices and rushes back smiling to avoid hassel for me) but the brakeman serious, intense, in a low voice trying to make me understand---It's also like the restaurant by God the very restaurant of "Aunt Anna in Maine" dreams and part Washington D.C. when there was a glittering boulevard at night like New Hampshire avenue and sad scenes where I wander looking for Big Slim in the soft impossible mystery, courtyards, the marble insides of spectral hotels, stadiums of roar, river levees, corner bars with shirt-sleeved men jamming to the door, New Orleans in the air and rumors of the vast alcoholic America which also I saw glittering in the Pomeray dream of the Stolen Mattress and

115

the rednosed son of the wino---The meat of my Cortons
Pork Scraps was in great big gray lumps---When for a second I fear the brakeman is going to order Cortons or Johnny
smilingly offer him some for lunch because I know they're
still hot and have to cool in the refrigerator, I see the confident smile on "Johnny" (whoever he is) (Roland) who knows
all this perfectly well (about cooling)---Ronnie Ryan, Buddy
Van Buder, the whole world swims by, archetypical as plots. . .

IRENE'S DREAM AUG. 9, 1953
"Francesca---a piece of clay---I mold it, it wants to come to
life---it struggles under my manipulation---I try to tell others
that it is breathing and wants to live---Then it is Francesca
dying, as they come over---My sister Bessie looks at her, she is
worried about other things---I take the figure inside the hall
---it stops struggling to live---it is icy cold and rigid---I lay it
down---The nurse comes to take over---As I lay there I
smooth the figure---I begin to mold it again and she strug-
gles---I tell the nurse and she tells me to go away---She
believes in her death, as I am going to the door I see the figure rise, and as I go down the hall I look back expecting to see
it walking but the people in front are behaving as normally."

ONE AWFUL CENTRAL SCENE, it's in the parlor brown
and funeral and coffin-like, Gerard is dead in his coffin and
all my writings are racked like candle flickers in a file box by
the stuffed sofa in the suffocant gloom dark, literally writing
in my brother's tomb---but it's the awful silence, the solemn
ceremony of my papers all old some of them crinkled but all

116

familiar and now-I-see objects of a destined meaningful
TOMB of meaning laid out and racked for use and observation and filing in the room of death---and so as if I was
replacing life and sex by writing and death, I----antagonistic,
dual, doom---Relatives dont even have to be there, I'm sorta
alone with Gerard in the parlor playin my papers---There
was earlier a dream of incest with Nin, no acts of incest but
the understanding all night long that there had been incest
and we should be punished soon---like when we used to
take diving slides with the pillow across the linoleum floor at
Lilley Street flat at 11 P M guilty time----

A GATHERING OF BOYS, one in his shorts or otherwise
down on his fingers in a racing starting position and for some
reason he was demonstrating wrong and wanted to show
how he should really do it and correct his stance and meanwhile I--this annoying kid I dont know who maybe Fish
who hit me or some Nadeau Ladeau in the Road kept hug-
ging me and clinging to me from the back really affection-
ately so I couldnt fight him off and yet most annoying and
sinisterly personal, in the press of the crowd at the starter
ramp cage---

AN APPOINTMENT WITH MA AND NIN to meet
them at the Times Square Paramount to take them to the
show but instead I went to the Strand and came out late and
they were already going in the Paramount or home and I felt
no guilt----went upstreet 7th Avenue to Schraafts where
Irene worked in white employee dress making faces of dis-

taste to me conning her work over pan of chocolates and nuts under her bespectacled middlage bosses' continual scrutiny---as I waited for her a hoodlum ran by shooting it out with the cops, up and down the marble stairs as I tried to duck---suddenly it was all Billerica Street Lowell Maggie Cassidy's brother---Joe---swings---river---gray---sad----the little eternity street down which I struggled.

I'M MARRIED TO JOSEPHINE and with all her friends around in the kitchen she makes fun of me and my "writing", I'm there with all my manuscripts, gooping----a cuckold paramoured to a dike---I make up feeble stories and try to write them or act them out with disinterested friends---Later Ed Buckle or Buddy Van Buder comes to try kitchen window, sees me, says the publishers want another novel to look at (a falsehood, what he really wants is a jolt of heroin again and I know it)---a bleak laterlife with no balls, no joy, no Ma, no Kerouacism, nothing but the possibilities of the present ripened to full horror---without any of the charm now apparent---I'm like old Uncle Mike in the cubab tears of afternoon or that incredible teary old Canuck lush in the Papineau Tavern in Montreal who cried when we carried him over (called him over) and I was amazed to learn this lonely broken heartsensitive wretch was one of the richest men in the neighborhood---people avoided his big Weeping countenance and frank blue breton eyes---he was the one said I should drink Caribou Blood---Le Sang du Caribou---something Breton & Lost---

A FRIGHTFUL SUBWAY ELEVATOR IN CHICAGO---
it's in that same Eternity Park, broad, gray, scenes across the
way, like a vast Botanical Gardens---the people in the elevator silent---the gray news of the day, or eve, the Chicago-ness
something as bleak as that hollow-sounding marble hall of
eternity (men coughing) or the crystal chandelier eternity
where thoughts more or less meet---

THE SIGHT OF MA'S HAMPER, with cloth, designs,
sewn on, so clean and sweet makes me want to cry "I'll never
see anything as clean and pretty as that again!"

TWO SUCCESSIVE VISIONS OF MONTANA***---
driving, with Irene, past the snows, mountains, on the side of
the road are fantastic huge mansions with tall pillars and big
quiet fronts, closely packed like in Venice, tall, thin like in
Grant Wood, like Burchfield wellkept heaps and it's all in this
strange Montana--- Next thing you know I live in a ranch
style comfortable home in Montana---sitting with Ma
through picture window I can see mountains and snow, and
I say "And there's a nice little road, to go to the store, not far
from town," etc. all to her satisfaction, it's like the livingroom
of that house we'd sat on the wooden porch of looking for
flying saucers in the cold West moon---no doubt the corrupt
porch falling apart with me on cot, in "Phillipines" is up on
side of house---and so by same law too it's cold red sun
Maine of Aunts of Winchendon nearby and something raw,
happy, connected not only to women of baby birth few days
ago but ultimately to boulevards of Montreal of my truck-

119

driving honey-colored love New Haven pier crash days with pows of seas, dry muds, spiders, slants, pits, trestles, caves, necktie racks, skis, Swiss, red, rock, smosh, pot, pone, poll, pall, pill, pell, purl, pash, posh, Tim, Tyler, Tom, Reading the Daily News, Finding the Shrouded Stranger, the desert, the arrow, the rat in the *CLIMD* (paste that in ya hat)---the actual wooden house with red sun on grade school in the first morning of the world, when even on the canal there had been no activities yet, dew sat unruffled everywhere, no footsteps of any action had crossed the spit face of time, I was infant rising to chime the paradise. I'm on the road to heaven (this marks the first year of dreams, begun in Easonburg Aug.14,1952, and it is now Aug.14,1953 in New York.)

THE RADAR MACHINE IN THE SKY---which I saw in a dream in 1945 on Morningside Heights New York, a misty night like the night of the standing on the corner selling peanuts to people in the soft sad dormitory fog, they were wondering what was happening as well as me---as ever the West End Bar cast out its strange warm gold light on the sidewalk just as now---generations---just as in now-generations the San Remo on the most awful fognight and rainwild walls of sea shroud ice haunted ships with tragic rigging wheel and keen in the drownable bay you see the lights of po re mo shining on the corner of Bleecker & MacDougald and it's always reassuring nourishuring to know in this dream the maniacal angels do gather in one lit spot---but now I'm on Morningside Heights, I hear a strange hum of silence and dynamo in the sky, I look up, pale clouds part in a Souwesterly breeze, for just a moment now I see the outlines and racks of

120

some great structure in the air that suspends itself though no visible wings or propeller, it's just so hugely light and covers films of air with its intricacies of balsa-like skeletal skin ribwork, so that the air would support the thin lightness of it but yet I know it is made of strongest iron heavy as an engine and what supported it up there was that great gray power I can hear humming in the foggy night---let your engines roar and shudder and support 4-motored NAAS---this passenger ship to Chicago Camago Crapago for Porto Morto Rican migrators was powered by an engine so deep and so strong and so still and so doomed (YOOOOM---the shudder is on a very hi frequency and so soundless, unnoticable at first---no static in its traffic---a great flying hot house with no glass, no flowers---black as racks of ark hell mara----sneering at man, po man---came from nowhere, everywhere, long befo atlantis--- will destroy us, support us, blow us buddha damn up---was invented by scientist men---by man)---I knew some new end was now promised of man, maybe he will no longer die, but lie in this machine and fly slowly thru the sky dirigible horror for---test tubes---but all that pure nonsense because all it is, is, something come to watch us and record our every move for reasons as yet unnamed as yet unspecified, just as, a real therapy never ends, or at least has silly many years and years to run before some statement can ever be mustered (ha!), some light (oog) vouchsafed---so black radar shroud-machine is a mystery wow still but I have seen it---in other words, urgh, I dont know, mad, and the dirigible prophorror may be comes after the "light" (o argh naw shat) the so called blody gory moody mady parady out light, crastapouch, explanation which anyhow will serve and save no one from the cracking open of his skull in the rocks of the cemetery I say. So hang yr radar machines and on a higher hook Lord God of Hosts for krissakes I do beseech dee. T'aint nothin but the sound of celestial farmers snappin their suspenders in the dawn of an already ended day, and for no other reason but porches with dark spiders crawling around to find the time of the light of the ouddl. But this is nothing compared to real and well-writ dreams, like:-

THE BIG FOOTBALL GAME, we're all going to the Navy Dry Dock like big ones I once saw Liverpool Narrows of New York on sunny day with my father shipping out and all the boys were in the auditorium---for the game, it's Columbia U. versus teams from Rook, and Lou Little is coach---but as we rush to the scene from those eternity stone lockers and showers of the underground gray dressingroom like the clattering how low wheesh wooo! echoey latrines of the Lowell High School basement it's very late, we arrive just as the kickoff takes place, I see them in the striped field, the straw---I'm in the car with four or five other players includ- ing White who'd broken his leg with me in October 1940 but was better now again and after all these years back at Columbia like me, for a go-back to old fail-trys, for reason of his own, grimfaced as a conductor or a Civil War General, same thing---I have a kind of subsidiary uniform with red in it, brown, tassels, somebody got it for me, their uniforms are pure varsity blue--We go over the shining Hudson, come to the drydock that sways slowly and gigantically like the East River Jim Inside Cratchit Barge I saw later today (howp), we drive alongside, see the kickoff, rush in sleekly thru the gate- gawping crowds (O the other night dreams of side rawl houses, what is the Omening of it?) and I look to see them if they're amazed to see the carload of great late players!---like Thanksgiving Lowell Lawrence the gray furors at the gate, at the Lowell goal line!---I have to sit on an end zone bleacher and cant get in the game, in fact Lou Little, the coaches, the school, nobody even knows I'm on the team, I came straight out of a dream into this reality, my chances are so slight, really so impossible to get in the game I dont consider it for a minute but cheer anxiet-ly hysterical and--At the half I go inside the bleachers under the concrete grandstand is a great manyleveled superstructure like the Hospital or Hi School or Back of Theater Roominghouse of the World perhaps even a Castle, or Great Boat, like the interior of that U.S.Navy training house-home-boat at 28th and East River New York so vast, leveled, windows, Colonial oldstyle planks on an iron hull, like Julien's reformatory and like Jersey City piers in the long high eternity unbelievably drowsy afternoon I must have spend in there, among the Arabs, high, the Hospital and Sorrow Enigma of it---but gray now in the bleacher hous-ing, stones, dissipid, dank barrels, spewm, ugly, like latrine house---in the huge levels and noisy corridors (celebrating fraternity trouchdown drinks) I'm standing by a barrel and a dumbwaiter---wildhaired, big headed, hydrocephalic, stupid, an insane idiot in a madhouse not knowing what to do with my hands---my girl Judy Garland consoles me---"You'll play yet!"---she's part of the big weekend the team'd been having that was why we'd in that limousine showed up late--- Greenie White had gone in to play, he'd succeeded with the girls too, I not---So I who'd come impossibly with a lump in my throat tears in my throat tickling from the nasal hoping to play in the game in my makeshift uniform (snirf) (slob) the coach not even knowing of my existence now was left inside the concrete grandstand World Underground as the game ended, shots popped and everybody went away, for weeks till Judy returned across some Mexico Gray, and found me now crazed catatonic still by the same barrel---my little cat child had just committed suicide, down the waiter shaft he'd jumped, long black hole to some ambiguous safety outside this cave of death I'm in now, with daylight showing--- catastroph'd eaten him but I'd as yet to follow suit in the pact we made concerning the shaft, the egress to the river of hope that pathless its somber tide under giant bridges of Immortal Afternoon was also a shining pure impossible dream, to resurrect the blind, heal the leprous-skinned, still the fancy hand, calm the fever, gawp up the mad---Judy Ginger gently reminds me I owe her $5 from the football weekend---I havent got it---Dead kitties are poor---

IN MEXICO CITY WITH MY MOTHER---I'd taken a long walk from South Town to North Side in this Montrealish Dream Capital and it was very easy because all one fantastic slope thru traffics, all I did was skitter down steep concretes on flying feet sometimes not touching the ground, while cars in second had to grind down---Strange Mexico City---Ma and I are on top of a great hill, we go shopping to the bakery, there's fog ard coldness "Just like Frisco!" I tell her--- "and the hills too!"---The bakery is sad and drear, she goes in the front door, I go in the other which is connected to another building---I advise her to buy simple pastries without icing---A long line of Indian girls or people are lined up at the cheap counter like the Negresses

124

in Merkels---I'm almost secretly wishing I hadnt brought Ma
to MexCity, I'm worried because it's so much like Frisco---
Ah, it's beginning to miss

LUCIUS BEEBE IS USING MY ROOM in the first floor
apartment---he has his son with him, as I'm preparing to go
out for the evening and taking a few things with me like razor
etc. into the adjoining room to ablute, his boy is already retir-
ing in the sack and Lucius who is not the real life one at all
but *is* supposedly Beebe but shorter, friendlier, a visiting dig-
nitary from Shmolorado etc., he's in his undershirt shaving---
I go in my side other room like Huck's room of the other
night and discover I have to go back and knock for something
I forgot, which I hate to do--- "By the way you do know
Manley Mannerly in Colorado" I say---at the door--- "No"
---"Why he told me when you're in Denver he takes over for
you"---"No, not in the least, dont know the man"---he looks
like Mannerly---Earlier I was journeying across water and
New Orleanses of Sadness and up along the roarsome lone-
some Mississippi with populated shores---some kind of great
blue bay or gulf, my hands cupped over the wave to see---
Doomed to travel always in America, road rail and waterscrew.

MA AND I ARE IN CANADA or Maine looking for a
house, we are in the suburbs, go down a steep skittering hill,
I go ahead sliding on my ass on the concrete roadway, slowly
---In front of the house my foot sinks completely in
a rubbishy yard, I curse---it happens twice---Ma is looking
for the doorbell----it's gray and strange depressing ends of

oilcup-flicker suburbs in coldwave grave North---Later it's at Crawford St. the little fat kitty runs out into the traffic of the street with the mother cat, I've yelled at them a thousand times not to do it, to Ma I say "There, look, they'll get run over sure!" and sure they do, I see three cars just miss, the whiz and whirr of auto, the strolling cat, then finally a whiss and whir leaves the little one flattened, another and the mother is flattened, "There, I cant look! What'd I tell you?" Later we take them in and they crawl around on their bellies not dead but dying---in the yard of the house my foot sinks so swiftly and as if something underneath was sucking me down, like an evil grave, that's what made me curse!

BIG HORRIBLE ACTUAL EXPERIENCE of hot flaming death, end of the world cataclysm comes and hits New York disintegrating all buildings and I'm standing around waiting for it to happen and for how I'll feel when it does---It *does* come, I'm standing in a New York courtyard, the whole city and everybody is swirled to the right and as if flattened and whirlwinded out of sight in a searing mass like the collapsing house in Las Vegas flats---Doom in the air so awful, people'd been talking about it for days, now suddenly *rumble* the visitation arrives in New York and everyone's in ecstasy-anticipation of the actual final stroke of death---Everything disappears in disintegration, I with it---but my consciousness doesnt seem to disintegrate---

WALKING ACROSS THE MISSISSIPPI FIELD to the ship with Georgie Polock, Whitmore, the Chief Steward, I've

126

already been fired but dont care or that is replaced and my replacement's around but I feel good, beer, and am goofing with the guys---In the stroke of doom---Then it's Julien's house right there on that field, and Irwin and I visiting him, wondering if he'll go to Houston, and he makes a funny little speech "Kerouac when Ah goes to Houston which Ah never can do Ah dows it all outs my-a-n-n---when Ah bah---" but smiling and inviting us to sit down, in his house, which is like a gas station, and it's a pleasant afternoon

IN SOME KIND OF JAIL at first, all the hoodlums are being lazy beside individual beds in a big dormitory with windows overlooking New York---it's "Rikers Island" and I've been arrested on some drug charge---I look at the gu ys who've been here for six months, I understand their waiting and the goofs meanwhile, the relaxing---all they have to do is wait for their food---Later it's really more like a hospital I'm in, in another ward, the beds are white and in rows, not all set closely Chinese style in all directions pointing like in the 'jail'---It's a mental hospital now---There are needles---

TERRIBLE JUNKYARDS OF PITTSBURGH or Boston with one sweeping high hump hill over which the rail train goes, on the way up someone says "Say, can this thing make it?" and the car's crawling slower and slower and almost toppling back upside down it's so steep---Earlier the train had swooped at some little hill rack on the run between "Boston and Albany" where again I'm working with a "team" of railroad men and we're deadheading to "L.A." to work there I don't know how long, and that same brakeman or tagman with the glasses is along and we're all buddybuddy,---when the train hits the sharp dip, in the wood, outside Albany, along the water, the tie-pin brakeband breaks, we have to go fetch it in the sand and repair---But those junkyards, a massive city of it, my mother and I are walking over hot sinking rubber fields with curious hard pieces across holes bottomless--- looking for the city too much dump junk to negotiate, and crazy trains---up and down like a Coney Island, all melted, rotted, humped junk---Later it's the Richmond Hill house, a man next door's been arrested for growing "beet dope" and selling and using it, Buddy Van Buder is telling me this and to another girl who keeps leaning over me telling me useless excited stories when I sleep in backyard on a cot with the cat, pretty though---Rachel is rushing along the ramp rack on her house to yell at waiting friends in a car--- Seems the tag team is staying here at Ma's with me but I'm in my cot in the silent red dawn thinking, telling my cat, "I don't wanta work "---Unpleasant arrangements and invasions of my once-peace in Richmond Hill

GIGANTIC SAND MOUNTAINS of the railroad, a hospital or big brother infirmary nearby, the sun, a yawning cave pit---I say to myself "I knew I was going to work on the railroad again, but I'm afraid really afraid I think of these sheer drops, peaks, trestles,---" The rails lead into sweet All Lowell laid out below in some March sun, in fact here there's the daily noon move to clear the mainline for the hotshot passenger to Boston, I see the ancient conductors and proud young brakemen of Lowell in blue uniforms jabbing in the breeze by the engines---I'm up in the sand cliffs seeing this, working freights---Later it's my writing desk, typewriter, paper, novels---I uncover the old Cannastra Finistra paper roll of Sal Paradise ON THE ROAD novel---I'm talking to a man and a woman, she's going to Mexico, is a parent, says from now on she's going to really live and enjoy genital sex, there's something vaguely futile about her as though she'd been making big final decisions like that all her life---*selfishly* like me---the futility of the Bohemian decider and undecider trying to find hedonistic formulas to happiness in an ascetic ball of globe covered with unhappiness---In the sand pits there'd been a hegira of adventures with my mortal enemy who was trying to get me to fall but b' god in time after time of clever formula and slow painstaking ah-bedeardoed acti-vishmity ah done laid him onerous bones and all on his rack and pit pot bottom plot, aint never seen him since, 'ceptin I remember his face, sad figure on hill, distant hostility like something in the wind, sadness of his pinpoint soul dement-ing to me like a rock thrown from the universe of light---but as I say I succeeded in somehow avoiding him and making it and now I'm alright, I had to struggle through all such hor-rors to get to peaceful railroad securities---It's the shroudy stranger in a white B Movie serial shirt---in his earliest Lowell Lineaments was *Fish*---the kid who punched me---

A HORRIBLE NIGHTMARE JAMES WATSON is wait-ing for me in my big house on Salem Street with the countless rooms, has come to visit me, we forgive each other for spats of past---Lo! Ah! Uurg! he has become a physical fiend, his voice has a gurgling mad wild quality, he speaks in irresponsible screaming Dr.Jekyll Mr.Hyde cries---his legs have become short, no longer than 2 feet or 20 inches, it looks like he has a tail inside his pants, his body is long (so his general height remains undiminished)---now I realize with fiendish pleasure why it was possible for him to come to see me since nothing matters any more---nevertheless he still writes and probably greatly now---I feel sorrow---He's in my living-room, fiending and cursing and shooting sparks in carrying on an ordinary conversation with Madeleine who is naturally disgusted with him and has come to see if I'm going to make her, I'm licking my lips and looking at her breasts and for a moment we're alone in the kitchen and I want to put her down on the rug---I'm somewhat afraid of Watson but what can I do?---Later Irene is running a little restaurant across the street in Richmond Hill where the railroad men have been in the habit of going for coffee 24 hours a day, a kind of San Luis Obispo but in Richmond---across from Mrs. Whiteheart---Irene's presence signalizes the arrival of other Negroes in the neighborhood and suddenly I notice the railroad men aint patronizing any more the place, only beat Negroes---it constitutes a new invasion and change---people are sulking---strangely, as I sit by my bedroom window with Irwin Garden, I hear among the chatter of gangs of hoodlums on the street the words "Cody Pomeray King"---they've been reading *Visions of Cody*! ---Deni Bleu distributed the manuscript---I feel worried, Irwin is awed--- everybody is reading Visions of Cody and being amazed by it, it is a great comedy ---I begin thinking I should send it to Boisvert---I go into the new Negro taxi stand across the street, at dawn, there are drunks, Third Street bums---it is now a Negro neighborhood but I'm staying---the house where malformed fiend Watson

130

came to see me is across the street, sad, Autumn falls in its windows and makes them rattle, I'm afraid to look---His transformation into a Fiend does not surprise me, now I understand everything that had happened and the reason for his strange angry dependence on me---

I'M IN RUSSIA among the teenagers, in a little sort of candy store---I've journeyed far, this is really Russia, nobody knows--- "Wow! what will they say when they hear about the Teenagers of Russia!" ----There's a colored kid with a funny Raskolnikov visored trolley conductor cap and crazy Russian hair sticking out, he's the hipster of the gang--- There's a neat redhaired kid in a buttondown sweater just like a kid in American Hi School---There are two girls----It is dark, cold, thrilling on the great northern street outside, chimey pots smoke---The kids jabber in Russian as I in the eternity high dig them---I go out, in the street I find a beautiful carved ivory switch click knife and put it in my pocket proudly---I will tell the cops I found it in Russia---In an uptown bus I sit next to two Russian ladies chatting first in French then in Russian about the Underground as they notice my darting eye---Finally I arrive and return to Maine to great family reunion, the Baileys, Ma, Northern Maine Pines, everything. . . . .

Russia's young hipster with the stovepipe Raskolnikov Trolley-visored cap is a Negro like La Negra of Mexico City, now 14, or 16,---his hair sticks out and down from his sooty hat like straws, like a "Mardou" wearing a trolley wiper's cap in Russia with a whole street behind her, only an excited boy interested in girls and Russian weed---

WOODY HERMAN's having a big band session in the basketball hall, Roy Eldridge is with him and while someone is
playing a tenor solo Roy keeps holding out his breath with a
long held rasp for a gag---going "Aaaaaaaaaah"---so the tenor
man slows down the tempo incredibly to make Roy do it
even longer and everybody laffs---Seymour is there, is back
from England, watching---Roy has made still another new
comeback with still another new Herman Herd---Across the
street lives Spencer Tracy, I just heard a story that he was continually high on T, that one night he had his girl and per-
suaded her to undress and she threw her legs over his head
and there he was "Tied to the goal" and he said something
funny---I'm sitting in the Horace Mann schoolyard, there's
Bob Whitmore with some girls, I go over---there's been the
brooding presence of the Mississippi all night too, rafts, joyous jam sessions up and down it, scenes, gray vistas---And
Spencer Tracy's cottage where the rain cried, the cottage in
the backyard of my big birthday party house, sad sweet little
cottage where Gerard died and my wife was supposed to live
and now Van Heflin's there while I goof up and down rivers
and at jam sessions---*Man*

THE GREAT SHIP AND ATTIC OF THE WORLD
where I am with everyone else, all of us like children in white
nightgowns---I have my post in an upper part of the rack
where the old wooden rungs are falling out, I rush up there
to find out what I've done wrong---My buddy Scotty
Boldieu has disappeared---and done something wrong---
Everyone is sitting in a sort of classroom, *en jaquette*---I dont
understand what's happening but it's all serious and lost and

132

the authorities seem lax and cruel to leave us wandering around in this rambattered hulk and old lost all-pot no one to chide us or complain---I really dont care or know what this place was but we---somebody---

I've come out of the hole with languidj---

I'M SUPPOSED TO GO TO SEA again, Deni Bleu comes to get me in the gray house of tears---I start eating great amounts of food for some reason, salads, mayonnaise---he's going to get me back on the Carruth, he's made arrangements with Georgie the Polock, but on the pier street I see the ship is some other---A big colored guy is working in the pantry, I tell him I was pantryman originally and changed to saloon and shouldnt have and "I'd like to work my way around again to the pantry," he replies (also smiling) "You're gonna have to buck a nigger"---No sign of the little ratty steward yet---

WALKING THROUGH PAWTUCKETVILLE with Irwin and Bull, Riverside street's become that long Kansas bound brilliant hiway to the Americas, cars go by, prior to my great voyage I walk down, turn up Sarah avenue---Going up Gershom (we pass my dreamhaunted lost house of childhood there) I say "Iddyboy and I used to do this when passing the Social Club" (running backward against fence, bending it in) and I rush up and hit the fence head on with a tremendous jolt & noise amazing everybody and myself who forgot to turn and hit it with my back---the fence bends in cracking, too---curious guy rushes out, we three run around the cor-

133

ner, they hasted up Moody on Destouches candystore side, I'm on Textile Lunch side gleeful---We meet at wrinkly tar corner after a brief stop in old Destouches' store---Nobody's explaining the trip of the world to us but there's the spectral Riverside hiway offward going as if God had been a malicious creator of dyers and sufferers and hopeless throatchoken ant ish bedazzled *ess* in this impossible brilliance heart & horror of the hole on high---Gad I wish I could find my way out of these dreams as in--death's beginning to occupy my thoughts again---Straj!

THERE'VE BEEN BIG EVENTS & family reunions in New York and I got $1000 from the publishers at the same time I was offered a job selling books in a company car and some other job with it but I go to Mexico to "start my homestead," by bus---On the bus are Halvar and Peaches and three little ragamuffin blond kids who cry and play with passengers and are neglected by their parents as suddenly I'm dozing somewhere "near Kansas" and I hear a commotion, the bus stops, I go on dozing but wake up finally just in time to see the little boy is brushing something off the floor of the bus near the drivers' clutch handle, brushing up grit, crying in a strange emotionless strangled despair inhuman unreal & short, just one cry---apparently he's puked and this stopped the bus and his mother who's been in back seats talking and playing guitar with people is letting him clean up himself far from helping him---I think "No wonder he puked after those pickles and those shmickles at noon and God knows what he had this morning (what his foolmother gave him)" ---While we're stopped Hal the father all blond and white has stepped out to pee, he too is unconcerned, and now as the bus is ready to start up again he steps back in arrogantly down the aisle floating digging all the ladies with a perfectly defined hard-on in his blue slacks sticking way out and he knows it---I despise him---I think how he thinks I'm going to Denver again on some other fiasco plan but I'm only "going through to Mexico" I think proudly and I wont even give him the satisfaction of knowing this---of course we havent talked at all on the bus & suddenly I despair and want to go back to New York and *take* that book job and park my car on Wall Street while I'm picking up my samples and sell mybooks to my "driving student" clients while I'm at it, and make it, take care of my children if any with concern not like these conceited useless Hals and Peaches but it's too late, the bus is almost in Kansas, we've been traveling for days, hard, slow travel and trouble---even if I cash in my ticket at Kansas I'll have lost $36 and the return fare will cost $36 and leave me $80 and it's all a stupid big fiasco, and there's Hal with his egomaniacal hard-on flouncing down the bus-aisle---the world is drearily repetitious of itself---

I'M HIDING MY LITTLE GUN from the cop, a snubnose revolver, black---I'm in a flophouse, have just been talking to the girl and the child and directed them to some place on the Brooklyn Bowery of the old Movies and Fears of Falling ----Spectral Els to Moonfish Mansions with Hubbard, that Metropolitan New York so vast and brownbrick---now in the flophouse I'm sitting on the floor and I see the cop coming in so check on the bums,at first I hide my piece under a cardboard casually near my things---but I decide he'll casually find it and casually almost drowsily and unbelievably both of us bleary he'll take me tenderly to jail so I hide the gun down in the trash of a waste barrel in a little sink room near my pallet---

ON A SUNNY AFTERNOON IN LOWER EAST SIDE New York just like the real one I've been digging this summer around Tomkins Square with Irwin & Irene, and not far from that Julien-Reformatory-Sunny-Tenement Ship which finally I in real life saw docked at 27th and East River (the USN Training House Home Old of the Sea) (with colonial superstructure woods and innumerable windows of eternity) ---near these things, and at about 9 or 10th Street near Avenue B, I went to see a doctor to be treated, he had an assistant with him, first at one office then another on Avenue B itself on 10th he gave me a shot of penicillin and then prepared a syringeful of morphine---"Dont give me too much of that Doc"---He pays no attention to me but keeps talking to his assistant: "I have a hunch about this case" (meaning me) "I'll give him so and so grains. . ."

"But not too much Doc!"---

He fills a big load and says again "I've got a feeling about this case"---and I realize he means I've already raised my resistance against M with previous illegal shots and he knows it by looking at me, at the "case"----the assistant acquiesces and bam, he shoots me but to my scoffy surprise it's just a muscle bang and therefore wont harm me in quantity and I dont say nothin---

FOR THE USE OF LITTLE CHILDREN DOING
NOVENAS a railroad bus parked in front of Ste.Jeanne
d'Arc's, I go up and ask the attendant if I can get a ride back
to Boston on the train bus (it's one gray big coach car)---
"Can I deadhead to Boston in this?" He wants to know
where I been working, it takes me a long time to think and
say "Watsonville"---He's skeptical a little---I show him
papers, old deadhead slips---Inside, the children are praying.

RETURNING FROM LAKEVIEW, Irwin and I and some
other kids, night, we have to walk, a couple of dubious passes
fail to stop for us---in the infantilism of the dream I fear we
cant walk the five miles which is like fifty and was like 50
when I was in cribs and heard of Lakeview---we go down
great tar hiways,---to snowy Lowell, we've been motorboat-
ing in the gray mystery, picking beads by the shore. . .
        Finally it's just Hubbard and I and some
other kid who'd been involved a long time in some mansion
domicile drinking Nescafe and talking to old men who would
leave us money, and some madhouse bits---now we're out on
that tragic railroad earth with lamps, we have a train, ready to
go, I'm counting from the rear and Bull from the head end,
we meet midway at a circus car with orange tigers in paint and
Bull who's been counting says "Ten!" just as I do at the circus
car, it's a 20 or 19-car train---we have a guy with us who
looks at his watch saying "What's that extra man doing?"---a
tag man of circuses, a road foreman of engines but in the
dream an even stranger designation and duty he'll have---here
comes the extra man---I realize to my horror I didnt bring
my little handbag and so cant conveniently pack my Nescafe

and whisky glasses and books so I stick it in my shirt and Gad railroad work is easy, we're planning what we'll do when we get to Bay Shmore already and have no engine yet---

THE GREAT GRAY HOTEL OF THE WORLD, all night, with Bull, Irwin, Vicki, Subterraneans, Gaines in jeans and beard---Gaines is walking along the esplanade in jeans and full Bohemian but also Third Street bum eccentric beard, still a junkey, still having his income money for fixes----At one point a big skid row woman is seen going down the Canal Street with him to a small hotel---The big gray hotel is also a school, I have all my paraphenalia and cant find the class and wander around naked and innocent in basketball courts, among wrangling c rowds---It's one big dormitory, there are hints of sad Columbia Livingston Hall dorm rooms in September when the semester's begun but I'm not even enrolled---In a corner room I find Vicki, we go out together, coming back she walks off to leave me the cab driver---They tell me she's run up a bill---I count the three singles in my wallet and decide I cant do it---The house boys jide me as I walk off "You shoulda paid that cab fare, boy, her company's just struck oil and she'll start goin out with that other guy just in time---ha ha ha!"---the bellhops and pimps of eternity---I dont care---I go up, to Bull and Irwin in a room, during the night Bull discovers I have a sensitive nerve in my head at rightside back skull, he touches tip of it--- "Now I understand why you hesitated and grabbed your head last night when those people--" referring to earlier dim events---I feel my head, the nerve hurts---Bull is proud that I am so beautifully sensitive but warns me of danger from this nerve, I can

138

die from a blow---or wrong contact---We're strolling on a great ramp in Atlantic Gray fog, right outside the 10-story or 5-story windows of our room, the three of us---Bull talks in loud voice, Irwin shushes him pointing to open hotel windows---"Oh, *really*," says Bull annoyed "what on earth do you expect them to hear, my dear"---Later there are some Subterraneans in the room, they're reading my manuscripts, I'm a discovered genius, Irwin is telling them how on Saturday nights of my heroic writer past I'd *grab my head* from the great inrush of ideas and sensations, it seems I told this to Irwin myself---The listener is Gold from Frisco, who makes cracks---Another, blond kid is there, Don Johnson, half-awpedly listening and sometimes commenting---it is a great hive of conversation, rooms, studies of all sorts, absorptions like Vicki's in whose room are elements of the old Upper East Side Elevator Apartment dreams, of her at 1946 or 1947 ---Meanwhile Gaines has done something funny and once again we see him going down the esplanade in jeans and Augustus John beard, loaded----

I'VE GOT TO ESCAPE AGAIN, the Javert Shroudy Stranger has come after me warning of my arrest, it's a gray bleak landscape in California leading to some impossible Africas and out-of-town suburbs with little black-trees---I have to quit my job and run off---The boys are having their phoney paper revolution and are practicing at the radio microphones under the ramp of the overhead drive---I go to Erie N.Y. which is like the sad port I inquired about ships at, this time there are no blond Scandanavians and shipping but sad people plowing plowing up and down sidewalks that made me topple and a huge railyards like in Montreal at the foot of the steep hill street---"I'll hop a freight tonight, go south, get away for good---he'll be watching the bus station"---- Everything unspeakably sad and continuous---

DREAMS OF HEAT---Cody came to get me again from California, was immediately disappointed in me, that I wouldnt go back work on the railroad with him---It was at the Richmond Hill house, he came in early in the morning, went to sleep while I ran out in ferries and trains to some circus or sideshow in a muddy hilly street in New Jersey where I picked up on shit in a sinister atmosphere of mirrors, gypsy backrooms culminating in Manhattan at that old subway station marble office where the police were interrogating junkies and casually started questioning Bull about his arm marks and I was scheduled for questioning and examination at one (after the policewoman's lunch) and I had four or five arm marks of my own fresh from recent injections from doctors and otherwise, phew!---returning to where, at the soda fountain, I was told two separate girls had been looking for me, by the counterwoman, on that old Brooklyn-Lynn street and all this time Cody was sleeping at my house and getting ready to go back to the coast---When I'd asked him how he came, by train, how long he took, he said "Five nights and four days," sullenly, unhappily---

THE LITTLE CAT I HAD IN MY HANDS that had such a sweet sad little funnyface with gray eyes and finally spoke to me in a pitiful little voice, like Gerard's, "J'aime pas demain"

140

and I said "Moi too mon ange!" and felt like crying, like when
I heard Ma's voice over the phone yesterday in the New York
restaurant, my heart was moved just by the sound and loneliness of her voice, I'd left her alone the whole Laborday weekend and was calling at the last minute Laborday night to say I
was coming---that piteous note Gerard had, from her, and
which is in my own voice when I address little names to my
cats---this kitty was an angel, and spoke the truth---Also
there'd been parades around Irene and I in bed, June Evans
and Bull, June giving me a half-full bottle of rich tokay and
pouring a glass and spilling on bed, and Irwin with
Subterraneans out on Paradise Alley sidewalk in Russia talking to a Kosher Patriarch Golem, and Raphael Urso necking
with Irene every time I looked away and she saying to him ,
indicating me, "These old guys are peaceful to be with."----
and I'm tremendously jealous, she's already told me to leave,
it's dreary strange sinister and about to Fall----Finally there I
am waking up hitting Irene and Raphael reaches for me and
I grab him too, it's a drinking nightmare again

AS IF IN LIMA PERU but in Lowell up on Lilly Street there
are indignant Spanish fathers, scenes in a dark street, a flat,
something to do with a murder or rapine, in a high bleak
lonely country of the night, I come down from there heading
"back downtown" followed by strollers of hornrimmed intel-
lectuals who'd been seeing the show up there with me (it's the
same location as the Great Tolstoyan Dream), ahead are the
lights of the Boott Mills on the river, and the bridge---But at
Lakeview and Lilly I say "Damn I'm gonna dig my old scenes"
and there's Scoop's Store and two blocks from it I come across

141

the house I'd *froidly* com pletely forgot, a lil bungalow at present time has two sons repairing roof and yelling down to
mother in the dark but in the past was unmistakable scene of
Ma and I visiting somebody, when I was an infant---elements
of the Gerard-Died bungalow and the John MacDougald and
Miss Wakefield bungalow and all the bungalows---I believe so
strongly I'm (not) dreaming I find myself at 35 Sarah Avenue
and jump up to dark windows in snow and a baby starts crying inside, next door "Sure enough just like I dream'd" there
are Christmas lights in the Alice windows, but blue ones---
That lil bungalow was scene of death, brownmothed kitchen,
ancient rheumy eyed old Sax ghost place of Lowell Old all
smelling of Cubabs & Pain---

"WE HAVE LOW PRESSURE CLOUDS IN CAR-
OLINA" this gal is saying to me as we look at the sky, the
great intrusion of a stormcloud black and huge coming in on
a blue sky---just before, I'd been working the railroad with a
few men, I watched as one guy gave a sign and got up on his
Diesel and hung from the platform and gave the come-
ahead, he'd just thrown a switch---The gal is "trying to make
me" and I'm not interested in her, in "Kinston North
Carolina" girls---it's definitely in Kinston, and Ma is there,
and a house, Nin and Luke, the railroad, the guy on the
Diesel making the little come-ahead over his shoulder to the
hoghead four feet behind him in the cab, up on a viaduct the
engine is and I'm watching from the road---feel displeased, as
now---This is that Southern town of old, of rakes, girls,
night, Henderson-like and prophesied---now I comes the
dark low pressure clouds---

"THE POLICE ARENT LOOKING FOR ME, it's okay,"
I'm telling a girl on the street in Jamaica near the Long Island
Railroad station, street where Pat Fitzpatrick'd shown me the
porch post halfpainted between two houses, "Talk about the
brotherhood of man, Kerouac!"---"They're not after me,
there's been a queer murdered up the street, see---" and I
wake up horrified to realize the girl will wonder how I know
this---a nap in the couch dream after supper, to Television---
This morning also to TV I'd dream'd of Indian wars in the
New York State Massachussetts Woods, Randolf Scott, cab-
ins, lakes, Out Our Way horses and rigs. . .

I'M BACK IN SAN JOSE and California asking myself finally
what the hell I'm doing there as I have a fight with Cody and
Evelyn over something the very same afternoon I arrive there,
my duffle bag not even unpacked, the kids not even waked
from their nap---I stalk out, not even say goodbye to Evelyn---
seems I missed a ship, and wont work the railroad, and nothing's ahead of me but sad awful trips back east so out on the
street when I see the great Babylonian spread of Chicago-red-
adobe-Algerian roofs I realize and say to myself "Go to Mexico
with your last $100-----the peace of the roofs in the after-
noon"----and I take a cab, for no reason, ride further into town
like a jovial Big Slim hobo, till the 35¢ fare, when I realize that's
$5 in Mexico so get off, inquiring after the station---I was
closer to it when I got on the cab, I'll have to walk back any-
how---I'm going to Mexico in the great North American
afternoon---Later it's big harried rehearsals for a musical comedy collegiate or otherwise with many pianists, singers, confusions, I'm there in a sour frame of mind naked with books and

143

belongings, in this attic, I've--everything is done, I'm broken---
suddenly I start a fight with a big late harried pianist in floppy
clothes but a flailing foolish pre-arranged or pre-thought fight
---Those red rooftops of Chicago-Mexico in San Jose, which
I have never seen, their vastness, Fellaheen silence, like Italy,
Afternoon, Ah the world itself ends up saving you---

AMSTERDAM AVENUE ON A COLD SNOWY NIGHT,
right at Columbia Campus, suddenly I see the cloth caps of
bums shining in the pristine moonlight like ice, great silence
over all---Amsterdam becomes suddenly Moody Street
which also hath colleges---

A MAN IN A WINDOW, a fat man, a bay window in a
street in Mexico, same street where these hoodlums stopped
me to rob my duffle bag, Hubbard and I are cutting along to
pick up our junk and at crucial moment suddenly see the fat
agent in the bay window and I yipe a warning and Bull and
I dissolve in the dark doorways ending up together in a Blake
dreary YMCA, where scenes of undress and general mystery
occur in the graybrown lobby---Later, in the bathroom in
Richmond Hill, Bull is showing my mother his scars "and my
distended belly," he says, raising shirt and showing big scrolly
like Africa native decor scars on belly (like Irwin's appendix
scar) and distends his belly enormously out into a huge con
ball, accomplishes this by rearing little ass back---my mother
closes her eyes, doesnt wanta see---

BUSRIDE WITH IRENE down Moody Street across the
Moody bridge,I turn to talk to the young passenger brakeman, where the river is, is a giant railyard reaching clear to its
intensest center at the White Bridge Falls---there'd been a
flood earlier---but now, milleniums later, the riverbed is a rail
valley---and so I ask him "Are they hiring brakemen?"

   "No!" he says emphatically and immedi-
ately I smile my radiant smile and cry "Oh but they sure are
in California!" and it's understood that he's about to say "But
this aint California" and all around in the clear air of lost
Lowell I can sense the exciting railroads, the redbrick alleys
back of the Old Citizen, on the Canal, outside town in the
sand hills, in the river bed---then the sad people gathering
under iron clouds in Kearney Square nights, the sad darkness
of the old Lowell Sun lobby where in looking for familiar
faces and fumbling around I worry and wonder if anyone
knows I'm in town---and that Chinese Newspaper Mystery
on Schultes' corner, my revisitings in October so broken-
down--- La peine dans l'aire noire, the pain in the dark air.

   While I'm thus talking to brakeman Irene,
colored, sensing herself colored, is fidgeting in the seat and as
if to say "But why are you talking like this? What railroad is
that? What is this Lowell up to? Whom am I anyway?" and
all her sundry fidgetings in the public car of the world. . .

IN THIS SOUTHERN TOWN we've been, there've been
rooming houses, the whole world---it's like Kinston again
and still I'm working the railroad, we're out there making
moves and I keep goofing on the fireman's side and the other
trainmen dont even know where I am but my being a student

they dont mind---finally I do get up to the engine and have
to pass on a "shove" sign but realize en route I lost my, not
only my hat but my lantern, which I refuse to believe at first
---it's also San Luis Obispo because at the station the old conductor makes out a map for me showing how I can get to
their roominghouse and give the landlady this phoney excuse,
us, the whole team are going North to the City and
Conductor doesnt want landlady to withhold rooms when
we come back, and on the map it's a small town like San Luis
---When I say I have no car they decide not to send me---
Three nuns pass but the Conductor lets out four loud farts,
saying, "Well, I'm ready to pull out"---We go to a Mex niteclub for a beer and I sit there with the brakemen all buddily
lovingly entwined, on a bench or bin cover---a Mexican girl
is urged to sing, by a boy who kisses her, a boy with another
girl at table yells something, the first boy gives him a bad
look---I note this and explain it to the brakeman---Finally
(the brakeman is Crazy Fox) a big queen sitting at bar says
something cute and hoodlum resents it and in the silence
slowly empties his drink at him across the corner of the bar
as I wake up picturning myself throwing the hoodlum out by
the neck---I'd mournfully said "But I lost my lamp and my
cap" but they said "Dont worry kid"---I look around for the
attending engine where I must have left it, like that night in
San Luis Obispo I forgot a big lunch in a Diesel and went to
the Roundhouse to fetch it---It's Carolina, bright day---The
roominghouse was also Nin's, Southern town, Irwin was there
and wanted to go to Europe, Ma was there sulking about
something---The niteclub is like the one by the Pacific Red
car tracks outside Pedro Cru and I Xmas 1951 when Pachucos
bought us drinks---I had a girl earlier in the roominghouse,

played intimate games with her, in fact had ? girls in all and one met me at foot of the stairs to whisper intimately and when were we going to play again---?--tall, well built--- Sunday evening roastbeefs, lattices in the kitchen---

The John Kerouac Memorial Mental Hospital.

Rather, the Jean-Louis Kerouac Memorial Mental Hospital. . .

★ ★ ★ ★ ★ ★ ★

A BIG STRANGE WAR has broken out in America; about 400 or 4,000 Prisoners of War in a camp break loose and burn their way down the Mississippi towards New Orleans-- the whole country gets panicky, mobilizes, it seems to me to be kinda silly, it's that old gray war again only now right in our own country--- I go down to New Orleans in the general upheaval of war, at night in the great spectral glittering city I arrive at the boys club to meet everybody and there's Cody!!---and he's suddenly given up family and responsibilities and spiritually fallen apart and is a drunkard, a wino, red face and broken nose, tragic, dirty, young-old----I'm so astounded by this change and yet I think "He must look just like his father now!"---Dave Sherman, others spectrally are there too---cardgames---We three go stay at a guy's house, queerlike, John Bottle-like---he doesnt expect us but that very night is having a big queer party and we are welcome ---At the piano sits one of them, tall, dark, pockmarked, with a malformed hand, whom I address as *"Hands"* in requesting a tune and get a dirty look---We're in jeans, young, the queers seem to dislike us but I dont really (in retrospect) believe they could have---and meanwhile those tragic

147

Prisoners are fighting their way down the Mississippi leaving their dead and diminishing in numbers with every skirmish, every new broadcast---I feel sickened by the cowardice and hysteria of America become so blind as to misrecognize the freedom needs of imprisoned men "Communists" or not---the great pileup of arms and pathological propaganda on them---and Cody is battered, nose broken, fired from the railroad, a hobo, Cody Pomeray in his inevitable final American Open Spaces Dempsey Whisky bottle Night as always I'd dreamed of him and of myself---But now it's a serious reality and I realize Cody is going to die of wine and neglect---He doesnt talk excitedly any more but is silent like Okie---Later I go into my livingroom after a long sleep and my mother is sitting there with the furniture rearranged and some of it missing, bare, dark, sad, I say "What are you doing?"---she is brooding, alone, sits in the middle of the tri-angle of chair and table with head lowered in long widow's despair---she whose face last night I saw bending over my sleep with an expression of unfathomable meaning I know is love on earth---and who was ironing all my clothes while I had these tragic dreams---

BARBARA DALE AND HER HUSBAND at their new home in Lowell on the first floor of the Lilly-Hildreth house where I'd lived in my childhood of 6, Irwin and I go visit---same house, I am amazed, it's Christmas---from the yard B's husband (ostensibly Marlon Brando) calls down "Get some gin and water" but in trying to give us money I reassure we have it---and Irwin and I softly go to "Ralph's" store which is "still there" (25 years! on the corner) and old Canucks are

148

sitting in there in vast families in brown gloom---I come in say, "Une douzaine d'eu…d'oeufs--"---remembering to pronounce it right, a dozen eggs, and the old Bowlegs cuts out into the back to get em and is gone a long time---meanwhile one of his daughters, as if because tho I'm polite and smiling I havent taken off my baseball hat reaches out and snaps my bra-strap thru my clothes, against my back, which doesnt perturb me---Earlier I'd been in some Obispo training Monastery with Book Rooms and Monk Head Coaches looking for me---impossible, not to be found, and hiding and cutting around yards, out to the Barbecue Fields---etc.--- sheepish---Last night it was Joe laughing, leaning to tap me on knees, saying articulate Canuck joke, jumping up Hyah! hyah! and putting on hat to leave---as of yore---but there are Two Joes and I'm glad one met the other (hints of Cody, or Somebody) and there's a spectral lunchroom in rainy Stony Boston Chicago of the Dreamglooms where Joe and I go--- his car---the return of the old Joe of Salem street---

(incidentally B Dale and husband had a little niece who was playing a spinet piano behind a screen in the kitchen)

POP AND I ARE TRAVELING on some train in some bright land, the train takes a siding for some important scheduled Superior train and so for some reason big fat Pa follows me who in my own foolishness-follow-follow the "conductor" down some ramp to throw the switch so that as soon's the superior train passes (and it nothing but a Mail Car of Death self-operated, alone, gray, sinister) (cutting down the track silently) I help the conductor throw the switch (tie the,

149

lock the Mainline Switch) and he and all other trainmen watching are laffing at me, tho Pop is serious, so that when it's done and climb out of the ramp up iron rungs of a ladder and see the rear car (smiling trainmen waiting) so give the Hiball Sign to show I know speed and need to go---'mid laffter I start running in snow and soft rockbeds to catch up to departing train and have a real hard time and have to sprint like trackster (as they cheer) (and somehow Pop and the Conductor are left behind anyhow)---running, knee pumping, kidwise proud to catch up to that observation car slipping away---blushing in winter, realizing they laugh, an old old feeling---Earlier the train was a bus and Pa was Ma---Ma and I were going somewhere, sitting in hard backseat and people left and I grabbed a soft seat reminiscent of the time I preferred soft window seats of Broadway Bus with Ma on Radio City day, to back seats hard and with motor hot---

TRAGIC HATEABLE LOWELL again, winter, my mother and I have a new apartment or flat in Pawtucketville not far from Crawford Street---G.J. acting drunk and popeyed, plus Raphael Urso brash and bashing around for crumbs to eat, plus Julien drunk, plus Steen drunk are all in the house with me, I'd told one of them my mother'd make chicken for supper so they all invite themselves and I feel the horror, my Ma hates them especially G.J. and she aint even home yet from the visiting relatives somewhere in Lowell to see them---looking for something to wash my teeth with I find a little paste tube left over by previous tenants---When Ma does arrive she sits in front room with Manda and Pete (Step-grandmother and husband) and I have under the cushion of the sofa (to make it "even") stored my comb, brush and things and put a sweater on rag to "even" it out with the pillow---the red feather cover cushion, I'm fiddling with it---Later I'm at the big Rose Bowl game, standing at the goalposts commenting excitedly with someone in the brass ruddy last-glooms of late afternoon autumn dreams---the titanic shadows are colliding on fields---radios announcing all this bleak loveless universe and with its all annoyance and pain and eventual shame and the barefaced maltreatment you get in business associations and in love sometimes, I have but one consolation: the arms of my love on waking

AT A BIG "SWENSON" PARTY in his huge complicated hard-to-find-your-way-around apartments, there's been a weekend, drinking---We've gone down the street of some mixed-up California town (Los Altos!) and saw a colored girl across the street, wellknown, to whom one of our party called, "Come on over Joo Jee!"-- and she derisively said no, with a remark, waving, going on alone, the colored guy in our party emphatically saying to me "You should know Joo Jee, you really should know her---she's something---" and later the big banquet for everybody---hysterical eaters---I start in the kitchen with tidbits on the table, toast butter and crisp in a dish on a side board, various crumbs en route in the livingroom, ending up in the parlor where people are standing or sitting around in various attitudes of wellfedness, not saying much, picking their teeth, drinking black coffee, or port, or Scotch---I see a lovely pecan pie in the middle of the diningroom table and take a knife to cut a piece, which brings it to the attention of everyone else so that when I wake up we've all slowly silently stepped up a tempo at the pie, cutting, lifting pieces, dropping them, hands mixing and clashing and sweating as at gold, hands trembling in growing hunger as the more Swenson morsels are laid out and the better, the hungrier more desperate the dark voracious guests fighting now to freeload at the curious pecan pie "I discovered"---but the whole dream filled with the gray indissoluble hopelessness like a stone ---an emptybelly 3-beer nightmare, alcoholically lost, grim---

THEY'RE HANGING THE POLITICAL TRAITOR in my closet up in my room at Phebe Avenue, crowd watching from near the window and I (with friend) from near the corner---It's an old man like the actor Ray Collins, he isnt too scared, not at all in fact---The executioner puts the rope around his neck and for an instant we see a look of distaste (for the rope) (itself) (not death) on the face of the condemned old man---I stand horrified to see it's all "really going to happen!"---the hangman ties the knot and then with no ado puts up laboriously the body of the big man, I had intended not to "watch" but I do "see" and the rope tightens, the politician grimaces to choke, his body rises, silent---no complaint---no comment from the audience---I "dream" his twisted side down deadneck, not moved at all but curious---going downstairs then with Lionel to the parlor where I turn on the television though it's 5 A M and Ma's in the kitchen cheerily making her go-to-work lunch and chatting with also-up Nin---I say to Lionel "But he really *wasnt* all Ainti Fascist!" and it's my father I'm talking about, my father was hanged---My mother looks at me as if she

152

didnt recognize me immediately or what I was doing down there---The red livingroom rattle furniture of Lilly Street flat in 1929 is responsible for the horror, the hanging, the guilt, the old Victrola's just a new TV now, is all---the coffin that's never been removed from the parlor of the Kerouacs---*le mort dans salle des Kerouac*---

WILDERNESS OF VIRGINIA after awhile, the bus carrying me west to "Oakland" and on which I've been sleeping with head down on the top of the back rest ever since New York and so profoundly that some tall blond guy got on and sneaked into my window seat thinking himself in but I pretend to flop over and eventually he shifts to another seat--- it's the distinct Virginia woods and the bus goes through a little town with Alpine like houses every one inn-like humming with excitement and voices of eaters, I think "They come in old country cars from down every hill, to the taverns of town"---As on my great voyage west in August 1952 across Carolina to the Coast, the sky is blood red in a rainy dusk, through trees far across the marsh I see the remnant red fire beneath a lowering night, outlining thin birch and stumps of America-lost trees---On the bus are two young railroad men one wearing a passenger cap, they're "deadheading" up the mountain to a train, some train order station in the bleak pines---I'm going to chat with them after my nap---In my dream-nap I imagine the bus is going thru Santa Margarita and wish I was there, have nostalgia memories of Obispo and the little hillswinger's shack at the trackside at Margarita so sweet and peaceful---America is so sad, haunted, long remembered, itself a dream, what can Irwin

153

Swenson begin to know about the red dusks over the wilderness trees and the meaning of young trainmen in the hills, old shanties with stoves, the long old dream---Also I see visions of the war in Italy and see a truckload of American soldiers go by but in the Italian's naive picture of Americans they're all wailing together in one great bop band ensemble like Ted Heath or Neal Hefti band and I wake up realizing the Jazz Century I'm in and the thousands of dollars BEAT GEN-ERATION which M.C.A. Agency lost, is worth----the big issues jazz will be, bop, and how Watson has already begun to capitalize on it at my expense (using my anecdotes, phrases etc. and in fact further battening on the sufferings of junkey musicians)---I feel horrified and fear my Blake humilities which I can stand will become unbearable if worth millions to stealers like Watson, as if and just like, Christ and his thorns pounded into a golden Chalice, the Bible a Bestseller,---the Agony in the Garden a smash hit! Bitch! Poseur, sloth, fop & cheat---musty!

I'M EATING JUNE BEAUTY in a second story bedroom somewhere near the Bunker Hill Street of the White Horse Going East where the night before we'd been looking for secret dark places to ball, in the moonlight shadow of a house drawing up our open bed or vehicle but once started realizing it wasnt so dark and inside the house of the sad dim red windows maybe they see us (hints of Pauline Cole and I in the soft oral darkness laughing)---I'm not rich, not poor, happy in loves---Now we're in a daytime room and she's sitting on a stool like Irene's red iron stool and I'm kneeling wailing at her, she arches back with ecstasy, I chew & work

---suddenly I realize a whole bunch of workmen at the nextdoor roof can see all but they every one pretend not to be looking at all by the time (passion spent, blindness done) I look up, we have giant double windows showing the whole roof---also across the alley a woman in this morning is laughing, vaguely in my sexing I'd thought it was because she saw us but I didnt care---Still, now, she laughs as I goop looking around for possible watcher suspects there in the room of eternity with my naked beauty---

SAN REMO BAR is suddenly full of old Greeks who've hired it on a rainy Sunday night to celebrate a wedding---I go by and see them, drunk, one looks just like Irwin Swenson and bends anxiously and in great spiritual pain to someone in the heat of their communication---"But of course that *isnt* Swenson" I tell myself " because he has no outward pain and concern for others and tearful regard like the Greek, Swenson has that smile and that unconcern of income or riches, that *inward sleep* making him impervious to the bare razorblade of life---" "Speaking of the Devil!" I gulp as I see Swenson rushing up Bleecker---we saunter together to Fugazzy 's or just Sixth Avenue and I tell him (because privately embarrassed) exactly what I'd been thinking (omitting the income & riches part) when I saw him---Sad misty night in the Village as on those ghost mist waiting nights of the Columbia Campus and Radar Machine dreams

HITCH HIKING FROM BOSTON WITH JULIEN and Irwin, we've been to the Charles River---We're now outside

Arlington when a bus stops and we get on and ride a ways and ask to get out---Irwin and Julien do so ahead of me but I linger in back and by the time I'm ready to get off the crazy bespectacled busdriver's started up again---he turns around and comes back, tells me to turn the rollers to "Enright" to determine the fare (which no one's paid)---Still another time he turns---"Let me off here, there they are!" (my friends, in the road, walking)---but the old driver goes on---I've said to him "You wouldnt believe it looking at them" (he's asked if we were Harvard students) "--we're all Columbia students but the blond one is an editor, the dark one is a famous reporter" (or the like) ---the people in the bus are patient--- Holding my palm full of change the driver picks at it calculating, ends up taking all---

WEEKEND AT THE LOS ANGELES RESORT, I've been there and waiting for Bull and others (something about a train that broke in half and reassembled, recoupled, all four pieces intermixed and *turned* while in motion!) (railroad-turned, or cars rearranged)---now we're leaving and Irwin or somebody packs my things for me as I'm too distraught, into a hard suitcase---Marie Fitzpatrick's come in sexy dark dress, I've thought of laying her---Buddy Van Buder, a whole confusing high weekend in my sort of stone cottage by the sea in Southern California---Returning thence to the L.A. city, to Bull's pad, where he tells me "Gerard and Rose Gold were here earlier, I wanted to take a room in the Hotel Alamein with them to dig all the diverse characters in there that rush around staring"---he tells a funny anecdote about the Alamein which I dont hear because intent on my curiosity about the reason for Gerard's and Gold's visit---"this was earlier?" I say amazed---I'm some kind of well to do but crazy character in handpainted but spotted ties, like Lionel in L A

THEY'RE HITTING FUNGOES in the Bridge St ball park fields of my boyhood in Centraville---it's "Coach Frank Leahy" and the kids (of 10, less, and up)---I'm in deep left scrambling after long fouls in the great weeds lost hidden rubbergreen Rousseau wildernesses where the blacktape balls roll---I make several lazy catches, dropping some---The point is, I want to work up to the plate and get my licks but the "game" is desultory and unorganized and I even sense it'll never last long enuf to get to me and anyway no one notices my presence in the outfield, I'm as inconspicuous, lost, and anonymous out there as a 7 year old ballchaser---So I go, into yards, around tennis courts, weeds, etc. retrieving---and finally game ends and so I'm later walking around in the 'school' hall located at Hildreth end of the field (where eternity red barn) and there's G.J.though he's also strangely Irwin (Mouse has become Irwin?) and I say sourly "Them Jews out there got me all chasin the ball then quit, the bastard Jews" and like Irwin Mouse resents my sullenness and irrational cursing 'paranoiac' hostility to everything and goes off weary of me and I sense everyone else is also weary (like Lousy too) and I feel cold as a stone, abandoned, stupid, further irritated and incensed that now my own friends turn on me for a show of rages I always had and my father had, it's become "unfashionable" that's what---

157

IRENE IS LIKE MY MOTHER, or vice versa, where we're in bed or on bed and supposed to go to work but let the alarm ring, the clock drag etc. and finally my mother is getting up and confessing "I've dressed 8 times" (meaning mentally) and in me there's the great suffering of harsh getting up in the morning to work, bleak, hopeless to the bitter end---Suddenly in eternity I'm all involved with her in mutual despair-- "I wont go tomorrow either" she says, like a caricature of Irene suddenly going beyond and mad, as, if my mother ever did really quit work like that we'd all be in doghouse for sure---

LONG DREAMS EVERYWHERE---a house apparently I own and we come to it for a celebration, in the backroom accidentally I find Joe and a girl sleeping (at first dont know who they are, in fact my parents) so James Watson in the side bedroom prepares a sandwich, no a dish of chops and stewed corn for them---which I bring, being careful not to set down on new-lacquered bigtable near piano at far end but nearer bed on plain blacktop table with cloth---

A WHOLE BUNCH OF GUYS with me in some kind of Newport Bootcamp Barracks---I hear I've got $27 compensation waiting for me in the Commissary---we cut out to the cafeteria for sundaes, instead of my oldentime hot fudge I order strawberry with marshmallow---in the huge barrack sodaparlor shack the orders are repeated over a mike by a Chief Petty Officer---dumbwaiters carry iron rack trays up--- Anxiously I picture in my mind the hurrying hurrying flurrying hands of the sundaemakers upstairs fluttering over our

158

order of seven diverse sundaes---I watch the dumbwaiter, a
tray-box is coming down---Irene and I comment and watch
---but it's empty---only some little sad dumbkid comes down
and then yells up the noisy wooden stairs and so still I picture
the hurrying hands, the ice cream, the topping, the cherries,
nuts, the swift work like at Jahn's---I picture it and *time* it in
my anxiety to eat and so does Irene---meanwhile my com-
panions are big careless joking Boots or Seadog Brutes who
arent anxious for merd icecream---The center of the dream's
interest is only once rememberable and therefore once really
writeable and so from now on I ll remember the dream only
at this dreambook pad because everything of tonight's dreams
is lost, including a great awful sequence about a Beast, a
Monster crawling---lost at the first official recall of the pil-
low---because in remembering and making mental note the
brain is stiffened steadfast and no more opening (as of a blad-
der undulating) remains possible---merde!

$2.52 IS THE PRICE they're charging for the new French
bilingual movie in the movie house across the street presumably on Avenue A---the boxoffice is across the street, the girl
is telling me it's a "high class" audience---"You mean just well
dressed" I scoff---Meanwhile her boyfriend tries to talk thru
the little cage window hole---This is not the boxoffice but an
information booth, though people are lined up and Irene is
reading a paper and holding a woman's umbrella for her as she
stands in line---Okay, we go to the boxoffice at the foyer and
there's the awful price, this new picture has titles in French,
Italian, English, German, the works---I catch a quick glimpse
inside of a scene of a light-haired man gawping, the screen

itself is unusually white---The old tickettaker woman who is
the candy store owner old Jewess in Richmond, watched me
with averted eyes less I see too much (she's wearing slacks)---
Five bucks is too much for a show, Irene and I cut

MARY PALMER earlier, on a bus trip "from Lowell to New
York via Worcester-Springfield" with all Puerto Ricans living and traveling there now, Mary has a bunk and lays back
reading and I see her after the halfway mark arrival at
"Worcester" when with two Puerto Ricans I admired the
setting sun on spectral redbrick American walls---I'm going
to lie down with Mary, I cried "Mary!"---she doesnt mind,
moves over, but her jealous redhead boyfriend glares at her
and I cut out to back of bus for ordinary seat preferring darkness and solitude at window for remainder of trip to the
River of New York---a man is dozing in the seat leaving the
window open for me, I slip in

SOME AWFUL MANIAC is attacking me, keeps punching
at my groin with iron fingers, gnashing teeth, I cant keep him
away or understand him, no one helps me, I wake up with a
belly ache---Earlier Mickey Mantle'd hit a homerun in the
Stadium of Dreams, there where I was after our long drive
(300 miles) from Maine to New York and suddenly in the
gray luminosity there's all Lowell-Manhattan on its
Merrimac-Hudson shining and the driver was terrific---
Mary Palmer or somebody with me---and like driving back
from Lawrence of Salisbury Beach in youngdays and Sunday
afternoon there's redbrick Lowell still and the mills are quiet,

160

the cartons outside canal warehouses sit in long shadow gloom beneath those eternity smokestacks---the Homerun by Mantle is a ball I myself catch caroming off other strugglers, but an attendant wants it back---it's way up in the "mile high balcony" where I've been before---It's later in a backroom after some events in a frontroom having to do with truancy the mad bastard starts wrestling with me, nameless horrors like being tickled but viciously, I remember crying out "If there's anything I cant stand is someone who is queer and insane at the same time."

I GO BACK TO MEXICO BUT HATE IT, I'm with Irene----take a long walk with her down on San Juan Letran in the daytime saying "I know these streets very well" and figure on taking her to lunch in an earlier dreamplace I'd seen with Dave Sherman, which now I cant find---Somehow too I'm alone and carrying a white seabag and as I see two, three guys in the street I remember the dream of having my seabag robbed and hurry on---There is a long sad dirty Fellaheen street, I took the wrong road trying to return to downtown, I tell this to some guy in a car who's backing up but he's too stupid to care altho he understands and doesnt offer me a lift ---God the weariness, bleakness of my eternal mistake---I'm back in a, in *the* Mexico of Unreality---with Irene I figure I'll live in this tenement but when she hangs up clothes everyone'll be staring at her especially the soldiers in the last windows, American soldiers---I have a small sad temporary room near the old dream Medellin-Roebuck of original 1950 Weed Afternoons---Earlier I'd been in California and planning to work railroad there "out of San Diego" and make it, there'd been a conductor---all, all unreal and dreams---the voyages in between---Finally, alone, I *do* have lunch in some place, with a bunch of men speaking good English, I make a mental note to bring baby there---it's funny food, little cactus plants in pots, wet---to get there we've had to tread lightly thru highly charged organic water two inches deep and warned not to splash or walk too deep---This is the food of the great sad dangerous water---cactus peotl like little plants hot and steamed, brussels sprouts small and pale green, and one dish I have which is told to me as being the greatest: a kind of eggplant-looking or *boudin*-looking (French hot blood sausage) skin---or like Jewish intestine skin, etc.---I eat a big dish of everything thinking "Well I finally found a place for lunch anyway tho I wonder if the 'water' business is not just a lure to get customers and these pleasant men just restaurateur hustleurs"---While lost in the side sand road I'd seen the skyline of the city lost and twisted in another direction like the time I lost the center of San Luis Obispo walking around the elongated mountain---Mexico Shmexico this is too much loneliness and loss

BIG FOOTBALL FIGHTS---starts at parties but really in a field like Bridge Street haunted housefield across from Joe's where Ma and I go to watch scrimmage be photographed by Fred Dressler and another guy with small movie camera and suddenly (Charley Justice and others in the backfield) Justice is stopped dead at the line of scimmage, the ball bounces around, and guys start fighting over it at the wall-sidewalk sideline---and Ma and I who've been watching from a bush "Watch out Ma!" take hands and retreat---the fight spreads,

162

overtakes us, goes all over the field and into the street and up on iron structures and buildings and permeates elevators and halls---Everybody's slugging everybody, Ma turns into a little boy who wants to pee and I hold him high on a frightening girder as he fidgets with his lil pants in fear and men pound running and fighting slugging with fists on all sides--- Up in the elevator four opposing fighters start right in, in the rickety little lift, and the girl was sassy anyway so we all pile out in a hallway down lobby, I spar---"He's got the style to fight that guy!" laugh the two partners---a kind of maniacal ballet dance begins, in the fight, with bodies flopping--- Meanwhile it had been Lowell and I'd gone down the street to G J's cottage and he was asleep, night, about 11 o clock--- tan as a greek berry I see him (all the lights and the radio on!) face down on a white sheet bed, poor G J as ever tired from work and now living alone so that I mourn for his poor black robe mother tho she's just across town (this is about Crawford) ---and it's sad spectral night as of oil cup flares of ditches at edge of town---G J *is* like Irwin, he's a Lowell newspaperman and tho still a big champion Julien drunk has responsibilities, is married, holds his job down---I stand in the soft night road looking in, remembering all---All the fights and nonsense had begun earlier at parties where I'd been exposed and humiliated by some girl (in a marble station) like the LI Railroad girl, Irish, roundfaced, I think sarcastic---BOOM!

G J had furniture, a whole little ranchero concrete California style cottage "pitifully his"---all in little sad Lowell.

Now I remember it's not far from the "cottage of the Beland sisters" I'd had in dreams and in itself not

163

far from the woman with the Virgin Mary Altar (uniting streetwise Moody & Lakeview)---

A KIND OF SHIP'S CREW OF MEN all together in a cafeteria group where they've been eating, about 50, 60--- elegant people like Hubbard, W H Auden, many others, Swenson presumably---It's like the Lowell High School base- ment lunchroom so vast, dark---After I've been notified my time to work has come I go to the bar to eat, I'm sitting down with a group---Another pisses outdoors headed for the next bar, someone says "Why do they keep going to that other place?"---W H Auden comes in and for "the first time" is sitting next to me and I notice he may talk to me--- I've just written something brilliant---We begin talking about some joke drink---"Woman's piss" we'll call it--- "Only" I add (laughing) (heartily) "we'll call it by some other name---woman's urinary"---we search philologically---

OCT 14 '53---I'M BACK ON A SLEETY NIGHT on Moody Street or that is the street is covered with a film of white frost---I've been to Destouches' where people heartily laughed, then thought of writing the "wrinkly tar" corner of *Dr Sax* fame and thinking "I'll see Scotty and Lousy I wont be surprised"--- Suddenly I see "Duke Gringas'" young brother come clomping, I see just his shadow in the melancholy dusk, he's been walking all the way from the Library with books underarm *"like I used to do"* and I think: "I'll ask him, hey Gringas! Hey! Where's your brother Duke, Menelaeus?---" I figure he's a big scholar, also was a football star, unmistakably a

Gringas with his big clomp boot shoes fromming in the snow and his long Santoslike chin and Russian ears and gangly angle walk---I am very aware of the new generations of kids of Pawtucketville and look around, I'd just seen two others "like young brothers" of "so and so"---I head for Blezan's store conscious of the dream and determined to "make it come true" and the fine sleet white strengthens my belief in the unreality of the older "snow dream" of Moody but the thinner (more believable therefore) realities of this one---Kid Gringas in the sad dusk has that same sharp and humangrieving reality I saw in the "moonlight bum caps of Amsterdam" and many other dreams where figures stalk cleanly and sharp in soft gloom clouds of poor nap (H horror) brain

------

(real nights long ago when I'd go to Destouches for 7 caramels a penny and one had rocks and I'd chew that slowly over Operator 5 with the first one crossing the park, the familiar dust underfoot)

G'J'S AT HOME in Lowell, at his mother's, has matured into a funny conversational intense loafer------sits in the kitchen all day with the boys, one of them is Georgie the Polock who's telling him his usual stock of funny fantastic and murderous stories (like the one about killing three cops in a Marseilles air raid) only G J doesnt believe a word and immediately makes fun of him "There he goes O O O what a liar!" and I see a great slur of hope in Georgie's green eyes, they glow pale phosphorescent green and he looks at me, slitting them as if to say "See? I've finally found a man who fills me with great interested joy because he *knows* I'm a liar andI'll

never give in and admit to him"---"Ha!"---a great Polish
Liar telling Tales and there's all the slobs of the Kitchen Sea
believing in his bullshit tales but not hometown matured G J
in his Eternity Middens there--- What crazy buddies they
make in all this laterlife dreambleak---There is faint rigging
in the gloomy as-of-ships background---They are sitting face
to face in old age chairs in the middle of the room---I think
Scotcho may have been around earlier---

        I dreamed of the park too, "the familiar dust
underfoot" was a prophecy phrase of this dream, and there's
murder or horror and death in it, corpses,---the dry cornfield,
---a man, dead---adventures in the doom gloom,---Larry
Charity---not Larry Charity but Kid Taki---I've forgotten-
his-Name---the Gershom tenement blocks, the Omaha
garage, Riverside Street and the Giant Iron Tree---the old
Houses, the graveyards underneath, the Sunk Bleak of Lost

           Which now in solitude
           I dive into once more
           in own silent room
           of mind serene
           remembering
           the world

       ★ ★ ★ ★ ★ ★ ★ ★ ★ ★ ★ ★ ★

IT'S SOMETHING HAPPENING BETWEEN ME AND
POP, in Centralville---in the trellised rose sadness of the little cottage on West Street which had Christmas in its eyes
long ago we are closer than ever, it's he returned from the
dead and I'm grownup and thirty but we live in West St and
have profound absorptions together as others watch inter-

ested---For some holy reason the entire thing is kept from my mind in details, I can only say "J'ai rêvez d Papa"---

EATING LUNCH IN THE POLICE STATION are Bull and I and Raphael or somebody,---Bull is drinking some of the new coffee substitute with a funny name like PREEN, it has no caffeine in it and looks just like coffee---as he stirs and takes his first sip I watch and wait---"Well?"---He makes a face, "No good"---I'd just been reading an article about how there is going to be Prohibition of smoking in America and very soon---in a loud gleeful voice I say "Just like in the Twenties when people went to Europe to get soused---they'll all start goin to North Africa and places to smoke---and you know what they'll smoke---haw haw haw!"---and in a loud voice but no one of the cops in the sideroom care or notice, they're in a dark room with wet film, in shirt-sleeves---The scene slightly shifts as we're eating a big dinner now in a Mexico City cafeteria and my dessert is a little glass bowl of bread pudding on the sides burnt and sticking, at which I pick desultorily as we talk and Bull, getting up to carry plates back to the counter, without consulting me and maternally picks it up and carries it back as if he didnt want me to pick at remains like a vulture and get fat and I smile to think of it---Earlier we'd been standing around on the side-walk...it's some foreign country or other---As I consider the fact of everyone giving up smoking further and further into hiding with my Opium Pipe---this is the 1% top part of a vast 99---Ag!

THE DIVEBOMB PILOT, he's way up in the sky ready to fall and open his chute,---it's me---I fall a long ways but aint scared and there's a long way to go judging from the landscape so when I do open my chute I feel I've made a mistake and will spend all afternoon floating down to earth---I've my cat in my arms---

Later down on earth I'm working among boxcars and sheds with a bunch, "in the South," one fellow paints two boxcars dazzling silver and one blinding gold, so bright you cant look at them in the sun---the fellow is big Ned Weaver of the South redfaced and puttery with brushes--- "How can we work those cars now!" I think pettishly---Other events---around Easonburg Crossroads---Ma---

THEY'VE ALL BEEN READING MY LIBRARY BOOKS in the cafeteria-classroom and now stolen them, books I'd got at the Mexico Library on the sunny boulevard across town so now I'll be fined horribly since the books are gone forever so I think to myself "I'll have to leave town eventually, the mere thought that any of these hipsters might return any of those 4 books is sheer arrantry, grang---" or such, and the teacher the oldlady up front has finally gotten everybody to quiet down for the afternoon study period and there is silence, I cant leave and go act on my lost books or otherwise goof up and down that sunny library boulevard where there'd been plenty of nice girls---Wig---Bull---others---Raphael's sitting next to me at the schooldesk, we'd just been love rivals but now it's all over and quiet again between us---I'm young, free, irresponsible, haunted, in fact though a little bemused and carefree quite happy---etc. I'm something else I cant place, some kind

of blank sunny joylessness of oldness but mysteries and prophe-
cies and hints of wrong I wont listen to any more

BIG FIRE HAD DESTROYED whole blocks in New York
so they're excavating and filled in cement foundations and
now are driving holes down in for foundation rods and I'm
trapped on the high slipping bank of sand and rocks trying to
get behind the fence but afraid it's too rickety and unsafe to
grab---very high up to look down---An old foreman comes
along and tells me it's safe to catch the fence---He keeps feeling my ass, inspecting my blue railroad handkerchief presumably for come---Earlier I'd made an appointment to meet
Uncle Joe in the railroad station, the Pennsylvania, at the
information booth,---we're going to Nashua together---I
know I'll cry all the way all the time and he too---There he
is in a far corner of the station waving at me as if bashfully
and uncertain he's waving to the right person---I'm at a train
door, he's in a ticket corner, neither one of us in the right
meet-spot---I go on over---This was arranged during a big
weekend at Aunt Clementine's house which was just like the
one at 'Fortier's' last night when I slept on the double bed
with Donnie---Sitting in the kitchen all the relatives---Poor
sad Mononcle Joe with his black umbrella how I wish I'd
have known him in my maturity---what stain of sorrow is't
fills a grave in Nashua now---along side the other vast stain
of sad spot of Pop---and the little inheriting one, Gerard---

IN A SUNNY HOSPITAL of many levels and with the sun
shining as in May I'm having a conference presumably with

Malcolm Cowley and the boss (Harold Garden) and nothing definite comes of it but just talk about the ms.---but then when I come out, in the ante room lobby, Phyllis Johnson is at a desk like a secretary and says "Well Jack they've accepted your book today" and I'm awed that Cowley never told me but just didnt mention and probably paternally humorously keeping the good news away from me---So I go out walking in the sunny yard like Kingsbridge Hospital and bareheaded in the springtime warmth I walk floating light and happy into new success like the time, the May Day Boisvert accepted Town & City---Later there're events around a Jersey Central track, people, engines, houses---at the end I'm looking down the street, we're all ready to go, the kid is looking at me curiously---cant remember---the details were long and went on all night---

NIGHT ON PHEBE AVENUE IN THE SUMMER, midnight stillness in the sky, I've just been to Billy Hampshire's house and am walking home five houses up and thinking about my sleeping family behind the windows and the sleep in G.J.'s windows too when suddenly after the sound of a dull boom I happen to look up in the sky over the sandbank, over Rosemont, and therefore over Snake Hill further and there's the remnant of a comet just exploded with yellow lights spilling and falling some en masse in sprightly groups straight down like angels falling in the black cup void---I dont know whether it's fireworks or comets---Boom!---another one, is expanding like a fireworks, dissolves yellowly, the cluster of allied stars races downward burning in the whirlwind black, I have that usual old fear they'll not dissolve before they reach

170

the earth and crash into this silent Phebe Sleep for Holocaust
and Armageddon. . .an old dream---Later it's day on Phebe,
I've been walking around my old mapped Pine Brook and
Woods and on the way back on Sarah Avenue picked up a
likely looking crate for my radio and wood for my fire from
a carpenter's pile near a being-repaired fence (there's his saw)
and I dont even worry whether he or others might complain
if I took this wood, I'm returned to Phebe Sarah and the 31
I'm again a child and steal wood)---My cat Rondu is in the
parlor radio chair (my father's)---not his chair properly but
the one facing, at the other window (and this is the same
house of the jet bomb attack dream)---I see the cat in there
masturbating pulling the counterpane with his teeth and
pawing the chair and I float up the driveway with my stolen
window---"Gi-don-du," I greet him so in a second whem
I'm in the backyard dropping the wood and talking with my
dog (leashed in yard) Rondu flashes in the grass in greeting,
s'left masturbation to caromp with Master and Dog---it's
evening in Pawtucketville---Earlier I'd been around in the
Sunday Morn Sun and dug old friends, Salvin,---Later I was
down in the New Orleans again thinking "If I get a ship with
N.M.U.I.'ll have to hide my S.I.U.discharge and with
M.C.S.hide em all, and after all if I do get a ship and rush in
the gray sweat hall all day with Union papers by nightfall
when I *do* have a ship there wont even be any place on deck
for me to sit and relax and stevedores slam crash everwhere
---fuckit I'll just go back to New York and collect my
advance on ROAD and write at home"---that same futility
of roaming for nothing all over, felt in the California Dreams

BIG FLAMING AIRPLANES TRYING TO LAND in the New York-New Jersey airport in broad daylight disaster two of them are floundering across the sky to crash in the meadows of junk---I'm watching from the field after a bus trip from somewhere North where I had a suitcase and a bag of big marbles (big bag) and stored them in the bus compartment myself in an attempt to save the marbles (for Lil Luke) after I'd goofed and taken a walk down the bus hiway city then saw I had to get back as soon as possible and only way to be on time was cab, more expensive than the bus trip itself!---so hurried ---and now in field the DC-6's falling in orange sweptback flame---Later according to instructions contained in the Almanac of Mystery and mark't on the Map of Bayonne I go to Bayonne to the Ottoman Temple older than America made of wood Byzantium in splintered gray cracks, so old, like the barges at Communipaw waters---I sneak around on dangerous boards looking for the altar, I can see all big glittering New York across the river---it ends up I'm inside naked with little Philip and someone else presumably my young sister and we're all naked, I'm trying to take my choice but at same time I'm concerned (because pale and infantile) with other things, like airplanes and meaning of Temples---It was an Arabic Pseudomorphic overlay on the rusts of Jersey that no historian'd yet noticed and it was so strange, it has to do with those knives and Burma caves of horror, something's deep inside, rituals of Snake and Old Sanskrit Secrets---Who was That He Man who wanted to fight me? I sure was ready for im

LIVING IN A MARBLE STATION hotel room, alone, I bring back piles of newspapers, junk, bottles, (some empty?), mementos---I look at the clock in the Jersey Central Lobby, it shows I have seven hours to sleep and one hour to get up the line on my train which pulls out of the station itself--- I've been talking with friends, Walter Pidgeon was having breakfast in bed, didnt look at me except on the sly---(that old queen)---Later I'm riding around in 'my cab', 'my driver' and I are eating our usual fried chicken and he's talking happily as he wheels the hack thru Frisco Streets and I'm afraid I'll eat all the chicken---got to watch my weight too and eat only once a day since occasionally for a few bucks he drives me to the racetrack where I run right up to the starting gate and hire myself out riding a horse in the race, *jockey*—I'm a lonely independent man with no ties, no hopes, bleak tricks to make a living, full of death, indecision, sedentary laziness and worst of all I dont know why I'm on earth and what I should do to satisfy not any craving inside myself but some kind of craving in the sky, the lostcloud sky---I'm like Lionel, or Bull, waiting by the ticking clock and like T.S.Eliot 'without hope'---My room is gray, fairly comfortable with a double bed, good chairs, dresser, shaded window with view presumably like Ross Hotel in Los Angeles looking down on 4th and South Main---My 'jockey cabdriver' is happy go lucky Frisco type who knows Charley M. Low and stood at Rose flowery Sunday morning race tip stands of Market Street with Deni Bleu on days when Hank was back from Singapore or Marseilles with money to blow and laughing "Hiah hiah hiah! You slay-y me!---Yaaah!"---

ARRIVING IN A MOUNTAIN COMMUNITY somewhere in California I'm told there's a new branch being built on the railroad---I see a whole gang of guys, five, working at a siding with some cars---"*Five?* why do they need so many guys on a tag team?"---Later when I do begin work on that branch of the railroad and have just rode over the pass huddled on the steps of the Diesel and we're pulling a cut of cars some passenger deadheading and I notice how the angle seems dangerous you'd think the whole shebang'll turn over but because it leans so far over and I can relax against my grip on the Diesel steps and whole back and so almost fall asleep right there in the open and a foot above the rushing track---(Yes, there is work in the little mountain town, it has dirt streets and dobe houses and friendly neighbors)---when I *do* begin working the guys tell me "What you saw was the tag team *plus* one yard switchman, that's why five"---I'm running after the caboose, I fiddled so long trying to hide my bathing suit under some old gloves on the wet greasy steps of the Diesel that now as the cut starts off for work and the fellows have boarded the crummy and I'm too far down the track to catch if hurry and then finally sprint as I may---and the fellows if noticing dont care any more, they've seen I'm a goof of the railroad---my career in the mountain branch wont be long and certainly not noteworthy---Mary Palmer and the two boys have visited me there, at my house which has a lot of people in it, there've been big dinners that Ma cooked, Cody, long talks---it turns out that now he's a little older and people've been paying more attention to him than Tommy because of his obvious inferiority sadness, Brucie Palmer has become spoiled and talkative and cuts Tom left and right and has even become his superior in the repartee---I forget the subject of the conversation around the big food table, but's in a wooden house in that mountain town, my house bought with money I had---

174

it's in the West---At some point some little girl is saying she heard of a disease called "Neb" characterized by the fear of your mouth and head catching on fire---Pop was around too, laughing gabbling I can see his big excited moist mouth out pushed to tell and eager and unselfconscious

HIPSTERS IN THE MOVIE, talking in the lobby, the head---I'm sitting in the front part of the low balcony with Irene and go back to get Ma her new seat with us but she's in the far back where old men sit and has a package (shopping bag) at her feet and is quite satisfied to see from back there, is annoyed when I insist she come get a better seat--- The picture is "Death of Mad and Hatchet Cranshaw"---we see it written on screen---I realize my mother wants to be left alone, doesnt want her position "improved"---

I'M GOING TO DRAW A BIG PICTURE FOR THE NAVY of the Rock Island streamline train coming into the Frisco City on a trestle over the blue water and a ship coming in beside it, one half of the left page of the big 2-page spread color-drawing will show the towers of the city, then the Diesel pulling only a few coaches, then the water traffic ---anyway I'm on a pier to do this and at one point just sit around waiting like at Merrimack Square the shoeshine of Five-and-Ten Back Corner but on the wood warp drowse afternoon of slap gulls with Nin sit and talk, something Navified, on duty, waiting, and also reminiscent of parts of the Boott Millyards, the loading ramps---Earlier and probably connected I'd been in the showers with all the Marines, I see myself there fat, I refuse to fight with any of the Marines especially the red haired one ("they have knife tricks")--- The 'sketching' having to do too with earlier, also in Navy or Marines, Robert Whitmore my buddy of the S.S.Carruth is showing me how he describes an apartment building when he writes, "the wander wada rada rall a gonna gay, *Zack!*" the flow of words and the releasing bop-sound at the end of a prose rhythm paragraph---we're laughing like hell---there'd been great events enroute and in and out of the barracks which at one point melted into Joe Fortier's big Bridge Street house and the great dream of Doctor Sax's haunted house

DOCTOR SAX'S HAUNTED HOUSE---it's night, I'm with Bertha and Phillip at the Fortier house, there are lights in the (now occupied and not wrecked haunted) house on the hill way up the other side of the street---I see the shadow of a pacing figure in the fireplace flickers golden livingroom, huge---lights in many windows---"Wow!" I say "Doctor Sax the actual now real flesh Doctor Sax or heir apparent to that mad title of my Lowell Dream is stalking up and down the parlor with the cocktail like mad Hubbard at cocktail hour or some frantic James Mason Lord"---the night, the gold light in some of the windows of the manse showing thru the thick pines of the bigslope lawn that rises from the sidewalk stonewall on Bridge Street---"Come on Phillip let's sneak up the grass and investigate"----We sneak across the street, in the moonlight, lo, there's a cut of old sad boxcars in the spur on Bridge Street, one of them's on our way so I push it, 'kick it' somehow and it rolls into the lawn-track of the haunted house and so fast and far I'm worried it's going to hit the deadend block or go over the spur mound and derail or even bounce back and roll back on us so with keen eye fixed on the floom of mist moon ahead I wait awhile before starting with Phillip shh to wiggle up the lawn---Now we're crawling, we come to a mound, under a pine, suddenly there's the proprietor Mad Sax himself stalking in the blind moonlight grass with rifle and revolver, we flatten and watch--- Somehow he's walking straight for us by mistake and suddenly he's even walking over the mound and coming down right on us and that's when I see the sheriff's Badge he's wearing and he's gonna step over us accidentally or sinisterly knowing anyway so I jump up and shout---the Mad Sax Sheriff begins yelling "Bang! Bang!" the guns are just toys but he's very annoying and keeps pushing me back and laughing or yarking savagely with maniacal Hyde-like intensity and I jump back in horror, he doesnt molest Phillip, there's another "sheriff" nearby to whom I plan to appeal for aid as I jump and dance back in the now gray afternoon grass before the thrusts and bang bangs of the teethshowing old maniac with toy guns and badge who's sore cause we wanted to sneak up and watch him pace in his Eternity Mansion at Cocktail Fireplace Hour---shouting and cackling at me like that maniac tickling me last week---

A LONG BICYCLE RACE TO LAWRENCE which I win---there's also a stretch where you run and pick up your bicycle off the sand road, which I rode swooping on the banks like a motorcycle champion in a carnival pit----the forlornness of those piney barrens, that sand road, of the puffing lone racer!---I win the race and come back to the big

house on Salem Street where June and Ma (reconciled) are
waiting for me, June is at the gate, beautiful, we whisper
promises of the night to each other---her body is firm,
warm, her breast spots stick me delightfully, she's as white and
openable as that veritable Oyster Girl---in the house she's in
the davenport sunporch sewing, Ma's in the kitchen with
arrays of pans and pots in a partitioned section in the middle
of a huge kitchen---Later June and I are shipping out, thru
some friends of mine "because I'm too crazy or too wild or
too something to be a deckhand" I'm going to be made
Steward, Chief, and there sit June & I in the Officers' Mess
eating with the Engineer Department Officers---at one
point the 3rd Assistant says "But no milk"---"I'll get you
milk!" I say "after all if I'm gonna be Steward"---the ship's
still in port, I run down to the stores and search frantically in
dark lockers and funny little big-covered-but-small-insided
iceboxes horizontally shaped (to the deck)---finally in a horrible burlap canvas bag prop icebox like the horror bag of the
Kafka nightmare hero dragging his dragon green be-but-
toned caterpillar machine burden bag across the gray strange
stage of eternity racks and dust, I find plenty of milk and also
new socks and all kinds of mixed up stores (I'd just in a
wooden icebox rejected half empty milk containers)---here I
find brand new ones (because I'd thought I'd detected sour
milk scabs thru the transparent paraffin cover)---here's all
new milk and I start to leave but the burlap bag has wrapped
itself and almost grown tightly around my waist while I rum-
maged and all by design, it's a Trap Icebox of the Ship to
catch culprits and have them wander forlornly on the bridge
with the big bag dragging around them like a robe of shame
but a great "holding the bag" or "draggin the bag" super hor-

178

ror Shame---I tug, it's tight around me, insistent, I'm trapped ---Earlier it had been great singing of the Rigoletto Company, gladness, I was there with them---and the words: "Cad Pa L.I. Canada"---

     (O that back-around-me sneaking straitjacket!)

BROKEN SLIVERS OF GLASS are stuck in my lip at the potbelly stove hall dance where Evelyn and Cody were and Evelyn wanted the stove so badly, finally in the height of the festivities I see her the whites of her pale blue eyes furtiving she hustles that stove right out the door no questions asked (to Cody's waiting Nash presumably)---but the proprietor does see her-- Meanwhile I've been involved with broken glass and every time (from a bottle?) I try to disengage a splinter from my upper lip it sticks in my fingertip too, awful stuff--- I have to go to the doctor in the steepbank enlistment field where all the soldiers are sitting in the grass waiting their turns one of them a young kid called the "Colonel" or something whom they make fun of, he wears red, he's going to Peru--- Here as at the hall there've been hints of somebody teaching us Spanish and "Honduran" and that it would be very helpful to us in the "future"---In the middle of all this the scene had shifted to the Lowell dump in Rosemont, Peaches and I play- ing at a big pipe on the water and sitting on it and using it as our swimbeach and the doctor just told her she had "menopause" which means we can bang all we want, we're swimming naked and I want to see her naked in her rubber boots, um---across the river in the Little Canada dump in the tragic red sun is Halnau up to some greedy foragings of his own in scatterdamalia reality---Finally I'm with the waiting

179

soldiers again but now on Wall Street waiting at "Edison's" or "Einstein's" door like registrants for the Navy at Pine, the guy ahead of me is the little bald Mexican baggagehandler later South City yardclerk Joe, grumbling like a soldier---the doctor's going to remove that glass from my lip?---I see a news review of Rosalind Russell's latest picture, I'm sitting at Ma Evans' in Brooklyn (stepgrandmother) and there's the pix of Roz sitting now on the sidewalk with big honey thighs showing and with honey cunt half tied-clothes, a bunch of workmen and a racehorse, and the director of the picture kneeling and pointing at the horse, the caption: "The Way The Big Money Points"---the director Franz Halz Newmann the great self-photographer of French Europe, shit---

"HER MILKY ENGINE BEGINS" is the sexy saying about the Ava Gardner beauty in the story---the Enguardiente Indians, "original inhabitors of California" and therefore obviously Pomo group of fierce organized fighters are going to raid a fort in 1850, we see their naked forms sneaking along the roof, it's explained how they set fire to the fort by placing dry bramble bundles under foundation posts---We also see the boiler rooms they're afraid to go into, the underground damp room where I thought of living but changed my mind---No white men about---We see the great Enguardientes practising on a pale green hill, cavalry charges on horseback, volleys of fusiliers riddling targets in one fire so you see the big balloons explode in popp ing smokes---Earlier we'd all been afraid of the atom bomb hitting over the Merrimac River and in fact I'd "daydreamed" it or it otherwise happened, dark gloom over all our souls as we wait hidden and huddled on Lakeview Street (facing from where I was born)---disaster and Armeggedon in the Dark Air of my birth, over the river of life---

        After the great tragedy of "Camille" the young priests begin playing touch football with the visiting Scandanavian champions in the street---they're sensational--- a great gang of nuns passes, en route to the pastry shop for coffee---the game is sensational, long passes, long runs, fingertip catches, cries, trolleys passing, it's a great *comedy*, and is the last part of the tragedy of Camille---I'm watching with Nin---it's like Liverpool Merseyside---

PUTTING ON MY SHORTS and undershirt in the hall knocking on Mrs. Whiteheart's door, I cant do it in the house because her son Jack is there talking to my mother---I hurry like hell to have the clothes on before my knock is answered but the fingers are muddy---Earlier it was the Rialto Theater, events,---And there'd been a great Tidal Wave which forecast the fact that all Long Island was doomed eventually to be washed out---We see houses by the beach ---we drive frantically in gray catastrophic afternoon---I'm with an older man, we see ruined huts and houses, we drive across great plains of sedge---People are moving---also a lot of New York City is doomed---(written long after I was awake and therefore not evocative of the haunt of the dream, not worthy of this book)---

IN THE PACIFIC ON AN N.M.U. SHIP, as pantryman at first and with a galley crew of 50 to wash dishes for, a cargo passenger ship, I got the job so fast I'm amazed and there I am in apron at the greasy sink among the yelling golden guys and staggering with dishes down the gray alleyway to the strange little pantry where I rack em up---and the ship is two days outbound for the Orient---nevertheless in some spectral cove another ship pulls alongside and I go out thru the port-hole and return to America ending up childlike gooking at the window of home on Gershom Avenue in Lowell in broad afternoon with a sheet a shroud or blanket over my head looking out on the street thru the gray dim cloth---looking out on the big tenement and there's a Negro work-man staring at me from his ledge trying to figure out what I am---it's the old useless hanging around the house not-working sick neurotic shipjumping school hookeying Ti Jean trying to find his lost brother in the parlor glooms---At the end I see the beginning of the movie Two Years Before the Mast with the same two old guys embracing in surprise in a trellised sea garden---

IN WATSONVILLE CALIFORNIA with my mother sud-denly (in the marshes outside, at around Elkhorn or Moss Landing that Steinbeck wrote about and where I braked on the SP) we see a flock of flying snakes, reminiscent too of those seahorses in the picture yesterday and green and with lit-tle curved-for-flying spine bodies and the faint suggestion of transparent butterfly whirrers and awfully disgusting---"C'est des cockrelles," my mother says with great disdain and disgust, "They're just cockroaches"---she's not fooled---they're cock-roach people impersonating as flying snakes and she's seen it before---At once I'm reminded of Irwin Garden (Pa called him cockroach), Hubbard, all my friends my mother hates &

182

fears and in fact one of the snakes suddenly flops over my neck "like Garden!" I think frantically dodging to run, "like the importunate advances of affection from my disgusting friends!"---the flock of snakes over the marsh fly away---

Later, right after, I see a vision of the Katzenjammer kid that had dark hair, striped shirt, he's pulling down a prize box from heaven on a rope and pulley, it turns out to be a mother with gifts---

PARENTS HAVE THEIR SONS BY THE SCRUFF OF THE NECK dragging them out of bars meek and ashamed, because they'd been drinking and wooing with girls in there ---it's a big Anti Teenage campaign, I keep seeing it all night in various dreams---I says to myself "Hysteria in America has reached that Hate Love pitch"---I see Julien and Bob Piriams, in Lou's little garage office---Piriams has that big

shnurf smile---

THE EDUCATIONAL STATION OF COLOR TELE-VISION is turned on in Boisvert's office because of the big snowstorm---also I see "Baruch" on one of these programs say "Just because a man keeps bad company it doesnt mean--" so I know the Red Witch Hunters will uncover the fact about him that he hung out with Communists and suddenly I real-ize the big thing that's going to happen, the Purge and I dont agree with it---Meanwhile I've thought of going to Adele Norales because I found an old list of What To Do's and it says six Pick up Adrians and Mondrians at Adeles' (print of watercolors)---She lives on the bottom floor of Livingston Hall where the son of the Mayor of Trenton use to live-- When Ma and I are established back in the Moody Street Textile Tenement I have the TV in my bedroom and I suddenly realize I dont want it there, Ma's in the livingroom bleak---it snows, it's holy, there's color television.

TAKING BIG WALKS AROUND LOWELL, Pawtucketville, the Textile fields---I come to the Long Island Railroad overpass at the boulevard, the tracks, little rickety wood cottage back ass around-Crawford Stree all transformed to big be-lamped traffic boulevards

THE GREAT SNOWY BRIDGE DREAM AGAIN, the Brooklyn Bridge and a few blocks down is "48th" Street where I wont be far from the other bridge, the clear starlight is on the city I always see with little white bungalows East & West and that great bridge of the Bourgeois I saw burn in 1951---there were children dancing on some stage, supposed to be learning dance steps in the spotlight, most of the boys had incredible long feet and were acting awkward on purpose doing the fox trot like big dopes---It was back in San Luis Obispo, I'd just pulled in one the bus, I was going right straight down to the Colonial Hotel and see the old guy about my corner room upstairs again. . .all that "tanned healthy boredom" again and that vague air of murder---A queer attaches himself to me as I get off the bus, follows me into the cafeteria where thousands are eating---it's that booming sunny western New Town

PA AND I BLEARILY on the seats of some passenger train sit talking about his illness and what they've been saying to him down at the Union, about which he is very vague---He's going to die just enough if he hasnt already---Ma and I discuss it---God how heavily he carries his carrion corpse around in these repetitious dreams, with what a hopeless, pale, almost invisible face, so joyless; so far gone from all hopes of the living and even from the bleak recognition of the bitchness of existence (which doesnt bother him any more he's so listless) (in fact returned from the grave)---This is our sweet Papa of starry night pasts when we grow up and grow old in this world the least of which you can say is that it leaves a bad taste in your mouth, like iron---Jawbleak gumming irons of no-hope morns, shit on the branch of peace---There was another, special high rack where I was hysterical---This was all dreamed last night and gone now memory-wise---Night before I'd returned to Nin's house in Carolina, Luke driving me up in the puddly driveway and Nin far from greeting me gayly asks first I help her with the suitcase then when she does talk it's but coldly and asking why I came and why dont I straighten out---bleak little wood white cottage in the open flats on the highway, dreamed and seen before, and big gray grass wintermud yard---and Big Luke makes no comment, Lil Luke dont care----there's also a dog---

A HENRY FONDA MOVIE about pirates at sea, but he's impersonating some kind of woman and we see him hysterically packing to leave the ship and pulling things out of his closet including such beautiful flowing silken scarfs some of them blue as night we hear women in the audience say "Oh

185

he's been stealing just the same"---and at the end the movie (strange enuf already) no makeup and you see him go down the outside stairs plain faced, graystark, and you know the movie will again take a piratical romantic turn when the *real* Henry returns from the pirate ship captaincy with makeup and well combed and will be standing straight, handsome and indignant in the middle of the girl's room denouncing the other Henry---the people who are putting on this movie over TV are already getting letters from viewers in Greenwich Village saying they never knew about this great picture and it's old, 15, 12 years old----they want to know the names of all the cast---an old undertrodden neglected film masterpiece of Henry Fonda's early past

MY MOTHER'S ENTERTAINING THE ADMIRALS of the Fleet on our little pier outside the house---they sit, have crabmeat spread, a small can of devil's hamspread, Ritz crackers, are in blue uniforms talking and my mother and also Alma Horan and others are there---It's that same Frisco Bay housepier where I was painting the railroad bridge picture last month, only looking the other way over the blue waters ---I'm sitting stupidly and probably semi-naked at the bucket of food and the crackers and I hear the Admirals thanking my mother for their hospitality and but want to cut out now to their own swimbeach for male relaxation and further conference---At the door of their pulled up launch a young woman who is my mother gives them the final serenade with a guitar, flirting with the youngest officer---

Earlier it had been gray dramas of hipsters also in Frisco, with Bull, Huck---Huck and I following Bull

186

and another to the "subway" (now it's not New York) jog a half block to catch up and then slow again to walk hurriedly and we talk---later we're on a high hill in the snow and as Huck starts down I say "How we gonna make it without slipping?" he says "Dont worry"---it's right around the corner from the Henri Fonda house---Later Bull and I have hot dope in our possessions in his groundfloor graypad, we see an agent lurking in the court and sneak out the back door, Bull drops a packet in a trash barrel, we hurry "phewing" how close it was---Bull finds great iron doors and pushes them open "Here we go, they cant get us now"---they look like the doors of hell---20 feet high---(the street Huck and I ran in was a Chicago-like Boulevard, with delicatessens, like Kingsbridge Road in Bronx)---

FURTHER, EARLIER HEAT WITH BULL, we're walking past the San Remo and he has his knife out playing with it and we pass two burly cops who do a double take seeing this and start after us, someone yells here they come! and Bull and I start running---I tear off and over the barbed wire fence tearing my clothes and shoes---it's located across from Fugazzy's but also in the Centerville and Lupine Road of the earlier dream when there were hills, red winter dusk, houses, some great unnamable sadness about the past and my birth, as I go up Lakeview towards Lupine and it gets darker and lights come on and there's a stone wall---going over the fence I sneak into the house, the cops missed me---but as day breaks light reveals a man sleeping on his back on the floor on blankets with a 6 year old boy sprawled across his chest---they see me simultaneously---I have my pants down and shorts down as tho shitting in what I thought was privacy and I start quickly explaining my good intentions---"I was with a friend who had a gun---not a friend but a vague acquaintance, see--- the cops chased us---" They're friendly, the guy even takes me to his family house where my father lies in his deathbed and he's really *me* old and dark haired, scowlfaced, I'm in bed with him---lots of relatives around the bed---the house is on Lakeview Avenue in the same tragic iron dusk Lowell---

WALKING IN A BEAUTIFUL EVENING SNOWSTORM up the narrowshovelled hill-house sidewalk of Centerville with the Four Brothers, one of them Allen Eager, jazz musi- cians, tenor men---I keep wanting to walk beside the great- est of them to ask him about music and "atonal" chords but he's deep in conversation with another musician and doesnt notice---At one point we're walking in a soft New York side city street, then Buffalo-NY-like woodhouse streets and stark trees, from behind em all I up and loft a playful oval drysnow snowball that plops near them like the plap from a tree---it's beautiful---I do get to talk to the champ Tenorman who seems interested until I use the fancy non-musician word atonal and his face and the others' faces blank up---I dont belong, I'm trying to be a poet in the wrong medium---

OVER THE GIANT JUNK FLATS OF AIKEN STREET and Laurier Park and Hoboken New Jersey of plane crashes and rust, in bright sunny day, I watch airplanes fly off and studied the stories of the pilots---then I go and find a dank vast hidden underpart of a Spectral World Barn or Dancehall and go in there with a child like my mother or Phillip Fortier and crawl over a big oval rock to find hidden lumber and carpenter tools against the dripping well which has a bulb--- Now I want to create a mystery fantasy in this rubbish cellar and suddenly begin to hear a heavy slow thumping---"The beating of a giant heart---A monster is hidden here!--- They're building structures for it!"--- Far off in the gloom plastered against the Great Wall of the Cellar I see the Giant World Crab but aint sure it's really just that or shadow, or something else more awful, more *under* may be heartbeating ---it isnt real, I want to make the Monster Crab exist so write the story---I see families adventuring in the rubble

WAR---HORRIBLE INFANTRY WAR that made me wake up in the night and want to take off for the woods like Thoreau---I'm alone in a kind of schoolhouse surrounded on all sides by the Orientals who are firing from 100 yards across the fields and from the woods in back, burp guns, rifles, a constant racket and all aimed at me who am so innocent and childlike in the dream all I have is a goddam "pow" voice-gun to shoot with out of windows and even when windowpanes crash and enemy points big guns in at me to invade I aim the toy gun, "brow!"---I keep imagining the rain of bullets entering my body, the pain, but it doesnt yet happen---yet so many bullets are being fired at the little schoolhouse which is part Bartlett Jr Hi but only firstfloor and like the Haunted House across Joe's and something earlier, stranger,---so many bullets I couldnt help being hit--- Finally it's a moonlight dawn and I have no real knowledge of how to get out of this predicament because suddenly I've found some real bullets and a real gun and I'm jammed a cartridge in but cant find the firing safety pin and an enemy pokes his gun in the window to kill me and all I do is raise the real gun and say pow---I had hopes of sneaking off thru the dark but in the moonlight whitening to dawn I can clearly see sneaking figures like Indians closing in---and couldnt make it thru them and out to safety, oblivion, beyond the wood---I wake up realizing I wish I were dead and thinking of the next war, I wont be able to live thru it, and thinking of the American soldiers in Korea bound hands-in-back bayoneted on the ground to real non-pow bleak winter frost death and blah I dont see why the West should suffer itself the indignity of living on the same globe with those Mongolian Idiots of the East, who came charging in suicide thousands in moonlight attacks and loved it---Pearl Harbor's just the beginning---They've given Attila battleships---I think there are supposed to be others dead, with me in the classroom---I dont see them or notice them in the strange general goldenness of the color of this horror and final despair dream---

THE BIG DOUBLEDECKER BUS TO THE PICNIC on the river park like Merrimack Park, all the kids are taken and we go bouncing over the entry driveway (from Christian Hill we've come) and see the people, rollercoasters (this little mind one of 2 Billion today and 100 Billion in history) (pfahsh)--- we all turn into hipsters and abondon our teacher and start blasting weed and shooting junk, young kids of 15 some of em, and finally in our wild party in our apartment in the park comes a blue uniformed cop but doesn't suspect anything, is only looking for Jimmy Johnson who's run away from the orphanage---has his papers with him---Jimmy has just shot junk, complains---Wig is there, we're all hep--- Finally it's like the Fortier house and after endless parties I want to make the big No. I hipster doll like Georgia or Vicki, she's on the couch with me and I havent made my preliminary move yet---

DROWSY AFTERNOON IN THE STRANGE San Jose yards, Cody and I are living in a caboose or house car hooked to the end of a drag pointed East, at the far rail along the platform---but there's something curiously like that Afternoon Julien Reformatory of East New York which I know also now to be the big Spectral Colonial Naval Ship at 22nd Street---the afternoon, the boys, the work, the dormitories--- and it's also the Third and Townsend Southern Pacific baggageroom and we're all working, as other trains ball through on schedule and Cody and I are strange trainmen---earlier in fact there'd been a strange accident of a freight in a middle-way small town, I saw the warped cars at a crossing, got on board to dig the damage---Finally after I wake up in my wood caboose and rush to the Christmas work along the yard cars the train takes off and outside at "Perry" (which is located like Perry but is really in Colorado) the ground of the prunefields is all bare and cracked open in a terrible drought and makes me sad because I'd thought recently of farming in this railroad valley---

LATER NIN AND LUKE have inherited John's Saybrook house on the Big Easonburg location but Luke has secretly given it up to live in a new white cottage with "modern" gadgets and furniture so I stand raging in the yard of the noble old house saying "*I'll* buy it myself!"---Ma's in the house, all that old brown Victorian furniture like Joe's on Salem Street and behind is a great beautiful golden wheat-field and it's really some other secret place in my brainmap having to do with long ago dreams dream'd on Hildreth St. in the Kellostone house, the wealth of woods in the backyard and old Maine Aunt Dudley dreams. . .the backyard fence, the field, the mystery play. . .the backyard of the Salem Manse. . .the rickety boardfence and the huge Rousseau jungle weeds and the thrill of the lil boy's mind---

I'M IN A CARIBBEAN COUNTRY racing over the water of the bay on a little boat which I push my feet out on and the harder and further I stretch it the faster it skims over the water---there are other boats, I'm a tourist---I come and bounce right on shore and go on skimming thru the streets and on the beach but noticing that the straw bottom is wearoutable---I walk in the narrow picturesque streets of the Carib village, wanting a woman---I see a strangely interest-ing looking but diseased-faced and old woman on a balcony and give her the eye, at first she pretends not to respond but then comes down after me---We go thru silent mysterious streets like in Victoria Mexico and the woman of the Fellaheen Hilltop Guitar---I am pleased that a man can always get laid in a Latin American country---

We get on the main street of the Village which is like the "San Obispo" Main Street that always runs into the town in exactly that manner---hilly, eventful---it changes to where Julien and I and presumably Irwin (or Bull) have been vacationing inthis town and had our car parked in front of the Monastery Institution or Charity School, in front of the salmon wall---but the Headmaster is frowning in the wall gate saying we cant park there but I find a semihidden sign proving we can, and Julien's not too concerned and's working with luggage and cursing---

Since we're leaving this land I wind up in "Russell Jurgin's" or "GeneDexter's" or "Charley Williams' " apartment gathering our belongings which got mixed there, the owner is out---I steal paper clips, look for useless stationery materials but deliberately leave unwanted shirts, socks (the purple ones), suspected pants (are they mine or his? the trip's been long) and I leave a valuable threesome of pictures one depicting Julien Love as Christ Crucified tearing and straining off the Cross but nailed tight so in a gigantic agony pose hanging golden and *mustached* from the wall of a cathedral and the reason the picture is so "valuable to Garden" is we see his large penis balling up in a loincloth and as viewed from below very erotic---this picture is captioned "By Elmont High School gang, 19--" and is marked J. Kerouac under to show who drew it. . .a great thing and I leave it for the occupant's concern---(showing spirituality of his rapacious-seeming visitors)---Rummaging in junk and pants and books all over parlor trying to take final things with me to final ends of the world---Ending up in a mess of hipsters and Dick Beck and going from one pad to another to connect and pick up green and a mixup of Television sets and I end up at Ma's house on Phebe Avenue, it's Xmas, she steps on the couch, sleeps, I unplug the tiny hand portable TV in the sideroom and take it to the parlor to face her couch but am accidentally plugging up (carrying) the electric stand clock instead---I'm in my pajamas, the house is littered with stuff (the stand clock is covered with expensive leather)---and all started from an innocent joyride on a lake---(Shape of the foot boat was like a paper sailer you throw to ceiling---it sure *went*)

WALKING DOWN THE TRACK at near San Jose with Phillip Fortier and I look back authoritatively to check if train is coming to impress the fat women (one of them huge) also walking the roadbed with the seriousness of railroads---ahead's old Pot Number So & So the Sunnyvale Local with same old engineers and fireman and waiting in a siding for the passage of the actually coming train----Phillip goes to wait by holding on to a rung between mainline and siding, I say "No, no never do that, always get out of the way, the Lark'll blow you clear off the track with just the wind of it" ---we go to a chickenwire fence over a gulch and stick our fingers in it, we're "safe" here, except that a new danger of the flimsy fence collapsing exists---

Later I'm in the San Jose yard office---somehow a union hall too, walk in on Al Damlette and Charley Low in Al's room and they're not pleased to see old S.I.U. me because of the strike---I end up on a ship and it's sailing across the blue sea and I dont want it---"Hey! I'm supposed to be workin on the San Jose railroad!"---Further and further the ship sails---it finally arrives in a Northern City, I'm with my mother in the airplane as we land, digging Main Street for signs of where---"It must be Portland Oregon!"---We take a walk on elevated sidewalks with grill floors and see dizzyingly down and fear it---but it's North

and keen and hills and snow---While landing I lay in the tail
of the plane looking contentedly at girls' legs to distract &
satisfy me in case we crash---flat on my stomach in the tube
of the aluminum tail---In San Jose again I have my typewriter and a typewriter case for a portable which I squeeze it
in to---leave it on a bus, cant haul it over the window, ride
the bus on the outside hanging on, cursing---finally haul it
out all broken---a mouse and her baby mouse had contentedly crawled out of my case, I watched on an East Santa Clara
bench thinking "This Eastern mouse'll have a Western
home."---The travails, hassels and nervous hagglings of it all!
----I wish I dreamed of the Pure Wilderness---

IN THE MIDDLE OF ZAZA GABOR'S DREARY gray
afternoon tea which is going on somewhere else in the big
sad house at the foot of Boisvert Street location of the old
St.Louis de France nun's house where Nin had her sad bleak
piano lessons on long red afternoons in New England winter and I played in the field of the Devils with my crunch
boots---I'm in the toilet hiding and taking a crap and another
guy a well dressed witty socialite like Kyle Elgins but dreary
comes in or's already in and disturbs me in my revery----I'm
trying to hide from the Russian Novel chatter of the ladies
in that Gray Lace Breakable Livingroom and I imagine the
dismalness of it as a little kid considering his aunts hordes of
em---At some other point in the farce and force of unsleepy
dreaming I learn that Zaza or the socialite man is sick and
been ordered by the doctor to drive every day to New Jersey
and eat pure cream ice cream, quarts of it and immediately I
wanta go along or get some too, be sick too---Had a chance

to get up at 8:30 and slept till Noon instead, for fear of what to do with all that morning---

VAGUELY IN A SICK DREAM a bunch of us guys are in an open space surrounded by watching crowds, a giant act of teamship and fellow-suffering duty is being enacted as each of us (tho casually and in the midst of continuing almost gay conversations) takes his turn in the center to receive the downward huge tho soft enough shock of some parachute of the sky, some battering ram of mentality and guilt but real, material, so as I take my turn just at the last second someone of my buddies saying "Jack Jack" I stand there and down it comes, white, big, flappy, and shivers my skull a moment in cottony recognition and frizzles my dream and having done its appointed slow ram of Eternity it rises up, bounces up high and far again, to almost out of sight, where it begins again the descent to earth (which it must *never* touch), where WE'LL be to receive it on our sacrificial skulls---Watchers say nothing, we talk and pass the time and even the stick, laughing, comradely, crazy together like a troupe of hot rod racers in heaven---

I HAVE A BARN in San Jose, a "farm," a brace of white ducks and ready to start feeding them in the hay and since it's my first day as a farmer and I haven't got all my equipment yet I go to the store on East Santa Clara and buy a few bags of salt peanuts and nuts and come back to sow them in the ay for my pecking fowl, feeling meanwhile so proud and happy that I can feed them, like my cat----but they're gone, temporarily disappeared, maybe run off thru the barn door and I'll never re-find them but I have hope and faith they're just in the barn loft above, asleep---Evelyn catches me in a doorway, blonde and radiante, and we lock in a passionate embrace---Cody is dead but his ghost lives on scaring me in her embrace---I shall take Buddha's advice about the other man's wife and keep my comfortable ducks and downy bed in San Jose---which are gifts from the Living Cody---

LIVID LIPS OF TELEVISION where Jack Carson is snarled at on the pier by surrounding gangsters---at the gangplank, with his girl---"Yeh? whatcha gonna do about it?"---I'm watching in the late stale re-sleeping dreams of up-late noon ---Earlier it was on the tidal boulevard located grayly and spectrally in the neck of arm sea land, gray, somewhere, with a mankind by the sea worried about the sea flooding---in this case no great wave, but a slow seepage and you see the Newsreel Streets inundated, and not far from those shacks where I found old cups and cake dough---A location and gray mysterious event in the universe---there were children glee-ing at the livid-lips screen with me---I'd just left I think Mary Palmer's two kids and was walking the street alongside another woman and her two kids and I adjusted to them just like that, immediately, casually, we started in on Jack Carson Comedy routines---It's as though the Tree & Wheel, or Tree Wheel, of Dreams, was a distant beyond-the-real-one hung gray and phantasmal in space which is the void of dreaming mind in sleep, Another Universe and Hint of further worlds---

WATCHING A RAILROAD MAN AT THE N.Y.C.R.R. UNDERPASS at 40th Street and 11th Avenue, a new Manhattan location never dreamed before and only remembered not after waking but two days later while watching there, only in the dream it was further uptown, way up on the Hudson River bank near Columbia or lower but without reference to the 'Julien' location---there was snow, a lot of it, you could see New Jersey across the river (that was the big sensation)---it was cold, I was alone in the dark with my lamp and making a move and it was just like that NYC brakie at 40th Street, the tic of recall that instantly rose in me---the location of the snow and tracks in the general spectral NY of little white bungalows up and down East & West (the dreaming cottage meadow across Baker Field)---the sense of railroading, tragic snow, the land, the Night West out---the big puffy miserable workgloves in the lip-hardened iron hard worknight, mouths steaming in the lantern glo----this the place where I'd seen snow in dreams 10, 13 years ago but not with the rail there---up on a bluff, and having somehow to do with that Riverside Drive that was Zaza Gabor's teaparty mansion street t'other night---

AL BINGHAM IS IN PRISON, but is a trusty and allowed to wander around in a prison suit or pajamas with number during the day---I visit him, we're climbing the steps to the iron cells and the area of the greensward yard hall---"Ugh" I say seeing iron gray bars as we come up gloomy steps together---He laughs radiantly and serenely---"That's just what Wallington said last week when he saw them---" Al is resigned, Buddhistic, not Christlike, like a Genêt hero quietly and hardly ironically enjoying jail, no complaints to make, or excuses, as tho he couldnt help being in prison but he *could* cease tormenting his mind *even here*---so I see his radiance and wonder at him---we come to the Yard Hall where all the other prisoners and their visitors are gathered some sitting on the slopey sward, some wandering around as in a Ginsbergian garden of Dolls, tender prisoners somehow, all in gray suits as 'trusties' and Bingham the kindest, most beautiful radiant of them and saintlike----all of it is so beautiful I find myself wishing I was in this kind prison---

AROUND A KITCHEN TABLE WITH THE FORTIERS, earlier, a big family reunion, Old Joe big and redfaced but now so old he's forgotten everyone and just sits at table bulge-eyed and not unfriendly---at one point my own father who's not decrepit at all, but is figuring out the horses at his desk in his room, in the gray one-story manse, gets a phonecall, or that is, I get a phonecall from old Joe and then I say "Hang on, Pop's here'll talk to ya" and My Pa hearing this picks up his own desk phone to talk to his old buddy but by gor old Joe is so gone he doesnt hear me or understand or care and I see my Pa saying "Hello Joe" into the speaker but apparently getting no response and hanging up slowly, bemusedly, eyes on his horse playing figures as tho it no longer surprises him that Old Joe is Neglectful sick---(had a tic there of the warehouse on Bridge Street but the front of it as seen from Bridge at about the rail-road crossing and canal and dreams there of rainy-mist nights when I take long walks from Kearney Square to Centralville, always that route, my shoes wetcrunching gritbles in the side-walk of Lowello dream ah---)

. . . .Earlier too young Joe'd been around, and left always tragic and going away and pale and heroic is my sweet Joe O Dreams, brother of my days and great Father of Cody in my affections to the World---Strangely the family reunion of Kerouacs and Fortiers was in Mexico, thus "gray one story (dobe) mans"---Ma was around,---In Pa picking up that phone was hope of life, non-death, rebirth of Kerouacs for first time for Pa's usually dream-dead---(to think they've given him a phone in heaven!)

THAT WILD CHICAGO-LIKE NEW YORK or 'rainy Pittsburgh' of Book of Dreams' first page---I'm stepping out from my 450 W 20 pad to eat a snack in a Bowery Brown Cafeteria like in the old Henry Street Vision of Joe when he and I among doleful garbage cans and amid plasters of city ruins walked, a dream as old as Russia with Joe stee-riding along purple popped to 'bout laugh 'Hyoo hyoo!' boots and all and in that Murder Garden gloom---now 'tis the other side of town but the same Bowery like darkness and after eating which takes me two hours and my thoughts so vast while eating that when I wake up and realize my mind'd run thru two hundred dreary mind-weary Finnegangs Wakes, half awake goofball sleep---somethin to do with a waitress girl, burns---I leave and head back home, to "First Avenue" tho geographically it's Eleventh Avenue West Side---going down bleak Boston-like black cobbles like the cobbles seen earlier in an afternoon redsun dream of Sheridan Square, Danny Richman and Bev Watson, I spy four colored girls rowdily walking under a lamp (like the lamps of the 59th Street New York small colonial Greekhouse Armistice celebration dream) (which I go to see Jack Anderson mysterious)---As I start trailing after them for sexual interest I notice four white girls following them rowdily but all with short haircuts and pants and Dikes---I follow---there are other prowling Greeks like me (in the pristine red city morning New York of brown-brick the Greeks of Sex)---it's like Boston and backa the Boott Mills---suddenly I realize I'll have to cut thru a restaurant to get to my street and back to my furnished room---I go thru a bustling golden cafeteria where a man rushes up to me and says a story about some blonde waitress somewhere who was so sloppy her sores ran while she served you--- "Pimples," he said---I exhibit polite response but blankly he rushes off, so had I just stared at him gravely as I really wanted he would have persisted with something else (O the grief of the Lowell bridge over the canal, the old glassbroken walk for lovers on the canal lock wall, the nights I've jumped down dere per dream and in real life as a real boy prowled with Dicky and Who Else and the dream of the Flood Oersurmounting it) (with raging whitesmash, river mouth grashin to show clash crash)---drash!---brash!---Aoooowayyy br-a-a-shhh----I move on thru the kitchen and out the back with instructions from Porto Rican scullions Late from the Chico Sea---I start up a flight of circular iron steps like the steps of Waterworks & City Clocks with fat Wipers in under-shirts by valves reading the Union City Journal---I go another flight, contemplate a third, at each level the iron door is locked, I keep thinking one will be on some level unlocked and I'll be able from the outside to descend to my alley---but no door iron unlocked, the higher I go the more futile my search for homeward---I'm trapped in the steel & maniacal contrivance of the city---gotta go down again, start from the rear---Find some way to unlock the levels of my mind & get on in---woke up in iron red dawn of workday (at Post Office Mails) thinking: "I dont wanta go to no California & at red tired dawn my engine's waiting pointed to Watsonville three hours away--"

GABBING AS USUAL, in the Lowell City Hall Square with presumably Cody I've failed to notice the reason for Lil Timmy's big trip in the car, he grownup, 5, dressed in lil blue suit, Evelyn his Ma's been primping him & priming him for the big day as I gab, so it isnt until the last minute when they're getting in the car that I glance at their plan-itinerary & realize as on belatedly-guilt Tea seeing "Religion" & names of places in the booklet that I realize Lil Timmy's about to (and Gaby too) be *Confirmed* in a sense, big day, etc., O god I bore even myself with useless detail---failed to notice the kid's big day in the car driving to religious in new blue suit, because high gabbing in City Hall so see Evelyn aint interested in anything but her kids, as proper, and I wake up saying "Aint no sense my going bothering out there," that is, interrupting their lil serenities gabbing about myself---lil serenities of young parents and new children and all the calmities & lil joys of the dust---For me it's immortality in a hut--

IN THE PARAMOUNT THEATER G.J. and Scotty and I are watching the ballet of the Black Men, sorta Negroes or Polynesians, muscular & graceful, reminding one again of the "Indian baggageman buddy of San Jose" (actually a big Frisco Portugese)---the muscles hard, shoulders round, thin, tight

veins, the dances un-effeminate but manly & beautiful, up on
the stage---It's that spectral Paramount Theater I'd taken Ma
& Nin that night of Irene's 'candy job'---Going backstage &
into areas of circular stairs just like back-restaurant of yesterday with G.J. and Scotty now I say "Let's have coffee, let's
meet, where will you be?"---"How about the Ritz cafeteria?" I interrupt G.J. who's trying to say "X" cafeteria which
is actually the right name and I know it but persist, saying,
"Well it's the Ritz Hotel over it," really it's the spectral Astor---
astral astor---so G.J. and Scotty nod, they seem (as in Lowell
Middlesex sad return saloon dreams) to be unsure about me
and as if looking at each other oddly--- "In a half hour" I
'suggest'---really hanging them & cutting out before they can
say no---cutting out in elevator to go backstage to borrow
money for coffee & donuts, if I fail in loan G.J. & Scotty will
have to pay mine---It's the backstage of Backstages, and since
Repetitious Paragon Paramount is also that Hugeroom
House of Eternity and stage of great confusions & racking
dusts & events commending itself to the activity of the whole
world---Later I'm a successful smiling New York Damon
Runyon young genius writer (like the me of 1949) in Central
Park with my welldressed hatted friends all smiling, chatting,
saying "Well where do we go now, what do?"---like Lionel,
cronies of latenight cafeterias, of talks & sweetfaced well wal-
letted well-relaxed Megalopolitan eagerness the only kind I
might ever feature again if I ever come back (because of $)---
to city for further sojourns---It's midafternoon winter and
we're all idle in the park & only slightly dissolute (of responsibility souls) and goodlooking, like a team of scenarists goof-
ing---like a bunch of Sigmund Rombergs---I fear G.J. &
Scotty were never there to meet me---

IN THE FRONT ROW OF AN OUTDOOR SHOW sit-
ting with 'my people' in the second row is Watson & his
mother & sister---there are goofings & jokes about cats & a
ball bouncing around---Later the group of poets cuts out of
the 5 & 10 heading down 42nd Street in the rainslick, I'm
walking alongside 'Louis Simpson' needling & goading him
about his literary ideas---I say "I havent seen anything of
worth in New Story except Genêt, the rest are all awful &
awkward imitators of the so called modern style"---he smiles
serenely & says something abstract about his proposed essay--
-I say "Let's run & catch up with the others up front" (Garden,
Lionel Lawrence) & start running & I take long sweet slides
on the red tile sidewalk rainslick (like Mexico), long slides of
15 feet, hoping Louis Simpson too will be amazed---

A BUG CRAWLING OVER A ROUND BARREL like in
the dream, eating 'peach meat' I think, as it crawls along, and
it is a person---this in deepest sleep woke up by the cat, proving the greatest deepest dreams are unrecoverable to the ordinary morning waking brain---The bug was probably me, and
so deeply involved in nutriment I didnt think it strange---
Later it was a long happy dream of the backyard in Phebe
Avenue and Jack Elliot the Singin Cowboy has made a record
which is selling a million copies & we're all together in the
happy yard, a new house there, at one point there are three
thin mattresses on thefloor of a cold hut & happily I pick
mine out (narrower but thicker) leaving no other choice to
the other two guys, Jack & Someone---All forgotten by
now, afternoon, saved so I could write "more completely"
and this is the sad result.

My mind, the Mind, is too Vast to keep up
with.

The bug was eating peach colored pump-
kin like meat that was very familiar in the dream & therefore
in some future world is already familiar---

CROSSING VAN WYCK BLVD WITH A COUPLE
YOUNG GUYS who're worried about the cops but I'm
older in that score and aint worried and tell them, and even
when the black and white cruiser comes down-road I reassure them, secure and free in my thoughts---and of course
the cops dont even notice us---

Dont beware
The anger of
The hare

SEX DREAM---Marie Fitzpatrick or somebody, and I, hot,
go down the cellar stairs holding each others' organs---I have
hers, she mine, as we descend steps slowly---We're gonna
look for a place to work---It's the basement of the Fortier
Hugehouse on Salem---I pick a little sidecellar coal room,
gray with ashes, dank, and stand her against the wall as we
wake up---Just sweet immediate wanting---she's slicking up
breath in her hiss hot teeth---I'm grinding my molars in
bighard girlholding grash---r-r-o-pt---We're gonna find a
place to gnash our hot and juicy parts pole into hole in some
hideout craphole of the great cellar, no one'll know, we'll
have bare thighs and write on chalk on the wall and smack

goosy flesh and have hot jumping juices in the ecstatic secret liplicking lollswallowing lip-lolling suckcellar hole, droop--- I'll grab her bare rumps and squeeze and dump in, standing, the straight pole, up her roamous slit, deep, she'll part warm breath to huff---I'll grang her---spew spill flood her inside belly womb---flutter my knees---tickle her top---accidently plop in, God.

THE HATEFUL SHIP IN THE HATEFUL MISSISSIPPI, I'm late returning to it and finally on top of that it's not the right ship and I stumble around the early dawn deck---my bunk in the messmen foc'sle---after sad bad events in presumably New Orleans, drunkenness---my own real ship's gone upriver---

HAPPY DREAM OF CANADA, the illuminated Northern land---I'm there at first on Ste.Catherine or some other Boulevard with a bunch of brother French-Canadians and among old relatives and at one point Nat King Cole is there talking with my mother (is not dark, but light, friendly, I call him 'Nat')---We all go to the Harsh Northern School and are sitting (like the gray wood room of Mechanical Drawing class in Bartlett J H shack) and the teacher is a freckled redhaired Scotchman and acts a little contemptuous of the Frenchies, has his favorite teacher's boy in the front row and he too is a sarcastic freckled redhaired British Canadian--- I've been close and talkative and like Saintly Ti Jean with everyone so now contemplatively I lean forward and study the situation, watch the teacher and his asskissing sarcastic prototype, and softly, in French, nodding, for I see it all and only because an outsider American Genius Canuck can see, "Ca-na-da"---(I say) Ca-na-daw---and my brother dark-haired anxious angry Canucks vehemently agree with me--- "It's always them!" they cry and I see that sarcastic non-French smirk on the redheads' faces, smashable faces, something hateful I must have seen on Ste.Catherine St. in 1953 March, that arrogant Britishified look---or from ancestors' memories of old French-Indian canoe wars---Had I gone back to Canada I wouldnt have taken shit one from any non Frenchman of Canada. . .took everything from Brother Noël and mourned---but God the fist mashed face of my redhaired English Canadian enemy---

This was such a happy dream, I woke up at 5 AM from the comradeship and glow of it---no anger (as now, afternoon) at all---I should have written it at dawn---it was Ti Jean the happy Saint back among his loyal brothers at last---That's why

OLD SHIFTS TO ENTERTAIN OURSELVES, G.J. and Lousy and Scotty and I in adolescent immortal years, but in New York, that part of it (Thompson St) where GJ & Scot & I strolled that Sunday afternoon in 1940 when they visited big Columbia Zagg at Hartley Hall and we walked. . . long red sun on the cobbles of lower Manhattan, we walked among the haunted buildings of Wolfe and blue architect-light windows of below Canal office and engineering and factory buildings, we saw pushcarts of Bleecker and down to Skippy's boyhood Vesey but innocent of NY then---ending we took pictures on the steps of Avery Hall, stepping smartly with

pipe, full of Walgreen Times Square sundaes and movies---
the last diligent jokes of GJ with Scotty and the dice in the
dorms, the last sad beer in Lions Den ere they jaloppied back
to what they thought were their 'gloomy fates' back in
Lowell---O what a great book I must now write about my
entire life!----that lower New York of that 1940 walk, only
now it's night, a bar, the influx of Porto Ricans in NY so great
that the bar is full of PR girls dancing alone in the crowded
jukebox floor, as we file doorward from the back room (as
Pioneer Club) (Boys) the girls ogle and wiggle and I push
thru the first one, (leading Zagg) trying to ignore them to the
instructions of Buddha---they are scraggly Fellaheen
brunettes---there are men sitting around laughing, it's the real
present downtown Lower Village NY of actual gay Porto
Ricans---I therefore lapse into thoughts and see Lousy, GJ &
Scotty latching each to a girl and devise a beautiful sad French
movie of love picturing them next day, each separately with
his girl in a room, the serious tragic lover to be pimple-jawed
Scotty surfing and actually in love. . . comic relief Lousy and
his funny girl. . .also GJ and his outrageous behavior and wild
girl. . ."I'll keep myself out of this book," I think seriously,
"it'll be better"---I picture the actual girls---

A PINE TREE HOUSE, needle green livingroom and
scenes outside Maine windows and the front room of the
Phebe Ave. house where Ma recently lay in bed as I brought
her a leather electric clock (toaster)---events of some kind of
intensity, so that when Evelyn appears in the kitchen radiant
as an angel in white silk dress with little leathery ties exactly
like an angel's trussed-in-sections dress and has the kids with

her, undressing them, and says "I've been spending the holidays with my people" I say "Oh" casually but am actually amazed that she'd been away all this time that flew in the pine part of the house---presumably Cody---

THE BIG POST OFFICE BANK is paying us boys off on Jamaica Avenue, it's gray day, marble floors, hot radiators in front of small caged cashier windows so it's a drag to lean in and enquire---I've already drawn but am rushed back to get $165 more, which will leave my balance at $40---I jump up on the radiator side to see the cashier better---guys are pushing all around---the Cashier has a definite joking personality and remembers me but says something about my high-in leaning so I jump down and apologize to guy pushing up near to me "I'm small"---we all peer into cage window as cashier counts ---Negroes who've worked, collected and spent probably, lounge around the lobby watching---I'm suspicious of their motives---So when I get my $165 I fold it four times and thumbjam the sliver into my watchpocket but then take my wallet and hold it in my hand as I walk outside to make any thieving watcher think the money's in the wallet--- A Negro in fact following me---Just like the white guy who was pushing up against the window and was with a rain brim weather hat with hunting or fishing look and like owner of a car and family, this Negro had a definite personality, pale brown, in a definite tweed style topcoat, with a definite anxiety following me down the street but ahead of me---Suddenly he wheeled to come to me (in the busy sidewalks) just as I'd for further fooling put the wallet in my thigh pocket with big elaborate gesture---I immediately roared at him "Gra wah!"

or something resounding and ominous and he walked right by me anxious-faced and full of sensitive perturbation as though he'd only planned to pan a dime from me or say something preliminary (or whatever including robbery) but now my roar makes him understand not only my fear and unavailability of my money but that I've been watching him all this time and have foreseen his move so he floats on back, whitened---

AN MG CAR or gametoy truck that I'm zooming across sunny plazas of Lowell on, by the City Hall, at first in almost (oldtime dream) Frisco like sunny bottom-of-hill plaza (that original vision of Van Ness or Fillmore hill as old as original visions of Deni Bleu in Marin City)---my speedy machine takes me around and I look up at the fading sun and see it has a few bloated stars as big as little suns near it and they're big (and round as globes) because bloating and waxing like moons at wane of day or at fade fall 'pon horizons---So I look and see the small swimming roes of fire in the fields of the globular moonstar and I'm terrified in that old Lowell dream of starry disaster. . .looking thru a glass as I ride swiftly in the machine I watch & ponder---realizing the star is huge for some recent reason but also just for wane-horizon reasons and the sun is faded, vague, orange---we come to an old house like the Ottoman Empire of Hackensack but across the street from Lowell Public Library and there I get off the car and wander around in further events with somebody, a distinct sensation of that music store nearby---I watch the seething pellets in the globe world-star, like orange spirochetae

THE LANDLORD AND HIS ASSISTANT come to the Textile Lunch tenement where Ma and I've re-moved, we're living on the 2nd floor instead of 4th so that watching from Iddyboy's Gershom house which we've also occupied I measure the space between passing man's derby hat and the windows of our flat in the tenement and it leaves fewer inches than you'd expect, so we're not high at all----I'm in the kitchen alone, loafing, the landlord canuck and his younger assistant have just finished some repairing and are leaving me a paper that I'm to deliver downtown to the Rent Loan Bank not far from the music store---they begin dreary Lowellstreet instructions----for the prodigal returner----I experience momentary despair and bleakness of being back and subject to 'laws of Lowell' again, so long desdone out of---The assistant is a definite snickering little curious Pawtucketville kid I'm bound to see that night in the Social Club alleys with Pete Plouffe and all the others and it's going to be just like Ste.Catherine Street saloons, beer, smoke, talk, bleak wintry city streets of Lowell Canada---not a happy or even interesting dream---So I was loath to even write it, and the sun star, and am doing it out of a sense of duty existence of which is reasonless at this late stage in my search for repose beyond fate and rest beyond heaven

WRITING DREAMS, TAKE NOTE OF THE WAY THE DREAMING MIND CREATES

THE ROOMING HOUSE ON THE BUSY TRAFFIC-Y FUMEY STREET in the seaside resort in Sunland, I was allowed to sleep on the porch and I hated it and when I woke up in the morning from my bad sleep and traffic was heavy on the Boulevard one of the roomers coming back from an all night drunk said to me "You're staying here a few days? She'd a never give you this porch cot if she thought you---she thought you was a one nighter" (as if I could have banged a girl on the porch in the starry boulevard night)---Another drunkard comes to talk---their definite personalities annoying, confidential, toothy, semi-setup bums of roominghouses in the crowded Void Universe and I'm disgusted---Later I'm working on deck with the Carruth Bos'n the Scandanavian and vainly looking for the grease can at instructions from a deckhand, the deck cluttered, and I'm in a Skidrow whitecap and paintsplashed but one of the deckhands nevertheless recognizes me, "Hello Jack"---I'm displeased, 'trapped,' annoyed by everything and worst of all unsure---the ship is not far from the sunny rooming house, that nameless lip of land nee Florida alias Cape Cod forever Cot Night Soft---All exactitudes of events forgotten by now, the little things the Bosun said, etc. These the creations of a mind trying to escape via inescapable methods of work & rent---Omen of the future, and of the fact, "You are trapped as long as you covet any desire" and now I desire 'setting up' Ma in California---

THE ANNALS OF JACK KEROUAC---Annals indeed---anal ones---the Mind wished and dream'd itself a spate of San Jose where I'm taken to the parking lot of work at a location I hadnt *daydreamed*, on that road leading North from Santa Clara towards the yard office and the airport---and because I'm not drinking or smoking tea my mind is very clear and I'm very friendly and direct with everyone and play with the

212

kids with a spirit of serenity etc.---gray but happy scenes, at the lot, where Evelyn drives me, and I see the cars, the departing park-er, the boss, etc.---but the Mind loses control in a scene in a toilet across the street from Cody's house and Cody and I are taking craps side by side in a double crapper, Cody is talking about an actor as I wipe myself with paper, he says"But you know he's queer, he blows the Kings" and I have my part on my lap while wiping myself, it's naked, and at the mention of these erotic matters I can feel the swelling so I hurry to wipe up ere it's a pole but get all tangled in the wiping and get some crap in my mouth, a piece, for some reason with paper and reaching in and pieces that stuck and logics about teeth---here I am surreptitiously trying to remove the hunk of dreamcrap from my mouth which is also full of toilet paper (I'd wiped it instead of below) and Cody's talk about blows is, there's me coming up and I try to hurry, a Comedy---I even dreamed of the taste of the dreamcrap, which is a sensation I can remember only in conjunction with the possibility of a tasteless peanut butter like that 'peach meat' the barrell bug was moulding his way through last week---Meanwhile Cody doesnt notice my dilemna and I'm not working on the railroad so aint worried about time---

DRIVING INTO THE PICNIC GROUNDS with Mr. Calabrese, little Luke and Ma and others I reach out of the car and grab some brown or yellowish coconut string meat and eat a handful, playfully---it's disagreeable soapy---also the officials of the Park have seen me and are questioning ('reprimanding') me, and Mr.Calabrese who'd already been very sore about 'taking what dont belong to ya' is now red-

213

faced silent about my casually helping myself to the park coconut pile---the first park cop (in civvies) is a middleaged tall sheriff-like Okie in glasses---"Why did you do it?"---I sit in the car alone, parked by the bird house between it and other buildings, the others having gone to enjoy the games, and listen patiently and a little sarcastically to these 'reprimands'---consequently the Sheriff goes off and another Reprimander comes, this a darkhaired man in a blue suit with little mustache---Alternately on his face I see twitching from slick to tough (polite and to outright rough) as he talks to me ("Why?") and tries to figure out whether he should treat me as a member of polite Sunday-driving families (O the time the dog bit me on that Sunday drivegrounds'.) (1930)---I watch him warily, consider if he does hit me he will be tough to handle, and dangerously brutal, but I'm ready and wait, feeling only one slight twinge of doubt as to my personal safety & capability---Before, it was the mind wandering its characters around some holiday boulevard like the boulevard of the Garver Farver Hotel of the World and earlier yet, Ma and I are in a plane landing and I'm so afraid it will crash (it *is* crashing, the Pilot has said for everybody to hang on) and it's that Lilley Lakeview field (Laurier Field) and also New England Boston Canal Bridge West with Mattapan Charley Rooftops and the Hostess, the lights of streets below, Night---My mother and I are arm in arm on the floor, I'm crying afraid to die, she's blissful and has one leg in pink sexually out between me and I'm thinking "Even on the verge of death women think of love & snaky affection"----Women? who's dreaming this?

SEURAT---the boomcloud pang pock boats

IT SEEMS THE BEAUTIFUL MADE-UP DARK FRESH
BEAUTIFUL PEACHES is coming out of the hall room with
the high door and transom and with her is a Lesbian, probably
Ricky, and so stunning & Maggie-like and darkly beautiful I
involuntarily open my arms to embrace her but check myself
and Peaches says "Hmf, if you're going to do what you like
then why dont you ever?" and haughtily or that is indifferently
leaves with the Lesbian---I've been in that room all night, ages,
gray anxiety, it's located in the City but what an Aunt Anna
dead Gerard lost truck frontporch soft soap gray city, and how
lost forever in my recall and forgot even that. . .as if I'd gone
back to Heaven for my old shoes---only final contemplation
will upheave the details of that lost life and I write it---

BACK ON SHIP AND THINK "I've dream'd it & so here
I am"---believing I *am* back in bleak real, and what a toil tub
and morons everywhere---I've done something excited or
overslept and missed my morning's dishes and everybody's
mad as hell---I'm in a gray foc'sle or stateroom with some
surly AB---I rush to the sink promising I'll do extra---"the
well dressed steward" will reprimand me later

THE OTHER NIGHT, HAL KIND. . .in a dream roused up
suddenly while reading the dialog about locality of Mind in
Surangama Sutra. . .the same scene in a vast hall filled with
attentive, eating Saints & Arhats & Bhikkus, but in Denver---

215

Thousands of anxieties in sleep, inflamed
visions of he restless oversleeping mind in a room of a house

IN SOME LUNCHCART I've just had a big hassel with
some people behind the counter---"casting my tears everywhere" I say to myself in trying to recall details and falling
asleep on it---anyway I feel sad and broken and suddenly two
stools from me sits down a customer, unexpected in the middle of our hateful tragedy, comic in arriving but nevertheless
a real flesh customer in our real-life diner---and it's
W.C.Fields,!!! I am completely amazed, red nose, strawhat,
Fields himself in real life has just happed to wander in---so
unexpected and opening such fields of redemptive and
cleansing humor I let out a joyful quivering sob involuntarily and W.C., hearing me, only partially glances and politely
as if sadly scans the menu in respect for what he supposes is
a boy crying next to him about something---and this respect
and sorrow so funny, he hasnt said a word yet but you know
he will---it was the materialization of Old Bull Baloon, the
living Fields, just in time for Sorrow---but had I written this
dream in its dawn, I would have brought you a message from
heaven about W.C.Fields for in heaven it took place---so
funny that he thinks I'm crying from trouble and sorrow, he
in fact clears his throat quietly, he sits (just come in) minding
his own business, he's all adrift in his own personality adventure and here he is led by the nose by fate to our humble mad
lunchcart---the incredible troubles and jokes that have led
him here!
-----Just then I was wakened from this dream by the cat giving me two touches with his paw, like wolves do in Indian

Tales, and the first time Rondidindu ever did this to me, tho he does it to my mother all the time to be let out---in this case he just wanted to sleep with me (or stop my snoring?)

A HIGH GROVE OF SUNNY BEE TREES the dreaming mind creates over railroad tracks in some hot Mattapan Noon or Boston noon running alongside ditches suggestive of old canal ditches of Duke Gringas Castle Lowell and all the greengrass waves lazy in the drowsy suburb and here are Lil Luke and me going along the track on some big travel which is also just playkids goofing for a day---Lil Luke pays no attention to my demands, he has a mind of his own, I'm mad and stomp my foot on the rail but he wont follow and I'm more like a kid than he is etc.---that Boston and Mexico Railroad of cross-dust Lowells---but arrived, the terminal trees not far from the *Sea!*

I REMEMBER JUST SCENES,---in that upstate dark spectral Albany I've over radiant highways driven to come visit the Pat Fitzpatrick-Marie couple and there's their house and it's like that old sad northstate dreamhouse cold in the winter unheated I'd been in with June---(Russia St.)----

Next scene is some cold old house like Watson's in Sarrington Fabrook with cold trees and pilgrim-haunted moon and moansqueek trees of cemeterial Puritanical Maniscal New England mixupery---all furnished, the house, and I'm proud saying 'Wait till Ma sees the house I got for her' ---I'm standing in a dark cold room, it's November in the soul (my soul)---

December they'll rake up a coffin from the ashes up front---

A GYMNASIUM, A REDHEADED GUY, a murder which I witness and then all night go boasting of it---the scene is Columbia campus presumably and Guy Green's around--- Truth is, the white ball basket had not yet been out of the view of the upper dwellers of the Fenway balcony when in a war of some kind I came and ran my rod around and matched mind with mind, finding in it the activity anxiety and also I wanted to be a college graduate and tried to imagine where and what benefits would accrue from a Diploma ---skip't the Army, ran out of town, saluted no flags, hid in the basement, made love to dark dolls, practiced dhyana in a Burma Cave--- "Owk the Kerouac & here he is, & Told," & I'm going around and make several pointed jokes about the famous war redhead murder which I witnessed in the reeds weeds and knives of a sunny battlefield out by Phillipine Park where the 3 Soldiers saw Snodgrass eating pussy and the Phellipaeen Kings came laying straw mats for the wounded Faustian Heroes of Moody Street and the West End Bar, a big huge grondualted I framshant hassel the size of all the dize wize nizers in the Potterst---cram! crash! crackcizy!---night followed sun,---I saw Guy, maybe Carlo the Porto Rican Hero, maybe Garden of whom ashcans of Henry Afghanistan St. and pink slip front-to-the-West bedroom murders of the sea, and Yucatan Blues (now)---the Vision of the red rust sun park gym all laid out in mem o ry---writ in its proper language---

(Speaking of 'Maries' and harking back to the second dream back t'other night it was that incorruptible

218

hot soft and wet gash of Marie Desmarais as she after long egrets and egressive folderols finally comes and lays on my Richmond Hill couch (in the livingroom) and I reach down and there it is ready to work, all lubricate---but first I must go to the toilet and leak and it's 6 A M and I wake up any- way---it's the dark and stank grail of the draven, high in the low dreamdark level cot sea or I mean smot flock blanket bot smot rot ran sea, also, can, ran, the Price of the Szelnicks is money changers of the Oogoo Temple---I dont like the hid- den sewer dank and holy's saved by scaramooch---as all chil- dren and childreyn ye are---

Revelations of the loose mind in Essence connection---)

WORKING IN THE OUT-OF-TOWN RIVER WATER- FRONT as strange longshoreman on the edge of a pier directing the dropdown crane to its vat where protein peanut Oil is churned, and to do so here I am acrobatin on the out- side of the rail and over the water and it is the same water of the waters of the 1943 Dream of Brooklyn Liberty Ship Pier which I dream'd because I had thoughts and fears of going back to sea, was being deceived by Iron Irrealities in the Discriminated Lapless Dark of the World and dove, or jumped ship, or suicided, and also as if with Julien on our Last Day. . .those waters, but in sultry Mississippi South---bunch of stevedores on the opposite slipside are laughing and watching me as I teeter and balance and wave for the dropt down rowboat to guide it---

RETURNED FROM THE HOSPITAL WITH EDDY
MACARTHUR (!) (little Irish chum, and from the
Gen.MacCarthur artilleries) we come to my house on West
St and I sneak around the back to see if anybody's home,
going thru the motions of darting low in the high dry crackly
grass beneath the windows but actually floundering in a
semi-effort to bend down head below window levels and not
bending nor rushing with any vigor and making a lot of
noise---looking into closed windows like the window of the
livingroom (dark, like black water) with its linoleum and
leather-thickwood furniture and mahogany radio---I blatter
down the backyard like this, along the wood fence which is
like the yard at Joe Fortier's the day I played the water games
around and around his house while he worked at grown-man
repairs---I see the little white doghouse---small woodshed in
the (now Phebe Ave like) yard and see it's got too many windows, openings, to be secured against winter winds for my
inhabitation and it's too small---come around, ring the bell
and rattle the screendoor, "front," but on a scaffolding to the
left, and high,---I see Eddy Mac waiting out front and Jeanne
Desmarais and a girl answering my summons (in shorts is
Marie)---they say "Your Pa is gone to get his briefcase" but
since I've so far only thought of my Ma I assume because
they dont mention her she's in the house, maybe sick in her
bedroom---I was too lacksaidaisical to be real Indian in my
sneak, nothing was real enough---the hospital was a madhouse somewhere

Death the bony owner---

SICK THROAT DREAMS, some virus that makes me swallow and swallow and it gets worse as I feel my throat's not there, as if cut out, so the swallowing swallows void and the more I try to swallow the worse it gets. . . .dreams that accompany this are of the infinite never-ceasing painful karma-activity of the discriminating brain picking up its harsh matter and tormenting out its cold subjects (which we keep calling life) . . .scenes in a Brooklyn like slum naborhood, every time I swallow it gets bigger, more complex, more painful. . .hoodlums, a lot of Sunday dawn action. . .in front of a poolhall-club at night, the big tree across the street, some of the details I remember (they are of a 'San Luis Obispo dream' nature). . .high up on a scaffold with Hal Hayes and little Hal Hayes as we're detected by the cops we start jumping to safety but little Hal jumps right down to the ground a hundred feet below---'No No!' I say as I watch him fall feet first. . .he seems to land unconcerned and safe in the sand, among a crowd---I keep wanting to be just clear and restful but Karma keeps grinding out these restless images, actions, I swallow in pain and it doubles like a hatching cell, the darkness multiplies, I see now how the mind should be (and is) and how Karma must end---Later Eisenhower or someone is in need of hot water in the upstairs of the Carolina school-hall so I go down to the cellar where Deni Bleu's been washing and get some water in a bucket--- In the sunny green field, beyond the redbrick school I want to buy a lot for my Ma's trailer, ask a farmer in a car, a sheriff--- Time's in the redbrick clock---At night in the surprisingly busy backstreets of the little Rocky Mount town I pass the broom wholesaler in his truck, young, and two old broom retailers arguing with him from the street, I see a pack of

221

brooms seven for 29¢---choking on life I see that the stuff of Karma is in Chinese called GHAT---it makes upon itself multiplying, in pain & sorrow---Where's everybody?---After Little Hal jumps, I fall, and as I fall and see the great height I realize this fall will kill me---Previous to going to sleep I'd daydream'd strangely of hitting flat on my face & bell y in a fatal fall from high, daydream'd the double *flapthwack* of brainpan digging brainpan slapping itself to death---the GHAT gets formless but still as yet more torturous---I get embroiled in GHAT entanglements of a hell underworld and wake up suffering, sick, take an anahist because my swallowing is feeding on swallowing and leaving me greater and greater need to swallow---Finally, as the pills work, round 2 P M, I with the window open and fresh air in dream of the 'Gabor Sisters'---one invites the other to join her in Australia while she gets her divorce---I see they'll refuse to recognize decay let alone awful GHAT and be 2 blondes smiling and yakking and being busy and active till they get oldish and fattish and still they'll pretend it's not happening and go smiling and clacking on busy lady heels to stores and finally they will be old and still wont believe that such a thing as sorrow has et them up, living continual self-deceptions with a smile and cosmetics to hide their horror---marrying, divorcing, remarrying---being the famous gay sisters to the world---ZaZa and Eva---never admitting their pain, horror, suffering, despair, evil old age, disease & death. . .the fruits of Karma, the rot of GHAT---pretending everything is the same,--- being Rumanian Slavic types a la Chekhov, that is, "weeping" instead of *understanding*. . .that life is not worth living and they should never have been born will be their final secret thought in the moment of the only deliverance possible to people like

222

that, death---poor fat shams with grown-old gams and gumming yams---blamming around in this World of Clams
                   I put ashes on the original
                   And it disappeared.

                   ★★★★★★★★★★★★★★★

SIX MONTHS LATER   JUNE 28, 1954
BRUE MOORE and I are at 59th St Boys Jazz Club and
we're going down to the Bowery to light fires in alleys and
he'll play his tenor horn---but it's sad October in the night
---cold, lost---

NOT LONG AFTER JOE MCCARTHY and I were at
that house on Riverside St at Moody, getting ready to go to
Bartlett Jr Hi together and I felt such sonlike loyalty for him,
we're in the back caucus room in presumably Washington
and he's mad at me because I banged my beerglass while talking to him on the phone---"You just did that deliberately,
you just have no excuse" but I want to know what difference
it makes---others are watching us---Mac says something
final that I dont catch but it is one of his tough cappers---
"What did you say?---*sir?*" I ask, wanting to be respectful,
and he seems to soften, wants to explain, the others are
impressed so much so that one tall guy invites me to his high
school party tomorrow night, thinking that I am now a
bonafide McCarthy fighter because I made him explain---At
the door of the hearing rooms in some kind of Arizona
Parade Town with plazas, a little workingman calls out to Joe
"Hey Joe when you thru woik?" and he's such a wild little

223

boozehound woiker you'd "think" it would damage Mac by association to answer him, what with all the American Ladies and Evening Posts watching---McCarthy refers him to me ---"He'll get you in, the French kid"---I'm riding away with Senator Jackson and others in the backseat of a convertible, I hear this---I whistle with my fingers---The woiker rushes up the other street to find me just as I jump out of the car and in the crowd I'll lose him now (at the Big Square) and I've lost my car ride, but I feel proud that Joe still considers me one of his aides---

LOST BIKES, LOST LOWELL MOONS---Lupine Road nightclubs---girls all night, all kinds---I'm sent to see the 'girl I'm going to marry' in the little village of Salem witches, she lives across the road near the town square, I knock, a big well-built ugly broad answers the door and I think quickly 'O well she's built---really beautifully'---but it's not she, it's 'she's' landlady---my 'she' is in the back, in her own room, humble, is pale, thinner, I cant get a good look at her yet because the landlady is bitching about how far in the room I can stay, how long, though they're both young---My girl has a definite personality, I see the side of her pretty but pale, slightly pimply face and I think 'And she's very sad, and retired, like a schoolteacher, like Bev Watson almost' (lying on afternoon couches in countryhouse rooms)---

It all erupts into a gigantic party at the foot of Lupine Road---I'd been up there, asking questions of Ma about my childhood---now, on Lakeview, the big hotel is having an orgy, you can see couples rushing in and out, they're dancing on the secondfloor marquee, smoking reefers---

crowds of toughs hang around the entrance---I'd been away
awhile at the Brooklyn pier where Joe and I each had a separate merchant ship and slept across the slip from each other
though at one time during the night in my scary bunk I suspected someone'd come on board maybe Joe---now I've
returned to the Lakeview house where the old man had died
that Stonewall sunset, events in there---I rush up the stairs of
the orgy hotel and knock on a door, inside's a naked colored
tall beauty and a man, she rushes out to talk in the hall and
instantly I grab her and pull her muff up, holding her pliable
fine rump, and she responds and we almost do it right there
but it aint time---She too has a definite personality, tall,
knows me, calls me a pet name---I run down in the dream
and borrow a bicycle and pedal down the Californias to my
home---Evelyn's been away, hasnt cooked supper for Cody
and the kids---Cody is Joe, I borrowed his friend's bike---At
the station I yell at the ticketseller thinking he's shortchanged
---'O I thought the ticket was 45¢!'---absurd idea, it's $1.65
to the city---I laugh, run out before the change and the ticket
are ready, to check on my bike realizing it wont be there, it's
stolen---In the gloom I search, search, sometimes finding old
bikes without wheels, skeletons of bikes but not mine---In
the weeds. . .It's the backside of a sad place I've known---I
come back to the ticket station, its lights are out, as I come
the little street has feet of sleepers sticking out of drapes and
I have to be careful---Upstairs in the redbrick apartment I see
the lit windows of more girlfriends---What will they say
when they've learned I lost the bike! I look for the ticketsta-
tion light, fumbling in the dark, there's a light in back where
probably the seller's still waiting with ticket and change, on
duty, joking with late other men---

225

By the time I'm in the library and I see the white ass of the colored girl wiping herself in the shed toilet, and have found my old junks I'd left under the fiction shelf ---nameless semi-rubberbands and semi-foods---all the forms the Dharmakaya One-Essence assumes, in these raving human dreams---this raving human Dream this world--- While looking for the bike in the weeds a kind of moist bee-like pebble fell into the side of my shoe and I walked on anyway, thinking, "It's wet, I hope it isnt a living bee---it's probably a wet fruit or a wet pebble'---and I left it in---and it warmed up---

BOISVERT IN A 3RD AVENUE UPPER EASTSIDE BUILDING, when I leave I look back and I see where I've been the windowshades are missing---In Richmond Hill I find a little man pushing a huge load of chairs and sofas he's found on the street, whistling at his work he is---does it every day, 's in business---I find stuff too, two chairs and push on home but arriving in driveway Ma's not home only Marie Desmarais and I've lost a chair---In Frisco I'm going past the big hotel and to my surprise I see smoke, water, hoses, broken windows, and I rush by musing "Hm, s'been a fire I guess"---

IN A DISMAL STUDIO ROOM in New York my whole family Ma Pa & Nin and I have taken up quarters and "all got jobs" and here it's night, one dim light burning, we're conversing but it's a weird conversation, it seems I dont realize what I'm doing and involuntarily or carelessly (because not fearing wrath of women relatives and forgotten the father's because he so long gone in death) I'm rolling a stick of tea and talking right at them some wild excited inanities (born of T) they dont even listen to, rather they're discussing me solemnish and my father gets up and says "He's not worried about marijuana? Eh?" and he comes over to my side---I see him coming and I go blind, darkness takes the place of the entire scene, nevertheless now I feel his touch on my arm, he may have an axe, he may have anything and I cant see---I fall fainting dead in the darkness, with a groan that wakes me up and prevents me from being found dead (if there is such a thing as death) in my bed in the morning---for my blood stop't beating when that Shroudy Traveller finally got his hand on me---He's getting closer & closer----I know how to be beyond him now---by not being concerned not believing in either life or death, if this can be possible in a humble Pratyeka at this time

LATER VERSION---In a dismal studio room in the gloom of one dim light in New York presumably I'm sitting rolling a stick of tea in my hands, high, talking to my father my mother & my sister and it seems that I'm a defiant strange nut who doesnt care about his female relatives what they think because he doesnt fear them and I have forgotten how to fear my father who has been away in death---As I hold the joint in my palm he gets up and comes over---apparently they have been discussing me and I inhuman beast had been talking excitedly into their suspicious void and that subject was my lunacy with tea: my father comes to my side as I go blind, everything disappears, the scene has a darkness in it utterly but I feel my father's hand touching me (my father's) by the arm

227

and he is going to belt me, tho I blind,---do something, he was grinning when last I could see---as he touches me I fall fainting into death and wake up with a cry in the night, a whimper, that I hadnt I done it to pump blood in my heart I wouldnt be alive this morning to write this---The Shroudy Traveller is Pa! And the Shroudy Traveller is death.

AFTER READING ABOUT THE TRAGIC REDSUN LOVERS who got lost on an iceberg at Islip Drownpond by floating out to sea later to be saved or discovered when they crash into a lover yatch, and reading about the great Michigan football team which included Keith Jennison, the final paragraph of the football Liberty Magazine article enjoyed only by waiters in dentist's offices dismally with pain to hide, telling of the great defensive backfield play of Jacky McGee, I find myself with the team flying from New York to "Detroit" in a jet plane---Also I'm reading a clear, well illustrated article about jets showing jets shooting off spurts, and spurt-holes---the whole team neatly suited and tied in plush seats, as we come into Chicago and below I see familiar monuments and vast gray avenues of pain and wellknown dream location I say "Chicago! Hey look we're already in Chicago in one hour!" but everybody is so blasé about airplanes and I'm trying to tell the Aislewashing Attendant Pilot but he's too busy with his pail---We're landing at the airstrip but suddenly it's not an airstrip at all and nobody said we were s'posed to land in Chicago ("Air travel would be much safer if you didnt go landing around everywhere!" I think petulantly)---It's road outside town in a vast park, a straight road but here comes a bus---it moves aside a few feet for us

---we make a perfect 3-point landing, no bump, but we're going 200 M.P.H. on that damn road, a straight road though ---the bus keeps going its own way casually, it's a kind of brown Macy's delivery bus---Here comes a car---the pilot with his special cynical face as though he was a communist deliberately landing us at Chi to create a confusion, swerves aside close to the soft shoulders for the car and I picture us flip flopping over but we dont---My belt is tight on but nobody is concerned, leastwise the aislewasher standing in the aisle smiling---"You'll have to lay over till 3 this afternoon and get a plane via Porto Rico to Detroit" I hear, and it makes me mad to think this is all deliberate airline employee union confusion---We're landed.

WATERING MY GARDEN with a plant I've pulled out and now shaking, it had a tuft of grass "that Little Luke had planted"---now it shakes water all over and has a heavy "cedar" core which, when I've cleaned it of dirt and emptied it of water, is a neat wooden box with slit and makes a ter-rific little bongo drum---Aunt Loretta wants one too---

FLYWHEELS UNDER THE BOXCARS, so the old con-ductor is showing me "how to ride the rods" and crawl around the flywheels when in motion---We're at the Brooklyn Waterfront Yards and I've been "cutting the lines" on the floats with big machete knife loaned to me (as you'd loan a lamp) by the railroad---I tell them "I'll bring my own machete Monday"---the lines are not float lines, but ropes, or "rope-brakes" on the freights, which I hack and snap---We

229

go to the conductor's room in a brick building and I see all the seamen going in the other door and remember that door from long before when I was a seadog---I see listlessly the bleak brick dead alley, the iron door, the Negro Unioneers, and I think "All that hateful bunch of men in one trap, no wonder I hated going to sea."

LEO DUROCHER'S BASEBALL ARMY is encamped by the river, Iddyboy is the Campanella-like catcher and I'm in right field cursing him irritably for mistakes he makes throwing to 2nd for nothing but reprimand myself for losing my temper---Durocher is cutting off thousands of us, me included, I'm talking to him and his assistant about how lazy I've been and not trying at all, in a stone locker like of football dreams of Leo's like Lou---there are treks later in a brown field, like boot camps---"Aw go to hell" I tell Durocher and we almost fight---

FOOLING MY MOTHER all night long with stories about the young well-dressed Negro who starts big fires, you see him climbing around fire escapes of the night, with pipe in mouth, porkpie hat, calm---She's worries and scared---Come morning in our house on apparently Crawford St. I tell my mother "Hear those loud fire siren?---"Is it your nigger again?"---"No I was only foolin you, he doesnt do that at all"---but she refuses to disbelieve it now---I go off down the morning street, it is empty, silent and coldly red in a hill-cracking winter sun, beautiful, sharply real in the dream like a song I'd once known and lost and was now recovered heartbreakingly keen at my brain---that is to say, clean marselle of the red nike clat sun, the frost Raw, and I'm a little furnishing dike casiling down the easy mark---(here I tried to write clairvoyant subconscious prose but looked up from time to time at Giants and Dodgers on TV screen---pfft)

DREAMS IN ROCKY MOUNT   Summer 1954
IN THE GRAVEL COURT of an apartment on VanWyck Blvd. I'm standing, evening, I can see a vicious fight going on up the street, a crowd, and as I usually do I pay no attention, as tho it wasnt real, or within the purview of a Nirvana Saint ---but the fight rages across the street & closer, I hear shouts and suddenly I see it's a gang of hoodlums trying to control one whiteshirted maniac punk who's been attacking everyone in sight---As in a dream I see him running in the gloaming towards me---I see he has a knife---I watch with strange dreamlike detachment---He comes up, raises his knife to strike and still I'm detached action-wise but terror floods my realizing mind, fear holds me paralyzed and disbelieving--- Just at the last second I see Jack striking the face, I have left the body and am watching and it all wakes up---I may have been too late---Earlier it was a $4.40-a-week hotel room on Third Street Frisco, "cheaper than the Cameo," and I go in, up carpeted stuffy Skidrow stairs, past lonesome cockroach doors, but suddenly it's a huge mahogany University Club reading room with 100-foot ceiling and everybody reading, playing cards, smoking, though at the end there're several beds with sleepers in a bright light who dont care about privacy and probably pay $ 3 a week ------

BUILDING A SHACK IN A GARAGE in Richmond New York with scores of friends around---ridiculous---I havent got any proper lumber and one friend tried to make a door top with driftwood---I feel futile and must get money for lumber---Everybody drunk---it's really at the North Common in Lowell

LUNCHCART HANGOUT OF FUTURISTIC TEEN-AGERS somewhere in a room in Lower Centreville Lowell near the confluence of Aiken & Lakeview where lately I've been getting so many dreams of futuristic events and excitements (the Four Brothers, the angered father of Peru), big structures like pyramids in wood out on a sad Surrealist Worlds Fair plain---Deni is showing me a postcard he just received from my mother reprimanding him for his recent attacks on me---It is drawn in pictures, showing vehicular arrangements of people sitting and riding and their positions among the symbols and signs she's drawn---There are 2 other people, a couple---But suddenly I get the tremendous piercingly clear idea: "Deni I am going to Lupine Road now to see the house I was born in---" Deni, always unpredictable in that tremendous gamut he runs, as if innocently between malice and sweetness, is very impressed and looks at me with almost frightened eyes---"the house you were born in?---you hear that?" he says to the couple---And, because I've just realized I'm back home in hometown Lowell, I get a clear vision of myself going up Lilley and over to the cemetery at Hildreth then down into the Fellaheen Mystery of the wooden tenements down Aiken to Lakeview to the wooded hill of Lupine so bloodsoaked in lore sun in my brain---at the same time I catch suspecting that I'll never really go but hang around gabbing with these people---I live in Pawtucketville across the river and this walk will be on the way home---It's 4 P M sun outside---Suddenly it's night and I aint done it---

TWO DREAMS FROM APRIL CROSS COUNTRY BUS TRIP
TWO BIRDS START FIGHTING AT MY EAR on Bridge Street over the river, they increase their fury and are screaming and biting and scratching with a furious eerie lunacy---they'll end up picking my brains thru my ear

IN THE HALLWAY OVER TEXTILE LUNCH he's come, the Shrouded Traveller who followed me across the desert in 1945---he stands, in an ordinary white shirt, looking at me without expression---it's late at night and the light is on in the wooden tenement hall---He wants to reach out for me---
These 2 dreams are madness & death

HORRIBLE! Aunt Jeanne of Lynn is staying at my house over the Textile Lunch just as I'm coming in and undressing with Maggie Zimmerman for a ball---we're in the kitchen among litters of clothes, boxes---"Why dont you go away!" I yell at the old intruder who is watching us---"I will not!" ---I'm undressed right in front of her, lead girl to my bedroom---In there we start---I hear Aunt Jeanne still yakking and threatening in the kitchen---"If she comes in this room we'll go right on paying no attention to her"---But suddenly

I feel like insulting Aunt J, and when she addresses another complaint at us (and girl couldnt care less) I say "I'm not Jack ---that's not who it is---it's *Noël*" (her son)---"O Noël, is it" she says ominously "We'll see about that" and she goes to the phone to call my mother at the shoeshop---"Go ahead you old interfering fool!" I yell---When my mother comes home I'll have my bag packed and just take off---after I'm finish't with girl---

WHERE GOETH THE SPIRIT OF THE LIVING? that I should dream I'm going up 2nd Avenue in New York on a cool Summer night among the glittering lights, by bars where crowds of men all look up beer-in-hand at the TV fight, where boys play in the street and bump against me as I walk on hunching my shoulders to show how tuff I am--- where to? what final light ahead?

A MAN TIED AT A STAKE to be killed, the executioner sticks two little slivers of steel in his belly which doesnt hurt the man as much as he thought it would so that he waits expectantly, without pain, in curiosity and silence---but the wretched executioner has a thin smile, pulls out a gadget like a vegetable grinder or like a tin toaster that you put on stoves over the heat and lay the toasts on the 4 sides---it is a pre-arranged hooker for the 2 slivers of steel, an ingenious, ghastly, murderous invention of the beast himself---As the victim watches, still with that heartbreaking lamblike expec-tant curiosity he steps up, hooks the 2 slivers in the inside of the tin gadget, and pulls up---Some action takes place to

234

Hara Kari the man's entire guts, he lets out a gurg of horrified pain and twists up, tied, and dies---head falling down---

AT A TEENAGE HANGOUT or Village nightclub on 14th St near 5th Avenue in the strange New York night I'm with Ma, who wanted to come along---But it's a dim Apache sinister place and she's out of place but curious---A beautiful redhead is sitting with me in a booth with two other guys, one of them like Tod of Easonburg, big, thick, quiet---The girl throws two quarters on the table saying "Anybody wanta f--k?"---I leap at the chance, but there's some understanding that Tod is supposed to make it also (the 2 quarters) but he doesnt move so without looking at him and without having bought any beer I pick up the nearest beer bottle and up-end it and drain it and slide out of the booth pulling the girl--- We are walking down 14th Street at 3 AM towards Deni Bleu's pad, Ma is with us, tired---she wants to sleep---I suddenly realize I have no right to bring people to Deni's in the middle of the night--- "Better go home on the subway to Queens" I tell Ma---she's too sleepy, doesnt want to---the redhead is now a nonchalant Maggie Zimmerman walking along quietly with me---Next thing you know I'm all alone on the El in the vast lost Brooklyns, got so many things and junk I'm carrying and some ice-cream-fruit-salad-and-vegetable salad oil slopped together and melting in a carton, but good---I spill some on my shirt and am wiping it when (now a bus) the bus pulls up at Richmond Junction Stop---I wipe while the man next to me struggles out via my knees---Then I gather all my junks, my teamster transfer and rush to the front just as the last little girl is getting out---"Hey,---I'm getting out here!" I yell but the driver wants to screw me up and drives on, fast, flapping the doors shut---I yell and struggle down the aisle---He refuses the transfer on some grounds I cant hear---the passengers seem to be on my side and are yelling me instructions---The busdriver insanely shouts "I heard you say so-and-so, you were trying to bribe me, I'm going to have you hauled in the police court---"

"Stop the goddam bus!" I shout seeing now he's just a nut---He gets red in the face---"I'm gonna have you fined and put away"---He momentarily is frightening me with his imposing legal and busdriver authority threats---But I say "Stop so I can get out here!" and I dont have time to tell him I've got too much stuff to struggle ten blocks back with but he goes even faster---So I up and shove my heel in his face just as everybody's going to scream and the bus is going to careen---and wake up, my heel kicking in the air--- of the bed---

FATHER & SON EPIC, finally (me) the father is hopping freights East and meets his 10 year old son doing same thing --- "His face so covered with soot the father cant recognize him"---I am the little boy as well as the father---It's a place like Santa Margarita, in the mountains, a grove of woods across the track---A freight train is heading into a siding and I'm (with my pack) trying to decide the best way to get on so it wont be going too fast for the baby---I'm running at a slow dog trot for his sake, almost a slowmotion dogtrot---I waited too long because the freight headed in gathering momentum after the throwing of the switch by the head man but now it's balling thru quite fast, a long siding, I see that the hotshot pas-

senger is already balling by the upper switch and I get a dream
fear the freight will just hiball the gate and go on---everything
compressed and speeded up---but lo, even so, another freight
is coming down the mainline behind the passenger so we'll
have plenty of time to get on and I pick the second to last car
which is abreast of us now, doors open---There is no caboose
on the rear of this spectral train---At this moment as I'm running slowmotion to the open car with the kid I hear shouts
and see two dirty roughlooking bums hightailin it out of the
grove of trees with unmistakable intention to beat me for
what I got in pocket & pack---I have money folded in my
back pocket and stuff of value in the heavy pack along with
my lost blue halftoothbrush which proudly I've allocated to
my extra pants---"I have no knife!" I think with horror, no
defense, no rocks---As if alone, gibbering in haunted world, I
start running down a pebbly hillside but stop realizing they'll
catch me with my slow pack---I think of throwing rocks but
they can throw em back---I think of running for the open car
but it's stopping now and all this will happen in the passing
roar of the other freight hiballing alongside so nobody in the
world can hear murder and I think with horror of the impres-
sion this will make on the heart of the little boy---I'm all tangled in the molasses of self dream---wake up wishing I could
be Buddha and have no fear of selfhood, of the dissolution of
self, of pain and insult and death---

> If God were real everything would be honey
> And so everything is honey truly

A VICIOUS WAR with all the American infantrymen continually blasting away with their rifles but I'm the Company

Joker Imbecile who's always losing his gun and looking for another that works so in the midst of battle (on ramparts, hills, in copses, against enemy soldiers hiding) you hear me yelling "Where's my gun hey?" and everybody too busy to pay attention or even laugh---My sadsack soldier role---But at one point I look up and realize the vast ruin of a European town we're in, the architecture of the town clearly seen in the rubble---I'm lost and cant find my company,no one cares, it's a huge new war---

AIRPLANE DISASTERS(in this same war) have been recorded by a camera device that takes pictures of people while they're crashing you see their agony and even one shot of a man rolling over in smoke---(at the crash)---the device never breaks---We're watching a series of pictures---I am completely horrified because I identify myself and forget it's a (dream) device taking the pictures---Civilian passengers are shown in a writhing tormented assembly in the brave brown plane as it's hurling downward in the night to crash and kill them all---You see men looking at one another with expressions of intolerable regret---I watch one man looking down at the floor quietly--- as the others moan and pray and writhe---He is going to allow the crash to take him quietly---But as the picture goes on, closer and closer to the actual contact moment of death as the plane nears the ground, our hero has jumped up and is shout- ing---No matter who you look at, the face (women, children, men) shows something never seen before on that face and never to be seen again---Intolerable regret and great bemused understanding streaked with pale sashes of fear so great I myself tormented to see it---You see shots of the dying in the smoke

and flames, famous heroes in throes of agony alone not knowing their pictures are being taken or that anyone will ever see
this or that anything will ever happen again---It's the
Loneliness of Death, the selfhood of death---the fruits of self at
last and the pain and terror of it---Its hold was so great, the letting go of it is a great terrified wrenching---O if I could only
describe those faces, the eyes at last looking with a new, a final
realization of something---Their throats gulping when they try
to take it quietly, some sobbing in hands as the poor world falls
screaming to destruction---Og-----OM! Deliver all sentient
beings with thy diamond mace!

I GOOF, DISCOVERING A LONG PAPER BAR OF
SILVER worth a fortune but tore it up and shortened it and
didnt care and now my sister's fixing it, to get the money, so
now I want the money too---She's pasting it on the wall, in
her shorts, it's Sarah Avenue---it's a long paper tape of "silver
paper" found and reaped in the mines---
        Later it's Crawford Street and I'm not so
happy to be back there with family because it was scene of
adolescent problems, sadder, while Sarah was Blithe---I see
gangs of boys playing self invented baseball games on long
street by park, I see one gang standing next to each other in
lil circle with first base second base third base they can reach
with their arms without running and the pitcher stands right
in front of the batter delivering infinitesimal pitches which
when hit are transferred tinily to first by hand and game is so
small, a *city* game, take up no room---
        Something about Mike Plouffe---where he's
the new intellectual hero of Pawtucketville---Sunday morning

in the poolhall, and something about me recalcitrant---Ah that great and Venice-City of the war!---dry, blasted---

The fastest runner in the world is a colored kid with curly hair, his name is mentioned, he just beats everybody, the 100 in 9.2, only 17 years old---or 16---

Something which was kept clean and shiny all night long in these dreams is now gone rusty and I wake up and get up---a kind of chamber locker, polished by Ma, now gone red rough rusty

IN A YARD SO VAST are Joe and I when I'm to go get something at the house it's a long trek across the lawn on which scattered gangs of boys are playing long fungo--- shouting remotely---Joe and I were sitting against the wirefence when a stranger in a suit showed up and we both said 'Isnt that Dicky Hampshire'? tho because he was lost at Bataan we dont take our supposition seriously---Darker and bigger it *is* Dicky---"I knew it was you by the back of your head"---There is no elation of reunion or rediscovery just serious handshaking and calm Bhikku gravity and aloofness ---Joe is "grown up" and well combed and big---Later we're in my Sarah Yard and then something happens to the dream whereby I take and remove a wall of my mother's house to the other side of the street to "make more room" but now traffic interrupts the house and you never wanta go for water (to the kitchen) across all that traffic---There are 4 little Pinky kitties in the grocery store, I gather tbem cursing---I want to rearrange the wall and the furniture and the house together again before Ma gets home from work----that long dry tired lawn---

NEGRO IN THE ROAD in the South is offering to sell me 2 lbs. tea for $200---I tell him that's a good price---He wears a white shirt, we stand in the side of the road---Later I'm in some inexplicable ruin of Mexico with gigantic strange moving objects like boats passing in and out of the pyramid canal ---Had come to Mexico in an airplane with Nin & Ma, I looked down and saw white burros and White bulls in the grass and I'd said "That's Mexico" but then we began to fly very very low, over familiar American looking cities, I was also worried about our loss of altitude "no higher'n a train," I thought---Then I was in Danny Richman and Bill Wolf's Clothing store, they're in the back talking with people as I contemplate a sweatshirt I want to buy at once, or steal, and wear it as I come to greet them---Wolfe sees me eying the clothes---I'm naked from the waist up---There's a big murder case going on and cops, detectives keep coming to Ma's house to check on evidence, I'm in my room when the cop comes with my book and says "Page 7 here--" and goes to tear the first 7 pages out but I yell angrily "Dont *tear them*" ---"Dont worry I wont, I just wanta check on something" and shows me my name on the police register John Louis Detul and on my papers John Louis Detail---I say "Dont blame me, the Seargant forgot to put the I---see the dot of the I there?" My mother says "I'm not goin to Mexico, I dont want people looking at my papers all the time"---I get mad and say "O it isnt like that,there's only old cops and your tourist card and they dont even bother you!"---"Old blue bums"---The cop leaves and all the time we'd been talking and checking the papers I had a super long joint right in the palm of my hand, I'd just rolled it in my room---I even gestured with it in my palm and the cop saw it but wasnt sure it

241

was a white thingamajig or other---So now I'm hiding it
under a corner of the same linoleum I used to turn up as a
child to race my glasses of an incline---"The same linoleum
and room of childish fancies" I think, "which is now the
scene of my serious writings and grownup concerns"---

Those vast Gelatinous Drawbridges in the
Mexico River of Pyramid Squares, gray, I cant recall or realize how to say about it---but we were there, smiling---

I'VE GOT MY BIG NOTRE DAME N a red and white
sweater but I'm worried no one in the streets will know it's
for Notre Dame and I'm making plans to go there and play
football in the Fall even if I'm 31---"I'll be tired but I go to
do it One Season"---I live on Crawford St or Phebe and I'm
thinking "Now it's Sunday morning and I'm in Lowell---no
sense walking to Kearney Square or---I've seen all that---it's
no good on Sundays at Kresge's---the sad cars, the lil girls of
the movies---I can see GJ later"---Across the street is GJ's
house, it still looks the same---"I'll go to church, watch the
guys in front of Blezan's after, like in Doctor Sax"---

Some friend of mine is so tired he cant go to
the store with me but learning that I've just been playing football in the field he wants to try that, no matter how tired---

I see beautiful red checked Peaches resum-
ing her trip on the train, next to last seat in row,---my pants
are hanging on the hook behind her---I want to sit with her
but cant get her attention as she's talking excitedly to folks
across the aisle---"She looks much better now she's had her
rest---she was pale before"---

SOME CASTLE SOMEWHERE with dark and happy events that have to do with an airplane trip *over the road* from Frisco to Portland, the driver making amazing turns considering his huge wings---he even politely moves over for oncoming cars yet he's doing 200 mph and sometimes I think he's going to take off anyway but we end up on the road in Portland Oregon, we see it written in big letters---This trip is part of my big "one-day roundtrip to California"---The flight west is fast and pleasant, I'm with Hubbard commenting on it---Arriving in San Jose Evelyn and June Evans are there, I mention tea to Cody who tries to hide he's interested---June is curiously sisterlike, humorous as ever, seems to respect me now---There's something I cant find in my things on the floor of the extra room---I go down to the yard office which is also a Castle and sign up and work a quick trip at sun bomb sea war dawn and as I tell Cody later 'My eyes couldnt stay open so Conductor Devlin let me close them so I made the run to Watsonville digging it with my EARS--- (the Western Pacific crossing knock noise)" I think of adding later in the dream-slap-recap---Once again that strange silo or structure stands "outside San Jose near Coyote," like a coal chute, second time I've seen it, it was near those ravelled drought fields, near Eden and on the track actually---

June Evans, I seem to be in love with her and she's my love now---Arriving in Watsonville which is also like San Luis Obispo and War Towns I go across that dark field of the trains, register, and come right back, for San Jose, where I'm riding in a kind of subway with Cody and two brakies and Cody and I have our arms around each other's necks in great prophetic tenderness and I wake in the dream to this with joy---we're gonna get our T, I'm gonna get my June, he's got his Evelyn, Bull Hubbard's coming, "I've *heard* the run to Watsonville" I'm telling the amazed brakies who are new close friends of Cody's, with definite personalities, from Frisco, whom I'll intelligently befriend now, in the glad San Jose night---Yet I'm flying back East immediately! Onl y to be dream'd after the Samadhi on "Infinite Void"---

A NEW LITTLE HOUSE on the location of Nin's present house in the South, Ma & Nin and I move in and we're joy-fully moving the furniture and fixing the place---I got out in the backyard and found a pile of junk left by the previous family which is however all kinds of good expensive things like hand mirror, books, old electric fans, linoleum covers, ashtrays, flowerpots, even clocks, boxes of matches, pillows, clothes, cups, towels, slipcovers---I go out occasionally whenever I need anything to fix a corner of the house---I have my own room, my own writing-room also (!) and I'm gonna fix it up like an office with desk in the middle of the room receiving all the light from the huge windows, at which I'll sit like an executive all gray windy Atlantic days doing something---The house has those nameless blear tearful win-dows, golden, yellow, strange, always wanted it

A NEW CAR, a 1949 station wagon Ma bought, Cody is driving it for us, testing it, non commital, in Frisco---But later it's a lil jaloppy coupe and I'm driving Ma West in it, hot floorboards---There's a smalltown with narrow streets thru which we pass, like the narrow Strawberry Blonde Streets of downtown Nashua there's a great crowd of people on their

summer eve steps because of apparently the couple locked
arm in arm asleep on the church steps but on closer inspec-
tion by the tall storeclerk they are dead, he picks a shrimp
from the locker case in which now they are drown'd, immers't
completely, and smells it and makes a face, and so everybody
knows they're dead---My mind also said 'drown'd in Clams'
---or 'oysters,' like Ricky's oyster bath---Meanwhile on a train
with a rear platform elaborately railed we're gonna have the
big picnic and we've even set out little discs of light in the
track to light, so we wont fall over---the train's stopped and
it's on the California track---Ma has the lunch ready, Nin, etc.
a gay outside roast--- It's a very broad train, like ship poopdeck
and the rail is like the rail of the work flat on the New York
Dock Railway---Ma goes off to get something and it turns
out there's been a murder since, some people pass through,
joke with us, including an angry woman I inaccurately for
some reason quote as saying some drunken hating "You son of
a bitch" thing but to my surprise the railroad clerk also reports
unfavorably on her (to the investigators) going through a
funny routine of her, leaning against his cage and suddenly he's
a respectable woman imitating a slut so well you begin to won-
der---Crowds are coming so when Ma comes back all glad and
gleelike and innocent to resume our glad party, I have to tell
her what happ'd---Later I'm feeding Pinky Lee but cant find
his can of Fish and remember I'd gone and dumped it in the
hallway can which was accidentally slopped chock full of water,
so drowning into uselessness a little panful of cat meal---but I
go and resurrect the fish out of the water---It's a pile of
garbage and junk in the hall, it's some kind of feeble hotel---

        I was driving that coupe with great gladness
swiftly over goodroads, pale gray asphalt, lotsa curves, but good

double lane size, with white line, rough surface to hold the tires---"Goin to Lowell via Hartford and Worcester" I think

A DOUBLESIZE TRAILER some people had (pack-wagon) which is really a big useless Trailer with wood rails and no top, wanted to sell it to Ma and me---They stopped at our roadside house on the sunny dirtroad of the Old Shrouded Arab Dream---I advised Ma not to buy it---But these people were Okies Old and had an old man with em on whom I felt it incumbent on me to take pity so I mixed him a ice n water jug in the kitchen but it seems the ice is wine-encrusted or soaked and the glass jug is full of red portwine, so I plan on telling the travelers that I've made them a pot of Wine Water with Ice, a big glass at that and their dusty road travails'll be nil---The old man with white hair, I worry about him, I struggle to get the wine outa the ice cause I really want to help, refresh and please him---the hot sun is shining, it's summer in the Dream

RUNNING OUTDOOR TRACK on a gray cool day, the 120 yard or so dash around the final turn, on cork track, I negotiate it pumping as fast as I can go, I'm the littlest guy there and I have a little red uniform---The coach doesnt let us go back to the starting line over the field or track but insists that we walk in the concrete underground ramps that I complain to a fellow track man havent got any air---I see Big Paul Franco the 3rd Cook of the Carruth looking to get out from under there to be at the finish line, sweating, not complaining -- The Coach is making like-railroad-signs and

I cant understand them,tall blond co-tracker is responding with signs---arms off hips, etc., I complain "What the hell do they mean?"---I daydream that I'll win the dash and beat all the tall guys---

A PENTHOUSE IN THE MIDDLE OF A GREAT CITY RUBBLE PLAIN in gray Chicago, Deni Bleu's blonde mistress lives there, I meet Hank there---there are beds, candy bars, like-French-Movie scenes of architectural surrealist ramps out the windows, at one point Great Night falls over the Metropolis Dump like Hubbard's Tin Nightclubs Plain, the stars, the dim lamps, the hoodlum spaces where woolcap gangs roam in rubbly sulphur fields like Jackie Cooper and Jackie Coogan and Kid Gangs and rat fenders and maybe underground walkramps and like Bull says houses suspended from cables---Deni lofts his great happy laugh in the Towers, 'Kerouac you slay Me'---Something about a half an Almond Joy and a Half a Fifth Avenue---It's in the grisly downtown later among gray Pittsburghy crowds I'm walking with Ma and Hank to meet his tall blonde---He makes a phonecall in a booth, we wait downstreet for 15 minutes, he is goofling with his girl---

BANQUETS, GANGS, at a neighborhood party like in Chicago Mel Torme (I keep identifying that way, Mel Torme for some reason, the lil blond singer from Chicago)---but a guy is intimidating me in a room with a bread knife and in panic half awake I rush up and grab the knife by the blade and there is no pain for a moment as I wake up like to wince

247

then resume the dream and have the knife which I hold by the blade Commando style and sink into his chest but it doesnt hurt him and everybody is shocked as by a vulgar faux pas----me most of all---but I feel that "I've conquered my fear of knives" and wake up, spectrally neither victor nor saint in this hasslish mystery of emptiness

NICE FRESH APPLES, red and hard and juicy, fallen on the sidewalk on Van Wyck Boulevard and I'm coming along stuffing them in my pockets, finally my shirt pockets, finally no room I pick up a box found in a drugstore doorway and use it---There are also other red apples apparently bounced off the same truck but soft and no good and dry and I leave them there---I eat one of the good ones and surprisingly it turns soft and old ere I'm finished, tasting at the end like a ruined old plum---I barge across the porch with my loot and Mrs. Whiteheart, Ma, Nin, Luke, others are all there---Mrs. W wants to know what I got, wants some, I rush into house saying "I found some apples (and I'm keeping em)" (under my breath) "I've got only a few---" I say out loud but Nin has followed me and I say "I've only got enough for you and Lil Luke---When Ma comes in she can have hers"---there are multitudes on the porch---Nin takes two---

US KIDS SWIM OFF A GRAY PIER, dive off, I go down the street after emptying my pockets of old roaches and think "I better go through all my stuff"---I live in the Fortier cellar in a dismal damp room furnished like a vampire's castle---People visit me---I go to Danny Richman's and Bill Wolfe's business store and they're having a big argument about something they're fixing or trying to sell---We cut and measure it out, some nameless huge taffy, we taste it---Then there's a marvelous rack of delicate chocolates and flavors from all over the world and ground cinammon nuts and coffee fruits and they mix em all up in a big batter and bake and Coffee Cake emerges which is the most delicious thing in the world---"That's yesterday's unfresh cake," I say, "Can I have it?"---they don't even comment, I'm to understand they only eat freshly baked Coffee Cake---Bill says of a nut dropped "I'll eat it, they're askin a lot for it" and he plops it in his mouth as Danny does the mixing---I try a sweet bitter chocolate piece shaped like a little stove, from a box in the rack---the Cake comes out square, streaked with colors like a marble cake, suffused with exotic African and Brazilian flavors, crunchy with Cocoa nuts and Nutmeg Nuts and Crushed Chunky Nut---it's terrific---I hope they'll give me some, they hardly know I'm there----

THERE'S BEEN A TRIP BY BOAT TO AFRICA earlier, the grey West Coast of Barbary, treks in the interior, Wars around---that long Siberial Africa

HUGE DORMITORIES OUTSIDE PARIS for Jewish Orphans but they are so vast, numerous---my guide says "The whole underground hid in these things during the War"---the buildings are 15-stories tall, vast as Knickerbocker Village, black with whiteframe windows and there are endless rows and depths of them, millions could live there---

"There's that many Jews?" I thought---We came to the shopping center of activity and on the other side more of these
buildings continued---It was France, the same outside suburb
of Paris not quite Paris landscape---Earlier we'd been up on
Pauline's hill street (18th) in Lowell and there was a busdriver,
a baseball bat---it went to the snowy Lowell garages downtown and our jaloppy is being repaired by Mechanics but the
girl wants the 'twist key' I call the ignition, or the 'in-key'---
says she'll fix it herself, races the motor---my gang's been up
on Lilly Street Hill which is crowded with snow sliders and
sunshine and joy and those same great War Land Buildings I
saw ruined the other night, the world opening up joyously
everywhere now---"Let's go to Frisco!" I tell the gang. "This
minute!"---it's the Green Clunker, Gold is driving it---"First
we'll get Freddy" (who's sliding)---We start from the garage
through the gay Square---

I'M LOOKING IN THE MIRROR at my back molars and
I can yak out my whole toothiness jaw so's ya can see like the
skeletal hint of what's to be, the leer of bone teeth---the
Molars are huge and have a single verticle dirty line running
down em that makes me sick shudder to think Ive grown so
old-&-decayed & am such a skeleton---I snap my jaw back in

EVERYBODY MOVES WITH A STAMPEDING ROAR
when the time comes for all to go en masse to the great World
Premiere in the rain but there's only one car, one coach train
car, at the door, admitting just so many, & the car is soon full,
fact I dont even see it fill or anyone get in, & the Public

Address shouts "That's enough, that's the first load" and he's been working everyone up to a frenzy of excitement to get to the Premiere and now it'll take all night to even get the people there let alone raise the curtain on the first rainblear brownmoth mask---I see the theater, the night, the marquee, the empty street, the one vehicle coming like a worm in the Science Fiction or Crazy Mad Comic Night to discharge Martian Lilliputian passengers, First Nighters yet---"We'll all go!" is the shout in the Tortured Hall---I've been wreagling all night to wrongle myself a wrass to get in---Write!

I'M AT MY RAINY MORNING WORKDESK in shroudy Manhattan and I look down by the dock and see the Navy vessels anchored in the bay and the crowds of sailors walking on the water towards the land---I say "Everybody's learnt that trick now---it seems to be easy---too easy---it must be some simple gimmick"---

EASING OUT THE THROTTLE in the dreammistaken belief that I was cutting off the ignition I let the Old Clunker of Cody's coast down the 2 steep highways, going to get ice cream & only when I'm there at the bottom of the hill I realize the clunker'll never make it back up, maybe no more gas to boot, and I will have fouled Cody's lil extra car

GOING ON A TRIP TO NEW ENGLAND with Ma, in a bus, slow, long trip grinding up trafficky hills----a blonde woman, thin and almost middleaged keeps throwing herself

251

on my lap so finally I sit with her and try to feel her up but she wont let me touch but keeps annoying me with her false sexuality---the bus is so crowded Ma's in a seat with 2 others, one of whom sits high on a pillow on the arm---Ma wants me to sit with her, somehow we got separated during the long trip---I look out the window and see the dreary New England wood tenements and traffic lights "When do we get to Boston?"---Eleven hours of slow riding---Finally Ma is sitting in front wedged in and displeased in the world and I've got that blonde in her kimono and trying to feel and it's disgusting me to be so animal in a piteous world---

MICKEY MANTLE, he's on TV, at bat, the bat's in his hand when the fight starts and you see the cleancut young America Hero swinging the bat right at the guy's legs, cutting him down, you see flailing white uniformed ballplayers, explosions of violence on the screen

VERY AFFECTIONATE OLD DREAM OF HAL HAYES, Kafka novels, Raphael Urso studying, in the library, rows of books---Hal has a vast shelffull of books of all kinds, plus voluminous huge personal notes on music handprinted by him painstakingly in ink in vast ledgers that some hoodlum-type or boss or ambiguous intruder is leafing thru and wondering out loud, as Hal & his girl humbly watch---"Wow, is that poor Hal studying!" I think. "He knows as much about music as Nietzsche"---Meanwhile Raphael is reading by another shelf, head bent---I see the exciting bright covers of The Trial and The Castle by Kafka, I want to take The Trial home and start

an interesting new year of reading & study---I feel very happy
---the air is cool, Autumnal when I wake up---

JUMPING INTO THE TROLLEY on a rainy night in
Frisco, on Broadway going down to the 'Barcadero, that same
location dreamed before as in bright sun of sea-going day
now's in the drizzle of the Hilltop Frisco Russian Hill Dream
when I stopt on top during a long walk and suddenly felt the
awful spectrality of "all of us" being there on Russian Hill---
I get in the trolley behind a sailor just as the conductor has
walked back 5 paces to joke with the rear man, I sit down
(normally, not cheating) like a flash behind the sailor's walking figure and just then the conductor turns and sees only the
sailor getting in and doesnt even notice me and I've saved a
dime---which I think "I might as well" do, remembering past
savings like this---I'm working, because later I'm in my room,
workclothes all over, ben workin with Joe McCarthy across
the hot dusty infantry fields carrying enormous dufflebags---
When our day is through we see another batch of soldiers
lounging on tufts of earth near the barrier of the official
Army grounds and the big buildings---"You the boys from
Cranford I sent for?" says Mac---"Yes sir"---"Report at
10 o'clock tomorrow morning"---I can see they're gonna
have a ball tonight but McCarthy who's been struggling all
day in impossible travails in the hot sun is only going to allow
himself 2 extra hours of sleep and come right back tomorrow
---Now, later, I'm riding the worktrain across the hot dusty
flats, playfully dangling one foot near the ground, and I'm
thinking "I forgot my money and my Hinayane check in the
room?" and thinking "After another week a this and another

$55 catch-up I'll go back on the railroad up at San Jose"---
but I wake up on my quiet couch of Tao repose realizing I
only want a life of inaction and adventure every day---

GIANT ROCK SUPPORTING THE ENORMOUS
BEAUTIFUL CATHEDRAL of the World of Notre Dame
in Montreal-Lowell near the South Common and Ma and I
and someone else (Hal Hayes?) are looking for a Chinese Street
Ste.Catherine Restaurant to eat our big gay shopping dinner,
it's around Xmas and the scenes in the dusk are glittrous, the
mountainous rock, the steep cliff where I'd been in a long ago
dream and feared of falling to the flats below (the dream of
workin railroad on cliff above redbrick town, Montreal yet also
leading off to dusty roads to Mexico---& also I'd walked up
there along a rickety broken fence, right on the edge, the
buildings in the moonlight like Joe McCarthy's buildings in the
training grounds and General MacArthur's Hospital Buildings,
all these scenes in a Complete World to which I try to give a
mortal sense of name)---Very happy when I wake up, to put
my day-shoes on---and read Chuangtse

IN A POOLHALL I HAVE A FULL LENGTH SWORD
somewhere like grim dismal Lowell I don't want and also on
the floor's my machete blade, unhandled and rusty---the
Negro Cook of the Poolhall says "I cut myself on that thing"
meaning the old blade & meaning to be funny (because it's
dull) but for sentimental reasons I want to keep it and start
tugging at it from him---He wont let go----He's the
Wiseacre Chief Cook of the S.S.Dorchester who made me

get up and re-mop the Galley, the big Negro with his huge cook knives whom I'd told "Take your hands off me" when he tried to start pushing me down the alleyway---It's that guy, and grinners watch again----I wake up with horror of ships, wars, jail, compound terrors of this compounded terrible world---I dont think to use my sword---

JERRY LEWIS THE COMEDIAN is sick in bed in my apartment, my studio room in Upper New York and June is there, when I go out to do something quick, while June is out, O come back and find her gelatinously dream-ly half-inventedly necking with Jerry, you see the little lips, the heads bent over, but it's only when I knock over my drink at their feet which I'd left on my desk when I went out that I realize June has been drinking it and "wasting everything" (she had just spent our last $50 on some futile self-serious absurdity) . . .it's now I realize her betrayal, indifference and unconcern for me and so I cut out from the dream---Never even laid a hand on her while I had er---

"SHE LIKES TO ROMP AROUND" the jealous sister is saying of the pretty young 15 year old sister (or 16-) and I look at her, she's wearing lil rompers that are tight and white to her tan legs and running off, shirt tails a hangin low---I rush out the house to watch more, it's in a pine wood settlement somewhere, like Maine, there are lil brothers and tricycles around and other houses---as I watch Rompey now her shirts' inside the rompers, she's cute---I aint no George Sokolsky (when it comes to girls in rompers)

255

GOING THROUGH AN ABANDONED HOUSEBOAT
or muddy apartment on the side of the river with Danny
Richman I steal an old victrola top and take it with me to
town, where it's played but doesnt work too good and has to
be wound---goes unnoticed in the general rack and ray of
city excitement---There are movies, Ma and I get in---I'm
sitting on the ground, a guy goes by staring at me curiously
then sees my mother and they fly into greetings---he wears
glasses---Going back up the river with Danny along the bank
I'm mindful of how when the Yangtse floods you cant tell a
horse from a cow on an islet and I look out to the Mississippi
islets---dots---it's warm, the grass and bankside is warm, bugs,
I worry about tics, we cut along the levee grass, walking back
America---we go through that houseboat again and I think
of stealing the victrola but I've already done that---Afternoon
sun rays in goldenly through the ruined windows---

BACK IN LOWELL BUT DISMALLY trying to work on
the paper, where also Boisvert is and I get his promise that
soon 'someone'll' publish Beat Generation and I go to San
Jose and gladly tell this to Nin and Irwin Garden and Evelyn
but Cody's asleep and doesnt care---In Lowell I also see good
old G.J. but there's a dismay, a cloud, it's that warm radiant
Lowell where I'm back and I've been everywhere and I use
Lowell to back up my dreams which isnt what it's for---help-
lessness, wrong choice---Nin is apparently reading some of
the first lines of Beat Generation in the San Jose parlor but,
it's also the parlor where Watson and the piano was and the
piano table I didnt want dirtied and he's around somewhere
displeased---This is all because I went to sleep before I was

really tired---I woke up miserably aching with over-ness---I loft a big stiff gin and tonic and drink it all up and start getting drunk and suddenly I'm alone in the front room and want more---

LONG HASSELS ALL NIGHT long over some little redhead auburn-beauty living with apparently Mary Palmer and me & Irwin Garden and Bull, such a raving little one we're all in love with her and finagle around---I'm a drunk, I go down and run errands and make phonecalls---Ma & Nin are around too, earlier, it's all in New Jersey but all the time we're supposed to be getting ready to go to New Yrok and never gits underway---Finally Mary and I are all dressed, we're going to NY with Pretty One to see her Russian dramatic coach but (and other things, Mary's, my affairs) but at the last minute The Redhead lays in bed overlooking New Jersey (which is like that Deni Bleu suburba of Gray Towers recently, that Chirico line design of sunshine afternoon houses)---says she hates to see that old dramatic coach, sounds like Josephine, petulant, wasteful, egocentric---Bull meanwhile, has got tired in midday and's typically laid up in his room in bed as I go there and take my New York pants off the hook---Mary's on the bed with the girl, she's all dressed, she's trying to talk and persuade and like an old nanny mama and I'm disgusted because I wanted to yak with the girl and now I'll be alone with the old one with her baggy eyes and anxieties about Pretty---"O I wish Pretty would this"---and "that"---no fun---"Sneak back and go up the fireplace and see what she's really gonna do," I think later, remembering Bull in bed in the next room---But's a dismal group, household---Julien was around earlier, gettin me drunk---The pad has a front room and two bedrooms and is in the 2nd floor and has outdoor wooden steps--- The streets outside are narrow and twisting, like Pawtucketville around Gershom Ave., a triangle block with little houses and fire hydrants and silence, eerie---The girl had auburn hair, a little bit of a strange definite bulbous and pub and snub nose, dark eyes, a petulant personality, a young fulsome body--- Irwin Garden is the one she loves and we're all jealous---

I GO UP TO KIND LOU LITTLE'S HOUSE to have my sore foot cleaned and bandaged, he has a nice home like wealthy 2nd generation Italians in the suburbs, daughters, pianos---It's back in Lowell and I have a red rubber ball and I'm planning to go out in the backyard and wham it pitching it against my old backbarn boarded window and by God to see if it's still there I look out the window and everything is too dim to tell----But later the little fat kid wants to play ball and I tell him "Let's go out in the street, it's a softball and might break a window"---He complains about the neighbors living at the Desilets location---I have reveries about the old park and think of going to it---

MONTREAL, RUSSIA. Big scenes with parents in a building, involving the shiftless brother-in-law Eddy Jones, who is a taxidriver lush in this strange dark Northern Gloomtown ---All drizzly and gray it is, as Eddy and I who am 18 years old and still kid-like, start out in his cab to get something---Eddy's like a thin W.C. Fields---"Boy" he says "wait here till I get me a shot of whiskey---Now the trouble with your folks is, they're always pesterin somebody to do dis and do dat---What I like is my freedom, see?---" He goes driving all over town and finally at drizzly dawn on some street in the Russian Flats and whorehouse district outside town he comes up to a gigantic Street Paver Machine that takes up the whole road and is four foot high with racks for tar, run by an old workman---Eddy rams his cab right into it, brang, and the whole thing shakes and quivers and moves forward, not heavy---Eddy's having a big time and laughing and is drunk & crazy---Next he rams up against a panel truck and keeps pushing it back (it's empty) towards a pedestrian who's trying to walk in the street---and because the wheel is turned the truck follows the man in an arc---a panel truck or cab earlier also pushed, out of which leaps now a visored driver drawing out an evil looking revolver with a wood handle---"Hey" I say from the back of the cab "I'm only a passenger, take it easy"---he holds it by the barrel to use it as a slugger while the pedestrian has already rushed up and hauled Eddy out of the cab and is bopping him hard and professionally on the chin with his fists so I rush up to stop it and do so by yanking Eddy from the punches and holding him at my side---Just as the taxidriver's about to lodge *his* complaint the pedestrian to my surprise removes a gun from his pocket and calmly shoots Eddy one shot in the chest ---Eddy is surprised and feels the pain only afterwards, and falls---I'm suddenly alone with him on the dismal windswept drizzly street of dawn, not a working street and so not a person in sight up and down the gray reaches of its dimness--- Eddy is writhing and crying "Get me a shot of whiskey" --- "But where? how?"---I find myself all alone with a man whose injury may be serious but I cant tell and he wants whiskey and lies in the road in pain, sentimental, my crazy drunken uncle-in-law---I'm so embarrassed I wish I could go away---(But on the corner there's an allnight whore and gambling cocktail lounge, with blue curtains in the plush door) ----"I'll go there and get a shot of whiskey Eddy?"---"Yea, yea, but get a whole bottle, you'll spill the shotglass bringin it back---"---I feel in my pocket, I have just a $5 bill and I think"For poor wounded Eddy I can spend that final fin" but I get twinges of guilt and remorseful fear and greed-anxiety and hear myself saying "Have you got $5"---"Yea, yea, in my pocket, get it there" and he can, I have to feel in his pockets because he cant turn over and I look up to see if anybody sees me, thinking "They'll think I'm a mugger rolling a guy"---bills fall out, I take a 5 and rush to the corner in the gray mist, go in the bar---They wont sell me a bottle---"Its too late, what the hell 's the matter with you, dont you know that?"---It's dark in there, plush, blue, gold bar bottle lights and a dim piano in back and a few voices of people who've been drinking all night till dawn---I want to tell them why I need the bottle---They're talkin among themselves---"Gotta wait till 8, city ordinance"---I get furious at the world with its goddam rules and comment about rules and there's my uncle dying for a drink in the rain with a bullet wound in his chest, I grab a bottle off the shelf at the end of the bar and run out fast---"Let em chase me! Eddy'll get his drink!" but as I reach the partitioning curtains I dont hear a commotion on the other side, they're still commenting about the city ordinance and there's even someone chuckling so that instead of being chased and shouted and shot at, I'm completely in the clear with the quart of whiskey and Eddy's $5 bill!---I run out silently and up the street to Eddy---But he's dead---Standing there with the bottle and his five dollar bill in my hands, over Eddy who's just become forever pure, I cry in shame and bitterness

ALL KINDS OF DETAIL-UNREMEMBERABLE SCENES in yards, streets, houses, with loves of all kinds, girls, mothers, people---woke up good.

THERE'S BEEN A TOWER SET UP in the city to show where the atom bomb is going to be laid when time comes to blast the city---announcement has been made for next month, and evacuation begun---You see the city at night now, dark, under a dim moon, low lights everywhere from the diminishing and dimming population---I'm there on a sad tenement balcony planning my departure up the northern river to the right---All the Porto Ricans linger yet in doom'd New York trying to salvage one last month of tasting the rich leftovers of a once-rich city---trying to eat up all their Manhattan Love, their Manhattanana, before they have to leave forever---I look at the tower in the moonlight, it looks so sinister, guarded, shrouded, to die---

"RIDING TO PRECISELY THE SAME MUSIC as at the beginning of the picture," the movie ad says, "Turhan Bey is seen entering the crowded city of Havalah---" you see pictures of a tremendous phalanx of easy riders invading an easy city, with turbans on, the plain thereof---then, the "end of the picture" they're fighting sword, tooth, nail and horses' sthump through the narrow alleys of Halavah---"the battles are

261

Narrated by Jewish Commentators" says the announcer---An after battle scene is shown of war prisoners hanging by their hands from public porches and you hear a loud THUMP as in the dimness and streetmoil below the announcer advises you that "a party of executioners became impatient because behind in schedule and cut off the head right on the sidewalk" but I missed seeing that, just heard it---a molly vitriolic city Turban Bey did emancipate---they gag to gape at Gaza

TRYING TO WRITE ALL NIGHT at the cafeteria booth but wearing big thick Lowell Highschool Track red sweater and also shoulderpads of football, finally I take it all off and Ma who's talking with women friends nearby wants to know if I feel aright---"J ava sho" (I was hot)---Earlier Joe was in that Sunday House in Salem Street standing around longlegged, archaic, like a watcher in old rainy photographs---

"ONE OF THE NICE GUYS OF LOVE, MUSELLE" is a song someone's singing in a deep dream---

THICK SMOKE IS RISING from the dust heap over across the highway where weeks before we'd laid out some of our rubbish to burn and far from not being burned out it's gotten worse, a dog is barking next to it---Ma, Nin, Pa & Me go across the highway to see, from our big gray screenporch house---it's somewhere in the South----I'm annoyed by the traffic and try to sneak between cars to cross but they keep streaming mindlessly---

262

Cabooses on a winter morning spurt sweet comfort smoke---

You see the President of the Lions Club sitting among the boys on the balcony as the organ plays "Hold That Lion" and he's a got a crewcut now, his split teeth show even more, he's Bill the popular Prez and you see he's conscious of his new haircut and wonders what the people of America'll think of it---The camera swings up to the great ceiling and up to the prison above where prisoners can hear the music and the rally, you see wire caging and gray light---

BACKWARDS FALLING STAIRS and the steps only 3 inches wide---so painfully I'm coming down those, holding to the rail, slow, returning from the auditorium of the Negroes---It's a moonlit night, it's somewhere, I'm a seaman ---A colored acquaintance of mine is walking with a colored girl, they see me---I tell them "Their stairs kill me"---We walk along towards the great Auditorium where I live, where I'd been entrap't earlier for stealing jewelry and the guy wants to make the girl but she's going to a party so he cuts off at a little sidestreet with ruts in the dust and sleeping cottages and I go on with her----Soon I've got her hand in mine and teasing my finger along---She says she's going to a party of six people, at a cop 's house---"Are you the seventh?" I say---"I like to feel hands," she says---aint pretty, sorta fat, ugly, but sexy---It's New Britain---When they'd caught me earlier I was way up the giant steps hiding where the blond guy identified me to a plainclothesman, I darted through the embrous awe hall rungladders among echoes of the show, guilt, it wasnt me but my friend started it---gelatinous thefts---Now, walk-

263

ing in the moonlight, the auditorium has become my room
and I want to take her up there but she's going to her party

CHLOROFORMING MYSELF, trying to commit suicide
in the bed with either June or whoever the girl, who'd just
made the mother come with a masturbation---this mother
---I get dizzy and Inhale more but dont die and I'm terrified
to die but decided to commit suicide--- It doesnt kill me---
Indeed I would commit suicide she is on the bad being
jacked off by either June or me, and comes, it's like saved in
a bottle and we comment and laugh and are all young beatie
bob the darlin moon

BIG RIVER EPIC, we all come hegiring down the thick
flood, swimming with our gear, horses
           I'm a famous young writer again, in Lowell,
dont have to go to school, am coming down those steep green
woodsteps at the hermit's house on Riverside Street where
they've been making cement blocks and a whole new huge
cement house, the cementmaker up to his neck in a vat, almost
drowning, churning the mixture with an automatic beater
shaped like a nobby egg, like a machine tooled fistpounder, a
pagoda---the boss is there, fat, in shirtsleeves---Earlier I'd been
sleeping in the attic and Pa was around---Boisvert is around,
it's a happy dream of my young success, I think of going to
Bartlett JHS to look up Miss Dinneen---I've written *On the
Road*, is what (Ray Smith)---Earlier it was the baseball practice
at Yankeee Stadium where I played pepper with lil kids---Up
in my attic, it was a big house, all the aunts and relatives were

264

visiting...the old Aunt Jeanne Lynn-dream and Uncle Joe sad-dream all happified now by some pristine and joyous new quality in the air---Embracing this love I seek to sleep and sleep more, dream on, till, seabells toll my eyelids' lash obliviso ----Methinks with this chiselled death-profile I must be Gerard---the little Lowell joy city, Richmond Hill----the fame of the dreamer, unhappy notoriety of a drunkard---

The river is in flood, gray, we are swimming in file and sometimes rest on the shore---it's a long trip swimming from Lowell to Mexico under gray skies & along gray shores---

UP IN NASHUA, back on the farm, with Joe and Phillip, I've very happ y and we go along the old incredibly old L.L.M. Railroad tracks and see a freight pull by all the antique gray weatherbeaten boxcars made of wood like barns, old Colonials---all shapes, sizes---engine is of course an old steam pot & we kids (*kids*, I'm 32) go up and watch close as the head brakeman disconnects the engine from the train, pushing me aside slightly as I lean too close---a complicated hammering and yanking, turning upside down and hitting-with-hand that makes him pretend to wince with pain---he steps back to look down the cinders for his sign---- I push Phillip back who's too close---I'm going to ask for work on this railroad---"Any JOBS?" I yell up to the Negro hoghead or fireman and he yells yes and in the noise tells me something and where to go and I whoop and say "Thank *you* sir!"---We wander down the track to Nashua, happy---but later I'm being driven by Cousin Ovila to work in some watch factory at the foot of a street by a sandpile with lamps

---But it's joyous Nashua and cold winter'll soon healthily come---Earlier in a mid-dream nameless and awful I'm blowing or squeezing or otherwise getting long streamers of worm out of my nose in the paneglass window of the store and it's 6 o'clock Sunday dawn and early churchgoers may have seen me---

BULL'S BIG GANG OF DOPE PUSHERS have been in, now here comes the gang of buyers thru the backdoor, an ominous crew of gunmen, I know em all---the house has been swarming all day anyway, it's my Sarah Ave. house in Lowell, it's a bright crazy day---Earlier in Nin's Southern House I had a big roach on my desk and in trying to hide it from her under paper or taking it in my palm she kept suspicioning me and darting to catch my hand "Hah? hah? What are you trying to hide?" "Nothin, nothin" as I palm the roach nervously "I wanted this pencil"---She follows me into the kitchen eying me every move---It's a nice house, somehow also the Sarah Ave. house but I'm not much happier than I was in that house where I'm married to Dusty in the old paramoured-to-a-dike- dream-----Better go to a Sinaloa hut boy. . .(as live in the same house as old TiNin and expect to be free to hide roaches)

IN SOME APARTMENT IN NEW SHMICAGO I take a desperate leak into an empty pint bottle of Wine because other empty quart bottles have already been pissed full by Hubbard earlier---I realize half with horror in the dream gray humorlessness that it's my own old pint I'm using---I dont want to piss on the floor and create a great noticeable puddle in the girl's pad but so, my piss wells up quick to the neck and overflows welling abundantly and richly and too much all over my hands and down the sides of the bottle and on the hardwood uncarpeted floor---

UNPEARLIED OLD UGLY GRAYDUST TRAIN, the Zipper, ready to go to Watsonville Junction so I get on and roam inside the passenger coaches (!) and then it gets underway but the wrong way, towards the city, so in trying to get off I clamber down the rungs, but my large buncha keys' in my way, keep dangling from my hand and when I try to put em away in pocket (while on rungs) they wont go in but dangle half in half out and of course I cant lose em so I hold on precariously with three fingers grabbing the grabirons and train speeds up tremendously---I get to the point of the Gray Locomotive and come down, turning the ground and the train away from me as I quietly relax off, arm out kissing the rungs goodbye, foot out in heel-up railroader's balance, like a stylized dance it is---off & safe.

IN STRANGE SNOWY FRISCO I got down shortcutting behind Market but end up in the countryside among snow covered farms though they're still 'parallel to Market' but now a closed tunnel seals off my return so me and other guy go through the wood barrier door and come into vast underground caves full of escaped Oriental War Prisoners hiding out---we go on various levels, deeper & deeper more lost, among scrabbles of rock, dust, refuse, papers, crap, dank, drips, leaks, from overhead city---finally I find my two searched-for Orientals over a fire in the corner of the Vast Ah Cave Eternity and if I dont watch out they'll roast me for supper because there's no food down here---O what happened to the snowy farmhouses?

IRWIN EAGER recordplaying in the closed livingroom in Textile Lunch Tenement and I call it to Danny Richman's attention but he not interested---I go in the door and listen, I wish Irwin would play louder and more distinct but I recognize his greatness and his prophetic humility of volume, his 'quietness'---I got to go down the gray dank stairs where the Shrouded Traveler had been in white shirtsleeves,---down on the street level I stop and there all my dream life comes back to me in a solid wave, sad, gray, huge,---everywhere unending gray scenes and dismal---this is the price of sentience, the current of deaths and rebirths---O path of sweet Permanency, through what wood, what raindrop?

IN LOWELL I'VE APPLIED TO THE SUN, with Jimmy Santos presumably, for a job on Commentary Magazine and he's written back a big glowing welcoming letter and offering me the job but Ma is leery and says I shoulda stayed low because now that I'll be makin money and makin myself known others'll be wantin it---so I ponder not doing anything at all, svaha!---- Meanwhile there's been a play or I wrote or acted a play and the final scene is on with the hero father at the picnic grounds holding a big waterglass full of red wine, well dressed, with wife who says "You drink too

much" and I look at Nin and she says "Of course he does---"
This man has a son who is arguing with him about big philo-
sophical issues all the time---the man is in a tweed coat---
Now I'm with Joanna going up to her room, new room, in a
little narrow hall, I go in with her, as she bends to get something I'm pinned behind and we push together a little but
wanting her to think that I'm not vulgar but appreciative of
her sweetness I quickly throw a little kiss on her dress, bending inward down---We then neck sloosily, dreamily---She's
very beautiful and I love her---

       The lifespan of an ant is very short, and it
only learns that learning is ignorance---

       Walking into Lowell from the long alien-
ated "north side" not far from that circus cliff of recent I suddenly pass a square which is familiar suddenly as being some
old forgotten Lowell place I'd felt alien and never sought
to rediscover in my thoughts---somewhere in the mixups
of cathedrals, wooden tenements, railroad tracks and heavy
traffics back of North Woburn Shtreet and back of South
Common, up towards South Lowell, around to the east,
strange----my flash of remembrance is in the dream and *for*
the dream, for now I see there is no such spot in Lowell or
in mind but I made it up to fit the dream, showing how
the dreamer Mind is not concerned with such arbitrary
Conceptions as fantastic or non-fantastic---whether it took
place or not, all its thought memories are active, pulling out
of absent blue air the empty images of a dreamer world

DRAGON FEATURE STORY in the Lowell Sun, that I'm
reading in the Richmond Hill chair in the silence of my

269

dream---It's a front page story by "one of the innumerable Sun writers," this one a Greek I think, talking about the War but twisting in dragontails and buttons to make it a 'feature' type story (I can see through it)---But I feel impossibly sad reading it and thinking about my wasted writing career & Lowell

SOMEBODY'S GIVEN ME 7 tickets to the big new British Play but I'm not very interested but insisted on to go---Of course I have to pay for them too---Nin (is it?) gets me $5 to buy them, for some inane reason I buy two instead of one at the boxoffice at the far theater way out of Mexico City which has also cost me $2.20 to get there via cab---My cat, my wee pretty lil favorite kitty is out there sleeping at the curb near the cab waiting for me when, seeing one of my seats is way up in the awful balcony & that the "play" is nothing but a big technicolor movie & a fraud---Lo, my other cat shows up & I have both of em in my hands as I call for a cabbie on the Large Plaza of sadness---not thinking that I dont have enough money to pay back to town $2.20 and certainly not enough to back home where Ma, Pa, Nin & others live in a house--- The cats at first were stiff then they recognized each other and now they're wrestling in my hands as I call a young American-looking cabdriver---"How much to city?"---"50¢"--- "Wow---how much for a little bit further to my house beyond"---$?---"75¢"---"As you see I have to take a cab with these cats"---I get in his high lorry and wait a long time as he's apparently getting ready or talking to other cabbies and so long that finally the cats go to sleep in the woodwork--- Earlier my father and I had climbed around some ruined

270

fabled ancient stadium---I'm not sorry at all that I saw only
30 seconds of the great "Play" & spent all the $5---

HORRIBLE NIGHTMARE MURDERS that were perpe-
trated partly in my Phebe Avenue house but in some redbrick
mill district too, the carnage and beating so bad the victim or
somebody puked all over the floor and you see it mixed with
blood and apparently pieces of flesh and broken man---so bad
I wake up, in the dream, in the middle of a spectral over-silent
night (dread eerie silence in Richmond Hill suddenly) and I
sense the murderers are back and O it must be me and my
1946 red sawdust at the funeral of Pa in Nashua---!---but I'm
terrified, again as by Pa in the Going-Blind-Dream of recent,
and the murderers are near (Bull and Julien in New York
tonight!)---and I want to defend myself, get up and fumble in
the dark for those two old lost Kerouac iron bookends on my
Gerard green desk---I take one and close it in my fist---also
worried for Ma in her front bedroom there, sleeping or probably terrifiedly awake---silent like me as the Spectres pass in
the dark---the police had investigated, interrogated, mopped
up the mess but Man I tell you it dont help, it's what you got
inside the dark that murders & mares night to its silent sound
glad cook of Ho Boy rooster saving dawn---Dear

I'M LOOKING FOR A PLACE to sit and write quietly at
the baseball park and go around a fountain and batting cage
wire to a bench on the side where there's an old typewriter
& desks under a tree and here I turn into "Malcolm Cowley"
and start typing---but so old the Machine, to register letters

271

ya gotta hit it one finger at a time *hard*, which I do,---&
there's a sad young kid there, of 18, definite personality, curly
brown hair, thoughtful, as an interested old Man of Letters I
begin to interview him sympathetically and find he's a young
tender poet so saddened he doesnt write much, or some
such,---walked 2½ miles before I wrote this, so part forgot
---So he stares into space in my dream and I worry about
him----Who's subjective? Who's objective?

A WILD DREAR EPIC OF A FAMILY living in the far
North on a strange high seacoast whose waters come up and
lap the doorsill at high tide and in storms lashes the whole
house trembling---it 's like Alaska, the days are short, darkness predominates---I'm there with Ma & Nin and there's a
short sunny summer when we arrive, warm enough and
pleasant---"I loved it so much when it came, suddenly one
afternoon, six weeks, ago," is saying the old grandmother of
the house on a cold sudden dusk, "but now it's winter again"
---For awhile too there'd been playing around in the lawn
across the road from which begins the whole Ars Scotia
Wilderness that goes & goes, solid, all over the Far &
Hopeless North---the games in the yard were wild, with
white horses and roughplay, I get on mine and chase the boys
who've thrown bats at me and tackle them from bareback---
it's all in play but wild---Now winter's come back, the house
shakes from the blast and roar of the terrifying sea, the seas
saw terribly, you see it hungrily licking the kitchen door
from gray infinity like Greenland seas north of Cape
Farewell---the father os the house is a mad old miser with a
servant who hates him, you see them eating together a mis-

272

erable meal in a barn, by crazy candlelight, in the Alaskan Town---the servant saying "You *miserable*(fool)all your life has been wasted in this Northern Waste with your silly out-cries about the Days of Armaggeddon and your Bible, mak-ing everyone quake because you're crazy"------Suddenly the servant is no longer sitting in his chair next to the Mad Master who is glouring, but in mine, and I am become the servant. Meanwhile I'd been to the Alaskan town, with my girl, the only girl in the country for me---Looking for candy stores to make sure I can get enough gum---gay restaurants with beer and whole families and booths and Community boots and mackinaws, a man sitting on the bar stool with a celery stuck in it by a child---My girl (Maggie Zimmerman) and I wander among the barns of Main Street, the skies are gray iron---Now the master is being excoriated by the ser-vant in the Town barn Last Supper and then the big storm comes and lashes the whole little house and shakes it in night and you know the house is going to be destroyed now and the Master jump up on a high wagon and scream in the gloom about his Prophecy "In the days when the windows be darkened and the daughters of music are brought low---" and he's going to drown in the tide with his slave and you'll hear a Spokesman of the Epic say "Thus they drown'd together, he who lived in, and he who sought to live from, the waters of death" (the second the master, and you see a scene of the wreckage littered Sea) but I'm going to rise up and make a huge speech of my own for the benefit of the hearts of everyone and all the kind grandmothers, girlfriends, aunts I've known in this dear lil house is this drear North, I'll say "Windows-be-darkened-be damned, all he had to do was build his house on higher ground!"---anybody can see

Earlier, or later, I was trying to steal some yellow paper pads from the Western Union desk in the Marble Subway corridor but kept hesitating over how many till finally I decided to steal them all but by then the pretty secretaries began going from room to room though they paid really no attention to me and dug me

IN JAMES WATSON'S STRANGE BIG HOUSE IN NEW JERSEY, two hours or more by train and bus to my house, I'm an uninvited guest and left alone in the long low fireplace livingroom while Watson's Bedroom lights are on and he's there with wife---a "deliberate affront" but I dont leave because it's 2 hours to home and wont get there till One A M and I'm tired so I wander around the big barnlike livingroom looking at W's notebooks (like mine, like these little ones, with numbers) and on the wall a replica of his "Harper's Magazine Column" wherein he writes of his "boy-hood in New Hampshire" with many large photographs of trees and bushes and creeks, with his prose among---he aint about to come out from the bedroom either---it seems too I'd been or lived across the courtyard in another place, and had come here only because it was near but anyway I'm not welcome---a drear dream---I realize how much money he's making now, and I make nothing----Ah, this affront!

IN THAT FATED cold northern town I go from the mar-ble station of events as murky as spiderwebs, to Pat Fitzpatrick's house, day time, to see his wife Marie, for a f., I hope---no one in, I go in, eat a new slab of American cheese off a bedroom sideboard then think to call out "Marie?" and by God she replies from deep in a bedroom and no longer innerested in me as I tell her who I am---So out on the railroad track we're trying to make a joint that'll crack the wood gimmick that's holding us up and my cat Pinky's lying on the railbed watching and as we make a try he comes up and smells the thing we put on---"He'll get run over!"---but the move starts again, and Pinky lays down safe between the tracks,watching, the coolest cat that ever lived----We make the slamming SPROWM joint and Pinky blinks to hear it in his drowse------we make our objective, dust, I pass the sign, wild autumnal clearday winds blow, Marie F. may no longer love me but I got my cat and tag team and works of the Mind---

Later on the passenger train I yell with glee and amazement when I see the railroad men of a strange local kicking a gon down a dead lead into a derail and over to tumble tragically in a sand hollow, because useless---"They kicked that gon over!"-----The brakeman laffs and says "It's because the sides are wore out"----"The slats are run thru" ---it's 'Woburn'---'near Lowell'----lots of sand and new construction and wild excitement in the wind whipped day with puffclouds racing in the glitter blue---I think of the randy dark body of Marie in the bedroom and her sultry careless voice---soon we'll be in Lowell and I'll see the heart's desire scenes----a whole book in itself, God----When Autumn wins my heart again and makes me lose my love the trees will take the Dreams, Roads, Dharma Railroads and Bubbles of the Mind Sea and crash them back to Eternity

275

FRANKLIN ROOSEVELT JR ON TV handing out eggs ---and the drug that is sprayed from a strange syringe--- Roosevelt sticking his hand out of the TV tube in my house and I reach out and take what he offers, cracked eggs, a big bottle of Accent, garlic salt, Ma and I are talking excitedly as I take and so miss a few times when FDR reaches out a thing and because not taken vanishes into space---I rue the things I missed, gloat to see the ones I got----

------The kid wanted to be friends, we went to the hospital, got shot spray dope from the nurse ' s syringe, I'm standing there becoming completely drowsy and crazy in front of other patients watching as the nurse administers---It's only later the sailor turns sinister (after our stay in the Sarah Avenue Hospital) and with his friends under the Jamaica El (where the timber fire was in the El) makes suggestive gestures of a fight, how they'll all beat me up, he in the lead and already I got my escape planned

THE UP & DOWN WILDRAMPS of an unbelievable Brooklyn waterfront, with parts rising up like drawbridges and girders among and workers (I have a job, like railroad switching off the floats New York Dock Rwy. but it's a weird darkwork where we communicate across big holes in our upramps and sometimes it's hard to climb they're so steep, you get some kind of pay and overtime according to their steepness)---in night I am wandering, in white t-shirt, looking for my work team, finding spectral buildings like Squibb's or the St George Hotel but just wood mansions full of sleepers, closets, sexes, sheets, dank abandoned rooms---the foreman cant find me---Finally I find June Evans and she

immediately wants to blow, on the bottom step of the big
Rank Roadramp Tower of Babel---we, she starts---we smile,
hurry off---I lose her in the big house though she told me
what room she'd be in---I go a floor below, miss her, find her
finally much later after ship-like events and loneliness in a
maze of lost corridors of the dark mind's house---She's in the
sack but a kid is playing in the room and we gotta get him
out---She smiles like an angel with radiance from her dark
heaven---I wake up realizing all is a dream, especially the
Morning Waking---

DREAM OF THE GROWNUP MAN CHASING ME, I'm
a little boy in some town somewhere, homeless, I've done
some prank or vandalism and he's mad and wants to catch me,
wears white shirt like the Shrouded Traveler in the Hall---
upon Main Street near the High School he starts chasin me, I
run down thru the lawns of the school and over the iron
picket fence and down a side street to houses like the houses
of Gershom with leafy mysterious yards---There's a sandbank
beyond (primal, scene of world redsun birth) I got my eye on
---He keeps coming behind me always about 2 blocks away
but persistent and shakeless---I've really become terrified and
have to use every craft of child sneakability to completely
escape him *or else*---he's insane---I go into a house hall, hide,
as in old dreams, people inside dont hear me, I sneak around,
under porches, in rooms of perfect strangers---the angry
grownup is outside looking, looking, he knows *I'm near*---I
sneak out thru bushes to other yards of the dank houses of
death, and come to the open spaces of the sand shrub hills
there and I take off across a long hollow for the other end---

clearly defined country, with water beyond I'm sure, and "seen before"---in a gray north land---he 's right behind, has seen me and hurries nearer, knows I would take to the open from fear of houses and yards---What did I do?***** I hide carefully on the far end of the hollow but as he approaches (himself hiding) I know he'll just simply see me---backtrack may lead to ridiculous, going-further may be hopeless, I ponder and breathe hard---There's a lil old house at the hillslope, I invade it and hide among woodslats and wet sound---My Shroud approaches---I *know* he'll get me (woodslats and wet sound, that's masturbating with the twins at five), he knows too the bastard sooner or later he'll get me but being a kid I have great potentiality and all the world yet and left to hide in and cover with tracks--- Shall I go towards the mysterious old Chalifoux woods beyond where woodstumps I was born in redmorning valleys of life hope?---or sneak back snaky into town? (Who the boy? Who chaser?) Who objective? Who subjective? Who real? What real? All liquid phantomry in my mind essence dreaming, like life---Ha!

(Close your eyes to all danger & dont be afraid to die. . . .it's all imaginary & empty & great)

WITH MY CRAYONS I drew a marvelously beautiful scene of some buildings in late afternoon, maybe churches or stores but using pink and deep inkblue lavishly and very heavy with the hand I have put up a color of awe and mystery of the late sun on old stone that is so beautiful, something never before seen by human eyes, a work of art worthy of a DeVinci, a Rembrandt even----I'm amazed just a little to see I'm a great artist---Unfortunately I drew the picture on the TV screen "during a color broadcast" and now as I'm just about to show it to my mother the colorcast ends and ordinary pale luminous gray faces show and my whole masterpiece is completely wiped away---"Damn bastards changed!" I yell---It was a scene like Venice in the late Fall afternoon, blues & pink & stone salmon & awe gulp dark sorrow that made you think of Jesus & Magdalene

Earlier Nin was driving a new car, didnt know how, we came thru the sandhills, visited a bar where I drank brandy mixtures and hiballs and then I drive the car the rest of the way, to our house in Carolina

"WHY DO PEOPLE LIVE IN NEW YORK?" I'm thinking as I wait for the "14th Street bus" on a West Side street, after seeing the one coming up the Avenue was only the "31st Street bus"---I look down the lonesome pier street, over the waters, the Atlantic skies, the wild Porto Rican garbage of truck helpers, the people spindly and lost far up the endless avenue---tho it's not crowded right now at the supper hour I think "It's because it's a wild camp"---

"WHEN YOU CLIMB POLES. . ." It was a seashore town epic with families, I'm up in a tree or a pole for my own amusement but the father (Mannerly-like whom I just insulted in his attic classroom) cries "Fire! dont you see the fire from up there? When you climb poles---when any of *my* gang climb poles it's to spot fires and hurricanes" but suddenly he and his brood of brats realize the fire is close to their own house and they start running there and where I am I can

279

see it's their house indeed at that---Finally when the hurricane is coming they send a silent dead boxcar down the long peninsula rail, to block something---my whole life's imaginary worries had all swum by on the gray peninsula---

AT DAWN (after yesterday's initiation of One Meal A day-No Drink-No Friends "Western" device for Buddhism) a namelessly beautiful joy in my dreambrain concerning the Single Taste of all things, a transcendental sensation of Singleness in the Universe, a Solitary Ecstasy---Interrupted by the daily morning vulgar throat-clearing of the Fat Pole next door and yet I blessed him in my happiness and all anger had disappeared------Later my mind went ignorantly deeply asleep & consumed itself with visions of rough seas, seamen struggling with a lifeboat over the side of a freighter & suddenly all disappearing to drown and you dont see anything on the sea till a minute after the floating rowboat hulk 300 yards down the starboard stern, the men gone except for inky seablobs----- Earlier I'd been in the old Sun Building in Lowell and asleep upstairs & some man, thinking me drunk, carries me downstairs to Kearney Square & I fake outness, a tender scene, he's got me like a baby-----then I walk on up to a lunch cart near the Y and up Merrimac Street and report my story to someone in the dark rainy day---evil weirdness of Kearney Square, the whole thing is nothing but a discriminated cerebral hassel and this I may say for the entire book of dreams of images to disturb its unbroken serenity & preoccupations with imagelessness though *how* this is so I cant tell yet in words that are in themselves discriminative hassels of arbitrary conception ------As I say, words, images & dreams are fingers of false

280

imagination pointing at the reality of Holy Emptiness---but my words are still many & my images stretch to the holy void like a road that has an end----It's the ROAD OF THE HOLY VOID this writing, this life, this image of regrets------------

FOR THE FIRST TIME---dreamed I climbed a gradual cliff from slope to slope and got up on top and sat down but suddenly in looking down I saw it was not a gradual cliff at all but sheer----in the dream no thought of getting down on other side---in the dream as always in Highplaces Dreams I'm concerned with *getting down the way I came*, or rectifying my own mistakes----and even though I know it's a dream, within the dream I insist I must get down off the high cliff I climbed--- the same old fear grips me in mortal throes---"But if it's a dream then the cliff is not real," I tell myself "so just wake up & the cliff will vanish"---I hardly believe it's possible, and, trembling, open my eyes & the dream is gone, the cliff is gone, the terror is gone---This is the Sign from Buddha's Compassion at last---In other words, for the first time I dreamed that I was on a high place & was afraid to get down but I knew it was a dream & something told me to wake up & the high place would disappear, & I opened my eyes & it was all gone
SAVED!
Buddha rectified by mistake for me-----
AWAKEN FROM THE DREAM
For a moment too I thought of jumping down to get down-----O pitiful reality! (but that would mean mortal pain, the falling, mortal horror, or, death)---
Also, in many other Highplace Dreams I knew it was a dream too, but insisted within the dream *on get-*

281

ting down----dream-activity in the dreamworld---dream-action down the dreamcliff---

The cliff seemed to be, and now the cliff doesnt seem to be---

Dream-analysis is only cause-and-condition explanation (such, as, cliff from symbol during waking day, like, murderer with knife because window left unlocked)---dream-analysis is only a measurement of the maya-like and has no value----dream-dispersion has the only value---Freudianism is a big stupid mistaken dealing with causes & conditions instead of the mysterious, essential, permanent reality of Mind Essence---(My only problem is how to practice the Eightfold Path day in, day out, as long as I don't live in solitude---) It's more than justthe high cliff of the other-night's-reading-Dante,---it's the high cliff of mortal anxiety---

SUDDENLY A BIG MARKET in Lowell with delicious things to eat at many counters on School Street near the old North Common, where Mike had his garage, and in there's Jim Bloodworth and Taffy Truman, eating, and I go up and say "Boys I've been working as a brakeman, anything on the B & M?" and they look at me askance, knowing me.

I'M AT THOREAU'S WALDEN POND HUT in Concord, it's evening and I can barely see as I try to examine some of his mementoe'd remaining personals including a little box of his old smokes, the box made of tearable soft cardboard like that of egg crate layers---a hip chick in a new convertible pulls up and is yanking her emergency brake with headlamps

282

illuminating Thoreau's wall as I yell "Keep your lights on, I gotta see this" because I dig her right away as receptive and cool and I cant see---As she watches over my shoulder I open the box and it's a little thimbleful of marijuana seeds---a little powdered marijuana tobacco, at least seems so and I think "Thoreau was High"---(which is certainly TRUE)---and I tell the girl what it is---She says "That stuff is hard to get"--- "Now no it isnt" I say with the authority of a great hipster "you can get it anywhere on the street (from any hustling girl)" I think to add, and in my mind the street is a great Chicago Drag glittering outside Concord & Lowell---Pretty Chick is awed by me---she tears the lil box softly apart for a souvenir, rolling it up into little ball---

(Dream'd in Lowell Skidrow Hotel, the "Depot Chambers")

WALKING ON TIMES SQUARE WITH IRWIN and Bull, at evening---scheduled to meet Huck according to my meet Irwin complains on the grounds that Huck is a criminal and his father doesnt want him to meet him and he makes his specific beef about "Huck knows that I'm here?" etc. so I get mad and say "Naturally, I didn't expect you to feel this way""and put him down this much"---Nastily he curls his lip at me, darkfaced, and says "You're trading little Jews this year" and I realize he means let Huck & Jewses (that Huck is Jew) (which surprises me, always thought Huck was German like the other night I dreamed someone telling me Shelley Lisle was Jewish) ---So I retort "It's your shit not Huck's" and go into the angry spiel about Irwin fucking up all over with his rejections & suspicions & fears & self-non-incrimination in the consequences of his own past & his new-found scorn & philistine pitiliness of Bull & us & I beef about these things at length in a raving dream of my own ending you see a gigantic 200 foot tree on Times Square in the night and point up at it saying "You & your father both, you've never bothered to find out the top-most branches of the tree that fed you,---" meaning you're just a lot of pavement-bound City Jews wandering around com-plaining about everything and rejecting it with dark sneers even as the tree of life its topmost pure branches goes unno-ticed---the tree of earthly pity---reminding me of the Herbert Gold story of how he hates his father sleeping in the bedroom, the snarl of it, the Jewish Hatred Dark---which I smash with a great speech about the Great Sad Tree of Earth----Hubbard is quiet and makes no comment because he couldnt care less, is thinking of his next jolt--------------------------

"COOL IT" I say to a gang of crazy boys I been playin on the rollercoasters with, as one starts shouting loudly about the marijuana exploits I taught them---"Ah hell, cool it yaself" is the answer from my disciples---We're in our shorts and T-shirts, I feel tired of trying to keep up with the consequences of the Beat Generation and all lugubrious in the dream---Wake up in Lowell Skidrow---

'T'is only in the quiet of the Sainte Jeanne d'Arc church on the great gray day of Nov.21 1954 that I saw: "The *Beat*ific Generation"

THE NEGRO DRUMMERS at a big jam session in a schoolroom where Ma & Pa & I watch with amazement, they are sitting in the center back seats taking alternate solos, the first guy seems great enough but the second pounds on his desk with the sides of his palms and makes such a thunderous fast roar the others wanta shush him for downstairs but he pays no attention and later the outdone other drummer comes to the seat in front of mine and wants to swap with a 'civilian' because apparently he doesnt wanta sit next to his enemy any more----Returning to my tenement pad with my child I am set upon by a Negro and his woman, "Come on with us, on the roof"---"Now"---"Come on, come on,"---a kidnapping---"No"---the woman backs up to fish in her purse, my kid hides in a corner, I'm ready for action and wake up

AT THE LONG ISLAND GRAYBEACH a big family reunion and event but instead of starting off on time I goof at basketball in the empty Y court, removing coat but not shirt and tie and I'll get all sweaty---I start playing my Self Game, the Kerouacs against the Kraps, the heroes of both sides---I hear juveniles screaming in another court---Then I hurry to the big Confused Event, riding the top of an outdoor subway or freight train right down the Queens Boulevard Mainline and hundreds of other kids are riding with me and it's started to drizzle, the outdoor fireworks at the beach will be a fizzle --- The Coach of the Children, Russ Hodges Serious, sees me and calls to me over the boxcars to help a little lost kid by taking him with me---I plan to agree---

DREAMS IN ROCKY MOUNT 1955 SPRING
SOME WORK IN A LOFT last night, near the Lowell

Depot, there I am sent upstairs by Joe to fill the bubble barrels with life juice and go up by the fire escape, am all alone there in the gloom but get unbelievably hungup and have all eternity to clown and delay like some Joe Jackson bum with falling-apart bicycle---All alone, as I feel and fret and fidget about what Joe'll think my gloomy hands glue to their indefinite and work---Nothing happens---I will be finished at dusk of the same day---Joe will fix sixteen spectral motors ere I come out of there---But he sends no emissary to check ---We've been laboriously all night over cars, fans, palms,---

THE GREAT ORIENTAL KALIFA is castrating the priests with an expression of tender sorrowful concern, he has a little clasp of silver that he applies to their parts as they go to him opening their flies (but away from the audience so you dont see the actual penises and how it works) but you do see the expressions of disappointed pain on the faces of the faithful who you might expect had thought the Kalifa would rid them of pernicious balls of eros without searing and wounding their conditional bodies so to the quick---I'm next in line, just as reluctant as a dozen others as it dawns on me what castration means---I refuse when glanced at compassionately---It comes at a time when I am about to stop renunciation and begin expecting and accepting everything again --- I get up and say "No"---In the next room are the Soldiers of the Brown East, marshalled to overseer the quiet castration of disciples---Two special young brownskinned guards (not in uniform but like passengers in a Mexico City bus) start whipping themselves up to a frenzy with speeches to each other and then come for me to handle me---But they're so ineffectual, I fight them off with that, without even trying and I go to the window and swing out to my escape ---One of my old hero buddies who'd been a Monk with me but previous to that a car fixer at the Lowell Depot Garage now makes a speech to the monks and guards of the Kalifa in the tenement funny drowse and rope lines of the court as I drop down on silken cords to the Fellaheen Mystery of Escape "He's such a great escaper, you will note this champion of the world can go down a wall without touching a wall" which indeed I'm doing but without half trying---My escape is clear as air---My enemies have no hold,---My personality is so deficient of self-nature I dont even touch the ground let alone the wall---Yet the pain of that silver nutcracker with the hand-around handle would have been 'real' I think, and hurry off---Besides of which, whether it's a Locomotive or a Holy Tree they'll bury me under, Emptiness is still the same---

As a chicken enfranchised of its egg, I cut off, in no direction, lyrically, light

A GRAVE LAD FROM LOWELL I revisit the scene of my old school, the second grade at St.Louis presumably---in other words, it's supposed to represent Billings School or St.Louis---in other words, it's not supposed to represent anything but itself---and so sad---First I'm in the cellar which is supposed to be the vast and dark St.Louis Parochial cellar where I remember nuns combing our hair with water from the pisspipes (the little wall falls) and the darkness, dampness, stone, so that nowadays my dreams of the Lowell Hi School basement which was not anywhere as dungeon-like are characterized by the damp gloom of the St.Louis remembered basement---I say remembered because in visiting St.Louis recently it never occurred to me to drop inside and re-see the basement which now in fact as I think about it cannot be located in my real discriminating consciousness---Where was it? the basement of that relatively little redbrick building?--- the basement of the Parochial Bazaar hall?----but there's no basement under it!---Where is it but in my mind?---But it is under the redbrick building and so much smaller than I dream and smaller even than the basement of the old High School Freshman Building where the vocational classes were held (wood benches, lathes, the wild Joes ready to begin a new day at their work which always seemed forced on them because they had been caught doing something bad and grownup in the misty gray Lowell)---I revisit this composited basement but suddenly it develops into a real cave, with dirt, dripping unseen walls, vast, but under the school and the fur- ther I walk the more it begins to resemble those big caves underneath Market Street in Frisco that I've been dreaming, where recently I found two starving Oriental Japanese sol- diers who were grubbing in separate cave rooms---how vast and like the cave underneath Laurier Field where the Big Heart of the Beast was thumping---then I come up to the hallway of the school, the wood planks, the doors to various classes, that sleepy schoolday sun pouring in and it seems I'm revisiting a heretofore completely forgotten "second grade room" which now glimmeringly I recall and cant believe it ---the utter lost-forever sadness of my unhappiness in one of the front desks of this room, the woman teacher long dead--- It's like the Billings School hallways in the background of the little picture of me at age 5, the same mothswarm Buddhaland goldennesses in the dust & and the shadows & the sun & the spectral quiet of Photograph.

AT A CALIFORNIA CAMP the Americans, on orders from the Russians who keep flying overhead in big planes threatening to drop the H-Bomb, have imprisoned a large group of people in a wire-enclosed trap and are preparing them to be the first victims of the H-Bomb Detonation right on the button. Meanwhile the doomed boys play basketball and even have gang fights. At H-Hour the people will be made to lie down in bomb shelters right under the bomb; some will be given certain shots, some not; offensive liquid mixtures to drink so the cause of your death can be traced like chalk through your guts---Everybody's saying "We'll all die of Mastoids anyway"----"from the concussion on the ears of the upper explosion"---My mother and I are there, trapped, so is Julien, Joe, many others---Ma and I foolishly came to California just in time to be trapped---At H-Hour fools with earphones will hysterically count off the seconds while people wait for death---it is sad---At the end, near the end, Julien and I are sitting together on a step---We have received no shots, we are among the lot who are going to be allowed to die straight without shots and for straight research of our blue remains-- It seems to me now that I have been taking care of Julien, who is like a helpless little brother, in many a life, many a rebirth---I am the Bodhisattva entrusted with his care---He barely begins to realize this, I can see, by his new silence and introspective respect--- I am writing a poem to commemorate the Scene---it ends with these lines:-

> The Silent Hush
> Of the Pure Land Thrush.

-------meaning Avalokitesvara's Transcendental Sound of Nirvana which is within and beyond the Bomb. It is a great Idealistic Poem and I finish it with a flourish of the pencil, beside the silent non committal Julien whose thoughts are bent on death---It is gray dusk, warm, withered flowers lay around----

> The Ground Divine
> Of Mortal Mind
>> I think on waking up---

I'M GOING DOWN THE STONE STEPS of the great Buddhist World Cave saying to watchers on the parapet "It's inward suicide"---and going down the Holy Hall ways with followers, to the big Reclining Face & the swarming dark full of light irradiating from the Center----There's nowhere to go but inward---The Cave of the World, the Cave of Reality beyond conceptions of sun, air, etc., contains the Well of Shining Reality

"NO MORE VICES SETTIN ON THE TABLE" I say to myself in Mexico City looking up from a long wild eyed rant with the pencil & the book---Pooh! I'll fly to Armour's Never Splendid Inherited Manor Borns of Pantaloon than be this hungbum writing-bum glooping & glerking & plerking in a blank room.

I'M RUNNING DOWN a sidehill & a goat-bull or cow-goat hackled to a long chain starts chasing me, I figure "All I gotta do is run so far & she'll reach the end of her rope" but instead of sprinting I keep twisting around to put my hand on the cow's head like Manolete appeasing & jibing the bull, but now this particular dream-cow takes bite painful bites at my hand & I twist to always afraid I will be butted up in the air, so foolishly I keep turning again (like halfback in flight catching bullet passes just behind over center & twists while running on delicate ankles that interlace as he goes one circle around with the ball hauled in)---but this is no hero football game, that cow is taking tragic Pink Chagall bites out of me & it's a night mare I dont even wake from with an issue decided---Besides what's the issue? Empty cows.

PREVIOUS, EISENHOWER is president of heroic America thru gray decads up to 1980's and we're all amazed to see him champion childlike cause after childlike cause, arms folded, a Saint, & I like him.----Cant afford to hate him 'cause I'm a child---Passing new paper laws, deep dream laws applied to childlike civilizations on an arbitrary gray map called the world---I cant remember the details of this bottomlessly gone dream, on waking I had no recollection or wanted more even of the barest details concerning what the Lincoln-like heroic laws were that E. passed but it seems I knew him in a dark house where's a Tolstoyan dance going on & events & crash! ---nobody loves me 'cause there's no me.

I'M SITTING IN THE WINDOW of our new kitchen in Brooklyn & as I gaze happily at all the golden windows of the tenements in the soft & fragrant dark outside, like the dark of California, my Mother is telling me not to sit in the window with the light on or the Snipers'll get me, a new secret juvenile organization dedicated to shooting people in windows---but I dont believe in the existence of the Snipers so I sit there, glad to be home anyway---And later I'm walking down Brooklyn Cow Street with Hindenburg & Huck the hoodlums of Times Square who've become involved with me again & come to get me at my cellardoor---This white dream we're having is truly inwardly and actually as peaceful, and ultimately, as the meditations of a devout priest in his church at 4 o'clock in the afternoon---as he gazes at his breviary, or through it.

LOST ON NUMBER 6 in the feature race, a gray, he broke good and was ahead in the backstretch and people commented on the goodness of his jockey but midway No.8 got at him and they all dove home close and he missed by a nose ---I was high on some weird tea that made me drunk like crazy so that I had bet all my (own) money (not Cody's) and lost $45 which I woulda regained on No.6 had he won, so I gotta go back home to New Orleans broke---Surprised to wake up seeing myself gamble & lose

I FIND CODY IN THE RAMPBACK at the race track, he solemnly shows me his new theory of how to beat the horses, it's an English newspaper clipping and the whole thing is worked out---Earlier Garden also had a theory, about snakes, insects, worms, and for proof he takes a hairy caterpillar and eats it as I *ack* and then like a child I can see his whitemush openmouth as he chews semi-seriously, it's on the high tenement of Mrs.LaMartine's porch in Centreville Lowell

                Theories shmeories!

         . .new ways of losing and uglying

MAYBE THE REASON WHY PEOPLE DONT WRITE TO ME ANY MORE is because I'm such an out and out bum----Tonight,or rather this gray morning, I dream'd I was in and out of apartment houses presumably in N. Y. on shady maneuvers (to get a place to sleep) with Deni Bleu and other tramps also trying to get coats---at one point I'm riding along on a sky elevator and I see what I remember to be James Watson's pad but the kitchen with its new brownwood furniture is different (far shot from dark sad brown wood of Lowell Kitchens long ago dusks)---because of furniture I think "Oh it's not his place!" but on calling and investigating it is, but James wont receive me, he's been in there 2 years with his girl "holed up" loving and writhing and writing---I sneak around doormen into foyers of the city, I'm wearing a suspicious overcoat, no hat, no morals, no scruples---not a thief but a strange gelatinous nameless mooch, a hanger onner, a parasite, a city wart, an apartment haunter, a sneaker-in-halls, a mattress- bug, a voyeur of orgies, a disgusting stale spectre---a dream drifter---at one point I'm hitch hiking up at that endless hopeless hill highway the other side of Bonny Brae---no rides, I sneak in subsidiary fields---Finally with a round quarter I find my way to a lunchcart near the r.r. station which has drastically reduced its prices in half, and would have gone in anyway from weariness and so with all the other customers,---Ice cream a dish is only a dime, I order it from the new queer counterman assistant who is a big good looking frank fairy who gives me the ice cream but forgets to hand me my 15¢ change because a boy at a booth has presumed to pull his leg (manfully) by saying "I'll suck your big juicy cock anytime" and Our Hero jumps without shame over the counter & goes to sit seriously in the booth to discuss further, as all the men notice and smile---So I figure I'll wait and get my change and meanwhile buy a 15¢ dish of hot pudding which will be free at the pay-counter when I remind Lover Man---as I'm taking my tray and silver with women in come two railroad guards one of them 300 pounds, and they pull up antiquated sorta car-seats to the counter and sit low to the floor facing it, waiting to be served, wearing old button down sweaters and guard badges and smoking pipes in the ray of the afternoon sun pouring into the busy lunchroom---

THAT RECURRENT DREAM WHERE I'M ALWAYS IN CALIFORNIA in Frisco, and have to travel all the way back and have no money---I see a woman suspended in mid-air giving her son a strange rich pie thru a window of a wooden Frisco building, which he accepts graciously over the rushing traffics of the street, and I think first of Evelyn (Pomeray) in Los Gatos and the sad trains there-to, then I think of Ma in the East (N.Y.?) and how I gotta go home for Christmas---There've been events all night, a bloody season, Irwin Gardens everywhere, Codies, et ceteras, I've had my up-to-here----it's time to go---wearing that seedy old top-coat and my muffcap over my ears there I go driving down the spectral boulevard in an old car (it's actually Cody's '40 Packard) and I think of hitch hiking all in the snow and decide, "Wyoming? No! I'll just drive all the way, at same time get this car home" (it's been given me)---What will I do for gas money? from hitch hikers---I'll work! "But if I work I wont make it for Christmas!"---the whole spectral hump o the continent's ahead a me, ephemeral as snow, awful as Edom,---my Arcady of Ribs, my Troy of Bones I'll crack and Waterloo on such a hopeless run and as if not remarmant & cartchaptoed enuf and once again and *again again!*----but here I am already,driving wrong way on the Oneway boule-vard and seeing I cant turnoff I make a neat proud U-turn and go back where I started from still debatin how to make that 3,000 miles east,in that miserable coat and muff hat, driving slow like an old man,sunk low at the seat---"La Marde"---and all on account of a pie.

What an arbitrary conception this Coming Home For Christmas is---I've done it twice now, and each time it bugged out on me---the first time my mother fell asleep,the second time she had to go to a funeral---big gay cities have huge sad cemeteries right outside, need em---

Rattling tenements and spectral girls (I call em tenements,I mean the wooden houses of San Fran)--- (like the one Rosemarie jumped off-of)---this drear dream-ing of necessitous sad traveling and I wake up in a vast comfortable double bed in Rocky Mount in a house in the country with nothing to do but write Visions of Gerard, wash the dishes and feed the cat!---and pop the Book of Dreams---Cant remember the haunting taunting earlier

295

details of this dream, the girls, cops, floors, sex, suicides, pies, pastiches, parturiences, wallpapers, transcendencies---the stations, gray---Garden, who never laughs, mines information---June Ogilvie Blabbery Adams McCracken my girl--- June John Boabus Protapolapalopos the Greek All-Mix Lover ---Pain Twang---

PRIVATE SCHINE, the blond sad handsome boy who was on TV in the Army-McCarthy hearings, is, now, years later, *still* held in an Army prison-madhouse where they've been trying to establish his "insanity" all these years---for anti-McCarthy political reasons---You see him in green fatigues, standing with his interlocutor, before a TV camera,as they bring up patients, the first one vaguely in my dream I think a gibbering idiot, and Schine is asked: "Is he insane?"

"Insane"

Schine is weary, you can tell this has been going on so long it's like routine but horror.

They bring up an ordinary looking young lad in fatigue & cap.

"Is he a queer?"

"Queer"---wearily, and I do a doubletake seeing the kid.

Then they bring up two fellows together: says the interlocutor: "*Two immortals who have become mortal. Insane??*"

And Schine bursts into tears---

And it's that old railyard scene, nearby, near the waterfront, cold, the bakeries and warehouses, this hopeless world---

I rush to Joe McCarthy to tell him but he's helpless and hopeless too---in the marble halls of Congress

WE'RE LIVING BACK OF OUR OLD HOUSE on Beaulieu Street and as I come in I savor the "meaty" feel of the doorjamb, and inside's gypsy drapes everywhere and Ma's in the funny little ramshackle kitchen and I'm gonna take a nap in the back room---

THE HUGE CATHEDRALS AND OFFICIAL CITY HALLS of Mexico City I'm showing Ma as we go up the main drag, I'm trying to persuade her to come stay live there ---it's gray,vast,hilly,strange like all the other Ma-Mexico City dreams with a cold hilly dreariness and hints of American white cottages---The Cathedral is half a mile hi!

I'M WALKING WITH EDNA in the mud roads beyond Mexico City downtown,in the slums, we're looking ahead at the hopeless horizon we're trying to reach on foot, I dont know how many hundreds of miles it is, all I know is we better take a train or bus to get there, a bright El Dorado up ahead in the eerie rainy Mexico o' my dreams---But finally I tell Edna let's do it now, here, she keeps looking over her shoulder down the empty night street, we find and occupy a latrine and starts she wants to lower her skirt I say no just lift it, and we start, cant get in, but I lift her thigh with one hand and now it's so perfect she herself has forgotten where she is and I wake up rocking the whole bed---lost the wife of my youth, so I deserve these nocturnal tortures---Edna was young in the dream, too

At another point, back at that strange marble-building-hotel point of MexCity, I'm smirkin with myself that I'm gonna get a girl in the streets beyond where the first (1950) MexCity dreams were, where Dave Sherman had lost his pants---I'll have to find a new and special language now to begin describing the indescribable location-mystery of these dream-locations for they're important---in each of these locations lurks a mystery of *Character*, a *Vision*---

G.J.'S. MOTHER AND SISTER are cooking awful messes in a black and gloomy kitchen in Greek Mexico City that I eat, it's like a blue jello inside a rind of hog-glue-skin, and's made by putting the jello uncolored in a cloth bag with the blue dye and some sawdusty stuff and letting it stand (in the grime, presumably)---G. J. is so solemn and serious and hungry I fain would eat with him, and do---O where is the Lost G.J. of a Black Greek Mexico City dream?---he's a kid again,and has that crazy potentiality, potency, of language, of making me laugh, amazing me---outside are all those endless riots of streets and marquees of downtown and black gloom roads and alleys---

A Mexico City fit for Fellaheen Angels--- St.Gloom,---St.Wild & Crazy-----Some *Tibetan* remembrance, some *ghee* and tallow-kitchen for G.J.-SOUL and I when we were young in Darkland and I joyed to see the Light of his Gloomy Prophecies---as we go foraging in the rain for garbages and gangs---An *epic*---Connected with the raggedy *LaNegra*, too, who must have been our then-time Silvanus Santos and Bodhisattva Hero reminder---

MY DREAM NIGHTJOB for the past several years of dreaming, I'm going to it at night in a fabulous 4-story-high bus across the railroad tracks near that perennial Brooklyn like Pittsburgh like waterfront, around midnight, and as we bounce over the track I'm reminiscing about my railroad work right on that very track when they'd kicked a boxcar and I threw the switch after it, after it crossed over the points, and then I ran after it and clambered up and braked it to a stop before the deadblock---Proudly, and now as my bus arrvies at my nightjob destination "near Yankee Stadium" I gulp and start the great horror of coming down the fourstory busladder on the outside, my hands closing around the grab ladder into tight white fists as I look down at the lucky people on the rain glistening cobbles below---But I negotiate the last 20 feet by half swinging half flying down the ladder and landing in a graceful airy jump to impress workmen, who dont watch---In topcoat and good clothes I clack off to my midnight job (my mindnight job) which is at the office of a garage again,where I know my work so well I'm always deigning to be a little late---Enroute I pass a candy store where just as I'm to buy an ice cold grape soda from the drinkbox some other character occupies the tiny drink-spot before it and I curse---Suddenly I'm some sort of elder brother greedily eating his chocolate pudding and wont give any to the baby, who then, in a William Blake newly-discover'd poem, makes his beautiful complaint

"Is nature
proud?"
and
"Something not new, some-

thing not perfumed, something not new, something not perfumed" as he runs his cherubic fingers and counts the panes and missing-panes of the window by his crib with the dusty glass---It is a definite new poem by Blake so beautiful that at points the language of the verse fairly gurgles with babylikeness, just perfect---I can remember long innocent questions complaining about the elder brother's delectable avarice and then the wild witty takeoffs---Ah me---

SOMEDAY I'LL BE REBORN in that great city in another world system, in the past or future, where the single 3-mile high mountain stands against the blue sky---With all my compassion with me, all I'll need is the wisdom of the land

THE BRUNETTE OF MY LIFE---we're approaching a work factory that's shining in the night in a field, (Green School field Centreville), to look for work, when suddenly we start balling right in the grass---She's Josephine-Maggie Zimmerman like, and throws long sea surges perfectly of her loins back at me---Saying, "I'm going to sleep out here" and I'll go in alone and get a job for us after I come and she'll sleep sweetly in the field like a hobo and wait for me to wake her at dawn---My angel doll of long ago, whose blackhaired presence in my sunny afternoon bedroom I took for granted

HORRIBLE VAST ANNEX OF DREARY PEOPLES wrongling around with events and racetracks and a war's going on in which I'm a machinegunner and have to kneel there in the open machinegunning distant house-&-walls

where enemies hide poppin us, I get hit and wounded, it hurts, I'm dragged indoors and repaired---Tomorrow I'll have to shoot again---My machinegun is a portable with round pan, blue, curious kids and people mill around and I stand guard till the battle resumes---An ugly but wellbuilt and very young girl has been in love with me all along, finally I go with her to the house and she undresses but I order her to lock the door to keep the war off, forget all about sex and end up wandering by Bronx bridges with the gun among sniper houses

I'M IN LOWELL IN A CAFETERIA outside waitingroom on the corner on Kearney Square where the grocery now (I b'lieve) is,---in there is Dick Nietzsche---Shelley Lisle the hepcat of Lowell, at first a lil unfriendly then warming up as I ask him for some bennies and to arrange to buy me more, he dumps about 10 in my hand "Oh they're the new kind!" I cry seeing their perforated bottoms---He lives somewhere in the Dark Highlands like a dark Timmy Clancy of old Lowell dreams, later we'll go there and pick up---I swallow 2 with water at the little icewater fountain and my face lowered to drink pious eyelids fall on swarming death but beyond death Awakening Buddha Realization that earlier I'd been up the (Concord) River of Eternity (the true Mississippi), the sere shores, and I recall my Ma would be mad to see me get high and dissipate but *"It's the pure truth no matter what you do"* I realize piously drinking and outside it's gray Kearney Sq. so sad and same and strange with dead ghosts waiting for buses, and damp foyers of marble halls, and rain and bus stops and wetshoes---I dig Dick as a great new sad kid---

301

THE MERCHANT MARINE ACADEMY is drumming out two impostors who pretended to be officers on the ship, as a remnant of oldtime punishments the ritual now is to lead them out with a black velvet doublenoose around both their necks and march off the merchantship between erect files of cadets, to drums---I see the captain who is reading the sentence: "The squawk of the little very self which wanders everywhere. . . . ." . .tsk tsk such ignoble impostors. .

"THE IMMATERIAL MEADOW OF THIS WORLD you ask as with golden ash" is saying the pockmarked colored kid with glasses wearing a snow white sweater to which I am clutching unconscious of what I'm doing as he's turned in his schooldesk seat talking to the blond kid disciple next to me who wanted to know and I'm thinking "All this arbitrary interest of mine in *teachings*, 't' ends up I put my face close to ugly pockmarks and badbreath" and stop clutching at his sweater----Earlier the Master had just read from the Sutra:- "It is not so with the wise, the elite, they see unconditioned void perfection of freedom, but those who discriminate appearances are the 'niggers' "----(in the sense that he would have meant the 'niggers' the ignorant and simpleminded)--- nevertheless this pockmarked kid is the smartest---Where have I seen a pockmarked bespectacled black man dressed in snow? Gandhi? Jimmy Thomas? Some Jain in olden
incarnations i the wood?
i the immaterial
meadow of this world?

GEE! there I am 16 years old on the Lowell Lawrence Eternity football field, you see me in a clear old newsreel I never dream'd was taken, I see myself as I was then, have just scored a touchdown and I wear nothing waist up so you see my chest and biceps and well developed almost chubby belly that I breathe in and out fast, you see me looking around *fast* like Roy Eldridge and though grave I make silly jokes and rattlebrain talk so as I sit there watching I think "Ah even then I was a fool, a young fool Kerouac is all"----my skin is white, my hair jet black---I rue my personality's sillier earlier manifestation there on the screen---

DRIVING WITH MY DETECTIVE PUBLISHER FRIEND down a dry sand road that runs parallel to Bayshore Hiway but by itself in dry desert Pecos rocks and blasted arroyos of red and orange dust, we come to his isolate cottage, Joe Louis is there but leaves during dinner to go home to his kids---another crazy Negro is in the garage

I HAD A WHITE BANDAGE on my head from a wound, the police are after me around the dark stairs of wood near the Victory Theater in Lowell, I sneak away---come to the boulevard where a parade of children chanting my name hide me from the searching police as I duck along their endless ranks, keeping low---The parade of children is endless--- Chanting and singing we go marching into Mongolia with me with my white bandaged head in front
(dreamed the day after the publication of
ON THE ROAD)

303

AS CAPTAIN OF THE GREAT VAGUE BOAT I've neglected my duties playing around with passengers up & down a thousand spectral staircases, suddenly I realize we've been at sea three days with nobody steering, I go to the dark bridge house, try to turn on the lights, and suddenly a big Chinese Strange Freighter going the other way signals me, I reply with one pull on the whistle rope, VOOOM, then fearing that "one-long" will be taken for distress & my peaceful vague sea voyage captaincy disturbed by boarding officials and breeches' buoys & signing of papers I hold off I give another short pull, this time because of my hysteria the whistle just goes PLURP---So I steer, cant see, hope we dont ram ships---Arriving at a tiny port with a narrow canal I veer the immense front of the ship around curves hoping all that hugeness behind me isnt ruining villages---

DREAM Aug.24, '57 Orlando---Of my being in "Guadalajisco" which is a cool sweet bordertown where I'm so happy I'm decided to stay there forever, with my young chums, and my special little 10 year old chum who talks in Spanish to me with a definite beloved personality like G.J. or a son---The American has us carry his gear to the train 20 minutes ahead of time every day, pondering 'Do we need a whole *twenty* minutes?' but I (thinking him a Cody con man) start off anyway longstriding with my mantilla and hope the American notices I'm walking like a real Mexican---I stride off with my little chum, looking down the Mexican street at flowing robed people---The boy, like me, is naturally certain that no place in the world compares to the city of Guadalajisco, he also explains its wealth, not from "ranchos" but oil and I see a map

304

of Tamaulipas showing trucks hauling oil---Meanwhile the railroad train has a Mex passenger-brakeman who gets off full-speed train without effort, just steps off, on station platform at high end, without even any special step-off or fall-away or back-leg technique, just a miracle---and in fact he's so good that at the last station before the Terminal they *drop* (special railroad type of kick-in) his car and it rolls alone into station, fast, where he applies a hand brake and locks but before car is fully stopped (in fact still fullspeed) he's off, stepping miraculously to do business of platform with his blue uniform and tickets---You see sad Mexican ladies carrying babies off the train in little balls in shawls---I try to tell some American brakemen of the nearby Border American Railroad about him but they're not interested in Mexicans, one of them is an older, ragged, rugged, sad dark Cody who (as for years he's been hopelessly doing it) invites me on the hopelessly long trip to his house, which I always refuse (being a lazy Mexican) because of the distance the hassel and he knows I will but asks, as if angrily, and indifferently, anyway---

From that station the miracle Brakeman then's supposed to run the car to the Terminal on its own power, now the American Brakemen are interested in how this can be done, but the rail is too hot, the rods between the rails, the floor itself, me & the Mex Brakie (who has Chaplin mustache) demonstrate by walking over & up the hot rollers between the rails among the watching Americans---It's like a scene in Hell, before doubters we burn to prove---"See?" as we walk in waves of heat up the Terminal rail ramp---The details of this dream are amazing, I could write a full length book, like, Cody's face, which is unshaven, surly, but sadkindly still, inviting me with automatic hopelessness and assuring me for millionth time that I will be welcome with his angry-ing wife---Too, my Guadalajisco gang of Mexican chums is strange, each definite individual stamped immortally in my mind (in the dream), each so momentous, and the reason for my great lifelong happiness is the sweet swinging land, the fine clean city, the breeze, our job as daily porters for the Cody-like 20-minute American ('Cant we leave *fifteen* minutes ahead of time?' I ponder, but start off automatically, trying to remember if the American is really *Cody* & therefore a con man)---As to the Miraculous Mexican Brakeman with the Chaplin Mustache, his achievement is taken for granted in Mexico, he just steps off highspeed trains to do his work a little faster, he himself's modest & matter of fact about it and if I were to tell the American Brakemen (who wont listen anyway) they wouldn't believe it they are so unshaven, angry and sad, so American in their disinterest---Not only Cody but a taller surlier brakeman to whom I try to say "I was a Brakeman too, lemme tell you about this Mexican, amazing!" but he strolls off to chat with Cody and a group of dark shabby conductors not interested in anything but angry sad American affairs---So the Miraculous Mexican Brakeman goes on stepping off cars, with a little definite stamp of his foot, nothing else, a little tricky plap, flatfooted, his body perfectly still as the cars rage by then ease to a stop by which time he's already punched tickets on the platform for childlike Mexican Travelers who dont even notice it's a Miracle.

And after work you see him waddling down the little dusk road of Rural Mexico to his little adobe home with wife and barefoot kiddies, where he sits by the ikon and eats his humble supper, hat and all, as loving neighbors serenade him with guitars---

306

NIGHTMARE IN NORTHPORT---last night, the three who started off as Bull and Irwin and me naked, later steal in China and escape on the run in a big Movie Award Running Classic about running up over the mad continental mountain and down into the back of India, safe, except for border guards and the shopkeeping informer whom they jump and start murdering with knives and kicking in the face WHAP! & finally face to face glued with blood the hero pukes up yellow sticky glue puke that glues their faces together in puky blood so that when he looks up in disgust great messes like on top of pizza pie stretch and the brothers recoil and exclaim "He's Sioux Sick!" and I wake up in the quiet 4 AM and ask quietly "Jésus, pourquoi tu'm montre des portraits comme ça?" and meditate crosslegged realizing it must be an educational movie from another Buddhaland showing Bodhisattvas why to reject violence and how horrible ignorance which not only projects an outside world but grasps at it, fights in it---It was the only really horrible nightmare I ever had, got it from a bee-bite earlier in the day I think.

The actual description of that horrified yellow puking of China mixed with the bloody faces would make you sick

DIGGING GRAVES IN THE YARD, I've already dug my father's along the walk and the marks are still there but now (and also dug a woman's but didnt place her in) but I'm afraid I wont dig deep enough under the 3 feet of snow and now have to dig 2 for Jerry & Lola and say to two guys with me "Come Spring the snow melts you see elbows sticking out of the ground, gad what a thing to be buried in a black suit" and

one of the guys is suddenly tall looking at me in a black suit!
---Cold bony dream---

THE GREAT MOVIE COMPANY brings all its equipment
to the westside waterfront to film with Raphael in the color
panorama lead but as soon as they're all set up a disastrous fire
breaks out and they get the awesome shots in---I myself have
to shore up the fire in the barn with my books, like playing
tides with water---So the first day of the movie is the greatest ever but the second day shows what they'd already shot a
shoddy TV thriller with cars driving up for assignations and
Raphael rushing off with a message---So that another jealous
producer in black & white shoots his own epic TV'er in the
deep hillfields & you see the hero (me) peeking at the hider
who is sneaking down the hollow for the big yellow bag con-
taining the secrets of the great color panorama company but
he's caught by the two hoods & banged on the kisser---The
suspense is all about how they dont see me but as they come
up the long steps they wont miss so I leap out, turn into a girl,
& kick the harmless younger hood down the stairs after first
exhibiting my kicking leg which the baneful blond hood only
stares at---The director of this one is a bearded beatnik
bohemian producer---

Fact is, if I tried to explain every tiny detail
of these dreams there'd be no end---like, I remember (in the
dream) my father's trip down from Lowell before he died, the
crazy sodafountain where we'd eaten and you pressed a button and out came mashed potatoes with gravy---Emil Ladeau
telling me his brother Cy married a girl from North Carolina
and is now living in Montreal and dont I remember the time

he, Emil, drove me to Texas? And I dont believe that Ma is dead, nor Jerry and Lola who may be kidding me, tho I do say "They're the kind of people would have to die together, otherwise the other would follow the first in a few days, they love each other that way" so I begin to believe it---Graves, graves! I the Gravedigger! The girl kicking the harmless hood! Oh! Suspense TV movies! The mind is nuts!

> I woke up---
>   two flies were boffing
> On my forehead

LAST NIGHT driving along with Joe in some car part of the big happy Fortier family caravan, the sisters Doris and Bertha or Marie get out to see how we're making out but because there's something wrong with me I'm in the backseat like a chauffeur's employer huddled very low so they and no one else may see me, something wrong with my pants or something, and my head I keep or try to keep so low that my chin is all big choky doublechin against my breastbone---somewhere in the sad

HORRIBLE, I GUESS IT'S THE END OF THE WORLD, the clouds in the sky are soot black and turn to white as you look and suddenly they are dancing a little on a tilty horizon so, and like on a ship's deck I realize it's not the clouds moving it's the Earth & I tell it to the gang in the school yard "The earth is moving" and Irwin and I go back and stand together near the redbrick schoolwall to marvel that the

Apocalypse has finally come and we're together in its Moment---Meanwhile my mother'd followed people up the steep hill and tried to sit crawling out over the mile high seats and I had to help her---

AT THE TOP OF MERRIMAC STREET where the Canadian Social Club is G.J. is now a shoe salesman in a swank shoe store and I come in to fetch him off to New York or Boston, our big spree---We cross the Moody Street Bridge discussing Scotty---G.J. is well dressed and rich, in fact he's the manager of the store---We will go to the tragic tenements of nightclub alley Lowell or the raw cold streeties of Pawtucketville with abandoned houses---

WAITING IN A FIELD for the sun to go down, bang, as soon as it sinks red over the horizon it gets completely dark and I cant see---I keep tryin to hop the friend train in the dark and run alongside almost not seeing the switch stand at the last minute, but do, over the switch points and get on--- "Lost my hat!"---Go back and get it but as the train speeds off to Detroit I realize I've lost my lantern too, but not my gloves, bah

UNDERGROUND GENTLEMEN'S CLUB in "Charleston S.C." I guess with labyrinths of lounge private rooms with mahogany tables and chairs---And the kitchen hath many cooks and colored attendants who bring in four "lamb shanks" which are as big as full cow legs and have red stripes

but the best one has blue stripes and they peel off the (carefully) sickly corned beef filmy skin for the party of four
headed for an airplane---When I lift my hand to indicate
"four" in laughter at this the head boy with the knife scowls
nervously because the young curly haired head chef at the
extreme right is darkly displeased (like Random Cowan lour-
ing dark)---so I replace the cook knife on their counter &
cut---Then I'm in North Africa on the beautiful sunny paradise old land southern shore of Mediterranean wandering
among Arabs and Peace, "Jesse," I say, "this is the original cra-
dle of cities, this was Carthage" (there's a lane of piled sand
going out in the ocean for quiet Arab bathers) but she says
there are, there *is* an older site in Spain ("Santa Lilaila")---

Then I'm in the South with Ma and Lil
Luke in a pleasant house with trees in yard but directly in
back begins a little mill lane among Colonial windowless mill
bricks leading to a frightening abrupt drop into a stinking
river of dye way below and alongside is the pure Mississippi
--- Then in New York Bronx the boys skating start a rumble
and one has his spectacles jammed under skate blades---Then
Jesse tells me some guy slugged her, she's almost pleased, she
says it went right thru her head, I prepare to drive his jaw
thru with one mighty jab, my "Moses Blow"

POEM DREAM

All warmly huddled
  at the bow of our battleship
  we seamen in the Brooklyn night
    go sailing across the river

311

              to our dock
                  and I jump down
                  and grab the rungs
              because I want to jump off
              as soon as we dock
              but the huge ship blams
          into the pier like ferry
              blamming other shore, full
                                  of watchers
      and as I hang there hard
          ship speeds skims slimmer
          down endless watery drydocks
          where Negros wait way ahead
          & I hang for dear life
          staring at the huge black tires
          of our ship thinking: "For
              rolling undersea?
                  or for drydock roll?
                  O, dishes"

MY ASS NAKED sitting on a stool in the field full of people I'm reading some book and the Jack Paar show is going
on in the field but I dont care---Suddenly he comes up with
mike and camera and pins me down to have me televised
universally naked, I hang there like a helpless child till I hear
Julien's faint voice in back trees saying (twangily St.Louis)
"Dont let him do it!" so after a helpless moment I up and
throw him a feeble punch

                            312

IN THE DRACUT TIGERS HORRIBLE STIFLING UNDERGROUND MAZE I'm trying to crawl back out with my loot of tomato plants tied to my back and cant get through the final narrow hole, & cry---Ma is there and trys to help me, another woman in the window, they try to yank the gripper off my shirt as I yell "The spiders will be coming after their tomato plants, hurry!" & they laugh, finally they really laugh when she yanks at my fly shirt pin and I yell "*That* wont help"---Some humor! even I grin!---

Tomato plants thick and prickly fuzzy deepgreen for spiders and wont let me thru the dusty hole---

Vant to crawl out of uncrawlable holes---

THE 500 MILE HIGH WINDOWS of the Tangiers yellow light night---Starts with a Nazi officer leading me up a snowy hill to execute me via automatic shnortzel Luger and makes German jokes in the falling snow making me think "O why do these dreary sexual executioners always have to come on so dull with their tired-out straight jokes" and when we come to a house with a steep outdoor stairway he orders me to climb, which I do (it is the same stairway of the cops in Lowell when I had the white bandage that I escaped to Mongolia in, as children paraded in my name), I know he's going to shoot me in the back so I climb and wince to feel it but nothing happens and when I get to the top I turn and see he's having difficulty with his Luger---in the snow ---by the same mountain pass that those Chinese-Indians used to go down the India border in the yellow puke dream---So I escape into a V-cornered tenement room and look out the window and in the dream it says it's a 500 mile

313

drop to the street (tho you can see from yellow Tangiers nightlights below it's really 500 stories or so)---It turns into a movie which me and my gang are going up a long night boulevard of transcontinental bus travelers to see, after I buy my thin little ice cream cone I'm walking with my friends one of whom is in drag as the Thief of Baghdad hero of the story (worn out Gene Kelly), another is real out queer Genêt hero, and there's Irwin, Simon, others---In my dream I realize 'butch drag' for the first time clearly and sympa-thize---I'm kinda weird myself, as I yell something at a group of girls and they come on dikey with me on the boulevard---Gang goes into the immense 500 mile high balcony and it shows the hero at the window ledge of the top floor, then a boom descends thru the 500 mile high ten-ement to show the audience the enormity of the dancing halls and props all the way down to the street where fallers squash on newspaper sidewalk and we're sitting together in a box and Irwin in a cultured concerned complaint classi-cally angelic says "Oh, *let* them have a big ball!" meaning all these Tangerian 500 mile queer teaheads their halls and dancing balls in this weird Arabian nightlife town (sea nearby) and it's so funny I giggle wonderfully like Cody and the whole gang turns and guffaws to realize I'm still at their rear, guarding and digging---Meanwhile groups are leaving the theater and see us (such a strange group) and others nearby also strange, all boys, all intelligent looking, and say "Oh ho, you can tell it's Saturday night"

---In the dream I'm a cultured queer queen-king, part saint, beloved---On waking it seemed I remembered that girl on the boulevard in my previous life-time in England whom I must have murdered---I must have

been a queer in that previous lifetime or couldnt divine
about "butch drag" without experience in this lifetime---

I'M IN "FRISCO" and I'm going to take a nice walk but suddenly I'm simply walking on the other side of Riverside
Street near the park and as it starts to drizzle I turn to go back
just as the cop cruiser comes by ("I wonder what they'll think
to see me turn back just now?") and I go to the corner where
there's an ice cream cake store (where in real life only the corner of the football field) and I order an ice cream cake that
turns out to cost $2 and I only have $1---so I cant buy it so
the lady turns sinister (O a rich cake the size of a briefcase
with coffee ice cream and sherbert topping)---She takes out
(she turns into a man) a kind of hand grenade object (or pine
cone) with slits and starts sticking sticks in it, or thorns, and
Zap Plouffe is there, recognizes me and tells everybody to stop
fooling me---In the dream Zap isnt dead, we discuss his
brother Gene---I wake up from this Pawtucketville of the
Strange realizing Zap Plouffe never died!

TO GET DOWN FROM OUR APARTMENT to the
street you have to go down a ladder overhanging from the
top of the Empire State Building---I'm sick of the whole
fucking thing and refuse to do it again but Jesse does it---A
man had just tried it before her (going to work with evening
paper in his pocket) and he quietly dropped off and fell to his
death silently and unobtrusively---It happens all the time---
But I go down the safe way which is not indicated in the
dream and I'm down on the dark street strolling wondering

315

if Jesse made it---Turn around and see her a block up strolling slowly on the other side of the street---It seems Ma didnt make it and is dead but I dont believe it---(The same day Ma was scared coming down the attic ladder, dreams prevision in a strange tender way)---Jesse is strolling sadly in the dark not knowing where I am any more

A FANCY DRESSED WOMAN is remorsefully sneaking out on her wailing baby to step out with tophatted Shadows in the city night, she leaves, sneaks downstairs and just then a woman upstairs comes down tip toeing in stockinged feet to watch the neglectful lady sneak out---but I am sitting in the dark watching it all thru a hall window, I see the peeking woman's satisfied smile and know that in a moment she will horrifiedly notice that she was watched in the act of her Spy ---and when she does see me it's just a dim light on my face in the dark and what a leering smile I give her! she blanches

LONG DRAMA OF JUICY MONSTROUS BEARDS and pirates in old Gilbert Street (juicy delicious 18th Century beards) house, must be the hants of there, the little kitchen *was* an old house, & at the end there's a cholera epidemic and they send the little 10 year old girl to get the doctor in town but he'd always raped her---When the young sinister doctor (a French actor) is there ministering the bearded sick we see that the little girl has been molested again, or that is we know it, but we also see the cholera's hit her as she jumps off the chair and her older sister and mother demand a shot for her---The doctor says "She shant have one

316

till later, it's almost too late" and as he emerges from his lab we see tears in his eyes---

Why is my mind so dull by day with no delicious juicy beards and dramas like that

CROSSING MOODY STREET BRIDGE with a holy goat in my arms I let him down on the planks and he runs across the street and vaults the rail of the bridge clean down to his death on the water-crashing rocks below---I cant look---But suddenly I realize he's swimming beneath the bridge, apparently missed the rocks, and now I see him swimming strongly to the rocky shore---He makes it, comes in the underbridge ramp running to me and as I reach down fingertips to catch him in my arms he stands on hind legs and just hooves my fingertips---I know I'll get him by the feet, haul him up, and take him home---

that Lamb
(white)

I'M IN MEXICO PEERING INTO WINDOWS while neighbors stare, finally I ask one woman "A donde es Senor Gaines?" but I really mean Hubbard and shows me a window with Hubbard inside standing in the middle of his room surrounded by a dozen beatnik and hoodlum and other visitors ---I knock on window, he rushes out politely to let me in but I have my hunting cap over my eyes not even looking at him and go in---In the middle of the floor Bull (no room for himself to sit) expounds on guns and finally fishes out a small automatic from a silk wrapping & hands it to a young darkhaired hoodlum---Later, in his shorts like the famous John L. Sullivan boxing-pose photo in BIG TABLE magazine, Bull is advised by the Sergeant to report up the sandbank to his officers the "Allies"---Other guys in shorts are listening---I marvel that Bull is so sardonic with the sergeant & about the whole Army in general--- "Give my regards to the Allies," says I, "if you gets there" (imitating Charles Laughton for Bull's benefit & also knowing he wont even go) & Bull laughs but I lamely add *"When* you gets there," as always nervous when trying to be *funny* for Bull, & like in the door with the hunting cap he politely refrains from comments on my awkwardness---I marvel at the respect he gets from the men and officers of the world

A BIG 'BEAT GENERATION CONVENTION' is arranged in Philadelphia, everybody's there but they've erected a 300 foot tower of concrete which topples over & falls in the field, you see nimble workmen sneaking out of the wood board interior amazingly & some being run over as the tower is allowed to roll because they're letting the rabbits inside move it shifting their positions---I see Irwin & Simon but I'm not sitting with them---On the way back to New York I'm with one of the Conference officials and when I ask him what he got out of the conference he says "O I'm not interested in that, I just provided the concrete for the tower" and I realize he's just a gangster and he gets real mean and shows me how Frank Sinatra wallops guys on the jaw (holding my head and almost blasting me with his big fist)---I hate him---You next see F. B.I. men studying his accounts showing where a certain "Gleason" received $6,000 in the phoney concrete deal---

318

"We're interested in knowing who this Gleason really is"---They've trapped the gangster inside his house---In between I'd come down that amazing ski-run shaft street steeper than belief, the same as in Lowell sometimes, James Watson nods when I tell him I wish we had sleds, we're coming down via the endless elevated steps of upper Bronx New York---I get sick & almost die as I fly around a post (wake up with a neuralgic leg)---

Everybody at the conference had been sitting in pairs, in chairs, I forget the fellow I sat with but in the back of the hall Jerry Getty has been balling the beautiful Revlon Announcer Girl Starlet & I want some too, I find them comin out from a dark sewer secret door & she's naked & Jerry says "She's out of her mind"---I grab her warm naked body, she doesnt want me---I dont like her much

THE FLYING HORSES OF MIEN MO---I'm riding a bus thru Mexico with Cody sleeping at my side, at the dawn the bus stops in the countryside and I look out at the quiet warm fields & think: "Is this really Mexico? why am I here?"---The fields look too calm & grassy & bugless to be Mexico---Later I'm sitting on the other side of the bus, Cody is gone, I look up in the sky & see that old ten thousand foot or hundred mile high mountain cliff with its enormous hazy blue palaces and temples where they have giant granite benches & tables for Giant Gods bigger than the ones who hugged skyscrapers on Wall Street---And in the air, Ah the silence of that horror, I see flying winged horses with capes furling over their shoulders, the slow majestic pawing of their front hooves as they clam thru the air flight---Griffins they are!---

So I realize we're in "Coyocan" & this is the famous legendary place---I start telling 4 Mexicans in the seat in front of me the story of the Mountain of Coyocan & its Secret Horses but they laugh not only to hear a stranger talk about it but the ridiculousness of anybody even mentioning or *noticing* it---There's some secret they wont tell me concerning ignoration of the Frightful Castle---They even get wise with Gringo Me and I feel sand pouring down my shirt front, the big Mexican is sitting there with sand in his hand, smiling---I leap up & grab one, he is very tiny & skinny & I hold his hand against his belly so he wont pull a knife on me but he has none---They're really laughing at me for my big ideas about the Mountain---

   We arrive at Coyocan town over which the hazy blue Mountain rises and now I notice that the Flying Horses are constantly swirling over this town & around the cliff, swooping, flying, sometimes sweeping low, yet nobody looks up & bothers with them---I cant bring myself to believe that they are actually flying horses & I look & look but that's what they have to be, even when I see them in moon profile: horses pawing thru air, slow, slow, eerie griffin horror men-horses---I realize they've been there all the time swirling around the Eternal Mountain Temple & I think: "The bastards have something to do with that Temple, that's where they come from, I always knew that Mountain was all horror!"---I go inside the Coyocan Maritime Union Hall to sign for a Chinese sea job, it's in the middle of Mexico, I dont know why I've come all the way from New York to the landlocked center of Mexico for a sea voyage but there it is: a Seaman's hiring hall full of confusion & pale officials who dont understand why I came also---One of them makes a great intelligent effort to have letters in duplicate written to New York to begin straightening out the reason why I came ---So if it's a job I'll get, it wont be for a week at least, or *more* ---The town is evil & completely sinister because everybody is ugly sneering (the natives,I mean,) and they refuse to recognize the existence of that Terrible Swirl of Flying horses---"Mien Mo," I think, remembering the name of the Mountain in Burma they call the world, with Dzapoudiba the southern island (India), on account of Himalayan secret horrors---The beating heart of the Giant Beast is up there, the Griffins are just incidental insects---but those Flying Horses are happy! how beautifully they claw slow forehooves thru the blue void!---

Meanwhile 2 young American seamen and I study them flying up there miles high & watch them swoop lower, when they come low they change into blue and white birds to fool everybody---Even I say:"Yep, they're not flying horses, they only seem to be, they're Birds!" but even as I say that I see a distinct horse motioning lyrically thru the moon with a cape furling from his infernal shoulders---

A broken nosed ex boxer approaches me hinting that for 50¢ a job can be arranged on a ship---He is so sinister & intense I'm afraid to even give him 50¢---Up comes a blonde with her fiance announcing her forthcoming marriage but she interrupts her speech every now and then to wail on my joint in front of everybody in the streets of COYOCAN!

And the Flying Horses of Mien Mo are galloping with silent ease in the happy empty air way up there ---Tinkle Tinkle go the streets of Coyocan as the sun falls, but up there is all silence & the Giant Gods are up---How can I describe it?

(Written after a Chinese dinner in Chinatown!)

STRANGE STRANGE DREAM of me making myself into a previous masturbating tape recorded body which lies right beside me whacking my hammer. . .

DREAMED I WAS WAITING in a strange illuminated white bus terminal in New Jersey for the bus to New York, endless wait, and there's a beautiful but strange Chinese woman waiting against the wall---I go up to her & point out the two Chinese boys & two Negro boys also waiting--- "How's that for a picture?" I banter, and come to feel her girdle, which she doesnt like---"How old are you?" I ask staring at the strange serene oval beauty of her face & she says "Let us just let it go at that, I was born in 1863" and I understand counting immediately that she's almost one hundred years old & I say "I see, you're Tibetan" and she gives a slight nod with her eyes---The bus is coming at four and it's only three in dismal Sunday New Jersey

WE ALL STAND FOR A GROUP PHOTOGRAPH in the yard of the great Pine Tree Mansion of the Captors--- later we play in the field, a hundred of us, I see Cody giving the rear man's hiball sign to a departing freight train & places a little Brakeman Doll in the tracks who also cranked-up tinily gives same sign as the train goes off to the outer world ---We're all prisoners of the Communists---Finally they ask us back for that group photo on the lawn leeringly saying

322

"Quite a few faces missing!" which I notice is true as I'm the last one to appear & the ranked standers are depleted---But they wave me away from the picture contemptuously down the dungeon steps, I've been suspected of revolutionary or at least bugged tendencies as I yakked in the "Free Field"--- Down I go to my doom---An insane attendant down the brown stone steps has me sit temporarily in a cell which has a large pool of brown water in a big pan with shit floating in it while I'm to be processed by him but he leaves momentarily on a call so I rock the cell shiplike somehow & dump the brown shit water out into the dungeon aisle---But he gets back just as I'm doing it, picks up the "pan" and dumps it on my head and then on *his* head and we stare at each other dripping brown shitwater hair & I realize among other things that the attendants of the Lower Hells are so miserably agonized they want you to be the same as they---But meanwhile I understand that the Underground Prisons have women cooks & waitresses who need man-love so badly that they have developed a super secret subterranean system of their own to hie men away into sumptuous underground love-making apartments & the Authorities never know where they've vanished---The secret word is so secret & feminine, the tokens of admission to stud so mysterious, you can spend the rest of your captive life just boffing these luscious thin blondes completely secure & safe from harm---The "tokens" are supposed to be "food ration" buttons but they're really what the women gather in work and pay to be allowed to visit the hidden captive men-places to be laid---And the Captor Authorities are forever puzzled---The insane attendant with shit water in his hair doesnt even know what's happened to you after you've been spirited away from his jurisdiction, not to mention the outside Firingsquad Photographers of the "Free Yard"

JULIEN AND I CHARGED WITH CARE OF KID-BROTHER ROBERT in the upper house, Julien wanting to go out and hit the Greenwich Village bars, the Remo---I've never seen him that way before, eager to go out & mix in bars---I wake up in such a dead silence I think my window's closed, but it's open

(1957 BERKELEY)
ALEX FAIRBROTHER is propelling a little 3 wheel bike with a backbox where we all about 5 of us sit, some on top of others, down a dark hall in a West End Avenue apartment house in N.Y., we're looking for Johnathan Miller's apartment, 80A, cant find it, with the flashlight that shines a white beacon in the utter dreamdarkness Fairbrother is examining the doors of apartments 80 and 81 & there's no intermediary 80A of mysterious never-findable Jonathan---Meanwhile we're a little anxious the night watchman might be coming down the hall with his own flashlight---Earlier, rickety house shack on the sandbank cliff, we've been living roisterously in it a whole gaudy family but now while they're all below having a picnic I test it by rocking it & it falls to the sand below (*has* fallen, I dont see the catastrophe itself), I myself just float down to look at it upsidedown, one good legsywhop & she'd went---The house was so rickety I dont think anybody'll mind---(Nin was a member of this family in the golden sandbank)---

Later Alex Fairbrother organizes our moun-
tainclimb, I create a contour map showing two little mountains
of sugar & snow, our route by airplane from Brazil *little-ly* to
these Arctic mounts, it only worries me as I wake up that since
it's a one day climb we'll have to try to sleep at high altitude in
the *arctic*

IN THE LOWELL GARDEN I'M STUDYING the ring of
glue I put on the log to keep the bugs away from a sensitive
point, some are stuck in it, Ma comes along with a sausage &
says "I havent much money left, you'll have to buy the food
from now on" & in the road on the sidewalk a friend is staring at us, "O how are you?" says Ma indifferently---He points
to his wife, Ma's also indifferent to her, they dont come visit
tho apparently they had driven over to see us but Ma doesnt
care---O well, it's the book of dreams

"DIEPPE"---I'm on a train going from some presumed Le
Havre to Dieppe but in a southward triangle V, down and up
again, thinkin to change at Dieppe for the Marseilles train to
go where it's warm (Avignon! I think but someone tells me
it's cold & windy at night in that old Arles country) and anyway they remind me I only have $25 & cant make it anyway,
gloomily I realize I gotta get off at "Dieppe" and roam
gloomy misty Normandy fields all summer with my poncho
and "wait for my money from New York"---It's morning,
the field is wet with dew, pink sun thru rain clouds, only
when I wake up do I remonstrate with myself with "What's
wrong with a summer in Normandy?"---All I wanta do is

get out of Europe, go to America, get out of America, go to Mexico, get out of Mexico, go to Morocco, get out of Morocco, go to Hell

DEFENDING MYSELF TO A JURY OF MEN including the white haired old judge but I'm up in the air, in levitation, floating over them vociferously explaining why I am not guilty & they smile either because my arguments are silly or naturally that since I'm free of earth now who can prosecute?---As if, "Look at that absurd angel worried about things of the earth"---"doesnt even know he's free"---"goes on haranguing to explain his position and there he is free as air"---s'this means?

DREAMS DREAMS DREAMS---In a car after long walk down Boston Mechanic Oldchurch boulevard, me, Cody at wheel, Irwin, Simon, girls, my own 15 year old green eyed girl, they smoke tea without rousing me from apparent sleep to offer me some (it's my tea) so I roll it away in my white writing sheet and then---(interrupted in writing here)---my girl and I walk thru long muds and sand dunes and awful burr patches to the sea, I get sore at her for leading me thru burrs all the time, we sit there pulling them off shoes & pants then go into the cabin where Swenson is sleeping in one room, we have to climb over his bed in the window to get to our room, he tries to wrestle me down---I'm mad at everybody but end up with my baby in our bed for sullen long early sexings in the mist---And earlier the long raw subways, at one point I ride the outside of the train where it rolls outdoors & jump off onto a slippery bank made of scrapwood which doesnt hold me & I almost slip back under the wheels, I tell the conductor engineer to slow down till I scramble off (before the tunnel) & before that in Cody's house how sullenly we cease talking to each other & b god but what a difference between my conscious day thoughts & these night dreams pointing to the fact that I should live alone a bohemian life with a little girl---Distressing to know that I'm not doing what I want, ever

ABOVE ALL JOANNA showing her cunt thru a slit in her slacks to Eileen Webber & Eileen Farrier (Eileen Webber takes on a wild depraved dike face stark & gray mad dark) at their request, but Cody is bugged---Then (it's all one a barge in Lowell) I come to Mexico City & come in the "discouraging" way so I can learn it, the street into the watersides & huge red building walls, tourist Mexico of women stretching off south to an unknown Tehuantepec distance gray map--- I ride in the train with the Mexicans, walk catways, cut thru parks, come to movies---That raving mad high hill waterslap bleekboat buildinged roadcurve Mexico City only exists in my dreams lonelier than the real

O JESUS, THE WHOLE OLD LOWELL HIGHSCHOOL FOOTBALL TEAM, all of us watching old movies of our games, you see Norman the blond center being led out by the gang to the street to where Chet Rave is walking with his girl, to persuade Chet that because Norman is all busted up we need Chet to play, they even show him a wax covered salami in a paper bag saying Norman had his cock torn off which I dont know if it's a joke or true cock & Chet feels Norman's broken ribs & says "O, he's even got busted here!" so he agrees to play, this we're all watching at the front of some train (now) looking on the tracks up-rushing & I'm next to Christy Kelakis, tenderly we lean heads together as "Santa Barbara Yards" sweep by in a blizzard at dusk & I explain my railroad work then, leaning lovey like that in a tenderest moment of my dreams, Kelakie says "We wont see them any more" indicating the ghosts on the screen of our old team, & I agree, say "We wont see them any more" (meaning ultimate death) & just then the train (now we're in the tail car) begins flapping around curves, I yell "He's going too fast!" & sure enough our car disengages from the whole train & goes reeling after it by itself & then the last thing I see the cars ahead of us, have stopt & we're bearing down on them 80 miles an hour, we all wait for death, the whole team, silently, with our noses to the glass or some (as I,) wincing away

ON TOP OF EMPIRE STATE FLAT TOP HIGHSCHOOL SLEEPHOUR PLATFORM with Senator Shaft's queer son who wont let me sleep & keeps pushing me near the edge in his "ardor" I finally confess to him I'm afraid of height & please leave me alone & finally ask the attendants to take me down blindfolded---He is a delicate little pale Hartzjohn, the problem child of the school, had earlier bothered me in the assembly seats, a vast gloesome wock wartpat high school it tis---Below our platform the people & cars move about like ants in the haze.

Will Our Miss Brooks ever marry dumb Mr Boynton?

DESOLATION PEAK 1956

TONY CURTIS' SEX ORGY PARLOR where a woman in front of other women is showing me what they do to you, she starts by balling up my genitals in her hands & licking a big tongue over the hump of flesh, she is a redhead, a lil older than me, it's in some sunny afternoon loft in New York or Hollywood & they show me vast albums of longhaired curly Tony with all his secret boyfriends---Later a grayhaired queer gives me a 'distinguished' photo of himself which he hopes'll make me fall in love with him, it's the cover on a novel of his, with autograph, it looks a little like me with whiter hair---He is rich, has a wife, rich pad, patio pad with drinks, I go there in evening after long time spent waiting with Ma in some marble corridor---Where we commisserated with each other---

O I'M GOING ON A BIG HEGIRA which'll end in my complete subjugation of the senses in some solitude Buddhist Gray Wilderness & so I dont even pack tho but start in the rain on my motorbike (vaguely worried I aint brought my good stuff) & as I put-put down a long Princeton Boulevard-like street past schoolgirls who say "Is Jack Kerouac sposed to have a motor on his bike?"---"Sure"---I come to the place across the street from the Lowell Depot and go in idly to see what they got in the way of cheap notebooks to write on in the "wilderness"---By God I got all my goggles & raingear like the Jewish girl with the M.G.!---I'm going back to the world, the sweet hopeful world, tortillas & beans in the smoky market & I wish I had a typewriter!

IN THE HOUSE IN PAWTUCKETVILLE MY MOTHER & BLANCHE are talking about the tall dark man who left his *pissaw* on the chairs & then my mother whispers to me that Mademoiselle Bergeron called & is coming over on some pretext but just to smell around and gossip, we've just arrived in Lowell in a new house---Earlier on the couch someone'd been scratching at my eyes, some nameless sexless Rainey-Julien person

PATHETIC DARK LITTLE GLASS COUNTERS of the candy stores of Lowell but it's in "Mexico City" and I'm buying the Mexico City News on top of it but it's all small & ravelled up at the bottom but I want to see the latest baseball news, just arrived and the proprietor is dark I dont see him in the shrouds behind & maybe I'll buy some *velas* then go to the market for a tall glass of orange juice or mebbe of *guanajuato*---The paper says "North Cascade News"---It's a big dream of the whole mountainous dark ridge but graysilvered of North America & I wake up on a frigid mountain in the Cascades of Washington, cold morning---

BACK IN PAWTUCKETVILLE ON MOODY STREET, AFTERNOON, I walk along at one point naked with my "naked self" (the two of us naked) and later go to the Textile Lunch, "it's just the same" (that is, not at all) with big back diningroom and eaters I recognize & I see Pete the owner with glasses (it's him!) going on, then I peek into hallway of our tenement to see "just the same" wall-paper (?) & then the hall, the last steps, how "we always went down these steps

330

touching both wallpapered walls with our outstretched hands" & so the wallpaper stain'd & torn and as I go down I close my eyes in the dream & see veins of light in the dark & I think "Mrs Fortier is dying" (she died four years ago)--- But I *know* she's dying---But it is a strange dream, and earlier it was the same Moody Street where Irwin & I had sat at a dismal booth cadging drinks & there were today some Negro blows---All time up here on Desolation I've been revisiting Lowell extensively, Joe on Salem Street, in my making reveries of Sarah Avenue, etc, how Lowell continues to haunt me so, it's a whole intact Shakespearean universe in itself---

TRAVELING TO BOSTON WITH PA in some kind of car we transfer on a dark boulevard at night near "Arlington" and get to go on the "Trolley to Revere" but here I lose my Pa like Cody lost his on a boxcar (almost) and I wander around in the trolley station among coatstrapt travelers & mystery & Pa is gone, gone, gone---& he had disappeared so absentmindedly ---like the Pa of the Frisco Hills basement---I then go to "Coney Island" and as I come out of the el I look down & see the Dodgers warming up in Ebbets Field, I clearly see Gil Hodges & Duke Snider with their bats & as I jump down to watch from the sidewalk in mid air I see the sign on the sidewalk saying "Do not watch baseball from this sidewalk" so instead of landing I obey the law and keep on flying till I land in the bottom of an empty lot excavation where children are playing so I just go on down into the subway where a man inquires where he is of a little subway guard in blue uniform, the guard saying "You are in (Chelan) and you should be glad

& know it in the future," & he points & we see, lo, both the 7th Avenue & 8th Avenue subway trains waiting on different tracks to serve the Coney Island public and I run to catch my train---Later I'm gossiping with a svelte sophisticated actress and I'm trying to be foppish and namedrop Tallulah Bankhead with whom I was last night, in my dream I remonstrate with myself for being such a queer---"If you'd a been famous that's all that woulda happened, you lilting sissified fool"---It's at an iron fence in the Long Island night---Anyway I cant get in a word edgewise, of daintified amusing emphasis

ORLANDO   1962

VULTURE PEOPLE, a dream to end all dreams---really horrible---must write it down for the horrible record--- Begins me and two kids are hired to work in the mountains on the same "ridge" as Desolation (i.e., Mien Mo Mountain again) & start with a cliffside river crew who tell us two workers have apparently sunk in the cliffside snow and we must lean over sheer drops and see if we can "dump them out" or haul them in---All we do is lie there on crumbly snow a thousand foot fall to the river crumbling the snow off in slabs so big you wouldnt know if men were trapped in em or not---Not only that the bosses have special shoes on slid- ers that are holding them to the safe shore (like ski clamps) so I begin to realize they're only fooling us poor kids & we could have fallen too (I almost do)---(did)---(almost) --- As observer of the story I see it's just an annual ritualistic joke to fool the new kids on the job who are then dispatched to the other side of the river to slump off *more* snow from sheer banks in hopes of finding the lost workmen---So we start

there on a big trip, downriver first, but en route all the peas-
ants tell us stories of the God Monster Machine on the other
shore who makes sounds like certain birds & owls & has a
million infernal contraptions enough to make you sick with
all the slipshod windmill rickety details, as "Observer of the
Story" again I see it's just a trick to make us scared when we
get there at night & hear actual natural sounds of birds, owls
etc. thinking as green rookies in the country it's that
'Monster'---Meanwhile we sign on to go to the main mountain but I promise myself if I dont like the work there I'll
come back get my old job on Desolation---Already our
employers have shown a murderous sense of humor---I
arrive at Mien Mo Mountain which is like Bixby Canyon
(Raton Canyon in "Big Sur") again but has a large tho dry
rot river running in the wide hole & down there on many
rocks are huge brooding vultures---Old bums row out to
them & pull them clumsily off the rocks & start feeding them
like pets, bites of red meat or red mite, tho at first I thought
the eccentric old town bums wanted them to eat or to sell
(still maybe so) because before I study this I look & see hundreds of slowly fucking Vulture couples on the town dump---
These are now humanly formed vultures with human shaped
arms, legs, heads, torsos, but they have rainbow colored feath-
ers & the men are all quietly sitting *behind* Vulture Women
slowly somehow fucking at them in all the same slow obscene
movement--- Both man & woman sit facing the same direction & somehow there's contact because you can see all their
feathery rainbow behinds slowly dully monotonously fucking
on the dumpslopes---As I pass I even see the expression on
the face of a youngish blond vulture man eternally displeased
because his Vulture Mistress is an old yakker who's been argu-

333

ing with him all this time---His face is completely human but inhumanly pasty like uncooked pale pie dough with dull seamed buggy horror that he's doomed to all this enough to make me shudder in sympathy, I even see her awful expression of middleaged pie dough tormentism---They're so human!---But suddenly me & the two kid workers are taken to the Vulture People respectable quarter of town to our apartment where a Vulture Woman & her daughter show us our rooms---Their faces are leprous thick with pie dough but painted with makeup to make them like thick Christmas dolls & dull & fuzzy but human expressions, like with thick lips of rubber muzz, fat expressions all crumbly like pie dough, yellow pizza puke faces disgusting us tho we say nothing---The apartment has dirty beatnik beds & mattresses everywhere but I walk thru the back looking for a sink---It's *huge*---an endless walk thru long greasy pantries & vast washrooms with single filthy sink all dark & slimy like underground Lowell Hi School crumbling basements---Finally I come to the kitchen where we "new workers" are sposed to cook little meals all summer---It's vast stone fireplaces & stone stoves all rancid & greasy from a month-old Vulture People Banquet Orgy with still dozens of uncooked chickens lying around on the floor, among garbage & bottles---Rancid stale grease everywhere, nobody's ever cleaned it up or knew how & the place as big as a garage---I push my way out of there pushing a huge greasystink foodstained tray of some sort hurrying away from the big stinky emptiness & horror---The fat golden chickens lie rotten upsidedown on littered stone slabs---I hurry out never having seen such a dirty sight in my life---

Meanwhile I learn the two boys are studying a hamper full of Vulture Food for us & one of them wisely says

"Blisters in our sugar," meaning the Vultures put their blisters in our sugar so we'll "die" but instead of being really dead we'll be taken to the Underground Slimes to walk neck deep in steaming mucks pulling huge groaning wheels (among small-forked snakes) so the Devil with the long ears can mine his Purple Magenta Square Stone that is the secret of all this kingdom---You end up down there groaning & pulling thru dead bodies of other people even your own family floating in the ooze---If you succeed you can become a pasty Vulture Person obscenely fornicating slowly on the dump above, I think, either that or the Devil just invents the Vulture People with what's gleaned out of the underground Hell

> Beans anyone?
> (that pasty puke "Sioux Sick" muck I
> dreamed of in 1958 was all over the kitchen
> walls)
> (more information about Mien Mo)
> (mountain)
> (of the flying horses, remember)
> (which must be an Atlantean Nightmare)

PIERRE WARWICK & I in a new cafeteria where I steal long pies of cheese & short, when we try to go in the Men's Room a guy is playing catch with his son in front of it and the ball keeps falling down long catacomb underground toilet steps where after running downsteps you skid clear across to the other wall on the wet slippery floor---The guy is a respectable man in a suit---Pierre wants to know why he doesnt like him, or me for that matter, to assuage Pierre as we walk on ice skates over an empty lot hill & down the other

side right among the suburban bungalows I sav & devise something about the guy's "Shrivelled
opinion"---

We run into a bunch of guys one of whom is a decaying Val Hayes, that is with a hat & decaying teeth, to whom I explain my inner mental egoisms by saying "Like if I'm hammering a nail onto the end of the word 'Perfection' & the nail goes *froosh* as I miss, I say out loud 'Ah, Perfection's
End"---

I add that nobody appreciates this but myself, like all my books I've written---He understands & keeps grinning like Val as I say 'Heh heh heh' to be like Nietzsche's shrewd why-am-I-so-clever----Embarassing that I suddenly ask "Are you Val Hayes?"---He says no but it isnt quite true? ---With Pierre & others we stroll down a long corridor of life & come to a hoodlum leaning on the wall with feet out, every-body walks around his feet (a tall guy standing next to hood-lum also but I plow slowly right thru the feet & turn to see him (as I stroll on) exhibit a fountain pen which might be a shiv, with the posture of a hood showing he has a shiv---In my own hand is a harmless little baton six inches long, actually my little baseball bat I carved as a kid for hitting rollerbearing Repulsion baseballs---When we arrive at the cafeteria section of the corridor the queers in my party excitedly call me back to greet a Henry Hartzjohn eating at table (his back is turned, I think it's Henry, they're saying 'He's alone!') but as I go back the two hoodlums stroll by, I look expectedly at the tall one as if to say 'Well?' and wake up---(that's some long hiking in the woods Pierre & I are going to accomplish with our ice skates over little neighborhood lots on ice skates down to stuffy cor-ridors full of conversation & bullying)

(I try to explain to Val that 'Perfection's End' means that no matter what is going to happen when I hammer in the 'N' completing the word 'PERFECTION' it will have to be just that, Perfection's End)

I ALSO DREAMED that everything in existence was a total abstract ideal mathematical whole, i.e., like, by subtracting 740 from 1000 you got 260 which meant "Egg" more or less, & other figures, so if you wanted an egg you *had* the egg in its ideal mathematical wholeness & didnt even have to see it or eat it to have it!---The same with the universe, a vast Ideal you can have without seeing it, feeling it, tasting or touching or smelling it---Just thinking it, right there, yours *before* the being! Flashing back & forth in my head all creation was there before the asking or wanting---*complete*---& *abstract*--- (Mathematical Buddhism)

DREAM OF JULY 23, 1958
HUBBARD AND I ARE IN "BOSTON" near Harvard walking up a dreary street on a Sunday afternoon and I am asking for the "interesting" bars, he says there are none, but he does know about a weird place a few blocks away which isnt exactly a bar but a seance club where you pay money to have spotlights shined on you as your intimate revelations, the very things in fact you wouldnt even want an intimate friend to know about you, are spoken nay sung---So we go there, in a curious walk like our walks in Eighth Avenue New York 1945 or later in Tangiers when we'd dig the green sky of dusk, and go in and pay and sit down and they start on

Hubbard first a curious group of sortof FBI types begin showing moving pictures of Hubbard's past right over our heads and it shows Ernie McRorie with rods sticking out of his ears and little atomic twirlers twirling on the ends of the rods and Hubbard says "O my God" as tho he'd never dreamed anybody would ever had found out about that--- Meanwhile I sit shuddering for my awful turn---Suddenly they start to show a movie of the women in Hubbard's life and first you see a very slim svelte Edna cutting up Claremont Avenue, the respectable Columbia neighborhood, and then you sortof turn into a scene of Julien and see familiar sortof Cecily women (Cecily Wayne) and women so familiar you never know them, and finally the last woman is a slim beautiful dazzling June Evans cutting up the street and the movie is so powerful Hubbard and I are suddenly transported to the actual street in Fellaheen Mexico and we're standing there against June's door and here she comes in a light green dress, carrying groceries, followed by whistling amazed Mexican *machos* and Hubbard says to her "Hey June" and she says "After what you done to me, Hubbard, I'll be harder to get than that" with a flip of her ass she goes into her tenement door and the *machos* come up to us whistling and say "Who is that?? she no podemos speaka Spanish" and Hubbard says "Sure she can podemos speaka Spanish" and I reply it to the guys "Sure she can podemos speaka espanol" and the guys whistle in amazement, they'r wearing white shirts, and we stand there and we know June will let us in later and meanwhile across the street in the narrow twisted crazy night neons and cha cha cha of Mexico are old (around-the-block) New England haunted houses of old white cracked white paint, with stark trees of

November. . . . .It is such a sensational and sensitive and charmingly Garden-like intelligent dream I woke up amazed. . . . .